SLASH

NOW, SHE TRAVELS THE WORLD WITH HER MONSTROUS PARTNER AND FRIEND VLAD, HUNTING DOWN AND DESTROYING SLASHERS WHEREVER THEY FIND THEM!

IMAGE COMICS, INC.
ROBERT KIRKMAN — CHIEF OPERATING OFFICER
ERIK LARSEN — CHIEF FINANCIAL OFFICER
TODD MCFARLANE — PRESIDENT
MARC SILVESTRI — CHIEF EXECUTIVE OFFICER
JIM VALENTINO — VICE-PRESIDENT
ERIC STEPHENSON — PUBLISHER
TODD MARTINEZ — SALES & LICENSING COORDINATOR
BETSY GOMEZ — PR & MARKETING COORDINATOR
BRANWYN BIGGLESTONE — ACCOUNTS MANAGER
SARAH DELAINE — ADMINISTRATIVE ASSISTANT
TYLER SHAINLINE — PRODUCTION MANAGER
DREW GILL — ART DIRECTOR
JONATHAN CHAN — PRODUCTION ARTIST
MONICA HOWARD — PRODUCTION ARTIST
VINCENT KUKUA — PRODUCTION ARTIST
WWW.IMAGECOMICS.COM

WRITTEN BY **TIM SEELEY**

ART BY **MATT MERHOFF**
(HACK/SLASH VS. CHUCKY)
EMILY STONE

COLORS BY **WES DZIOBA**
(HACK/SLASH VS. CHUCKY)
COURTNEY VIA

LETTERS BY **BRIAN J. CROWLEY**

DESIGN BY **SEAN K. DOVE**

EDITS BY **MIKE O'SULLIVAN**

HACK/SLASH: Volume 3. First Printing. Published by Image Comics, Inc. Office of publication: 2134 Allston Way, 2nd Floor, Berkeley, CA 94704. Copyright © 2010 Hack/Slash, Inc. Originally published in single magazine form as HACK/SLASH vs CHUCKY and HACK/SLASH #1-4 by Devil's Due Publishing, Inc. All rights reserved. HACK/SLASH ™ (including all prominent characters featured herein), its logo and all character likenesses are trademarks of Hack/Slash, Inc. unless otherwise noted. CHUCKY and all related characters are ™ and ©, Universal Studios, 2010. EVIL ERNIE and all related characters are ™ and ©, Dynamite Entertainment, 2010. Image Comics® and its logos are registered trademarks of Image Comics, Inc.. No part of this publication may be reproduced or transmitted, in any form or by any means (except for short excerpts for review purposes) without the express written permission of Image Comics, Inc. All names, characters, events and locales in this publication are entirely fictional. Any resemblance to actual persons (living or dead), events or places, without satiric intent, is coincidental. PRINTED IN THE U.S.A. ISBN: 978-1-60706-286-8.

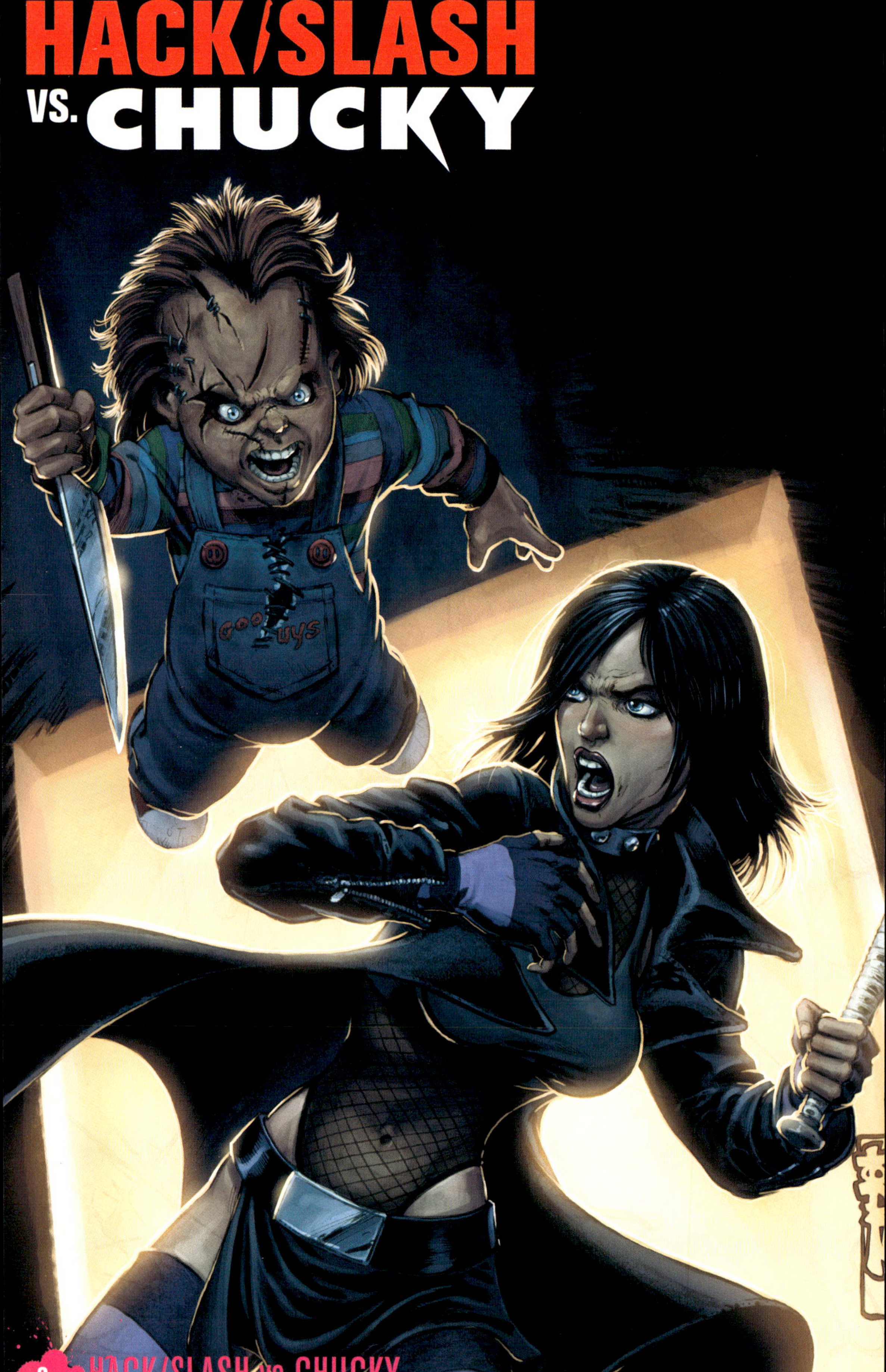
HACK/SLASH
VS. CHUCKY

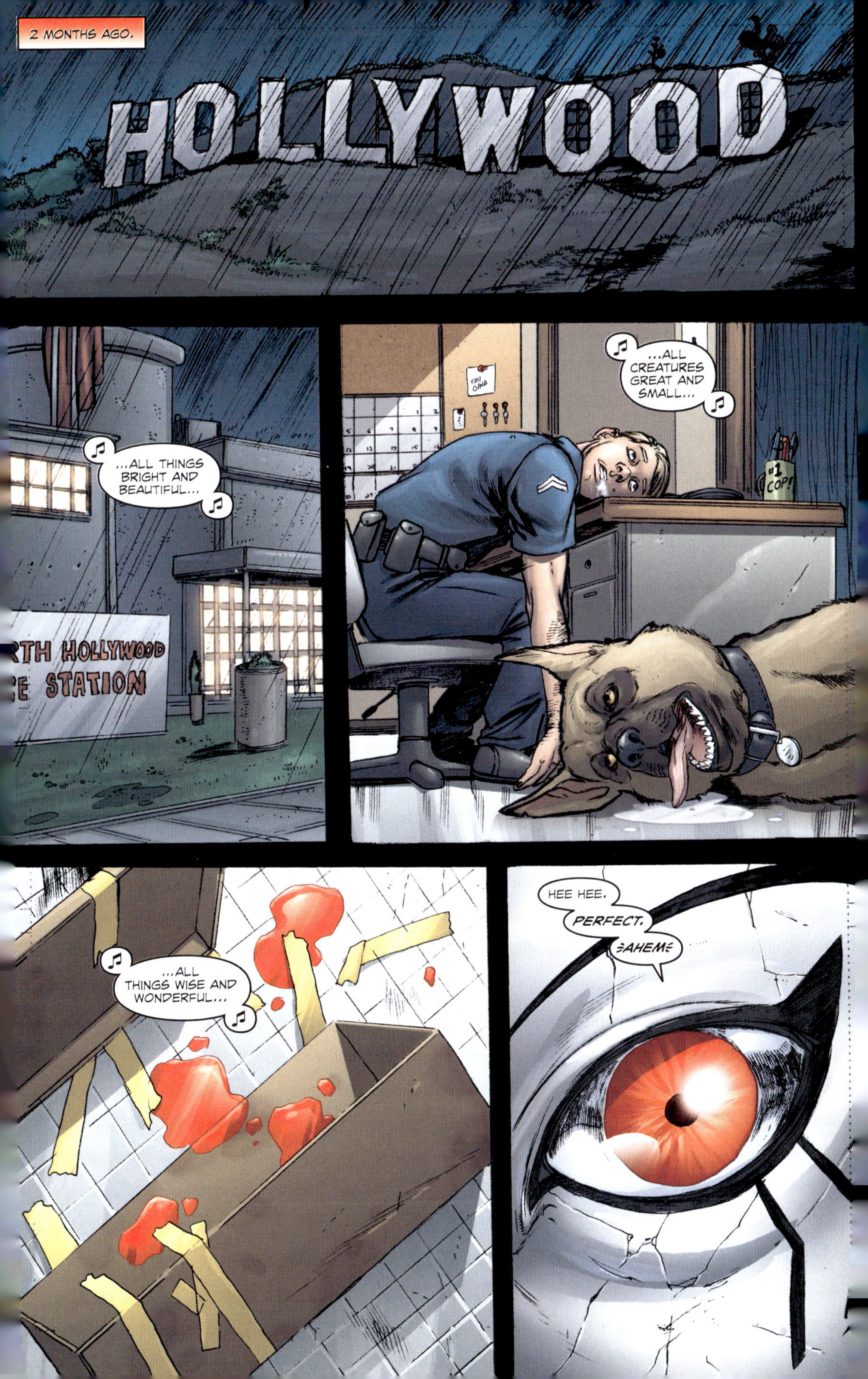
2 MONTHS AGO.
HOLLYWOOD
...ALL THINGS BRIGHT AND BEAUTIFUL...
RTH HOLLYWOOD
E STATION
...ALL CREATURES GREAT AND SMALL...
#1 COP!
...ALL THINGS WISE AND WONDERFUL...
HEE HEE.
PERFECT.
AHEM

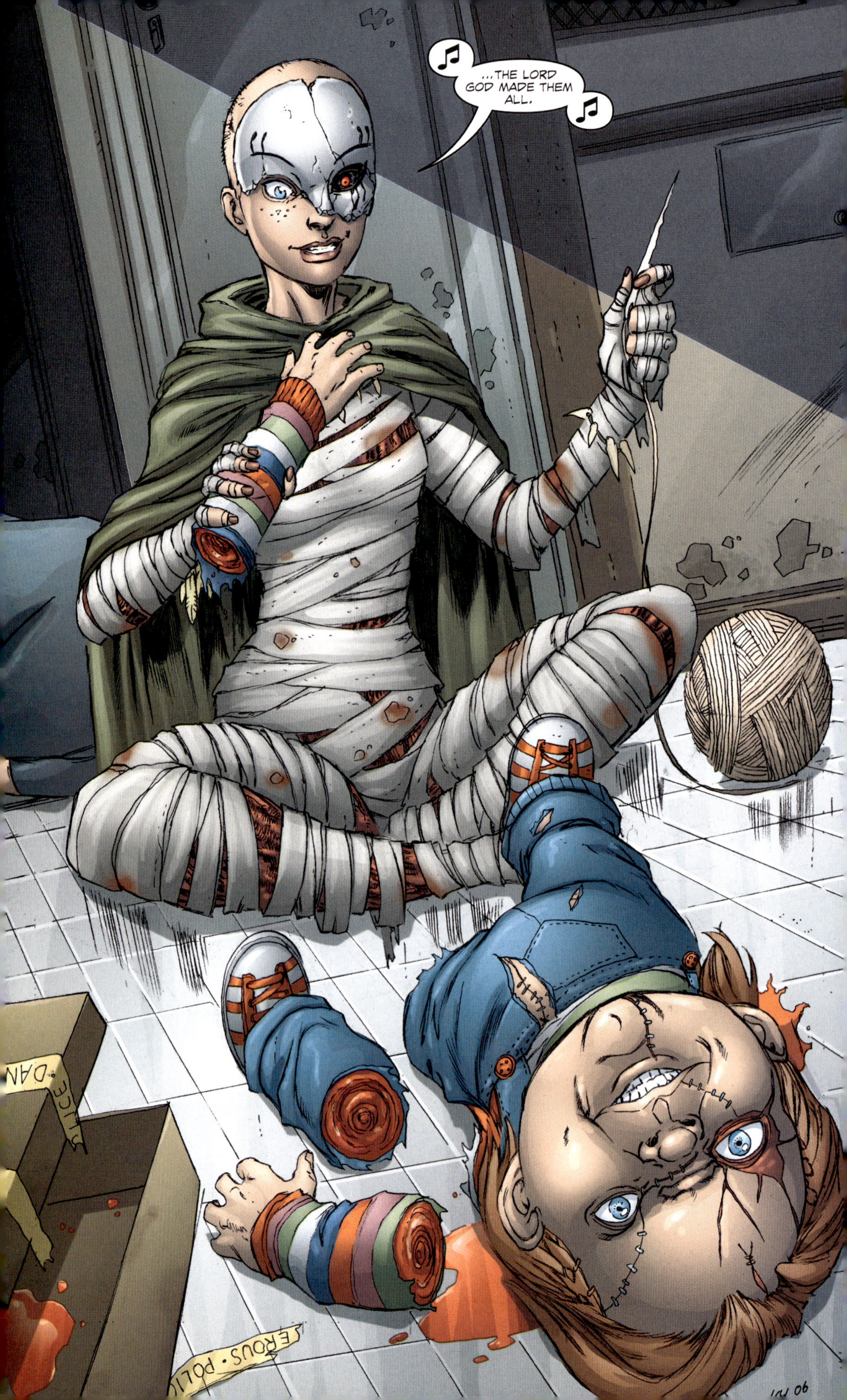
...THE LORD GOD MADE THEM ALL.

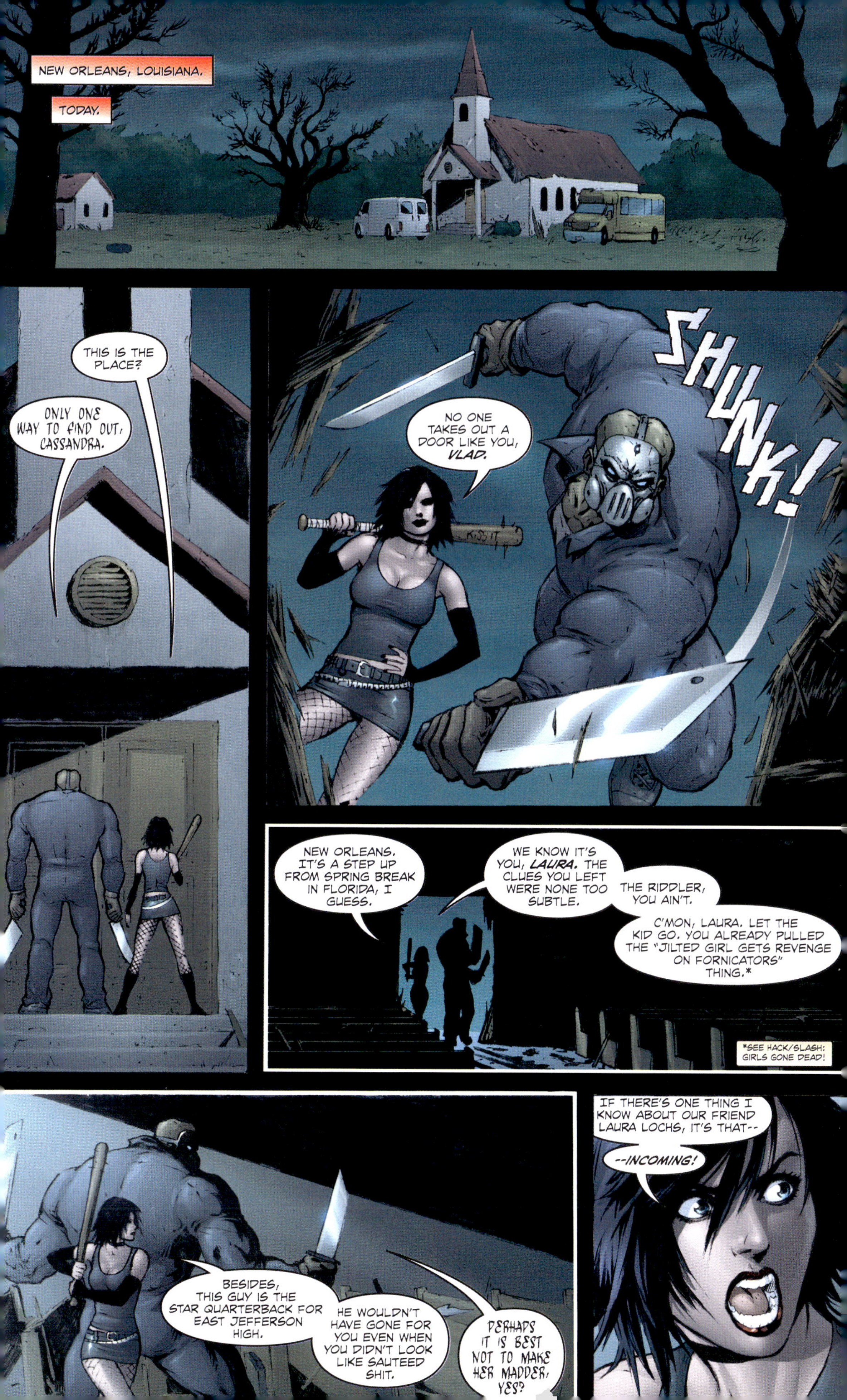
NEW ORLEANS, LOUISIANA.
TODAY.
THIS IS THE PLACE?
ONLY ONE WAY TO FIND OUT, CASSANDRA.
SHUNK!
NO ONE TAKES OUT A DOOR LIKE YOU, VLAD.
KISS IT
NEW ORLEANS. IT'S A STEP UP FROM SPRING BREAK IN FLORIDA, I GUESS.
WE KNOW IT'S YOU, LAURA. THE CLUES YOU LEFT WERE NONE TOO SUBTLE.
THE RIDDLER, YOU AIN'T.
C'MON, LAURA. LET THE KID GO. YOU ALREADY PULLED THE "JILTED GIRL GETS REVENGE ON FORNICATORS" THING.*
*SEE HACK/SLASH: GIRLS GONE DEAD!
BESIDES, THIS GUY IS THE STAR QUARTERBACK FOR EAST JEFFERSON HIGH.
HE WOULDN'T HAVE GONE FOR YOU EVEN WHEN YOU DIDN'T LOOK LIKE SAUTEED SHIT.
PERHAPS IT IS BEST NOT TO MAKE HER MADDER, YES?
IF THERE'S ONE THING I KNOW ABOUT OUR FRIEND LAURA LOCHS, IT'S THAT--
--INCOMING!

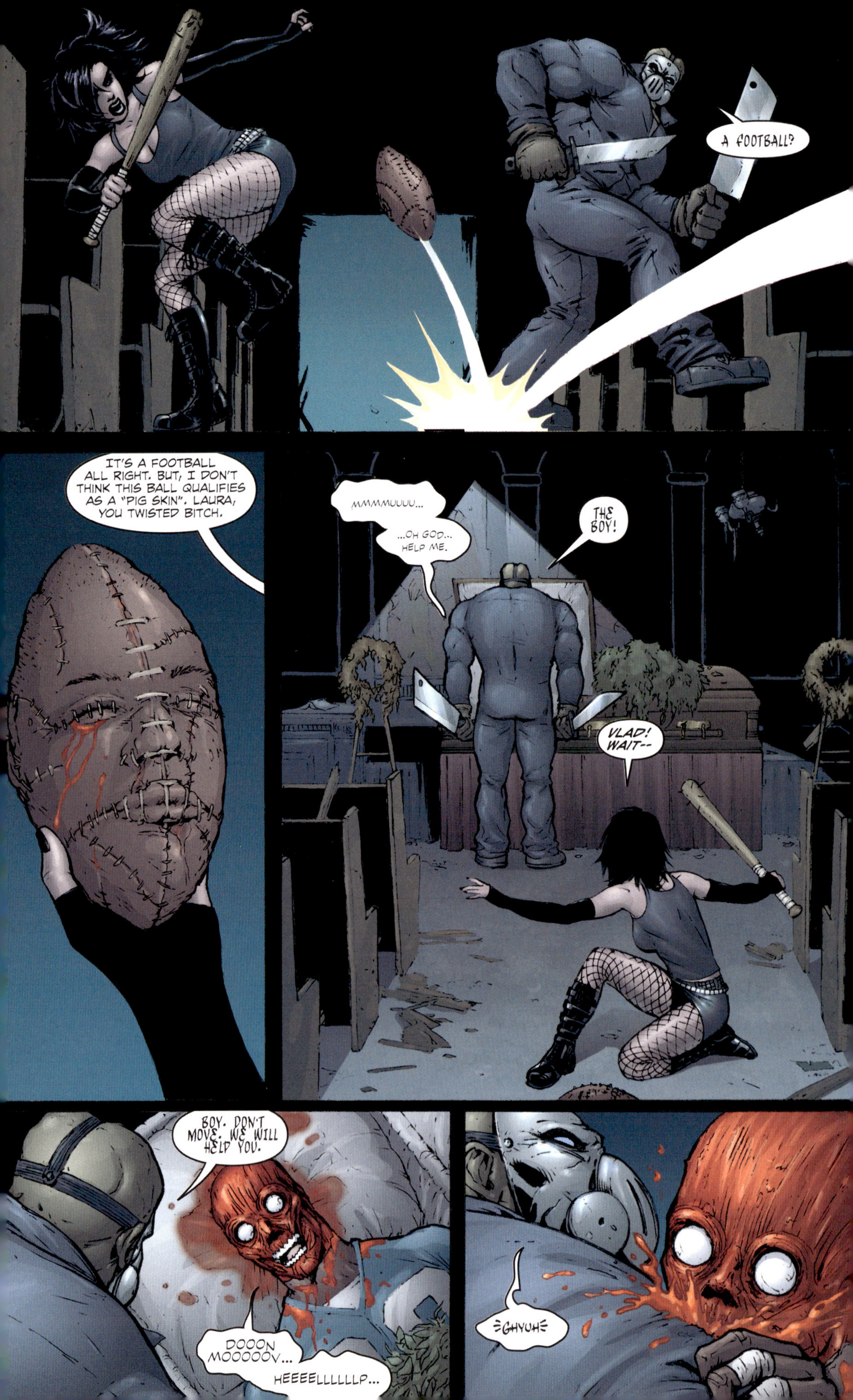
A FOOTBALL?
IT'S A FOOTBALL ALL RIGHT. BUT, I DON'T THINK THIS BALL QUALIFIES AS A "PIG SKIN". LAURA, YOU TWISTED BITCH.
MMMMUUUU...
...OH GOD... HELP ME.
THE BOY!
VLAD! WAIT--
BOY. DON'T MOVE. WE WILL HELP YOU.
DOOON MOOOOOV...
HEEEELLLLLLP...
GHYUH

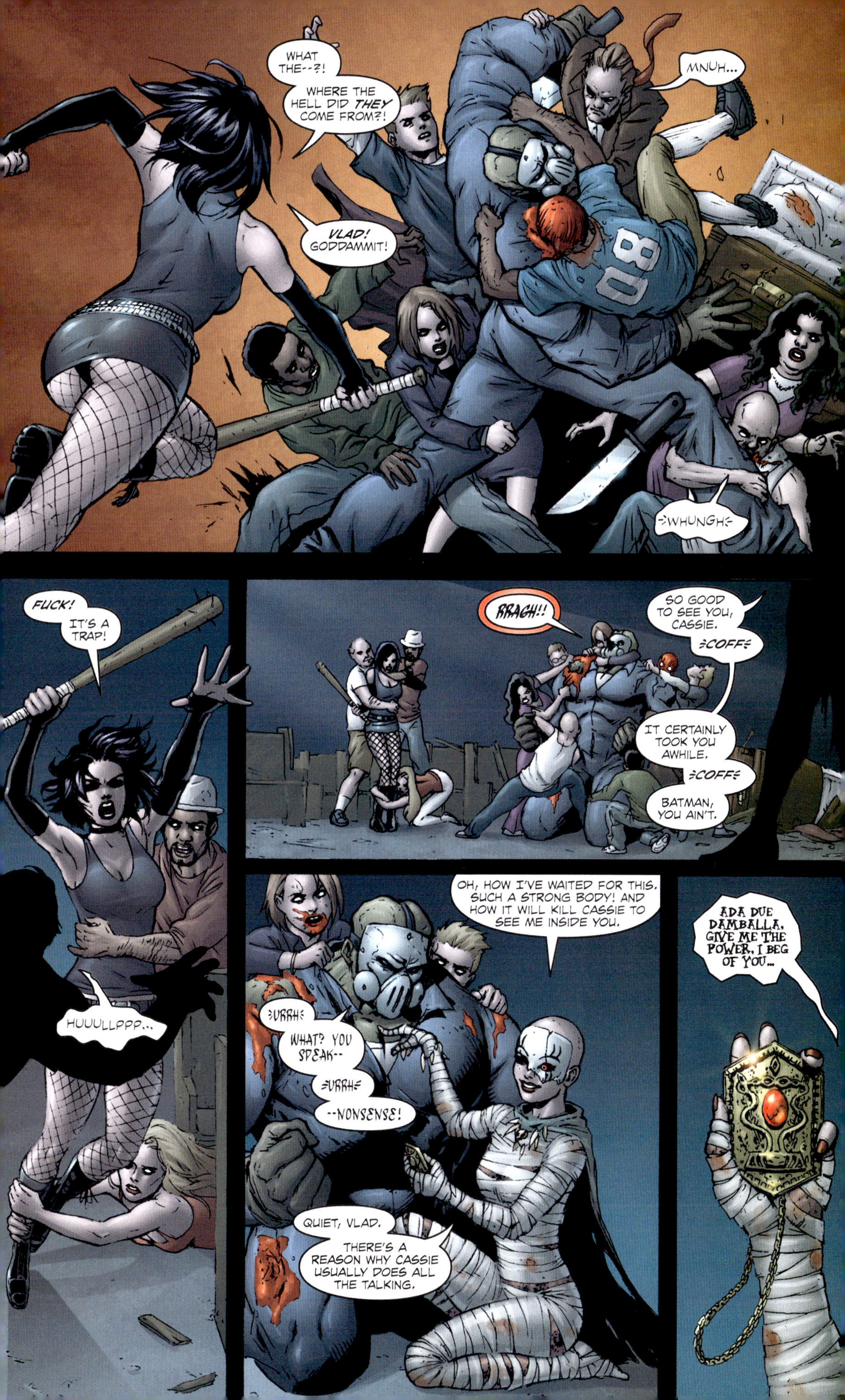
WHAT THE--?!
WHERE THE HELL DID *THEY* COME FROM?!
MNUH...
VLAD! GODDAMMIT!
WHUNGH
FUCK!
IT'S A TRAP!
RRAGH!!
SO GOOD TO SEE YOU, CASSIE.
COFF
IT CERTAINLY TOOK YOU AWHILE.
COFF
BATMAN, YOU AIN'T.
HUUULLPPP...
OH, HOW I'VE WAITED FOR THIS. SUCH A STRONG BODY! AND HOW IT WILL KILL CASSIE TO SEE ME INSIDE YOU.
URRH
WHAT? YOU SPEAK--
URRH
--NONSENSE!
QUIET, VLAD.
THERE'S A REASON WHY CASSIE USUALLY DOES ALL THE TALKING.
ADA DUE DAMBALLA, GIVE ME THE POWER, I BEG OF YOU...

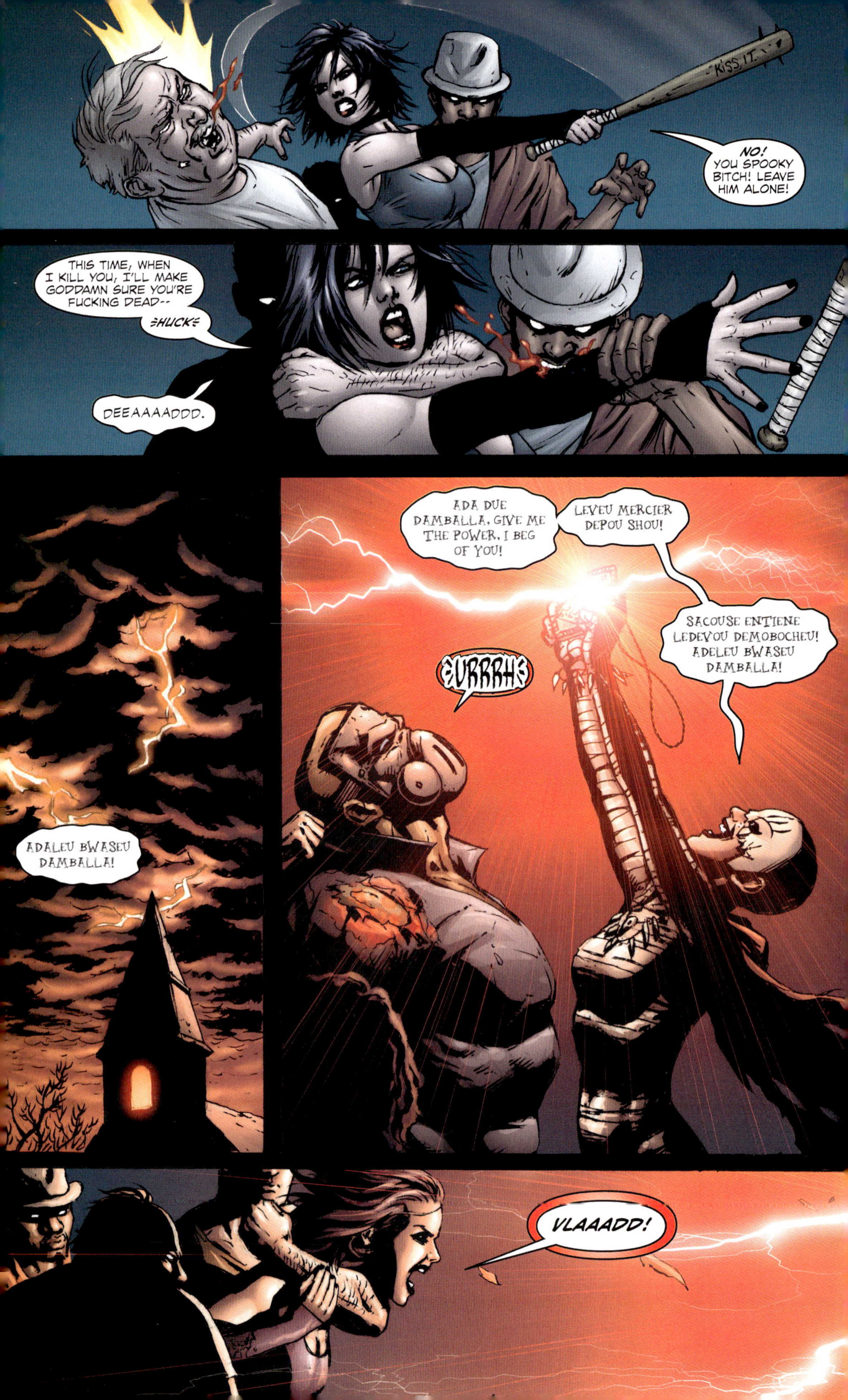
KISS IT.
NO! YOU SPOOKY BITCH! LEAVE HIM ALONE!
THIS TIME, WHEN I KILL YOU, I'LL MAKE GODDAMN SURE YOU'RE FUCKING DEAD--
HUCK
DEEAAAAADDD.
ADALEU BWASEU DAMBALLA!
ADA DUE DAMBALLA, GIVE ME THE POWER, I BEG OF YOU!
LEVEU MERCIER DEPOU SHOU!
SACOUSE ENTIENE LEDEVOU DEMOBOCHEU! ADELEU BWASEU DAMBALLA!
URRRH
VLAAADD!

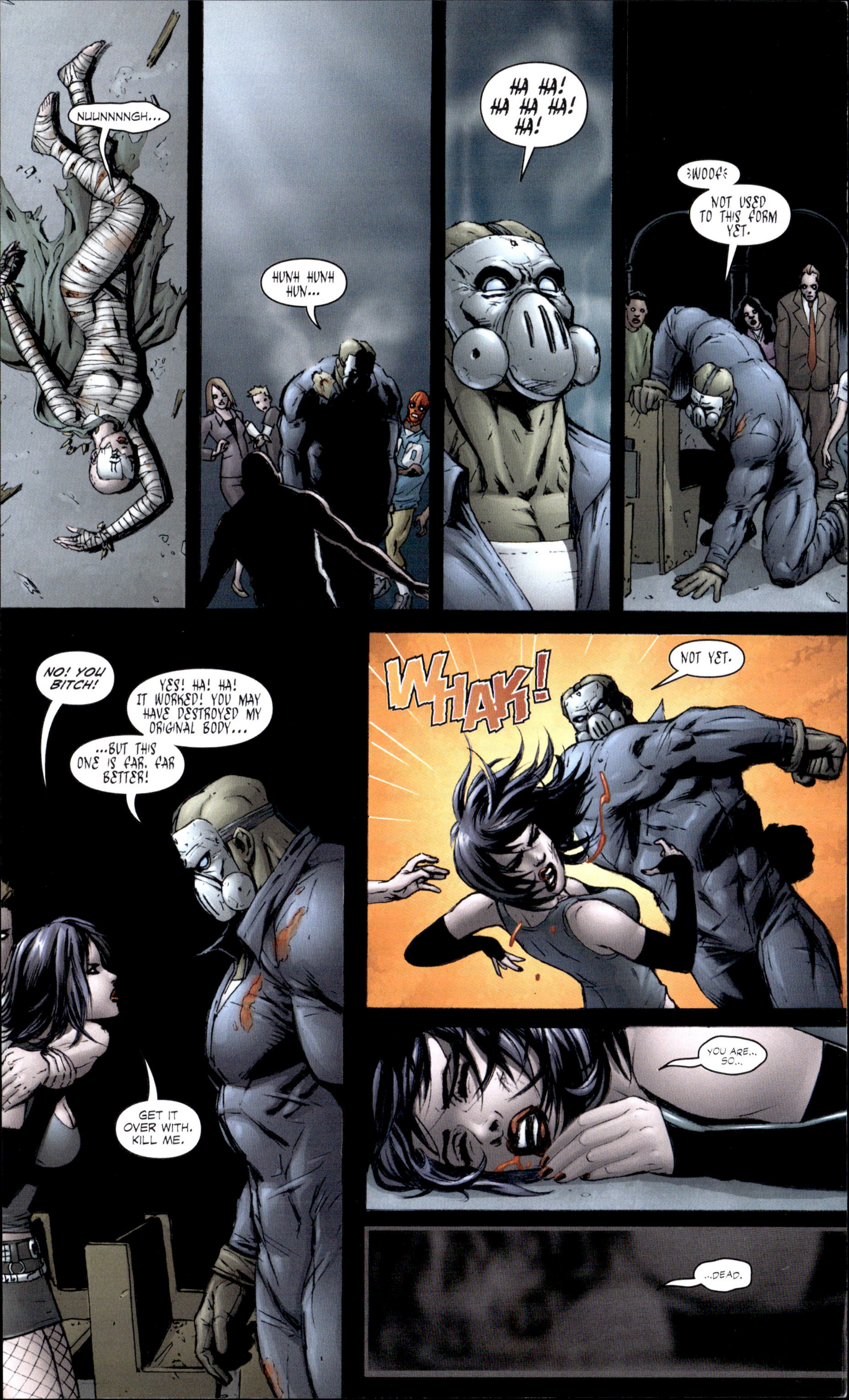
NUUNNNNGH...
HUNH HUNH HUN...
HA HA! HA HA HA! HA!
WOOF
NOT USED TO THIS FORM YET.
NO! YOU BITCH!
YES! HA! HA! IT WORKED! YOU MAY HAVE DESTROYED MY ORIGINAL BODY...
...BUT THIS ONE IS FAR, FAR BETTER!
GET IT OVER WITH. KILL ME.
WHAK!
NOT YET.
YOU ARE.. SO...
...DEAD.

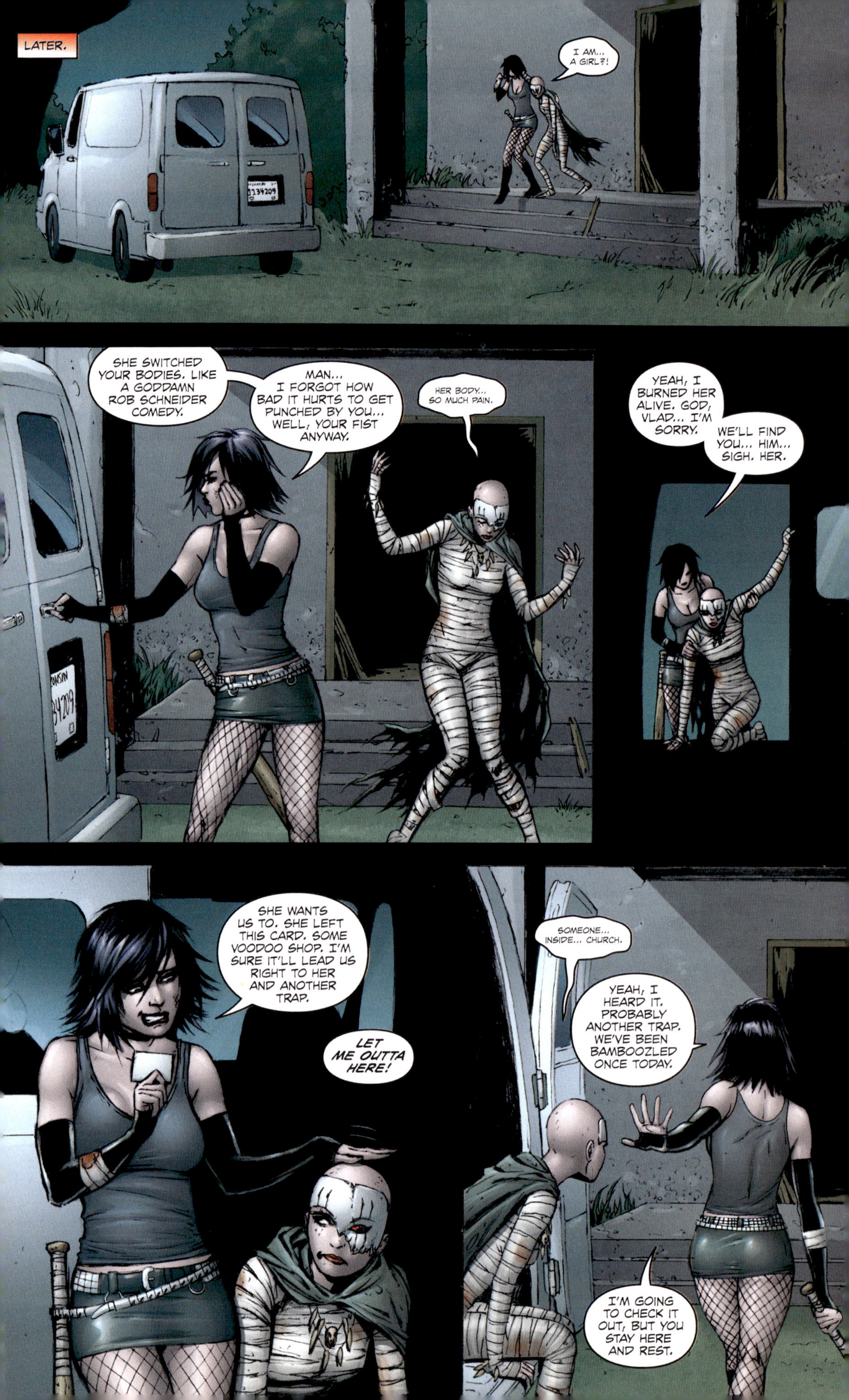
LATER.
I AM... A GIRL?!
SHE SWITCHED YOUR BODIES. LIKE A GODDAMN ROB SCHNEIDER COMEDY.
MAN... I FORGOT HOW BAD IT HURTS TO GET PUNCHED BY YOU... WELL, YOUR FIST ANYWAY.
HER BODY... SO MUCH PAIN.
YEAH, I BURNED HER ALIVE. GOD, VLAD... I'M SORRY.
WE'LL FIND YOU... HIM... SIGH. HER.
SHE WANTS US TO. SHE LEFT THIS CARD. SOME VOODOO SHOP. I'M SURE IT'LL LEAD US RIGHT TO HER AND ANOTHER TRAP.
LET ME OUTTA HERE!
SOMEONE... INSIDE... CHURCH.
YEAH, I HEARD IT. PROBABLY ANOTHER TRAP. WE'VE BEEN BAMBOOZLED ONCE TODAY.
I'M GOING TO CHECK IT OUT, BUT YOU STAY HERE AND REST.

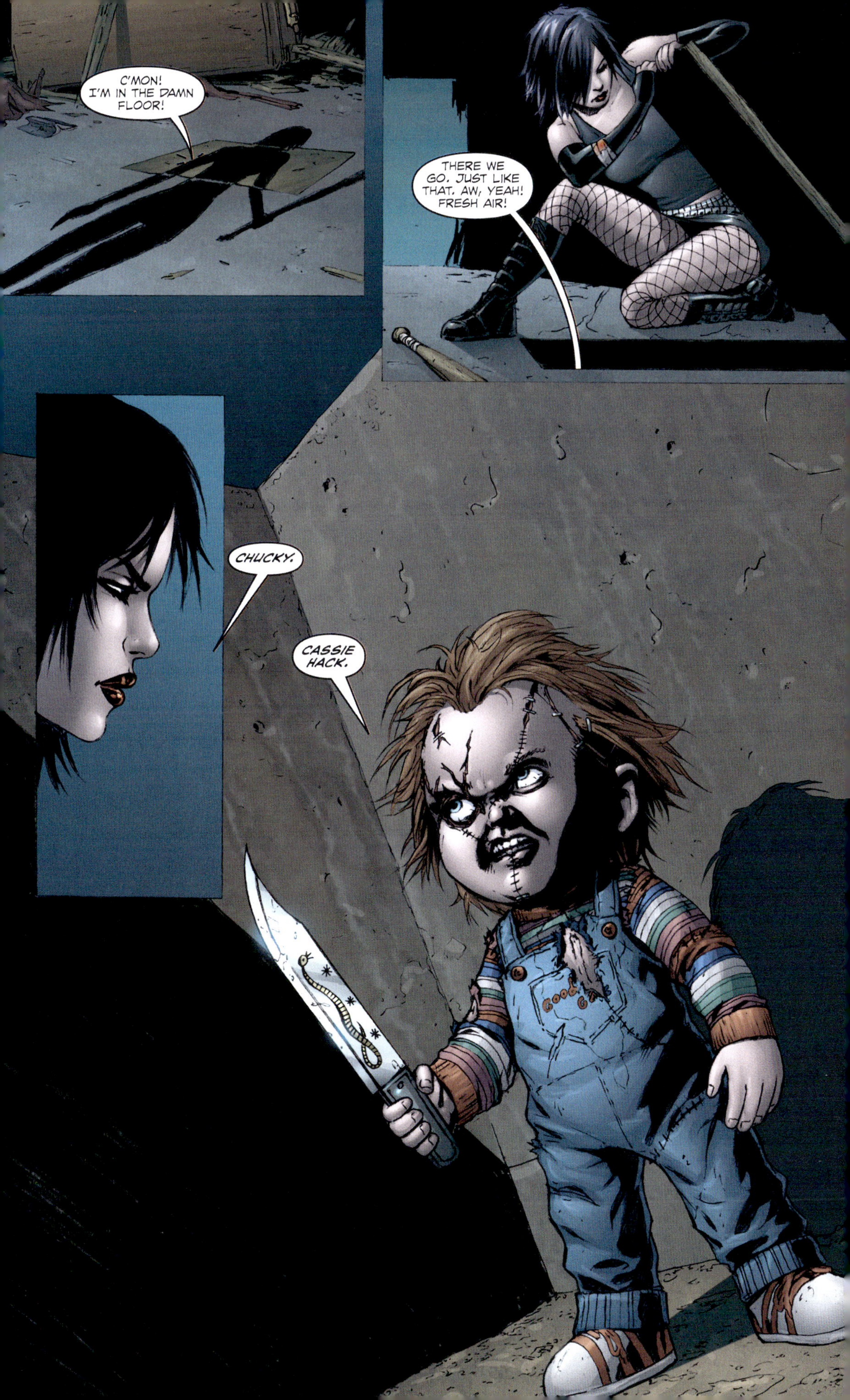
C'MON! I'M IN THE DAMN FLOOR!
THERE WE GO. JUST LIKE THAT. AW, YEAH! FRESH AIR!
CHUCKY.
CASSIE HACK.

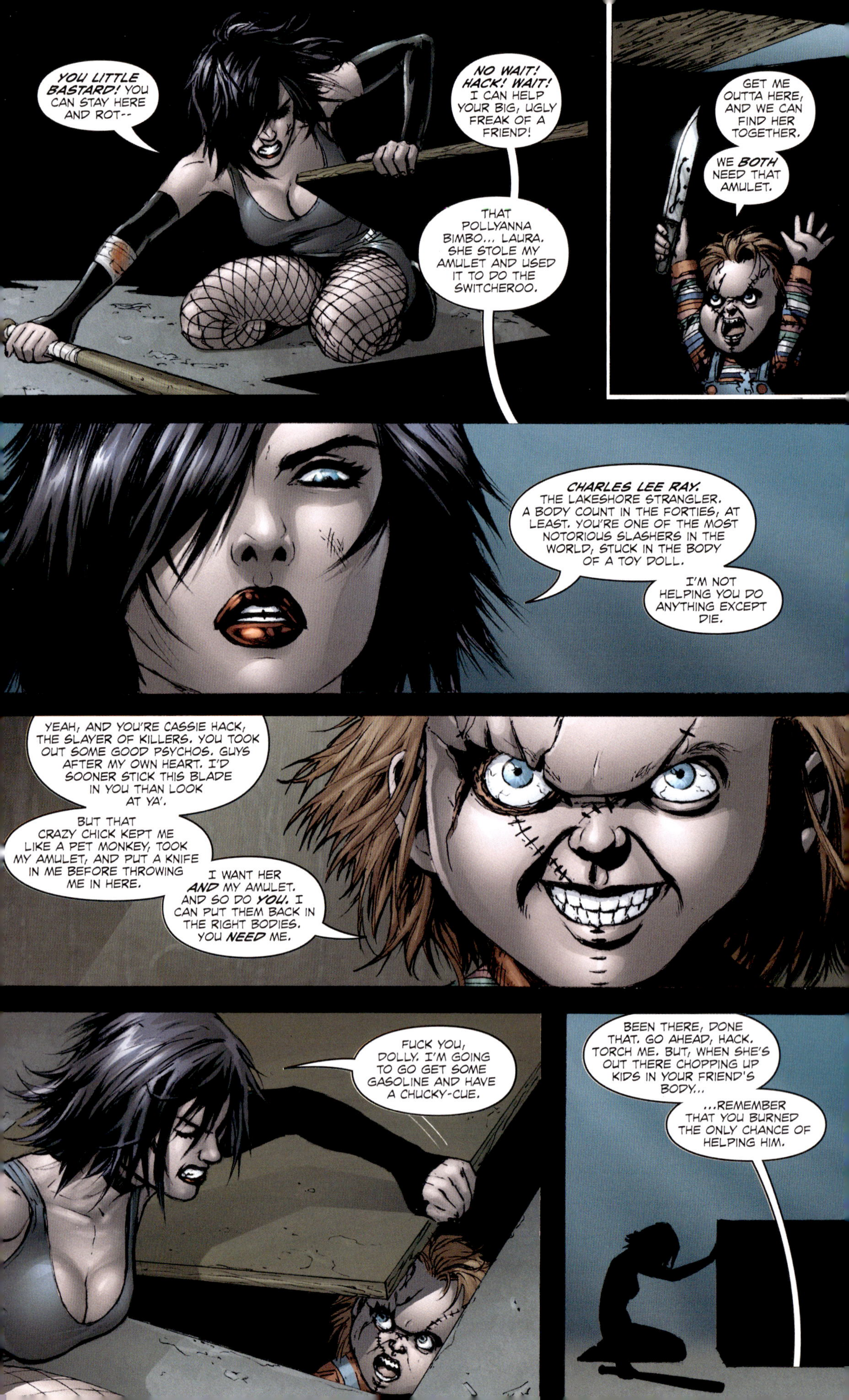
YOU LITTLE BASTARD! YOU CAN STAY HERE AND ROT--
NO WAIT! HACK! WAIT! I CAN HELP YOUR BIG, UGLY FREAK OF A FRIEND!
THAT POLLYANNA BIMBO... LAURA. SHE STOLE MY AMULET AND USED IT TO DO THE SWITCHEROO.
GET ME OUTTA HERE, AND WE CAN FIND HER TOGETHER.
WE BOTH NEED THAT AMULET.
CHARLES LEE RAY. THE LAKESHORE STRANGLER. A BODY COUNT IN THE FORTIES, AT LEAST. YOU'RE ONE OF THE MOST NOTORIOUS SLASHERS IN THE WORLD, STUCK IN THE BODY OF A TOY DOLL.
I'M NOT HELPING YOU DO ANYTHING EXCEPT DIE.
YEAH, AND YOU'RE CASSIE HACK, THE SLAYER OF KILLERS. YOU TOOK OUT SOME GOOD PSYCHOS. GUYS AFTER MY OWN HEART. I'D SOONER STICK THIS BLADE IN YOU THAN LOOK AT YA'.
BUT THAT CRAZY CHICK KEPT ME LIKE A PET MONKEY, TOOK MY AMULET, AND PUT A KNIFE IN ME BEFORE THROWING ME IN HERE.
I WANT HER AND MY AMULET. AND SO DO YOU. I CAN PUT THEM BACK IN THE RIGHT BODIES. YOU NEED ME.
FUCK YOU, DOLLY. I'M GOING TO GO GET SOME GASOLINE AND HAVE A CHUCKY-CUE.
BEEN THERE, DONE THAT. GO AHEAD, HACK. TORCH ME. BUT, WHEN SHE'S OUT THERE CHOPPING UP KIDS IN YOUR FRIEND'S BODY...
...REMEMBER THAT YOU BURNED THE ONLY CHANCE OF HELPING HIM.

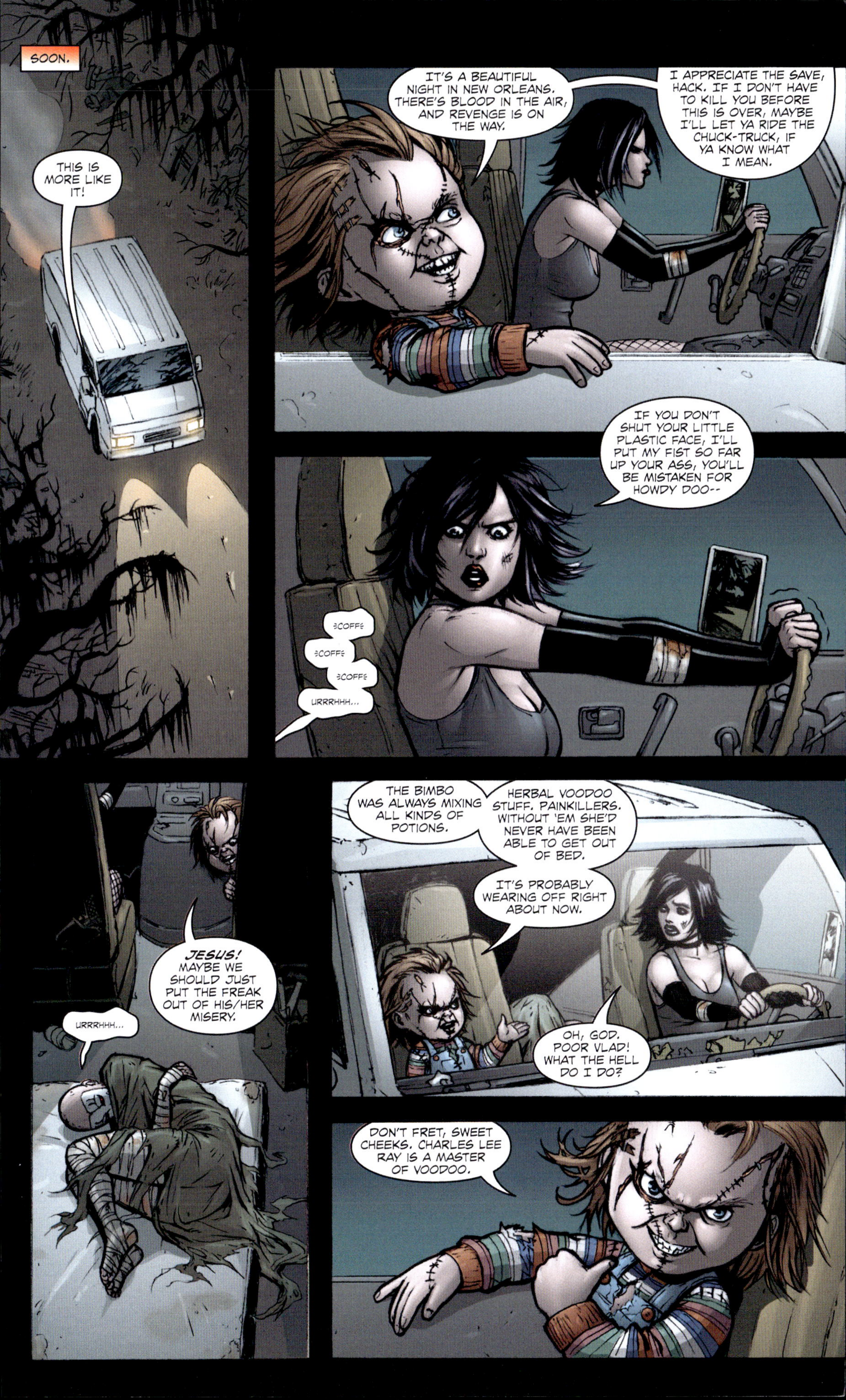
SOON.
THIS IS MORE LIKE IT!
IT'S A BEAUTIFUL NIGHT IN NEW ORLEANS. THERE'S BLOOD IN THE AIR, AND REVENGE IS ON THE WAY.
I APPRECIATE THE SAVE, HACK. IF I DON'T HAVE TO KILL YOU BEFORE THIS IS OVER, MAYBE I'LL LET YA RIDE THE CHUCK-TRUCK, IF YA KNOW WHAT I MEAN.
IF YOU DON'T SHUT YOUR LITTLE PLASTIC FACE, I'LL PUT MY FIST SO FAR UP YOUR ASS, YOU'LL BE MISTAKEN FOR HOWDY DOO--
COFF
COFF
COFF
URRRHHH...
URRRHHH...
JESUS! MAYBE WE SHOULD JUST PUT THE FREAK OUT OF HIS/HER MISERY.
THE BIMBO WAS ALWAYS MIXING ALL KINDS OF POTIONS.
HERBAL VOODOO STUFF. PAINKILLERS. WITHOUT 'EM SHE'D NEVER HAVE BEEN ABLE TO GET OUT OF BED.
IT'S PROBABLY WEARING OFF RIGHT ABOUT NOW.
OH, GOD. POOR VLAD! WHAT THE HELL DO I DO?
DON'T FRET, SWEET CHEEKS. CHARLES LEE RAY IS A MASTER OF VOODOO.

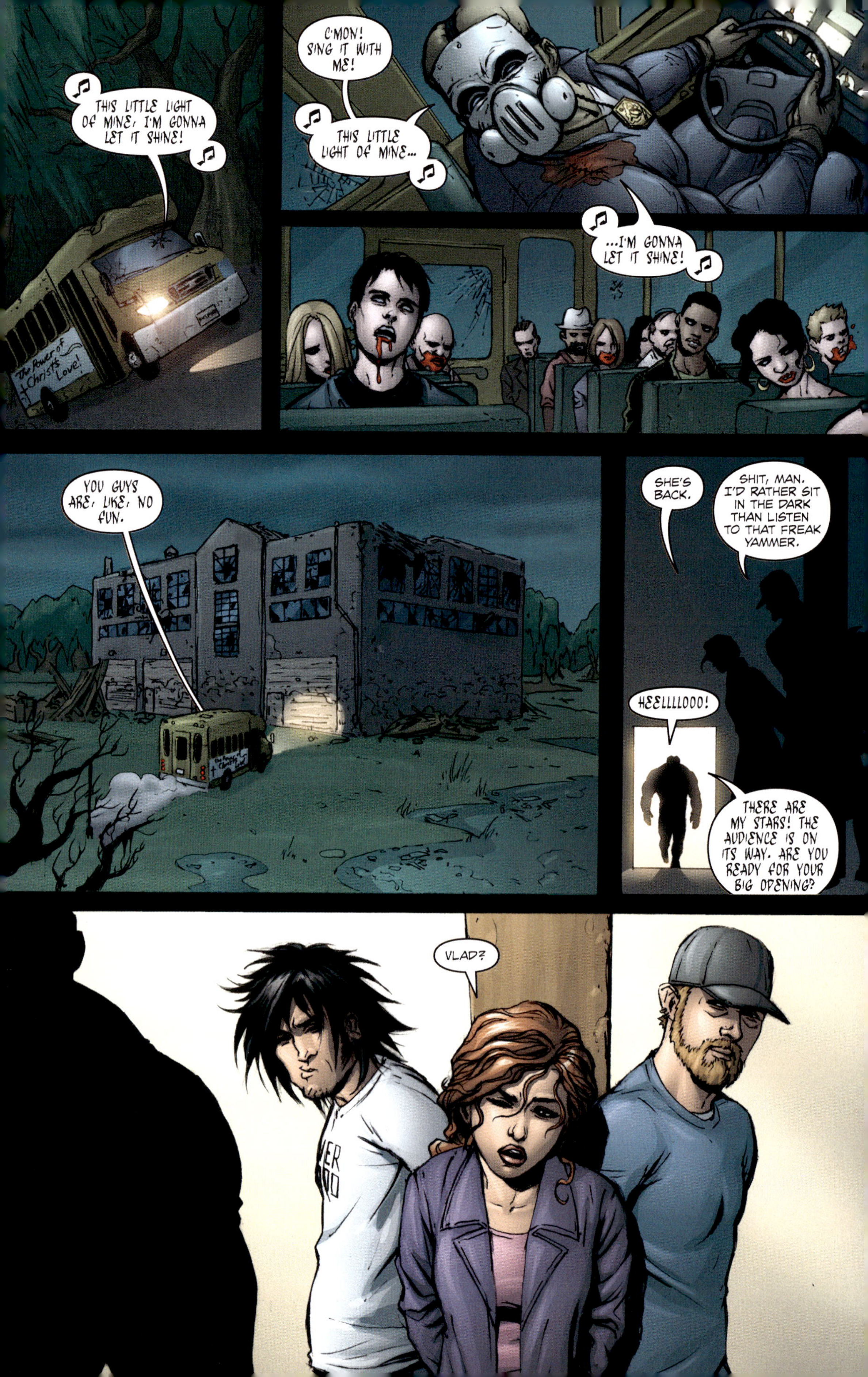
THIS LITTLE LIGHT OF MINE, I'M GONNA LET IT SHINE!
C'MON! SING IT WITH ME!
THIS LITTLE LIGHT OF MINE...
...I'M GONNA LET IT SHINE!
The Power of Christ's Love!
YOU GUYS ARE, LIKE, NO FUN.
SHE'S BACK.
SHIT, MAN. I'D RATHER SIT IN THE DARK THAN LISTEN TO THAT FREAK YAMMER.
HEELLLLOOO!
THERE ARE MY STARS! THE AUDIENCE IS ON ITS WAY. ARE YOU READY FOR YOUR BIG OPENING?
VLAD?

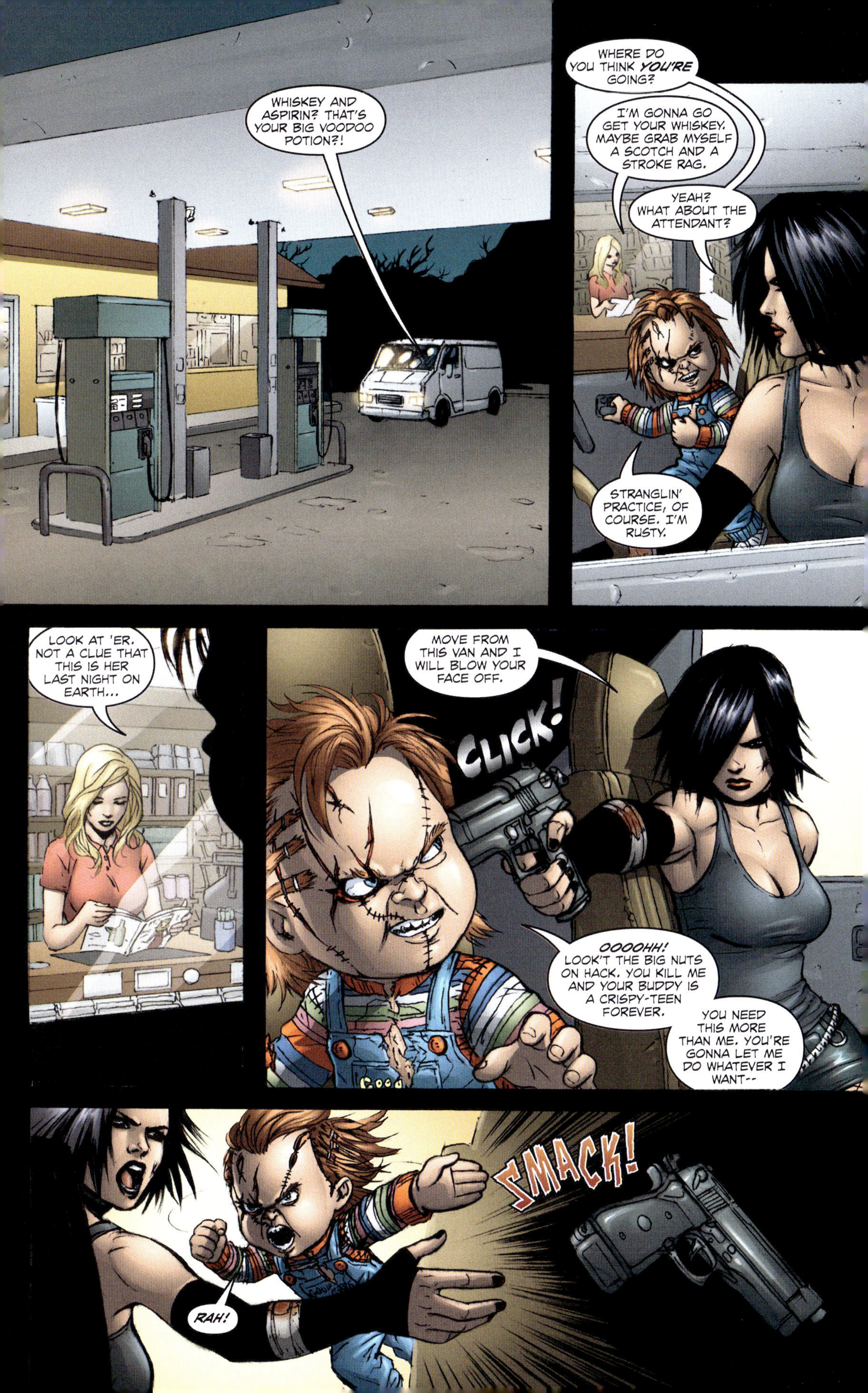
WHISKEY AND ASPIRIN? THAT'S YOUR BIG VOODOO POTION?!
WHERE DO YOU THINK *YOU'RE* GOING?
I'M GONNA GO GET YOUR WHISKEY. MAYBE GRAB MYSELF A SCOTCH AND A STROKE RAG.
YEAH? WHAT ABOUT THE ATTENDANT?
STRANGLIN' PRACTICE, OF COURSE. I'M RUSTY.
LOOK AT 'ER. NOT A CLUE THAT THIS IS HER LAST NIGHT ON EARTH...
MOVE FROM THIS VAN AND I WILL BLOW YOUR FACE OFF.
CLICK!
OOOOHH! LOOK'T THE BIG NUTS ON HACK. YOU KILL ME AND YOUR BUDDY IS A CRISPY-TEEN FOREVER.
YOU NEED THIS MORE THAN ME. YOU'RE GONNA LET ME DO WHATEVER I WANT--
SMACK!
RAH!

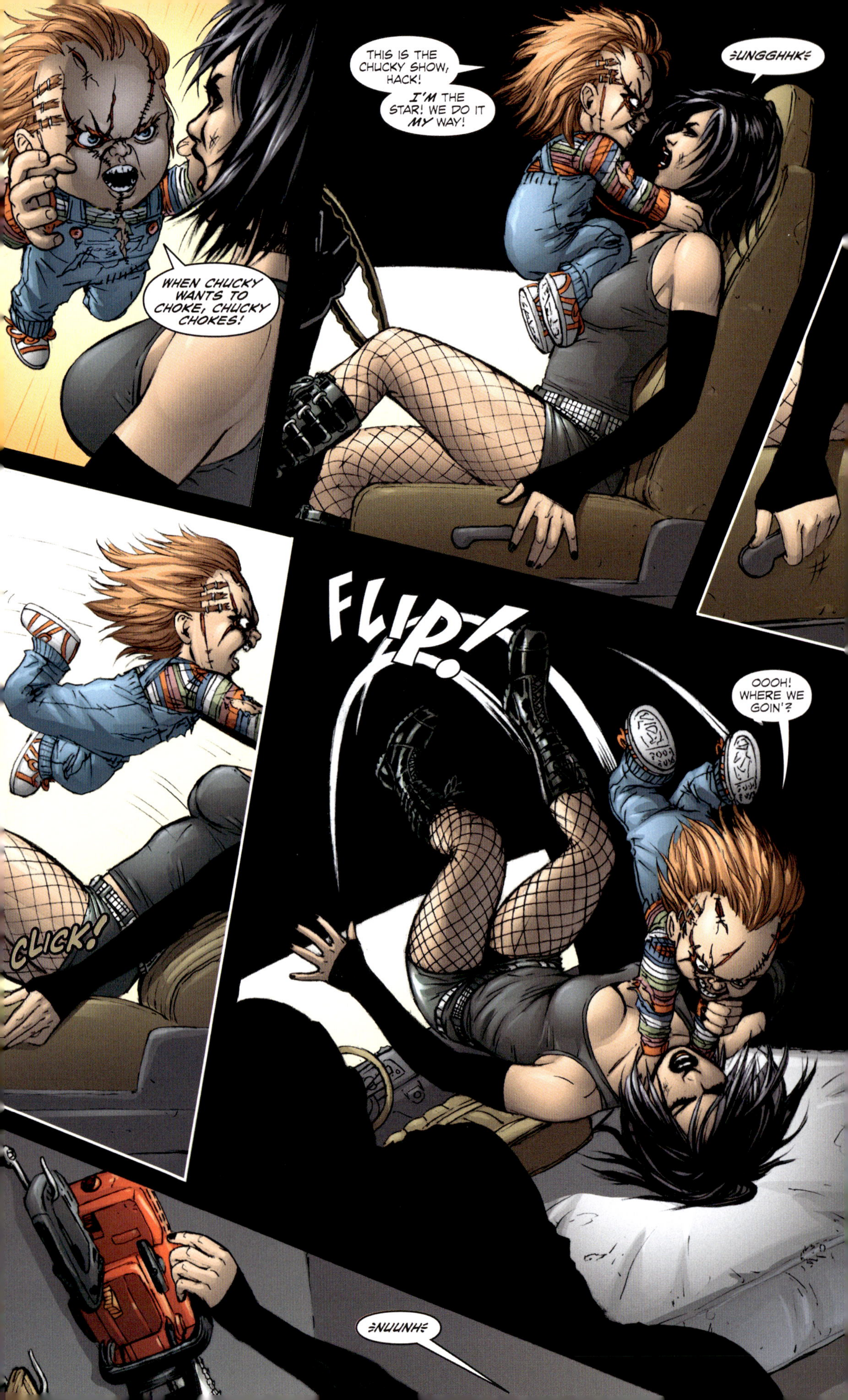
WHEN CHUCKY WANTS TO CHOKE, CHUCKY CHOKES!
THIS IS THE CHUCKY SHOW, HACK!
I'M THE STAR! WE DO IT MY WAY!
UNGGHHK
CLICK!
FLIP!
OOOH! WHERE WE GOIN'?
NUUNH

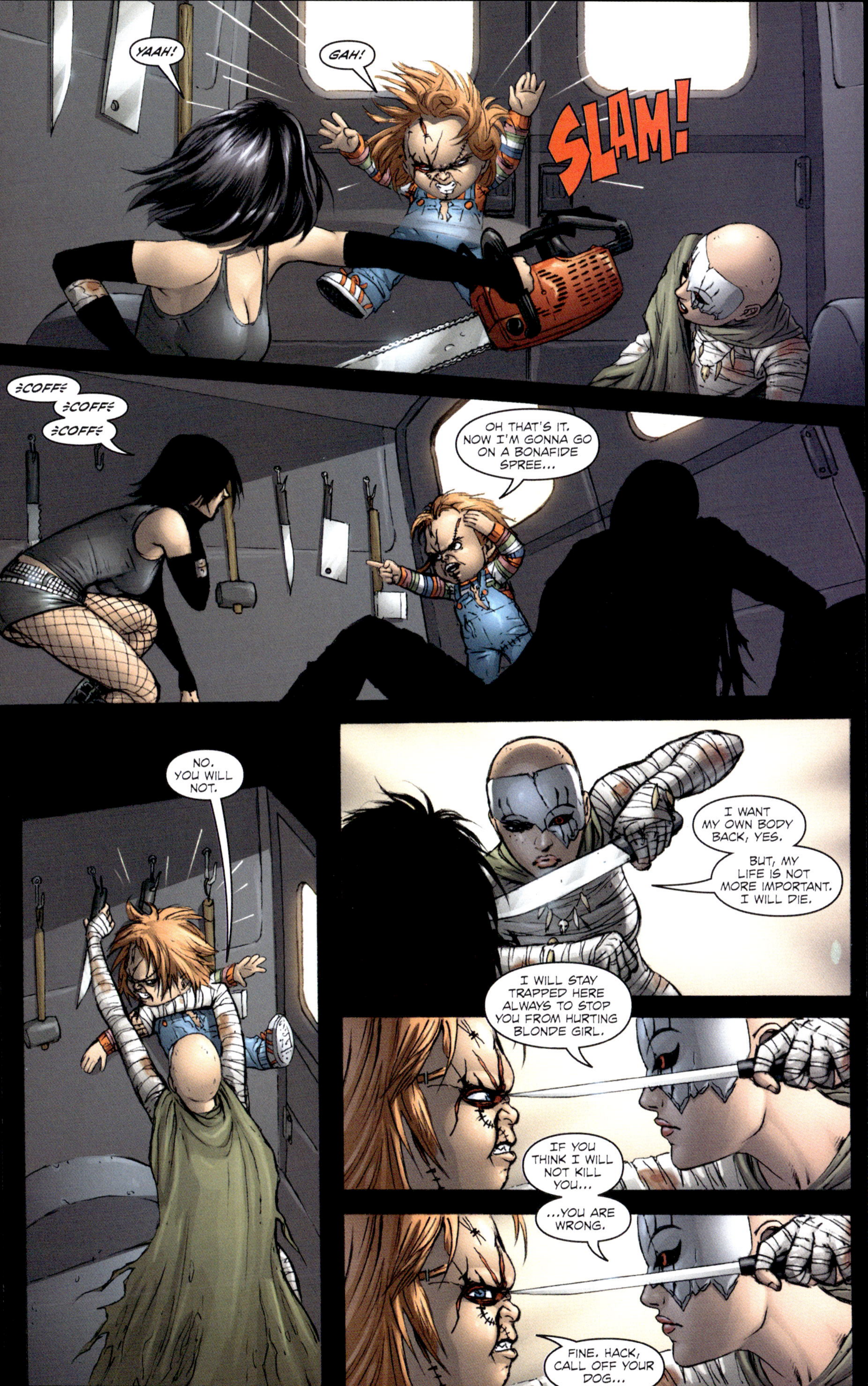
YAAH!
GAH!
SLAM!
COFF
COFF
COFF
OH THAT'S IT. NOW I'M GONNA GO ON A BONAFIDE SPREE...
NO. YOU WILL NOT.
I WANT MY OWN BODY BACK, YES.
BUT, MY LIFE IS NOT MORE IMPORTANT. I WILL DIE.
I WILL STAY TRAPPED HERE ALWAYS TO STOP YOU FROM HURTING BLONDE GIRL.
IF YOU THINK I WILL NOT KILL YOU...
...YOU ARE WRONG.
FINE. HACK, CALL OFF YOUR DOG...

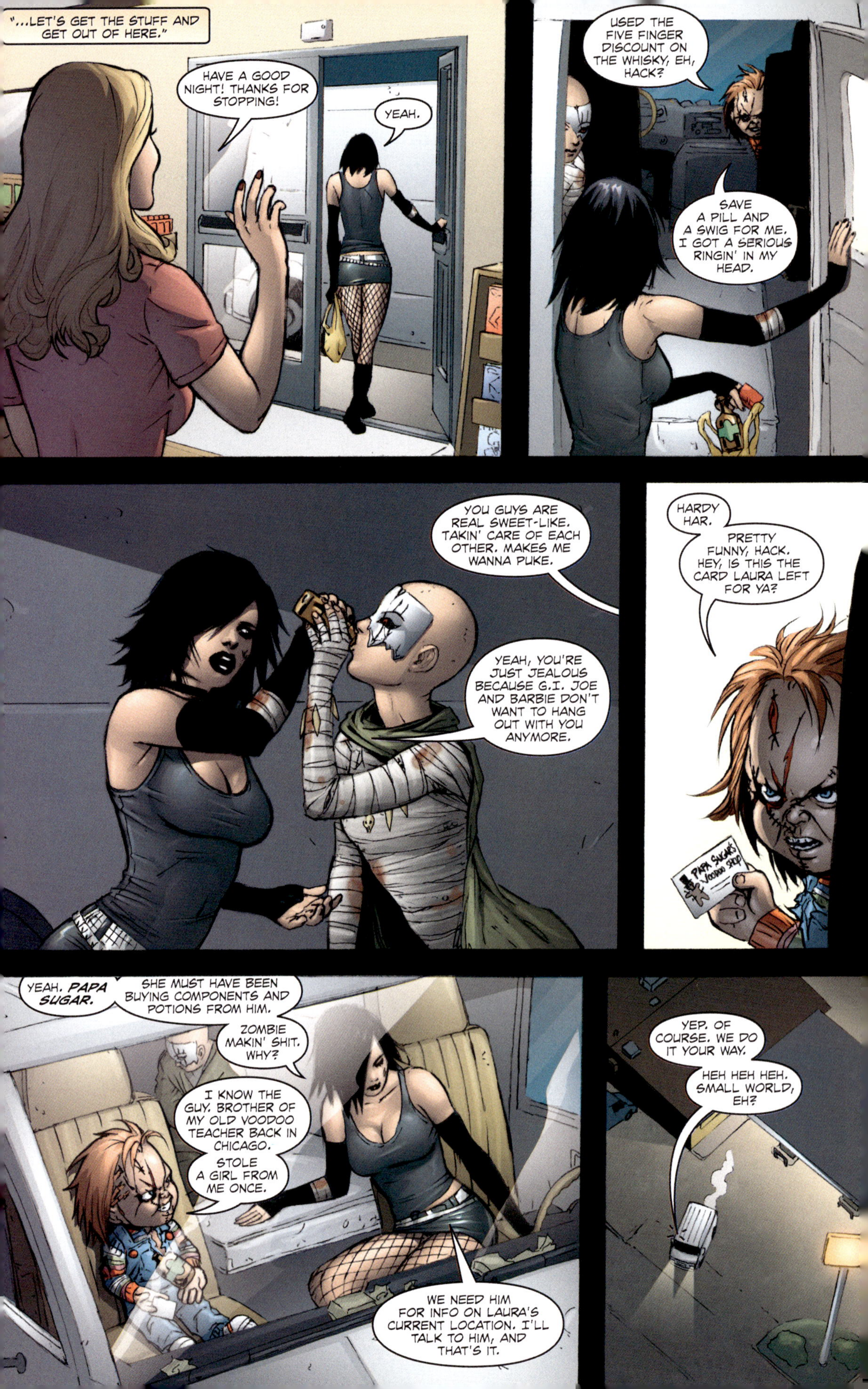
"...LET'S GET THE STUFF AND GET OUT OF HERE."
HAVE A GOOD NIGHT! THANKS FOR STOPPING!
YEAH.
USED THE FIVE FINGER DISCOUNT ON THE WHISKY, EH, HACK?
SAVE A PILL AND A SWIG FOR ME. I GOT A SERIOUS RINGIN' IN MY HEAD.
YOU GUYS ARE REAL SWEET-LIKE. TAKIN' CARE OF EACH OTHER. MAKES ME WANNA PUKE.
YEAH, YOU'RE JUST JEALOUS BECAUSE G.I. JOE AND BARBIE DON'T WANT TO HANG OUT WITH YOU ANYMORE.
HARDY HAR.
PRETTY FUNNY, HACK. HEY, IS THIS THE CARD LAURA LEFT FOR YA?
PAPA SUGAR'S VOODOO SHOP
YEAH. ***PAPA SUGAR.***
SHE MUST HAVE BEEN BUYING COMPONENTS AND POTIONS FROM HIM.
ZOMBIE MAKIN' SHIT. WHY?
I KNOW THE GUY. BROTHER OF MY OLD VOODOO TEACHER BACK IN CHICAGO.
STOLE A GIRL FROM ME ONCE.
WE NEED HIM FOR INFO ON LAURA'S CURRENT LOCATION. I'LL TALK TO HIM, AND THAT'S IT.
YEP. OF COURSE. WE DO IT YOUR WAY.
HEH HEH HEH. SMALL WORLD, EH?

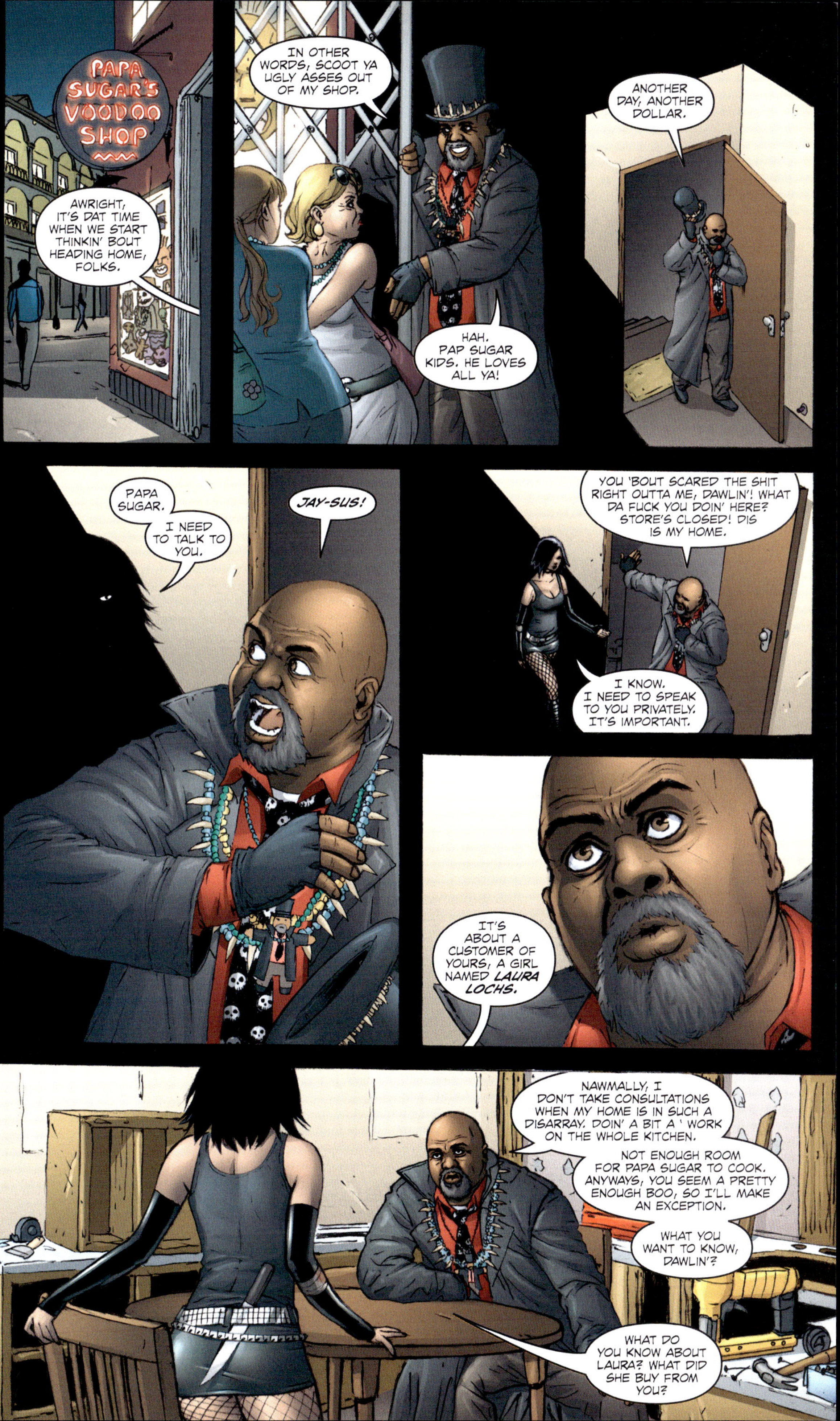
PAPA SUGAR'S VOODOO SHOP
AWRIGHT, IT'S DAT TIME WHEN WE START THINKIN' BOUT HEADING HOME, FOLKS.
IN OTHER WORDS, SCOOT YA UGLY ASSES OUT OF MY SHOP.
HAH. PAP SUGAR KIDS. HE LOVES ALL YA!
ANOTHER DAY, ANOTHER DOLLAR.
PAPA SUGAR.
I NEED TO TALK TO YOU.
JAY-SUS!
YOU 'BOUT SCARED THE SHIT RIGHT OUTTA ME, DAWLIN'! WHAT DA FUCK YOU DOIN' HERE? STORE'S CLOSED! DIS IS MY HOME.
I KNOW. I NEED TO SPEAK TO YOU PRIVATELY. IT'S IMPORTANT.
IT'S ABOUT A CUSTOMER OF YOURS, A GIRL NAMED *LAURA LOCHS.*
NAWMALLY, I DON'T TAKE CONSULTATIONS WHEN MY HOME IS IN SUCH A DISARRAY. DOIN' A BIT A ' WORK ON THE WHOLE KITCHEN.
NOT ENOUGH ROOM FOR PAPA SUGAR TO COOK. ANYWAYS, YOU SEEM A PRETTY ENOUGH BOO, SO I'LL MAKE AN EXCEPTION.
WHAT YOU WANT TO KNOW, DAWLIN'?
WHAT DO YOU KNOW ABOUT LAURA? WHAT DID SHE BUY FROM YOU?

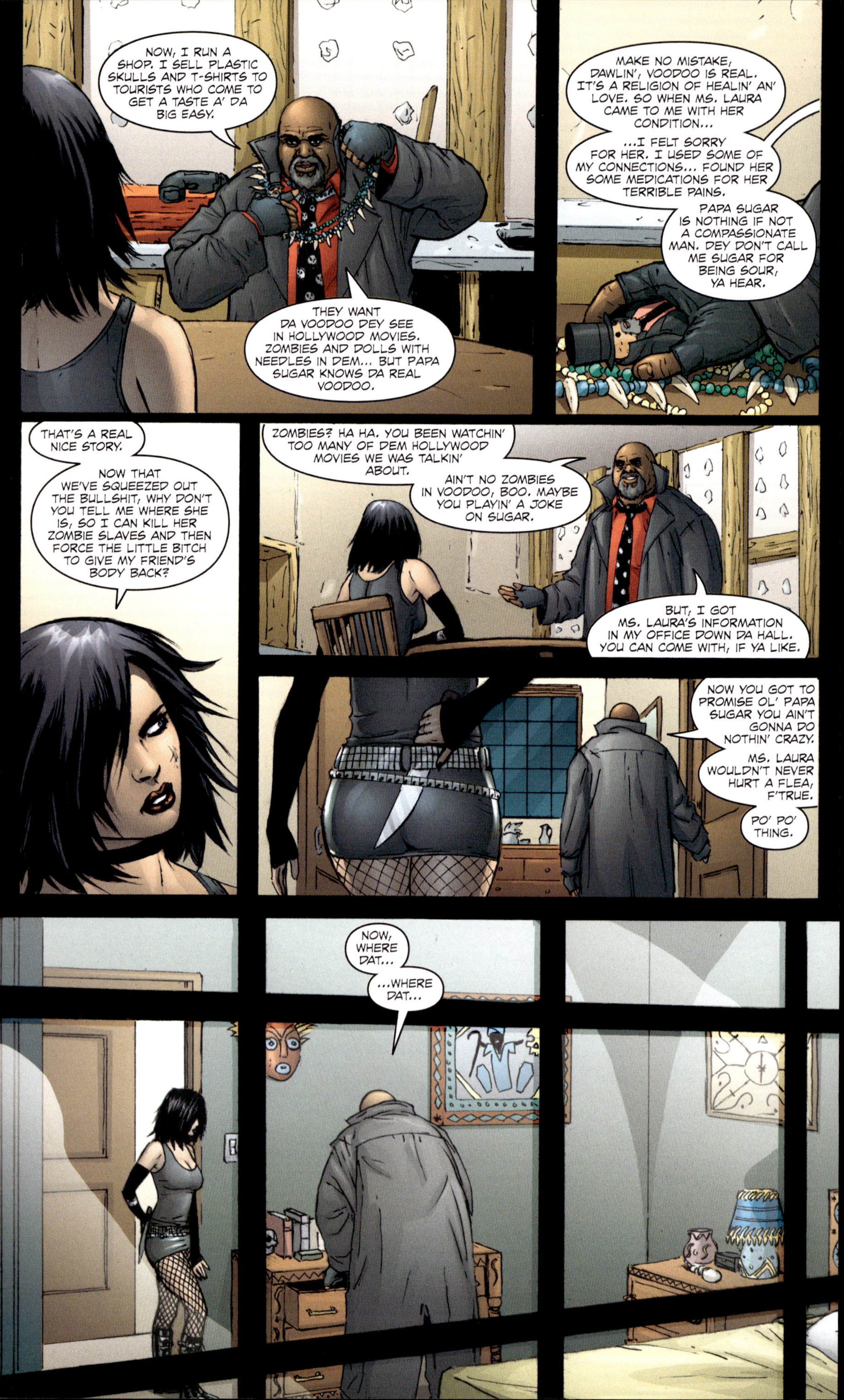
NOW, I RUN A SHOP. I SELL PLASTIC SKULLS AND T-SHIRTS TO TOURISTS WHO COME TO GET A TASTE A' DA BIG EASY.
THEY WANT DA VOODOO DEY SEE IN HOLLYWOOD MOVIES. ZOMBIES AND DOLLS WITH NEEDLES IN DEM... BUT PAPA SUGAR KNOWS DA REAL VOODOO.
MAKE NO MISTAKE, DAWLIN', VOODOO IS REAL. IT'S A RELIGION OF HEALIN' AN' LOVE. SO WHEN MS. LAURA CAME TO ME WITH HER CONDITION...
...I FELT SORRY FOR HER. I USED SOME OF MY CONNECTIONS... FOUND HER SOME MEDICATIONS FOR HER TERRIBLE PAINS.
PAPA SUGAR IS NOTHING IF NOT A COMPASSIONATE MAN. DEY DON'T CALL ME SUGAR FOR BEING SOUR, YA HEAR.
THAT'S A REAL NICE STORY.
NOW THAT WE'VE SQUEEZED OUT THE BULLSHIT, WHY DON'T YOU TELL ME WHERE SHE IS, SO I CAN KILL HER ZOMBIE SLAVES AND THEN FORCE THE LITTLE BITCH TO GIVE MY FRIEND'S BODY BACK?
ZOMBIES? HA HA. YOU BEEN WATCHIN' TOO MANY OF DEM HOLLYWOOD MOVIES WE WAS TALKIN' ABOUT.
AIN'T NO ZOMBIES IN VOODOO, BOO. MAYBE YOU PLAYIN' A JOKE ON SUGAR.
BUT, I GOT MS. LAURA'S INFORMATION IN MY OFFICE DOWN DA HALL. YOU CAN COME WITH, IF YA LIKE.
NOW YOU GOT TO PROMISE OL' PAPA SUGAR YOU AIN'T GONNA DO NOTHIN' CRAZY.
MS. LAURA WOULDN'T NEVER HURT A FLEA, F'TRUE.
PO' PO' THING.
NOW, WHERE DAT...
...WHERE DAT...

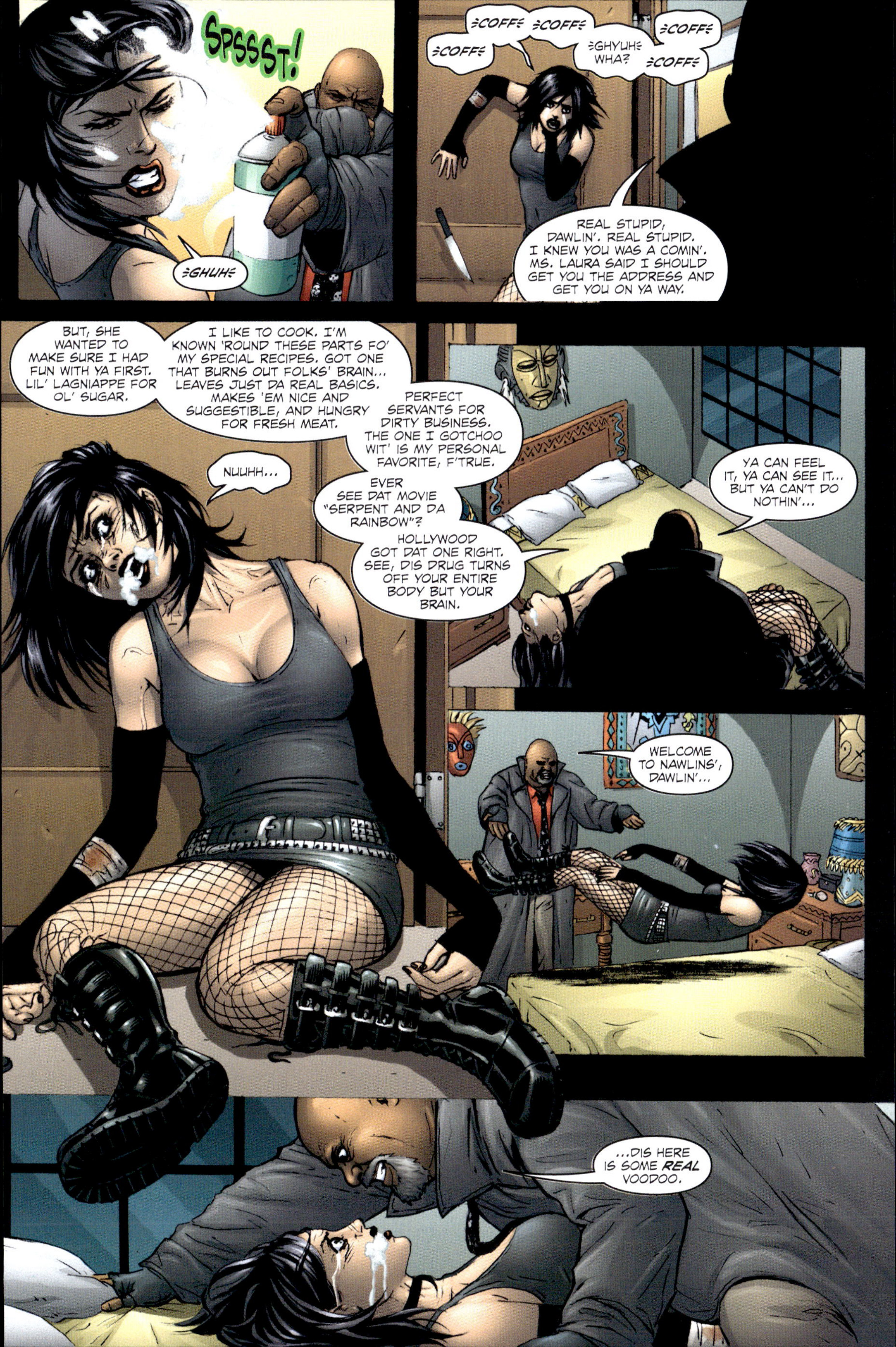
SPSSST!
GHUH
COFF COFF
COFF
GHYUH WHA?
COFF
COFF
REAL STUPID, DAWLIN'. REAL STUPID. I KNEW YOU WAS A COMIN'. MS. LAURA SAID I SHOULD GET YOU THE ADDRESS AND GET YOU ON YA WAY.
BUT, SHE WANTED TO MAKE SURE I HAD FUN WITH YA FIRST. LIL' LAGNIAPPE FOR OL' SUGAR.
I LIKE TO COOK. I'M KNOWN 'ROUND THESE PARTS FO' MY SPECIAL RECIPES. GOT ONE THAT BURNS OUT FOLKS' BRAIN... LEAVES JUST DA REAL BASICS. MAKES 'EM NICE AND SUGGESTIBLE, AND HUNGRY FOR FRESH MEAT.
NUUHH...
PERFECT SERVANTS FOR DIRTY BUSINESS. THE ONE I GOTCHOO WIT' IS MY PERSONAL FAVORITE, F'TRUE.
EVER SEE DAT MOVIE "SERPENT AND DA RAINBOW"?
HOLLYWOOD GOT DAT ONE RIGHT. SEE, DIS DRUG TURNS OFF YOUR ENTIRE BODY BUT YOUR BRAIN.
YA CAN FEEL IT, YA CAN SEE IT... BUT YA CAN'T DO NOTHIN'...
WELCOME TO NAWLINS', DAWLIN'...
...DIS HERE IS SOME *REAL* VOODOO.

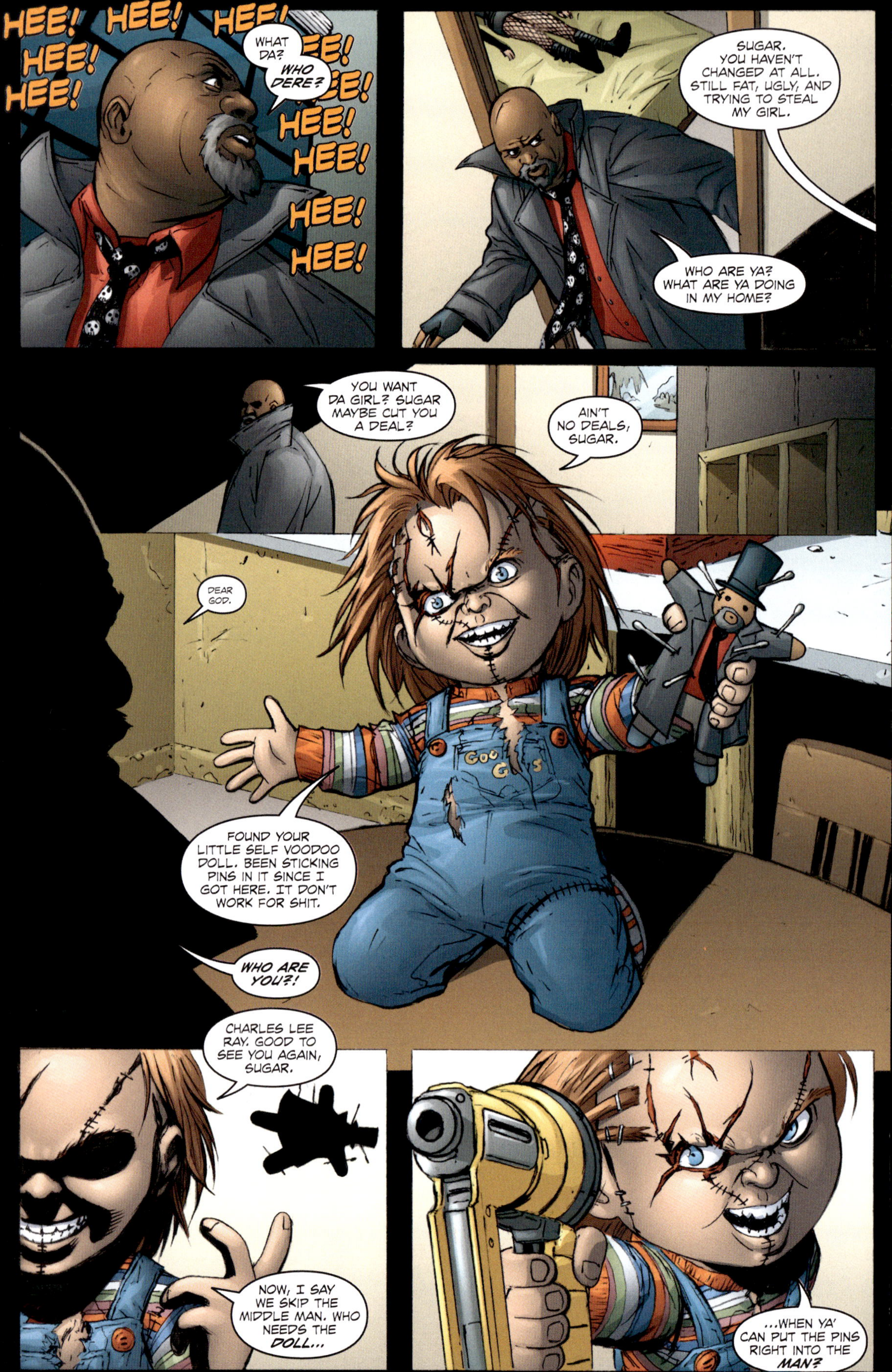
HEE! HEE! HEE! HEE! HEE! HEE! HEE! HEE! HEE! HEE!
WHAT DA? WHO DERE?
SUGAR. YOU HAVEN'T CHANGED AT ALL. STILL FAT, UGLY, AND TRYING TO STEAL MY GIRL.
WHO ARE YA? WHAT ARE YA DOING IN MY HOME?
YOU WANT DA GIRL? SUGAR MAYBE CUT YOU A DEAL?
AIN'T NO DEALS, SUGAR.
DEAR GOD.
FOUND YOUR LITTLE SELF VOODOO DOLL. BEEN STICKING PINS IN IT SINCE I GOT HERE. IT DON'T WORK FOR SHIT.
WHO ARE YOU?!
CHARLES LEE RAY. GOOD TO SEE YOU AGAIN, SUGAR.
NOW, I SAY WE SKIP THE MIDDLE MAN. WHO NEEDS THE DOLL...
...WHEN YA' CAN PUT THE PINS RIGHT INTO THE MAN?

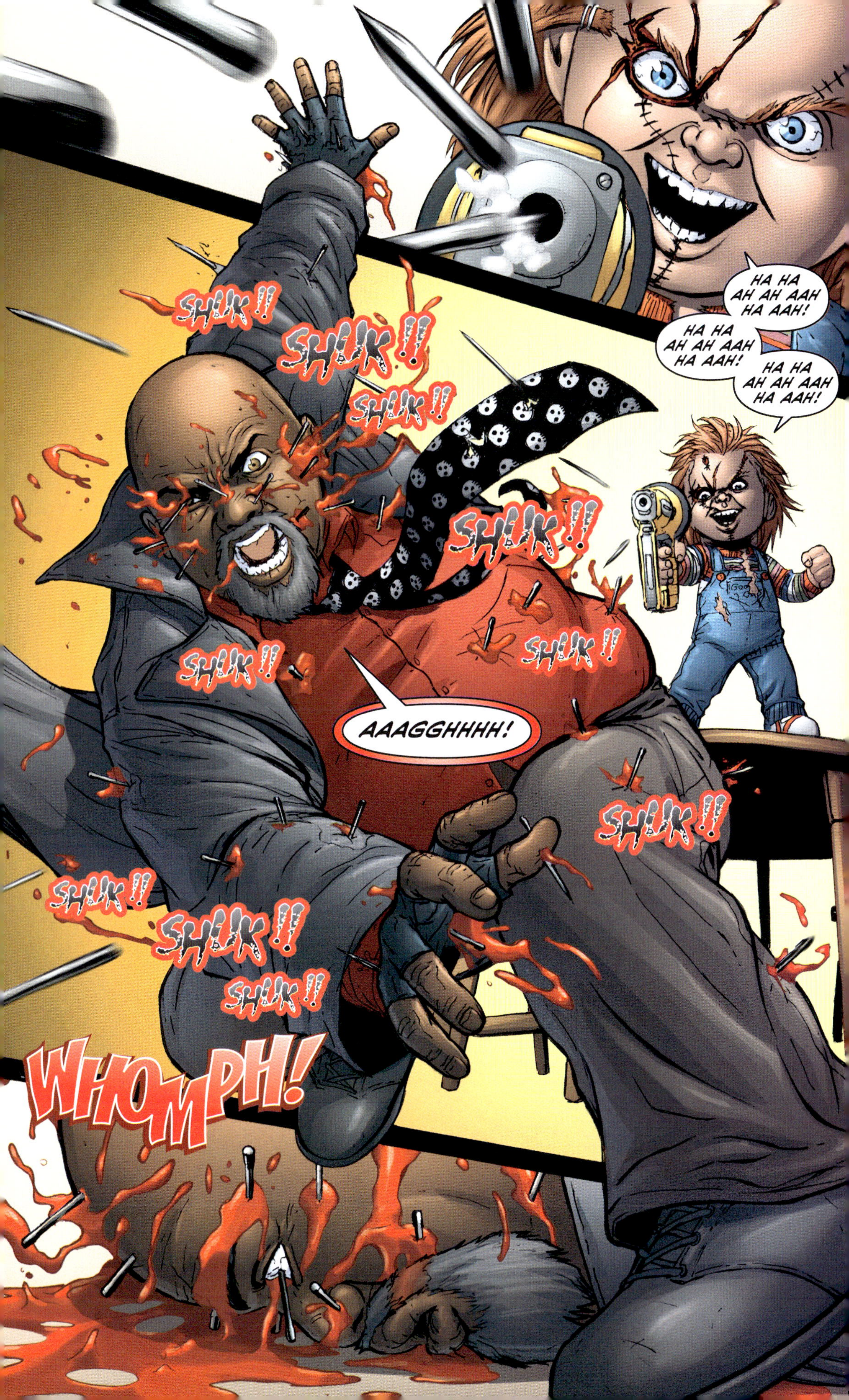
HA HA
AH AH AAH
HA AAH!
HA HA
AH AH AAH
HA AAH!
HA HA
AH AH AAH
HA AAH!
SHUK!!
SHUK!!
SHUK!!
SHUK!!
SHUK!!
SHUK!!
AAAGGHHHH!
SHUK!!
SHUK!!
SHUK!!
SHUK!!
WHOMPH!

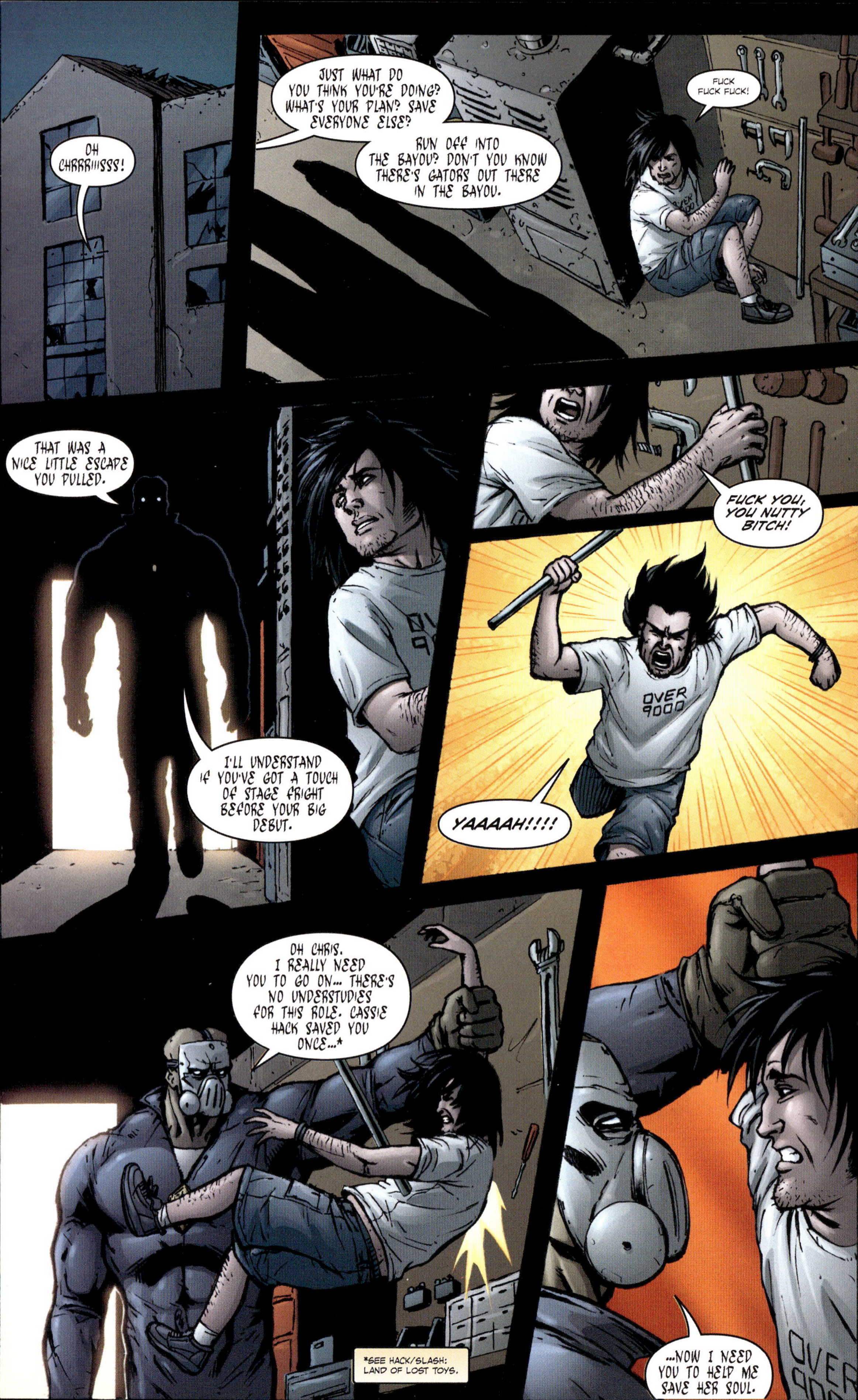
OH CHRRRIIIISSS!
JUST WHAT DO YOU THINK YOU'RE DOING? WHAT'S YOUR PLAN? SAVE EVERYONE ELSE?
RUN OFF INTO THE BAYOU? DON'T YOU KNOW THERE'S GATORS OUT THERE IN THE BAYOU.
FUCK FUCK FUCK!
THAT WAS A NICE LITTLE ESCAPE YOU PULLED.
I'LL UNDERSTAND IF YOU'VE GOT A TOUCH OF STAGE FRIGHT BEFORE YOUR BIG DEBUT.
FUCK YOU, YOU NUTTY BITCH!
YAAAAH!!!!
OH CHRIS. I REALLY NEED YOU TO GO ON... THERE'S NO UNDERSTUDIES FOR THIS ROLE. CASSIE HACK SAVED YOU ONCE...*
*SEE HACK/SLASH: LAND OF LOST TOYS.
...NOW I NEED YOU TO HELP ME SAVE HER SOUL.

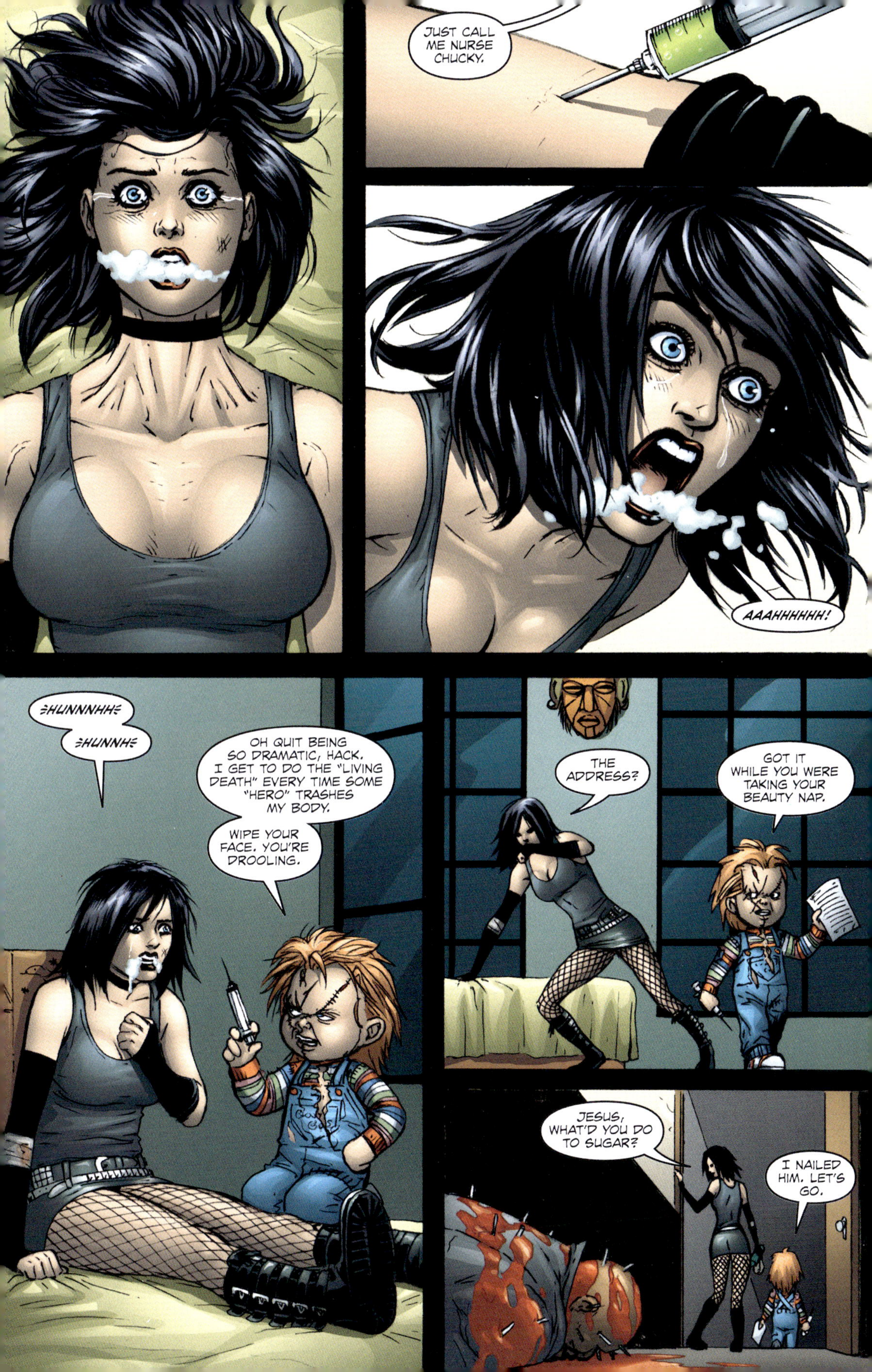

JUST CALL ME NURSE CHUCKY.
AAAHHHHHH!
HUNNNHH
HUNNH
OH QUIT BEING SO DRAMATIC, HACK. I GET TO DO THE "LIVING DEATH" EVERY TIME SOME "HERO" TRASHES MY BODY.
WIPE YOUR FACE. YOU'RE DROOLING.
THE ADDRESS?
GOT IT WHILE YOU WERE TAKING YOUR BEAUTY NAP.
JESUS, WHAT'D YOU DO TO SUGAR?
I NAILED HIM. LET'S GO.

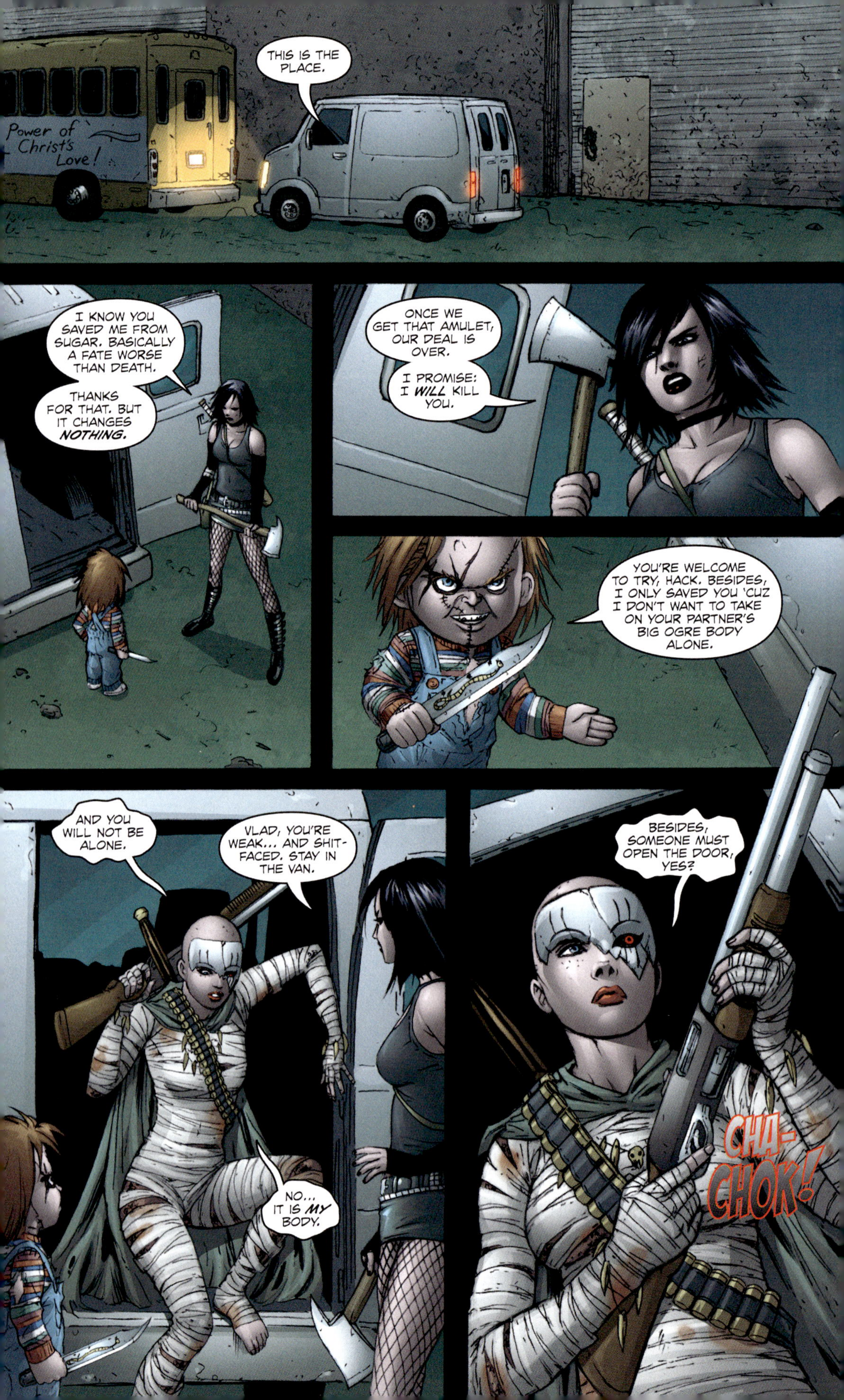
Power of Christ's Love!
THIS IS THE PLACE.
I KNOW YOU SAVED ME FROM SUGAR. BASICALLY A FATE WORSE THAN DEATH.
THANKS FOR THAT. BUT IT CHANGES NOTHING.
ONCE WE GET THAT AMULET, OUR DEAL IS OVER.
I PROMISE: I WILL KILL YOU.
YOU'RE WELCOME TO TRY, HACK. BESIDES, I ONLY SAVED YOU 'CUZ I DON'T WANT TO TAKE ON YOUR PARTNER'S BIG OGRE BODY ALONE.
AND YOU WILL NOT BE ALONE.
VLAD, YOU'RE WEAK... AND SHIT-FACED. STAY IN THE VAN.
NO... IT IS MY BODY.
BESIDES, SOMEONE MUST OPEN THE DOOR, YES?
CHA-CHOK!

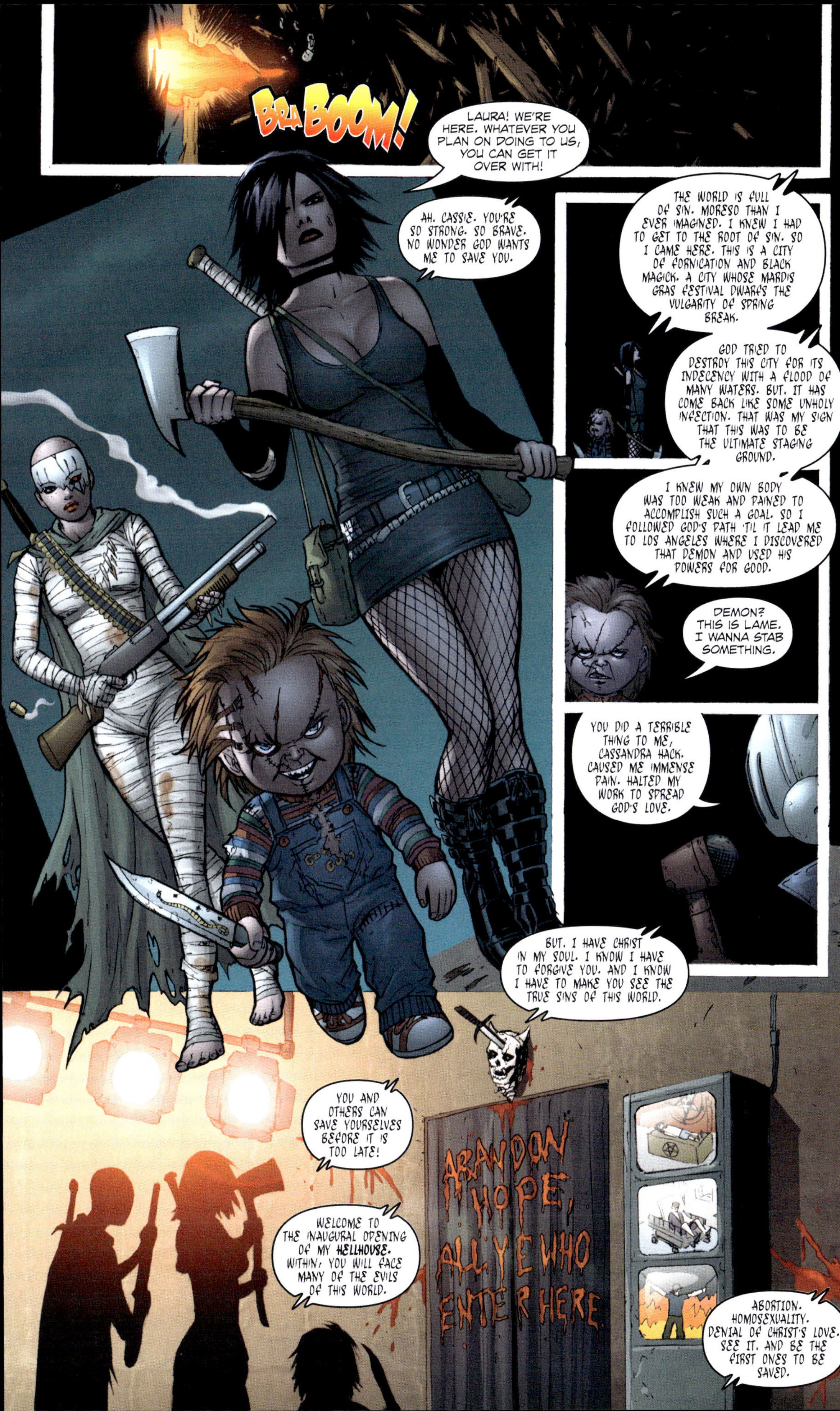
BRA BOOM!
LAURA! WE'RE HERE. WHATEVER YOU PLAN ON DOING TO US, YOU CAN GET IT OVER WITH!
AH. CASSIE. YOU'RE SO STRONG. SO BRAVE. NO WONDER GOD WANTS ME TO SAVE YOU.
THE WORLD IS FULL OF SIN. MORESO THAN I EVER IMAGINED. I KNEW I HAD TO GET TO THE ROOT OF SIN. SO I CAME HERE. THIS IS A CITY OF FORNICATION AND BLACK MAGICK. A CITY WHOSE MARDIS GRAS FESTIVAL DWARFS THE VULGARITY OF SPRING BREAK.
GOD TRIED TO DESTROY THIS CITY FOR ITS INDECENCY WITH A FLOOD OF MANY WATERS. BUT. IT HAS COME BACK LIKE SOME UNHOLY INFECTION. THAT WAS MY SIGN THAT THIS WAS TO BE THE ULTIMATE STAGING GROUND.
I KNEW MY OWN BODY WAS TOO WEAK AND PAINED TO ACCOMPLISH SUCH A GOAL. SO I FOLLOWED GOD'S PATH 'TIL IT LEAD ME TO LOS ANGELES WHERE I DISCOVERED THAT DEMON AND USED HIS POWERS FOR GOOD.
DEMON? THIS IS LAME. I WANNA STAB SOMETHING.
YOU DID A TERRIBLE THING TO ME, CASSANDRA HACK. CAUSED ME IMMENSE PAIN. HALTED MY WORK TO SPREAD GOD'S LOVE.
BUT. I HAVE CHRIST IN MY SOUL. I KNOW I HAVE TO FORGIVE YOU. AND I KNOW I HAVE TO MAKE YOU SEE THE TRUE SINS OF THIS WORLD.
YOU AND OTHERS CAN SAVE YOURSELVES BEFORE IT IS TOO LATE!
WELCOME TO THE INAUGURAL OPENING OF MY HELLHOUSE. WITHIN, YOU WILL FACE MANY OF THE EVILS OF THIS WORLD.
ABANDON HOPE, ALL YE WHO ENTER HERE.
ABORTION. HOMOSEXUALITY. DENIAL OF CHRIST'S LOVE. SEE IT. AND BE THE FIRST ONES TO BE SAVED.

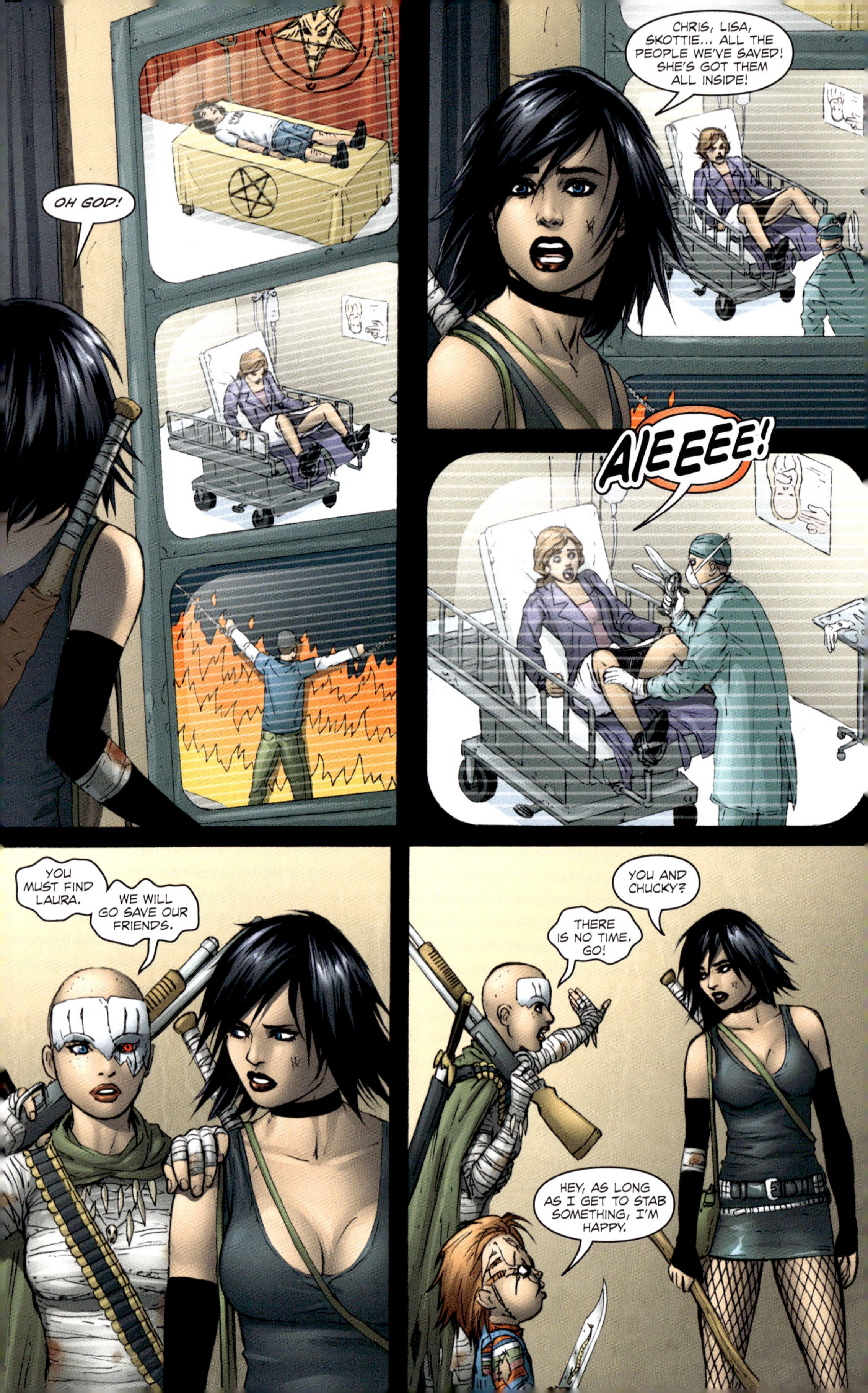

OH GOD!
CHRIS, LISA, SKOTTIE... ALL THE PEOPLE WE'VE SAVED! SHE'S GOT THEM ALL INSIDE!
AIEEEE!
YOU MUST FIND LAURA.
WE WILL GO SAVE OUR FRIENDS.
YOU AND CHUCKY?
THERE IS NO TIME. GO!
HEY, AS LONG AS I GET TO STAB SOMETHING, I'M HAPPY.

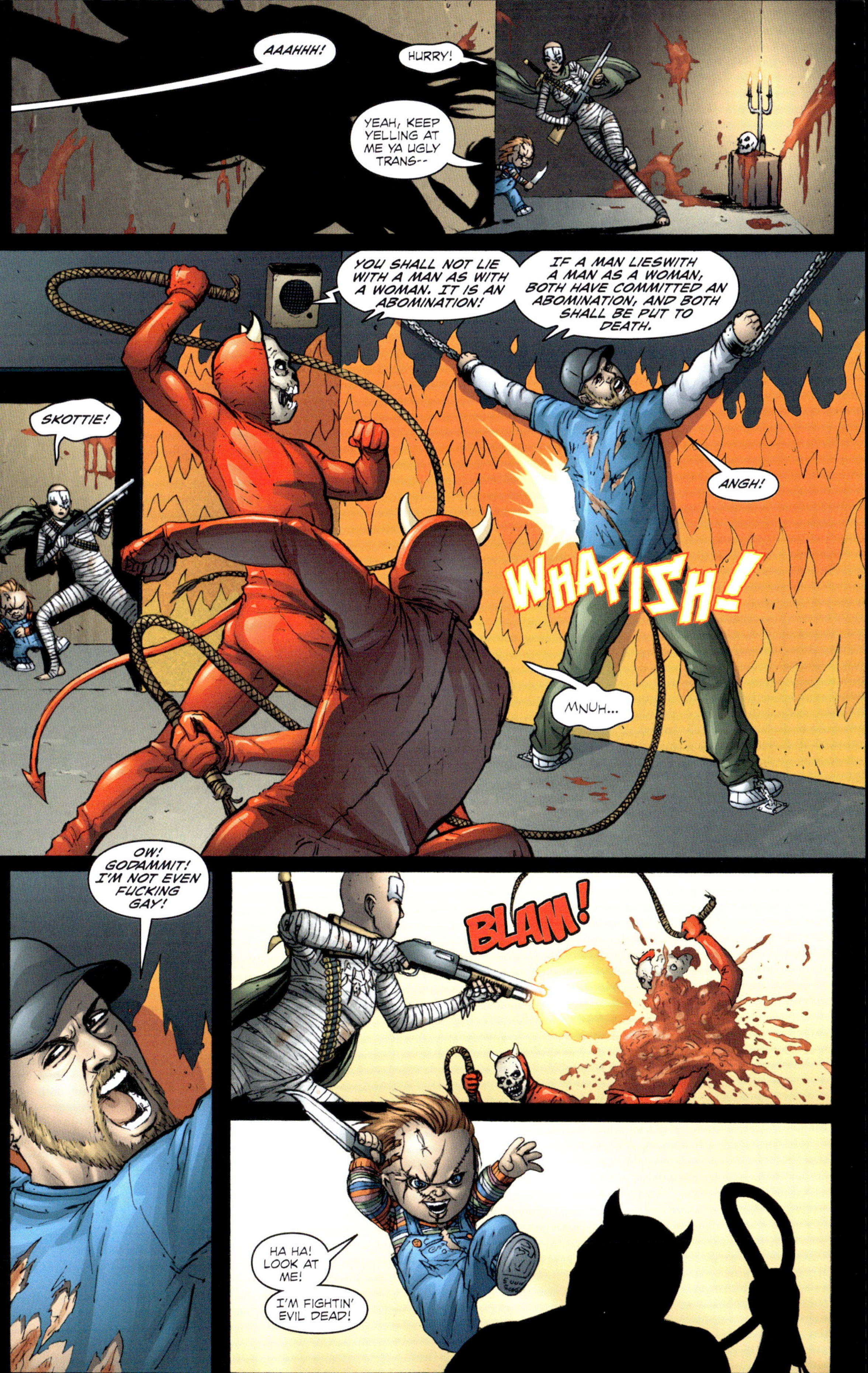
AAAHHH!
HURRY!
YEAH, KEEP YELLING AT ME YA UGLY TRANS--
YOU SHALL NOT LIE WITH A MAN AS WITH A WOMAN. IT IS AN ABOMINATION!
IF A MAN LIESWITH A MAN AS A WOMAN, BOTH HAVE COMMITTED AN ABOMINATION, AND BOTH SHALL BE PUT TO DEATH.
SKOTTIE!
ANGH!
WHAPISH!
MNUH...
OW! GODAMMIT! I'M NOT EVEN FUCKING GAY!
BLAM!
HA HA! LOOK AT ME!
I'M FIGHTIN' EVIL DEAD!

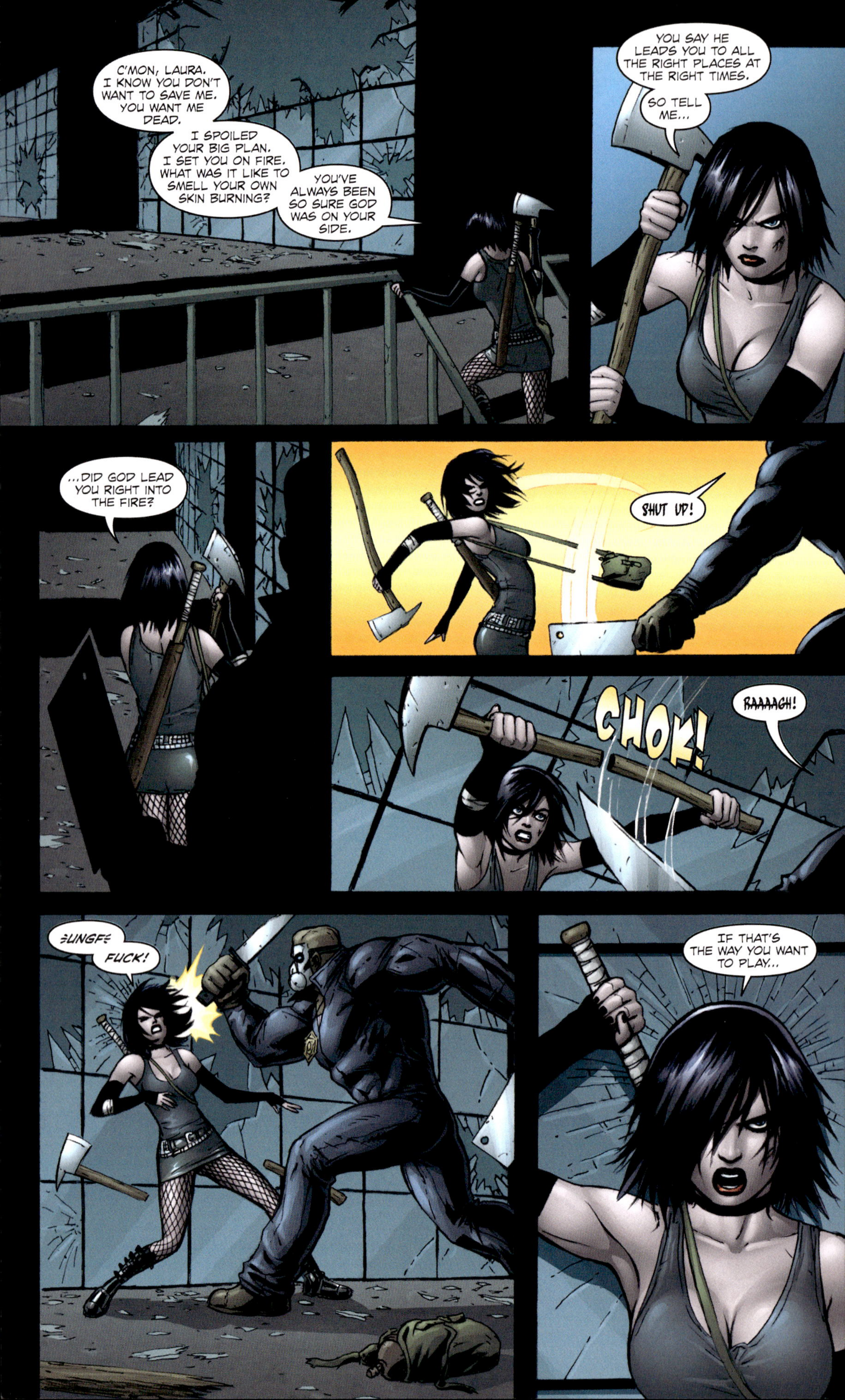
C'MON, LAURA. I KNOW YOU DON'T WANT TO SAVE ME. YOU WANT ME DEAD.
I SPOILED YOUR BIG PLAN. I SET YOU ON FIRE. WHAT WAS IT LIKE TO SMELL YOUR OWN SKIN BURNING?
YOU'VE ALWAYS BEEN SO SURE GOD WAS ON YOUR SIDE.
YOU SAY HE LEADS YOU TO ALL THE RIGHT PLACES AT THE RIGHT TIMES.
SO TELL ME...
...DID GOD LEAD YOU RIGHT INTO THE FIRE?
SHUT UP!
CHOK!
RAAAAGH!
UNGF
FUCK!
IF THAT'S THE WAY YOU WANT TO PLAY...

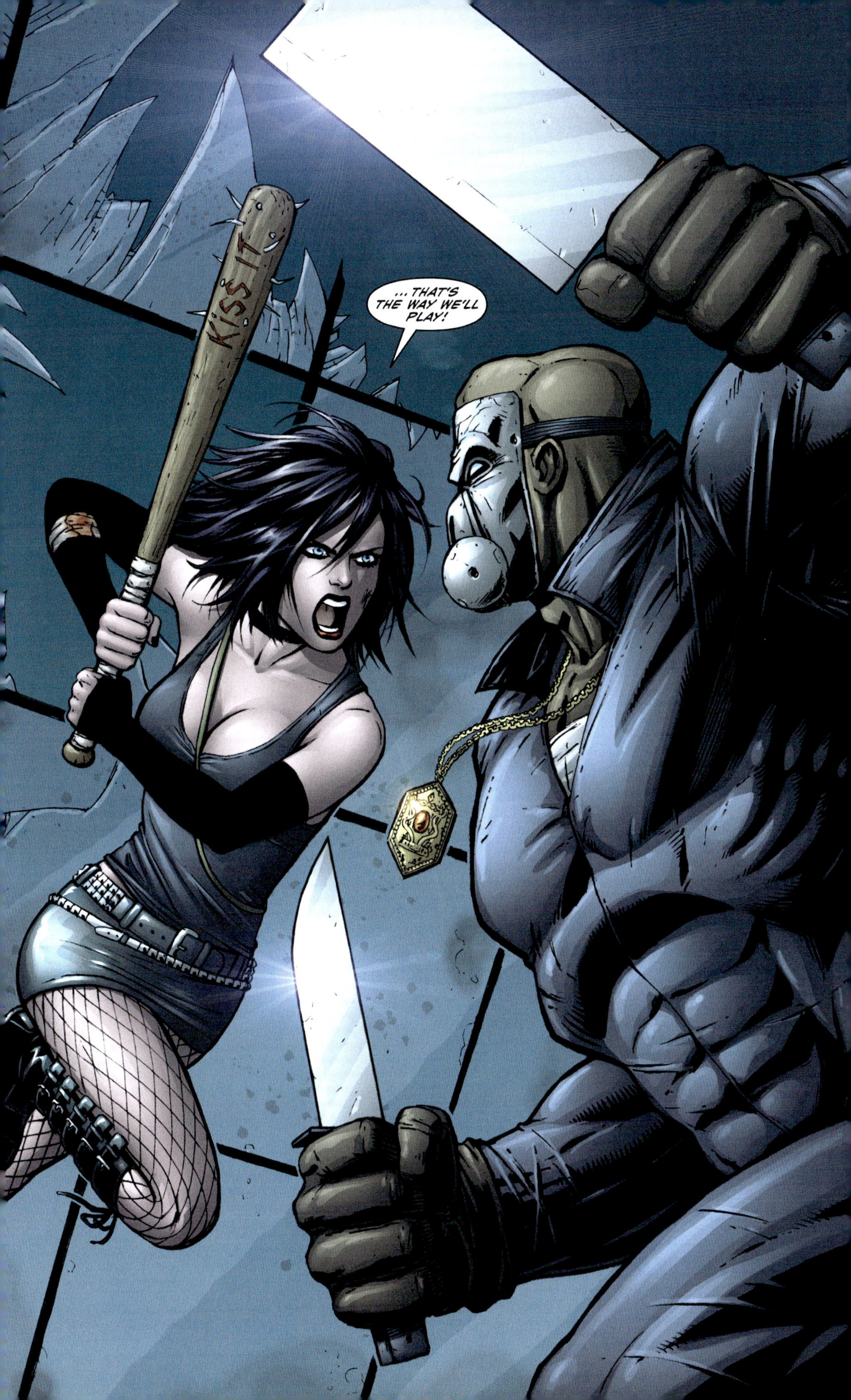
...THAT'S THE WAY WE'LL PLAY!
KISS IT

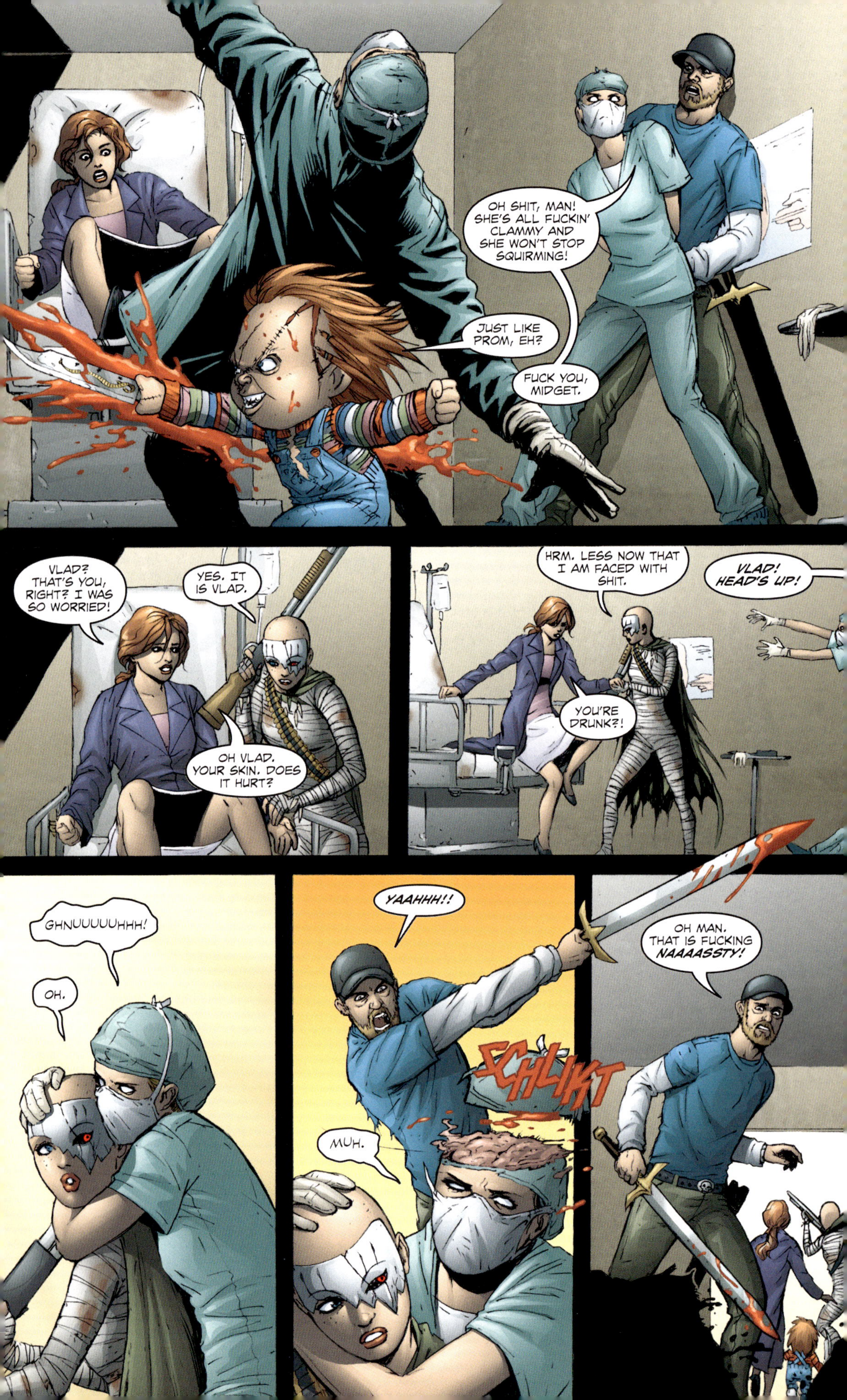
OH SHIT, MAN! SHE'S ALL FUCKIN' CLAMMY AND SHE WON'T STOP SQUIRMING!
JUST LIKE PROM, EH?
FUCK YOU, MIDGET.
VLAD? THAT'S YOU, RIGHT? I WAS SO WORRIED!
YES. IT IS VLAD.
OH VLAD. YOUR SKIN. DOES IT HURT?
HRM. LESS NOW THAT I AM FACED WITH SHIT.
YOU'RE DRUNK?!
VLAD! HEAD'S UP!
GHNUUUUUHHH!
OH.
YAAHHH!!
SCHLIKT
MUH.
OH MAN. THAT IS FUCKING NAAAAASSTY!

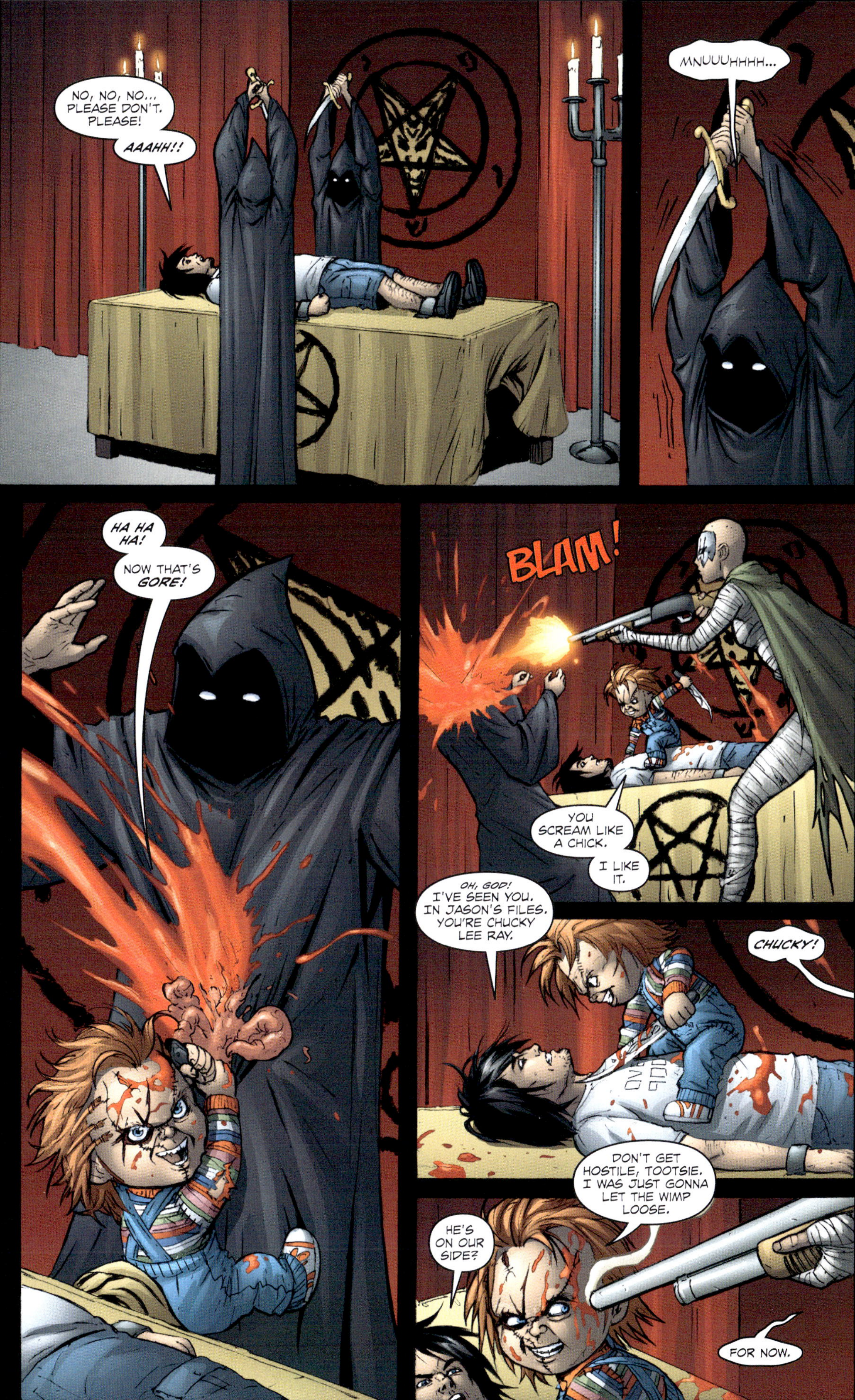
NO, NO, NO... PLEASE DON'T. PLEASE!
AAAHH!!
MNUUUHHHH...
HA HA HA!
NOW THAT'S GORE!
BLAM!
YOU SCREAM LIKE A CHICK.
I LIKE IT.
OH, GOD! I'VE SEEN YOU. IN JASON'S FILES. YOU'RE CHUCKY LEE RAY.
CHUCKY!
DON'T GET HOSTILE, TOOTSIE. I WAS JUST GONNA LET THE WIMP LOOSE.
HE'S ON OUR SIDE?
FOR NOW.

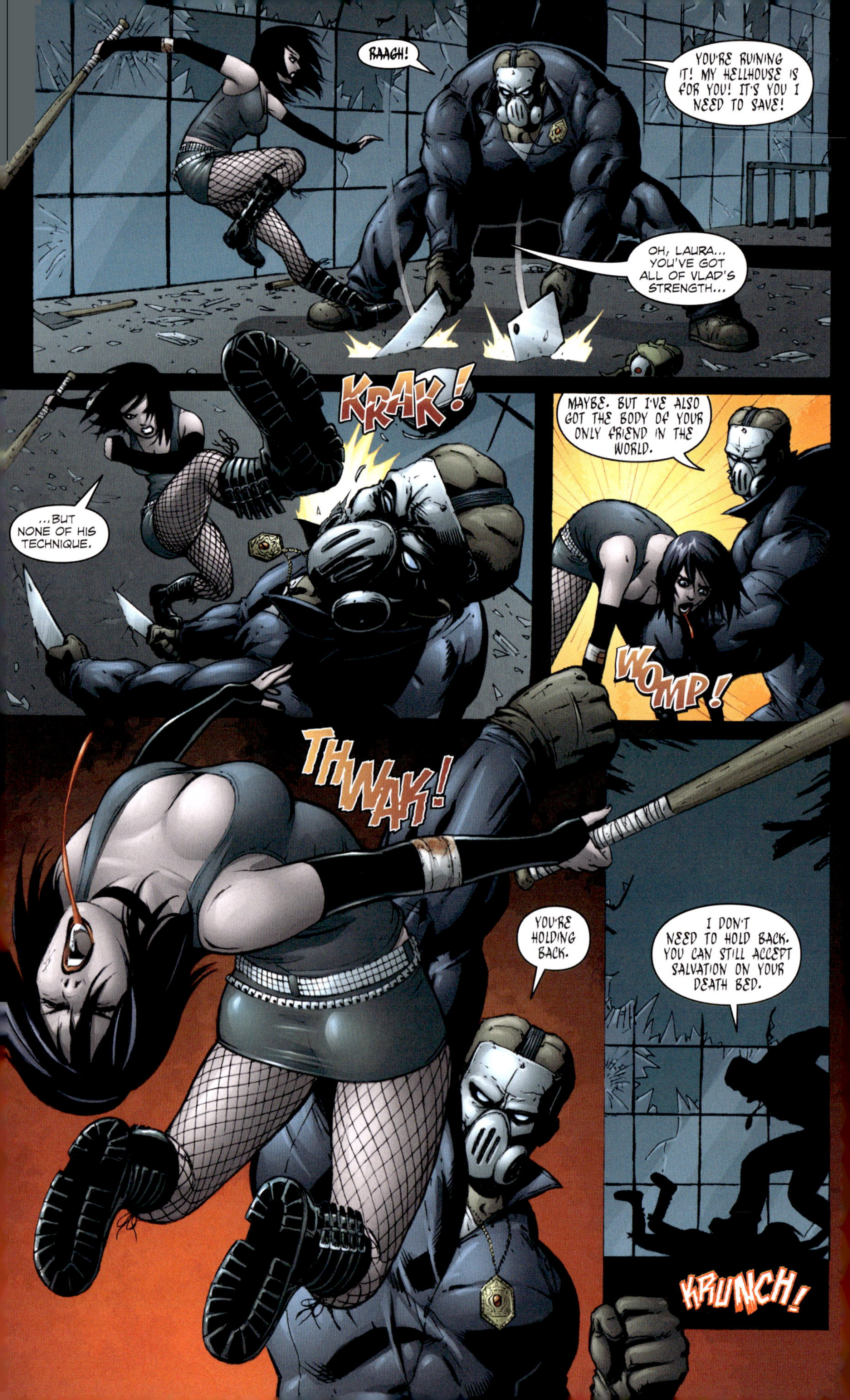
RAAGH!
YOU'RE RUINING IT! MY HELLHOUSE IS FOR YOU! IT'S YOU I NEED TO SAVE!
OH, LAURA... YOU'VE GOT ALL OF VLAD'S STRENGTH...
KRAK!
...BUT NONE OF HIS TECHNIQUE.
MAYBE. BUT I'VE ALSO GOT THE BODY OF YOUR ONLY FRIEND IN THE WORLD.
WOMP!
THWAK!
YOU'RE HOLDING BACK.
I DON'T NEED TO HOLD BACK. YOU CAN STILL ACCEPT SALVATION ON YOUR DEATH BED.
KRUNCH!

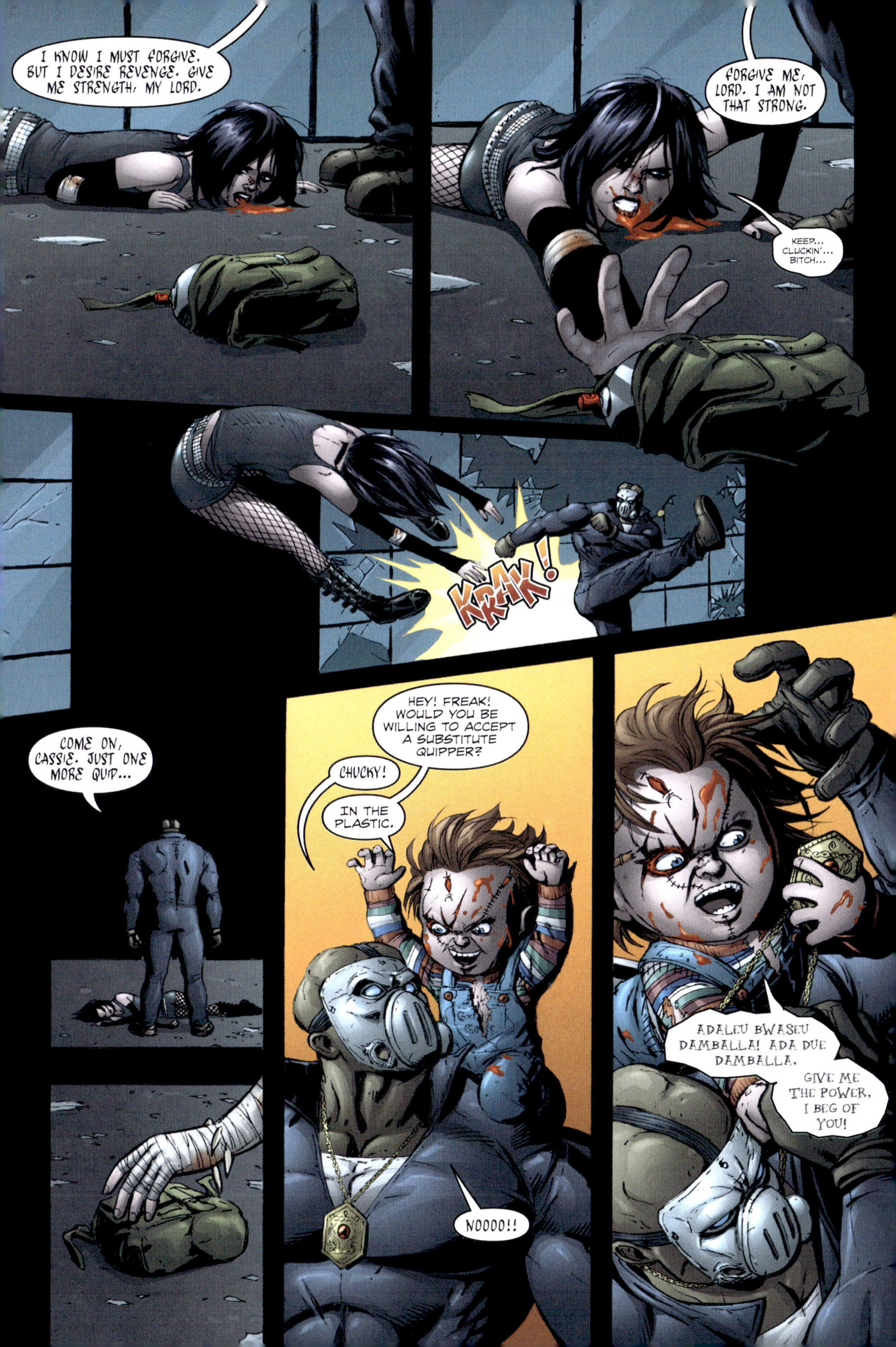
I KNOW I MUST FORGIVE. BUT I DESIRE REVENGE. GIVE ME STRENGTH, MY LORD.
FORGIVE ME, LORD. I AM NOT THAT STRONG.
KEEP... CLUCKIN'... BITCH...
KRAK!
COME ON, CASSIE. JUST ONE MORE QUIP...
HEY! FREAK! WOULD YOU BE WILLING TO ACCEPT A SUBSTITUTE QUIPPER?
CHUCKY!
IN THE PLASTIC.
NOOOO!!
ADALEU BWASEU DAMBALLA! ADA DUE DAMBALLA,
GIVE ME THE POWER, I BEG OF YOU!

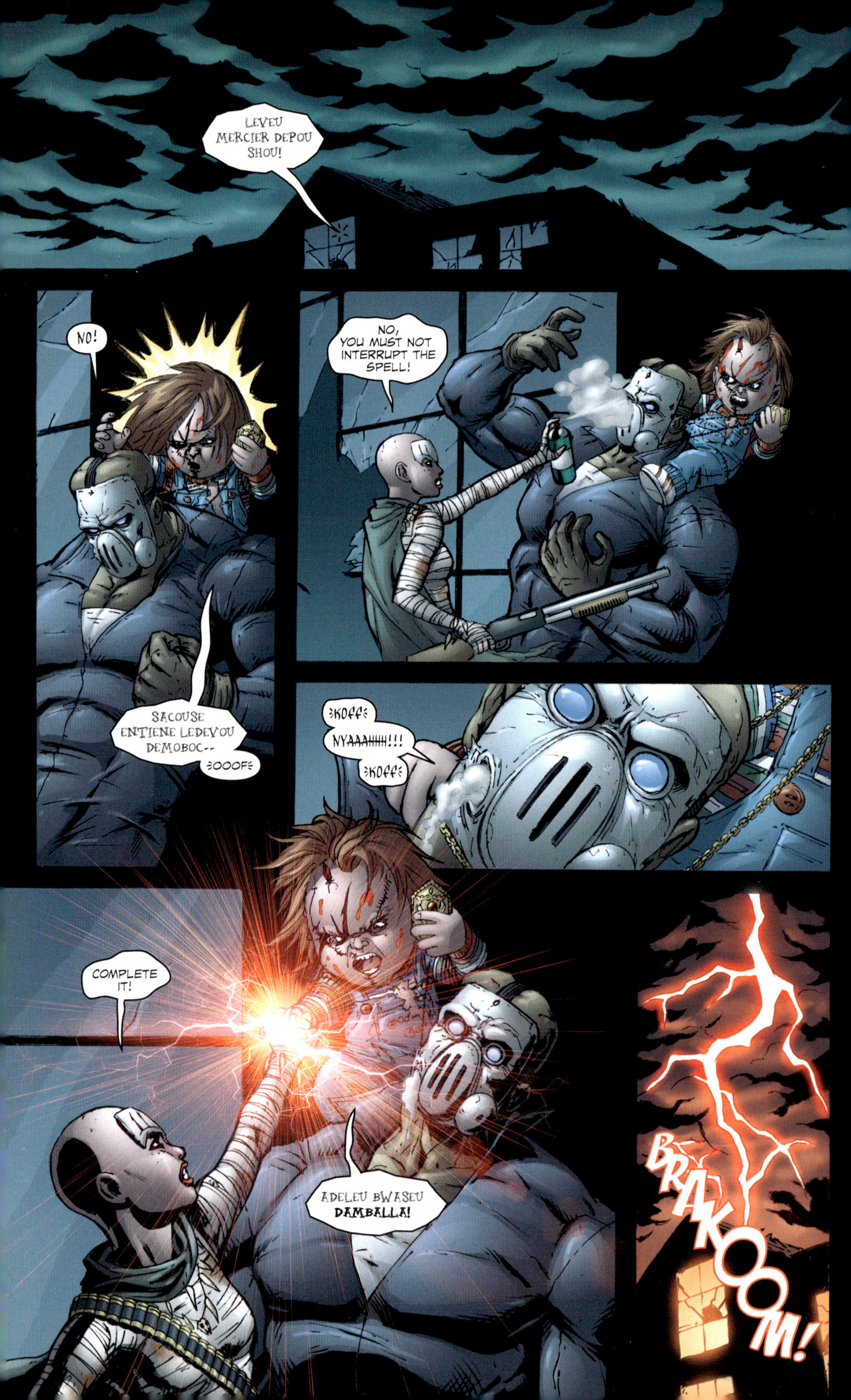
LEVEU MERCIER DEPOU SHOU!
NO!
NO, YOU MUST NOT INTERRUPT THE SPELL!
SACOUSE ENTIENE LEDEVOU DEMOBOC--
OOOF
KOFF
NYAAAHHH!!!
KOFF
COMPLETE IT!
ADELEU BWASEU DAMBALLA!
BRAKOOOM!

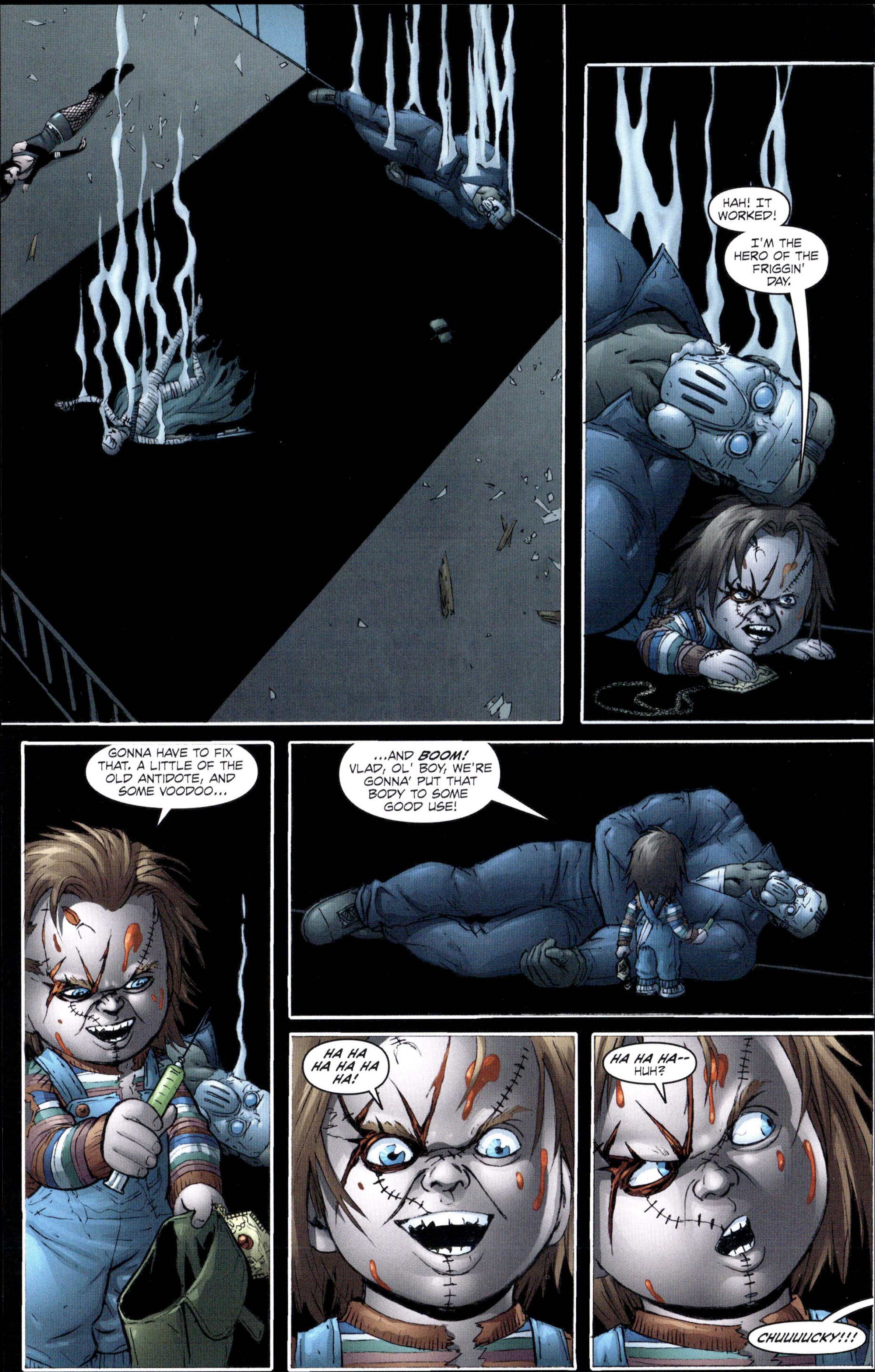
HAH! IT WORKED!
I'M THE HERO OF THE FRIGGIN' DAY.
GONNA HAVE TO FIX THAT. A LITTLE OF THE OLD ANTIDOTE, AND SOME VOODOO...
...AND BOOM! VLAD, OL' BOY, WE'RE GONNA' PUT THAT BODY TO SOME GOOD USE!
HA HA HA HA HA HA!
HA HA HA-- HUH?
CHUUUUCKY!!!

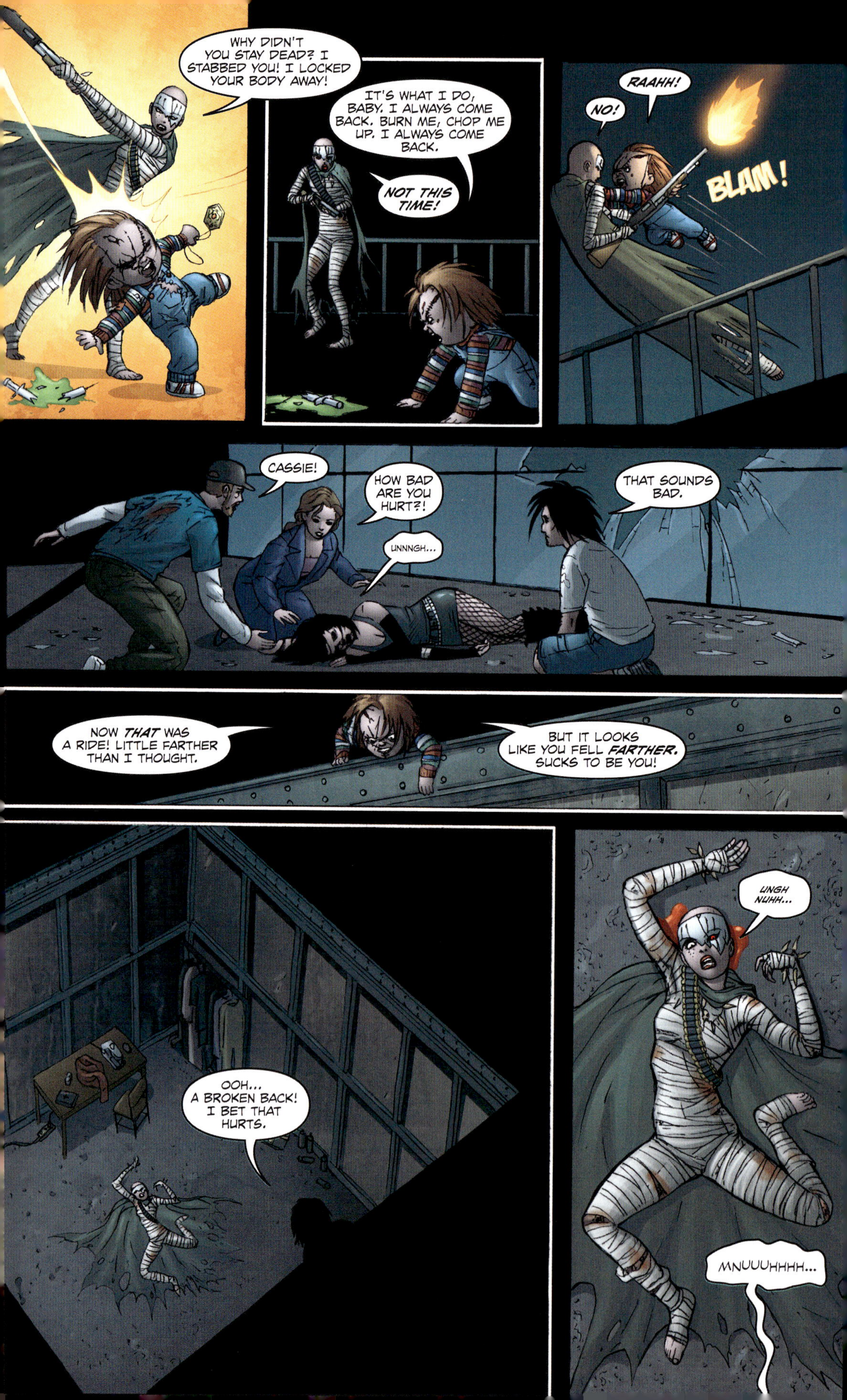
WHY DIDN'T YOU STAY DEAD? I STABBED YOU! I LOCKED YOUR BODY AWAY!
IT'S WHAT I DO, BABY. I ALWAYS COME BACK. BURN ME, CHOP ME UP. I ALWAYS COME BACK.
NOT THIS TIME!
NO!
RAAHH!
BLAM!
CASSIE!
HOW BAD ARE YOU HURT?!
UNNNGH...
THAT SOUNDS BAD.
NOW THAT WAS A RIDE! LITTLE FARTHER THAN I THOUGHT.
BUT IT LOOKS LIKE YOU FELL FARTHER. SUCKS TO BE YOU!
OOH... A BROKEN BACK! I BET THAT HURTS.
UNGH NUHH...
MNUUUHHHH...

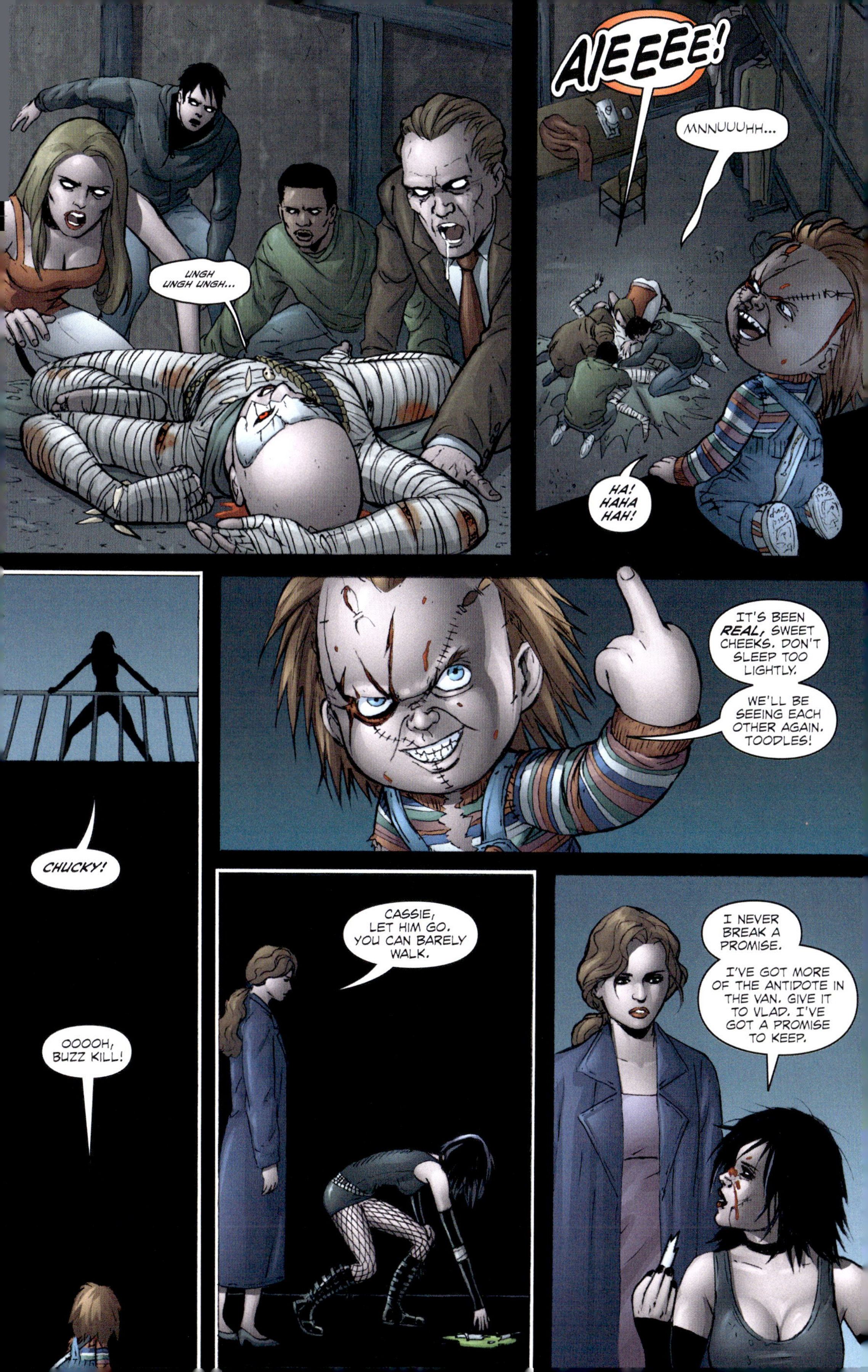
UNGH UNGH UNGH...
AIEEEE!
MNNUUUHH...
HA! HAHA HAH!
IT'S BEEN REAL, SWEET CHEEKS. DON'T SLEEP TOO LIGHTLY.
WE'LL BE SEEING EACH OTHER AGAIN. TOODLES!
CHUCKY!
OOOOH, BUZZ KILL!
CASSIE, LET HIM GO. YOU CAN BARELY WALK.
I NEVER BREAK A PROMISE.
I'VE GOT MORE OF THE ANTIDOTE IN THE VAN. GIVE IT TO VLAD. I'VE GOT A PROMISE TO KEEP.

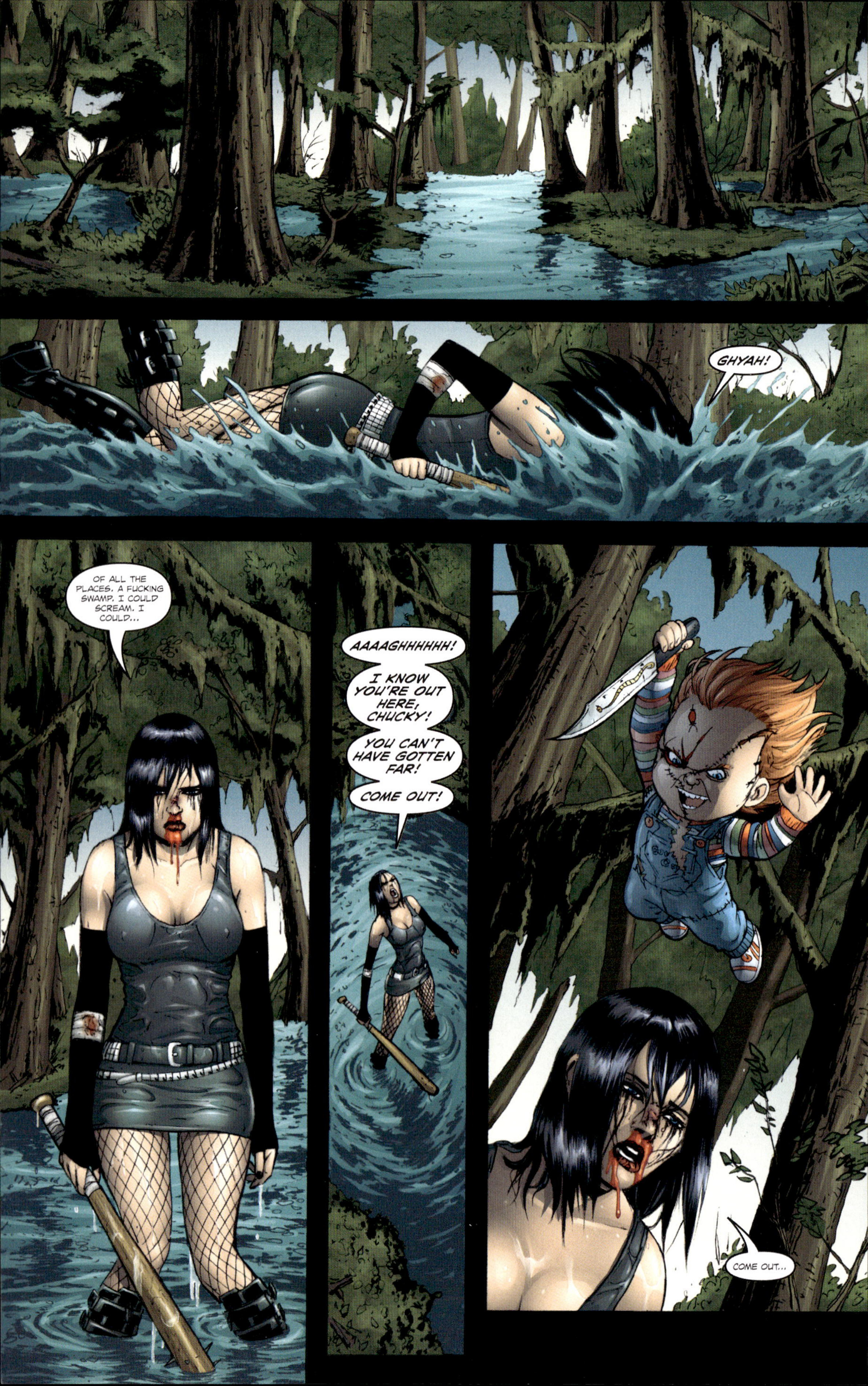
GHYAH!
OF ALL THE PLACES. A FUCKING SWAMP. I COULD SCREAM. I COULD...
AAAAGHHHHHH!
I KNOW YOU'RE OUT HERE, CHUCKY!
YOU CAN'T HAVE GOTTEN FAR!
COME OUT!
COME OUT...

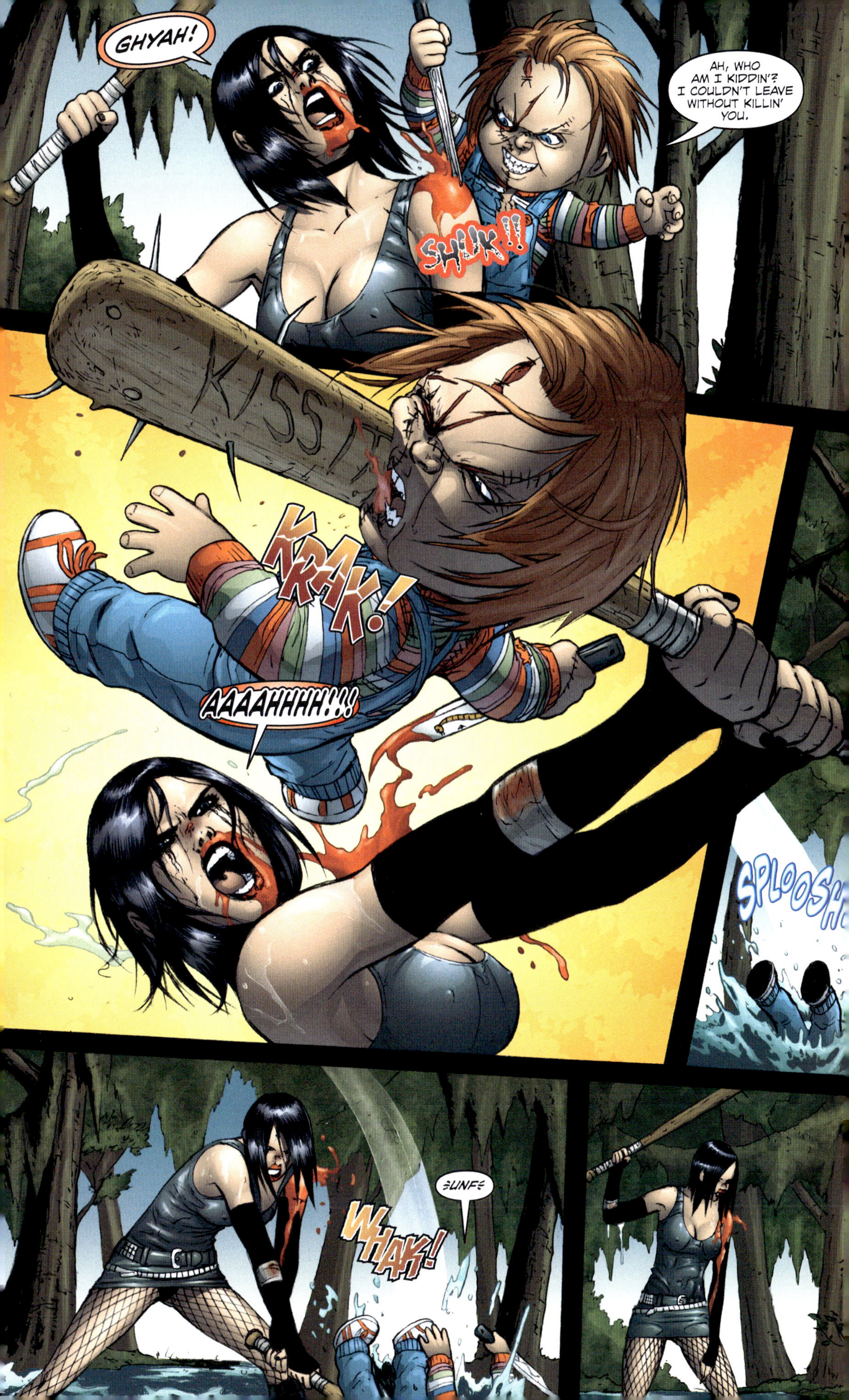
GHYAH!
AH, WHO AM I KIDDIN'? I COULDN'T LEAVE WITHOUT KILLIN' YOU.
SHUK!!
KISS IT
KRAK!
AAAAHHHH!!!
SPLOOSH!
WHAK!
UNF

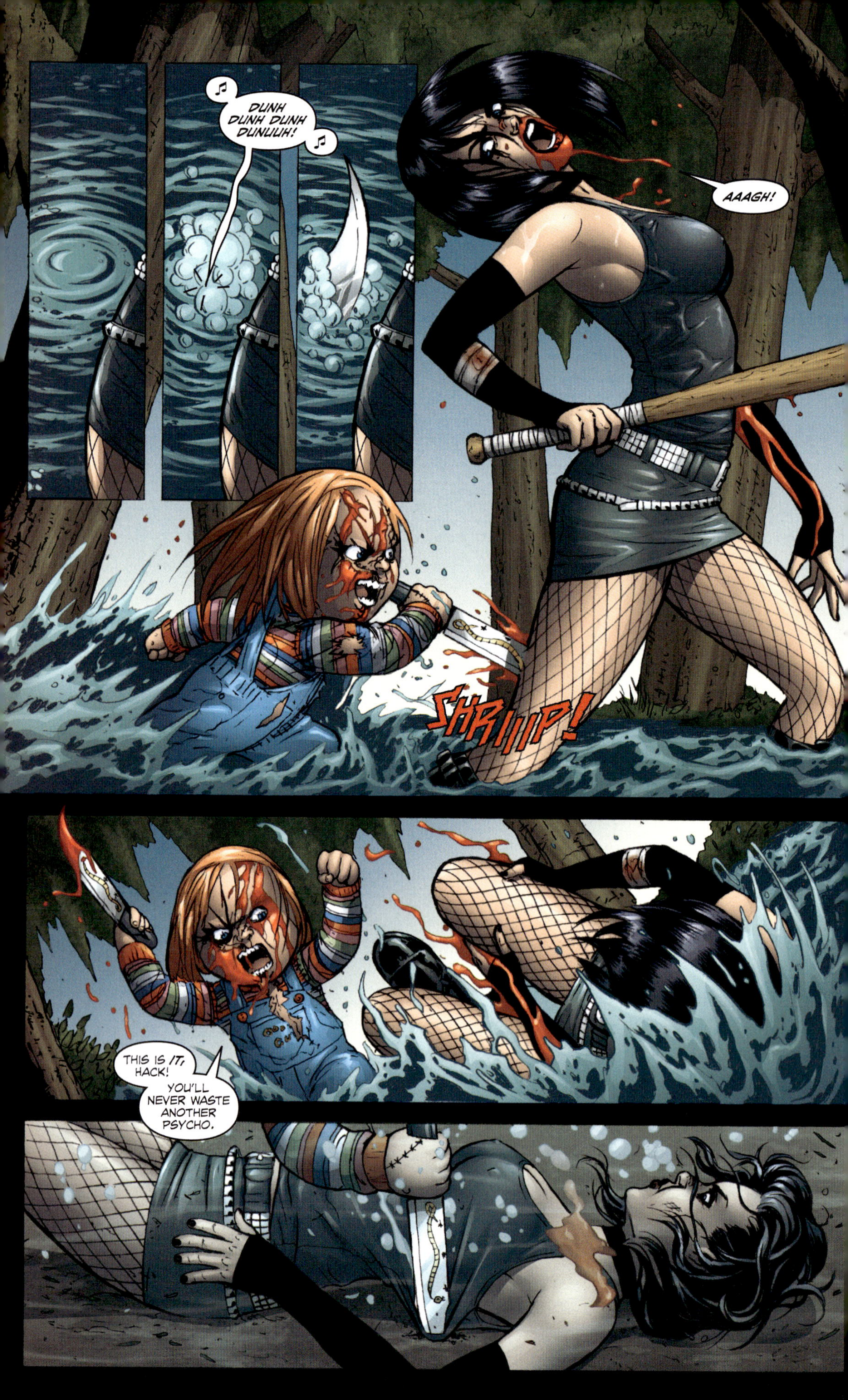
DUNH DUNH DUNH DUNUUH!
AAAGH!
SHRIIIP!
THIS IS *IT*, HACK!
YOU'LL NEVER WASTE ANOTHER PSYCHO.

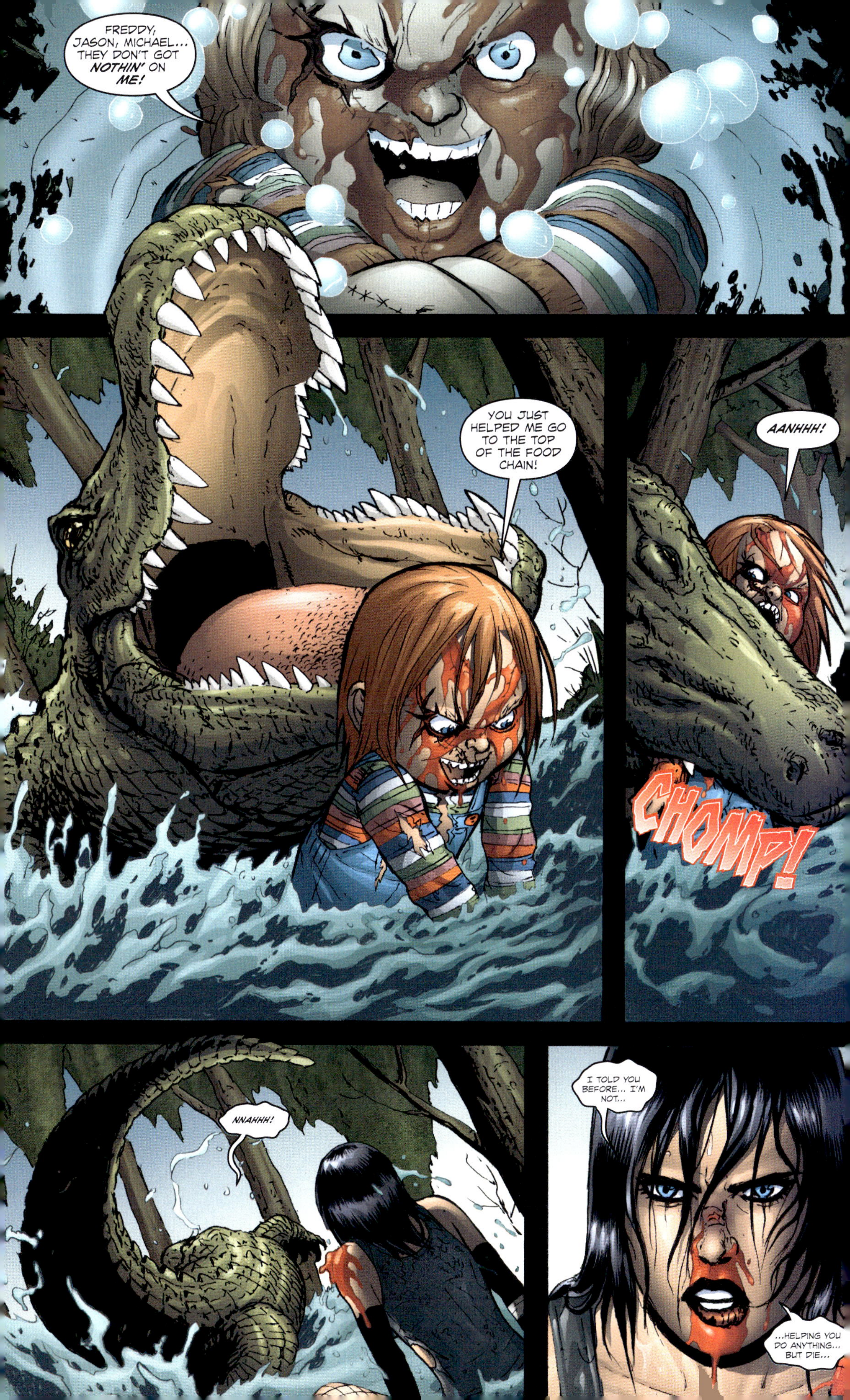
FREDDY, JASON, MICHAEL... THEY DON'T GOT NOTHIN' ON ME!
YOU JUST HELPED ME GO TO THE TOP OF THE FOOD CHAIN!
AANHHH!
CHOMP!
NNAHHH!
I TOLD YOU BEFORE... I'M NOT...
...HELPING YOU DO ANYTHING... BUT DIE...

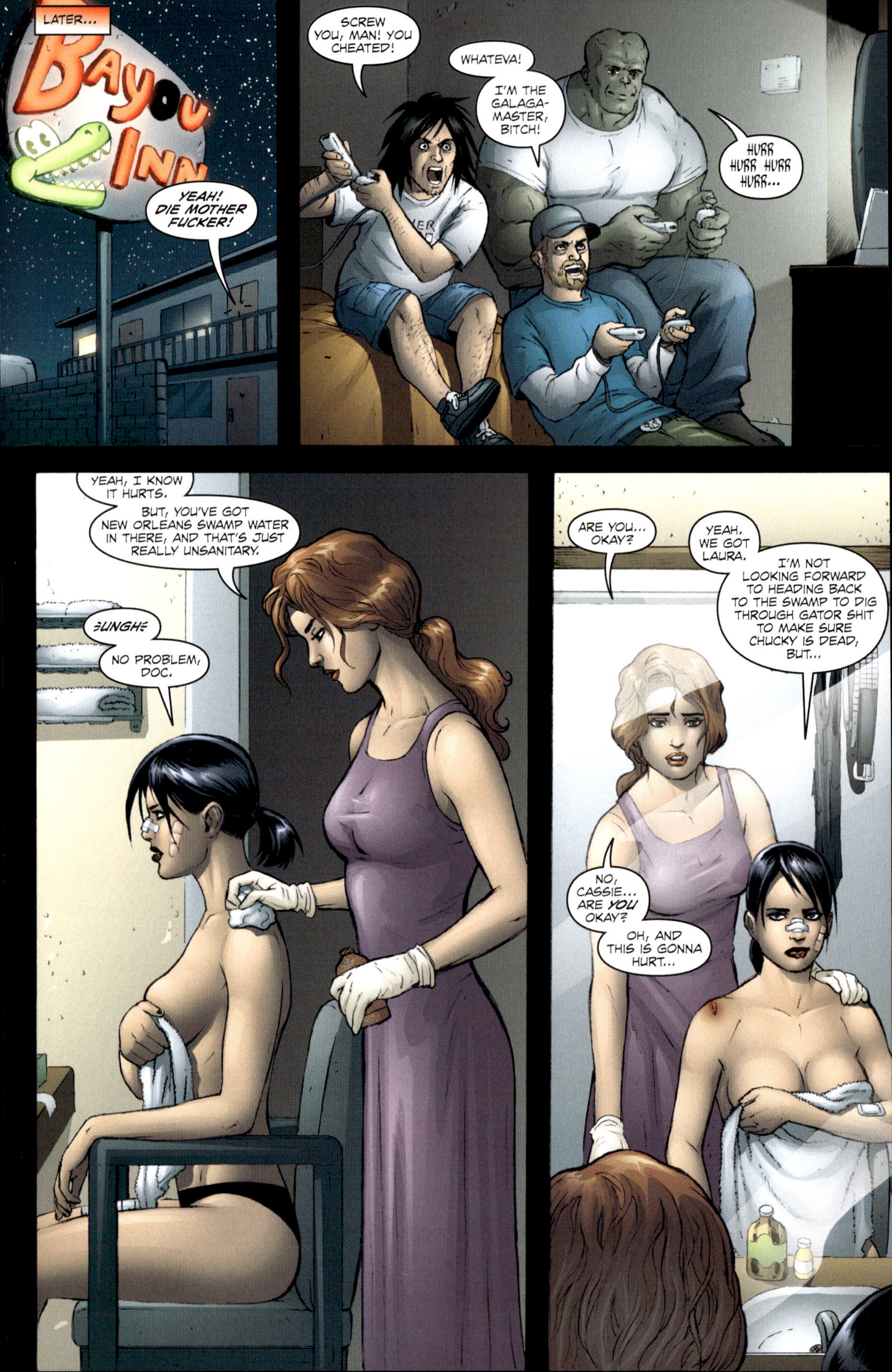
LATER...
Bayou Inn
YEAH! DIE MOTHER FUCKER!
SCREW YOU, MAN! YOU CHEATED!
WHATEVA!
I'M THE GALAGA-MASTER, BITCH!
HURR HURR HURR HURR...
YEAH, I KNOW IT HURTS.
BUT, YOU'VE GOT NEW ORLEANS SWAMP WATER IN THERE, AND THAT'S JUST REALLY UNSANITARY.
=UNGH=
NO PROBLEM, DOC.
ARE YOU... OKAY?
YEAH. WE GOT LAURA.
I'M NOT LOOKING FORWARD TO HEADING BACK TO THE SWAMP TO DIG THROUGH GATOR SHIT TO MAKE SURE CHUCKY IS DEAD, BUT...
NO, CASSIE... ARE YOU OKAY?
OH, AND THIS IS GONNA HURT...

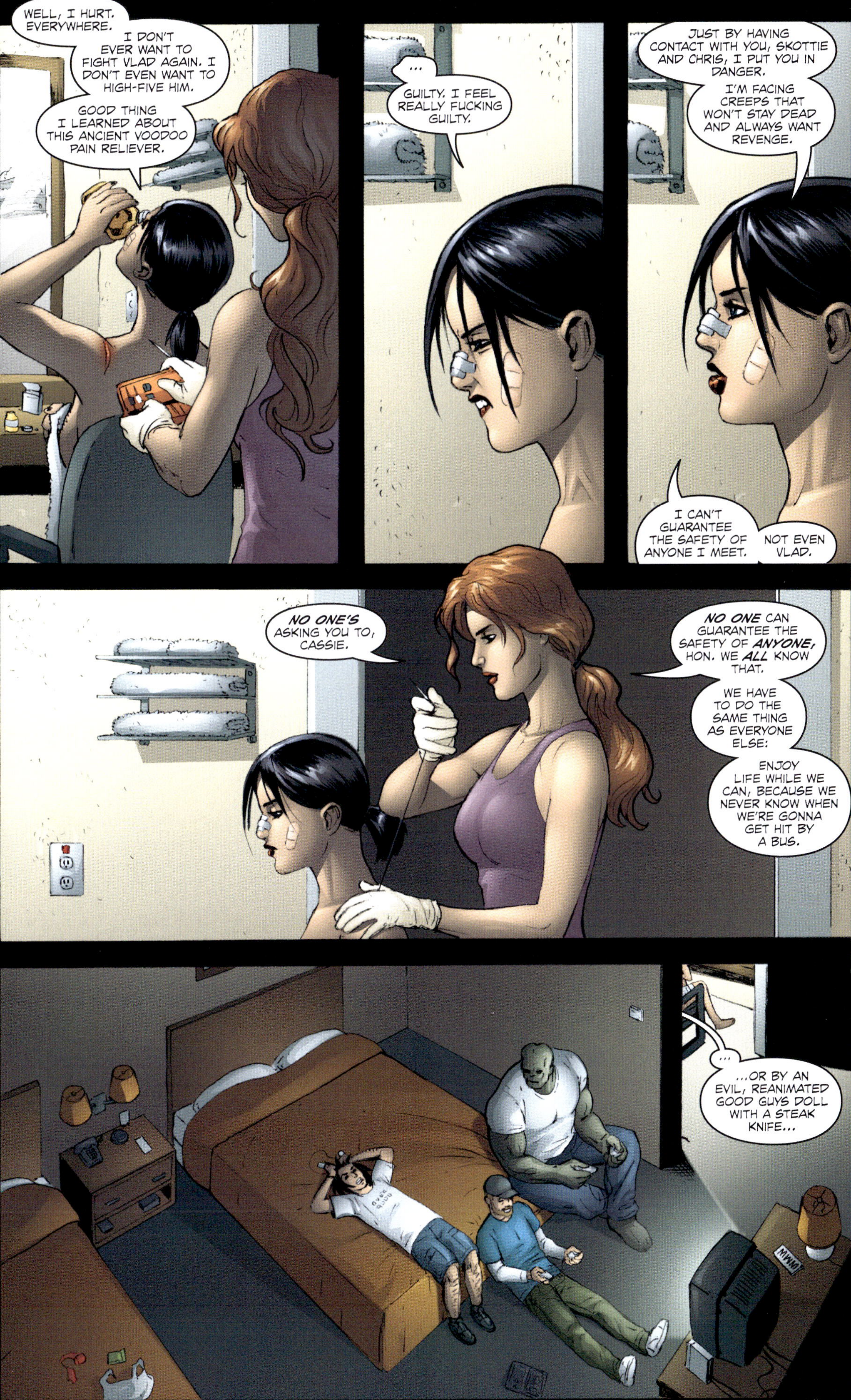
WELL, I HURT. EVERYWHERE.
I DON'T EVER WANT TO FIGHT VLAD AGAIN. I DON'T EVEN WANT TO HIGH-FIVE HIM.
GOOD THING I LEARNED ABOUT THIS ANCIENT VOODOO PAIN RELIEVER.
...
GUILTY. I FEEL REALLY FUCKING GUILTY.
JUST BY HAVING CONTACT WITH YOU, SKOTTIE AND CHRIS, I PUT YOU IN DANGER.
I'M FACING CREEPS THAT WON'T STAY DEAD AND ALWAYS WANT REVENGE.
I CAN'T GUARANTEE THE SAFETY OF ANYONE I MEET.
NOT EVEN VLAD.
NO ONE'S ASKING YOU TO, CASSIE.
NO ONE CAN GUARANTEE THE SAFETY OF ANYONE, HON. WE ALL KNOW THAT.
WE HAVE TO DO THE SAME THING AS EVERYONE ELSE:
ENJOY LIFE WHILE WE CAN, BECAUSE WE NEVER KNOW WHEN WE'RE GONNA GET HIT BY A BUS.
...
...OR BY AN EVIL, REANIMATED GOOD GUYS DOLL WITH A STEAK KNIFE...

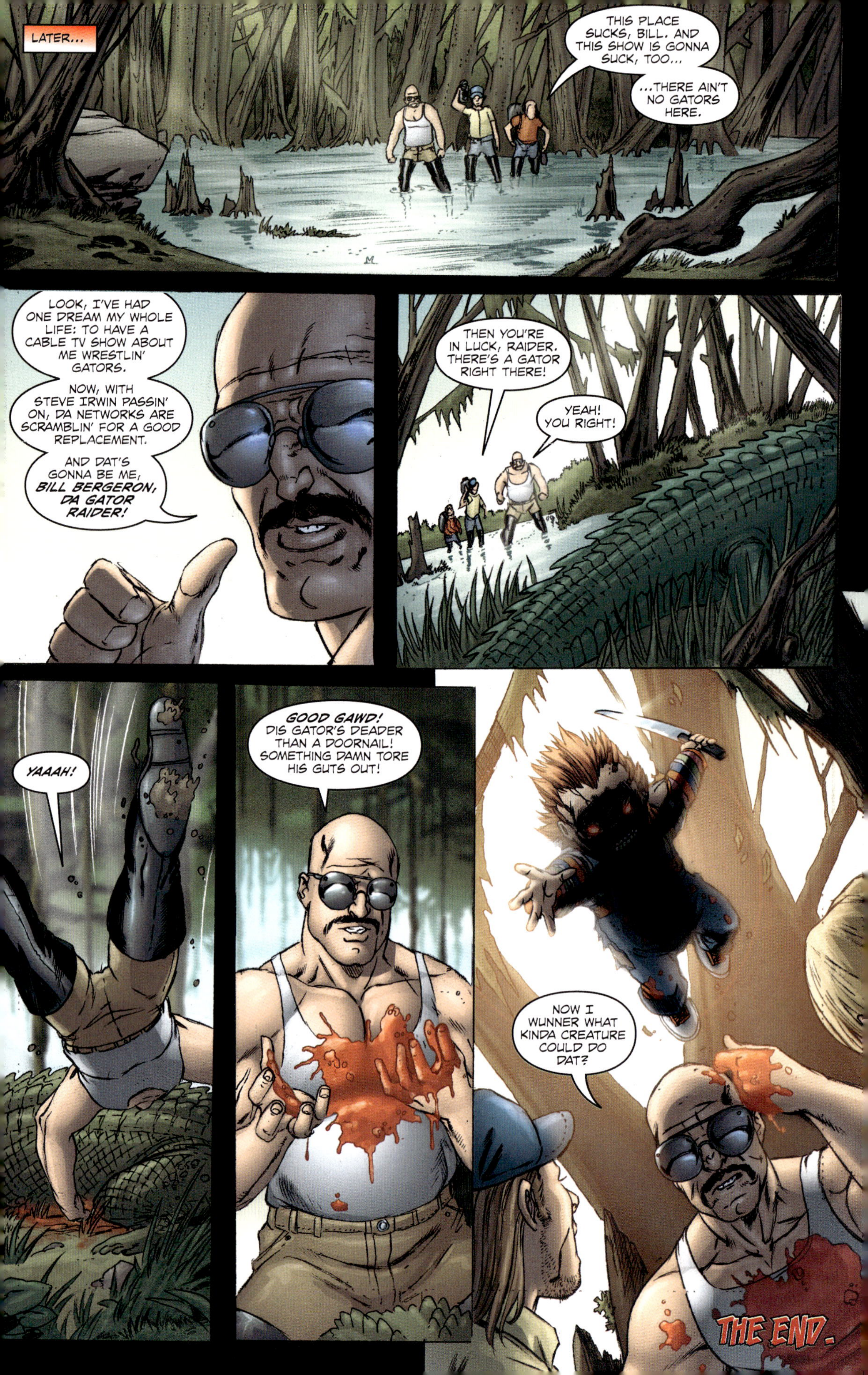
LATER...
THIS PLACE SUCKS, BILL. AND THIS SHOW IS GONNA SUCK, TOO...
...THERE AIN'T NO GATORS HERE.
LOOK, I'VE HAD ONE DREAM MY WHOLE LIFE: TO HAVE A CABLE TV SHOW ABOUT ME WRESTLIN' GATORS.
NOW, WITH STEVE IRWIN PASSIN' ON, DA NETWORKS ARE SCRAMBLIN' FOR A GOOD REPLACEMENT.
AND DAT'S GONNA BE ME, ***BILL BERGERON, DA GATOR RAIDER!***
THEN YOU'RE IN LUCK, RAIDER. THERE'S A GATOR RIGHT THERE!
YEAH! YOU RIGHT!
YAAAH!
GOOD GAWD! DIS GATOR'S DEADER THAN A DOORNAIL! SOMETHING DAMN TORE HIS GUTS OUT!
NOW I WUNNER WHAT KINDA CREATURE COULD DO DAT?
THE END.

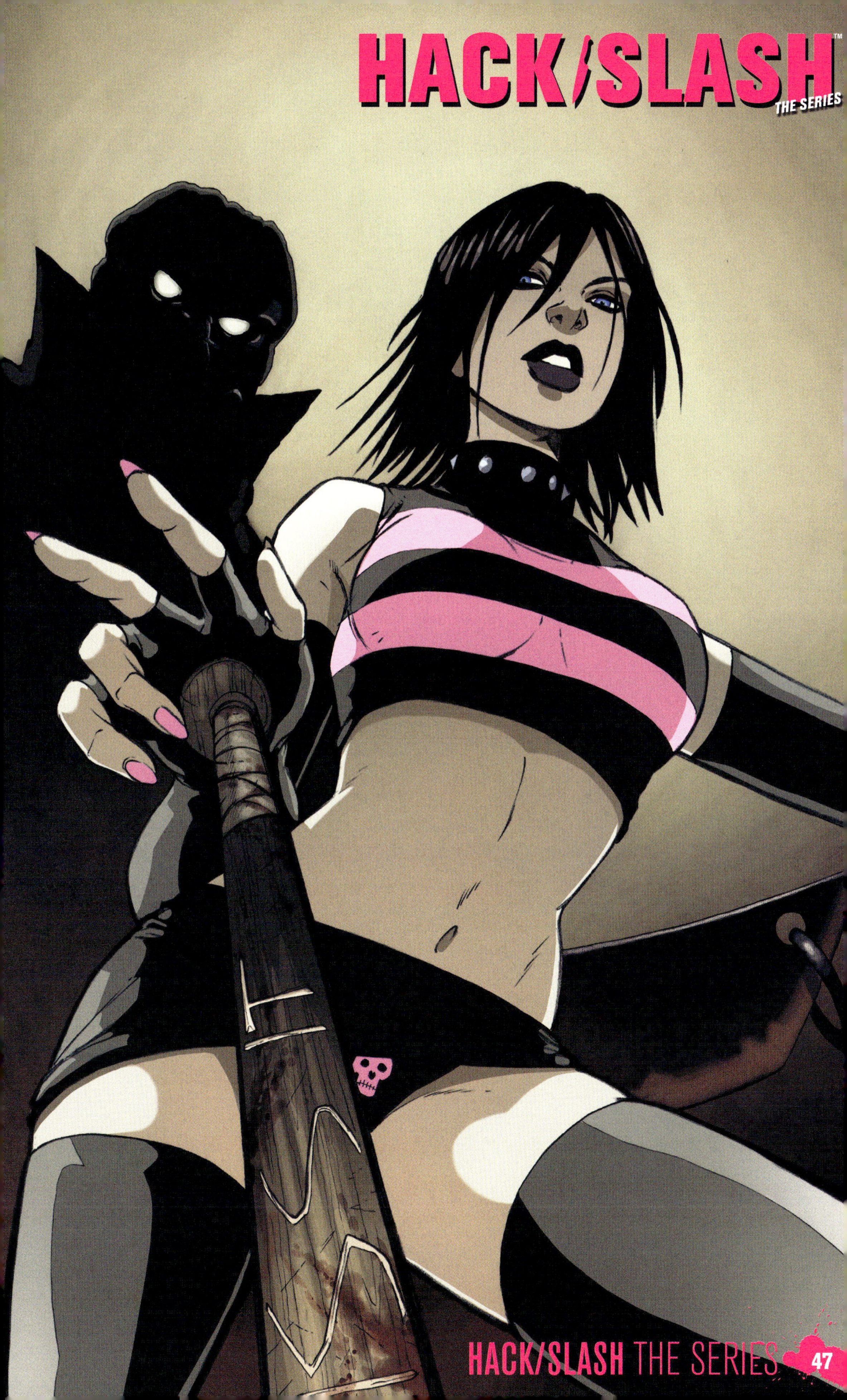
HACK/SLASH™
THE SERIES

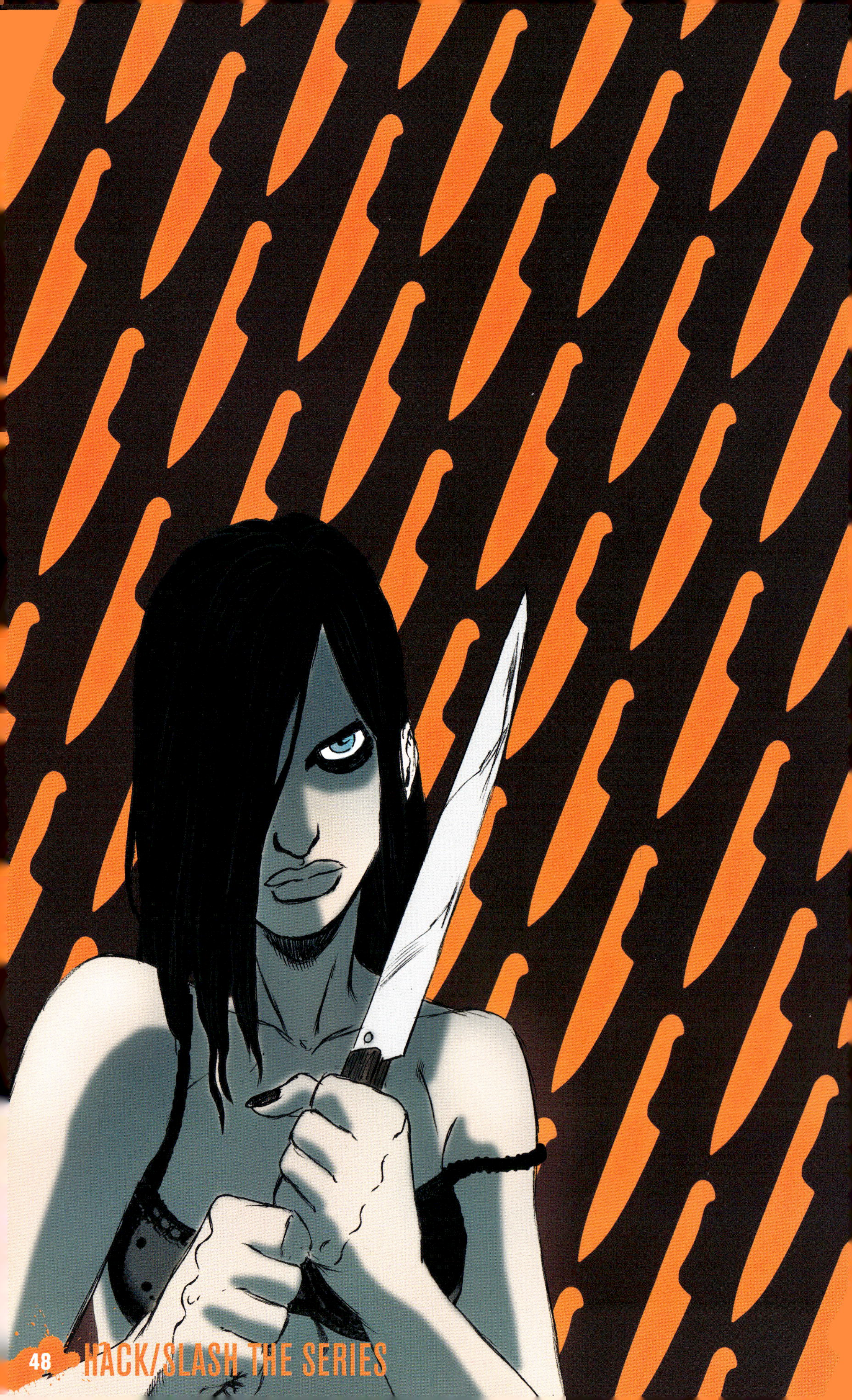

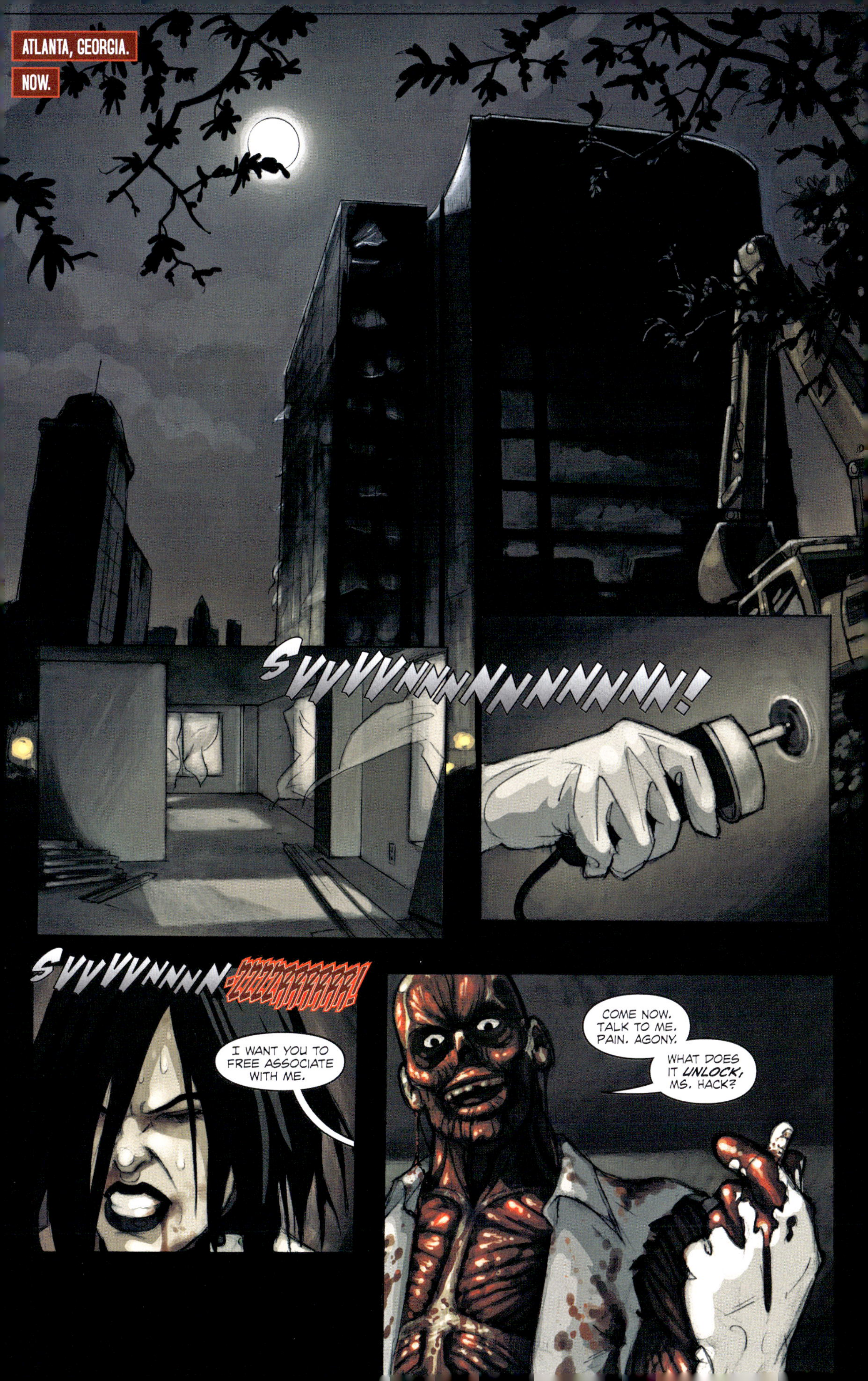
ATLANTA, GEORGIA.
NOW.
SVVVVNNNNNNNNNNN!
SVVVVNNNN-ZZZZRRRRRRR!
I WANT YOU TO FREE ASSOCIATE WITH ME.
COME NOW. TALK TO ME. PAIN. AGONY.
WHAT DOES IT *UNLOCK*, MS. HACK?

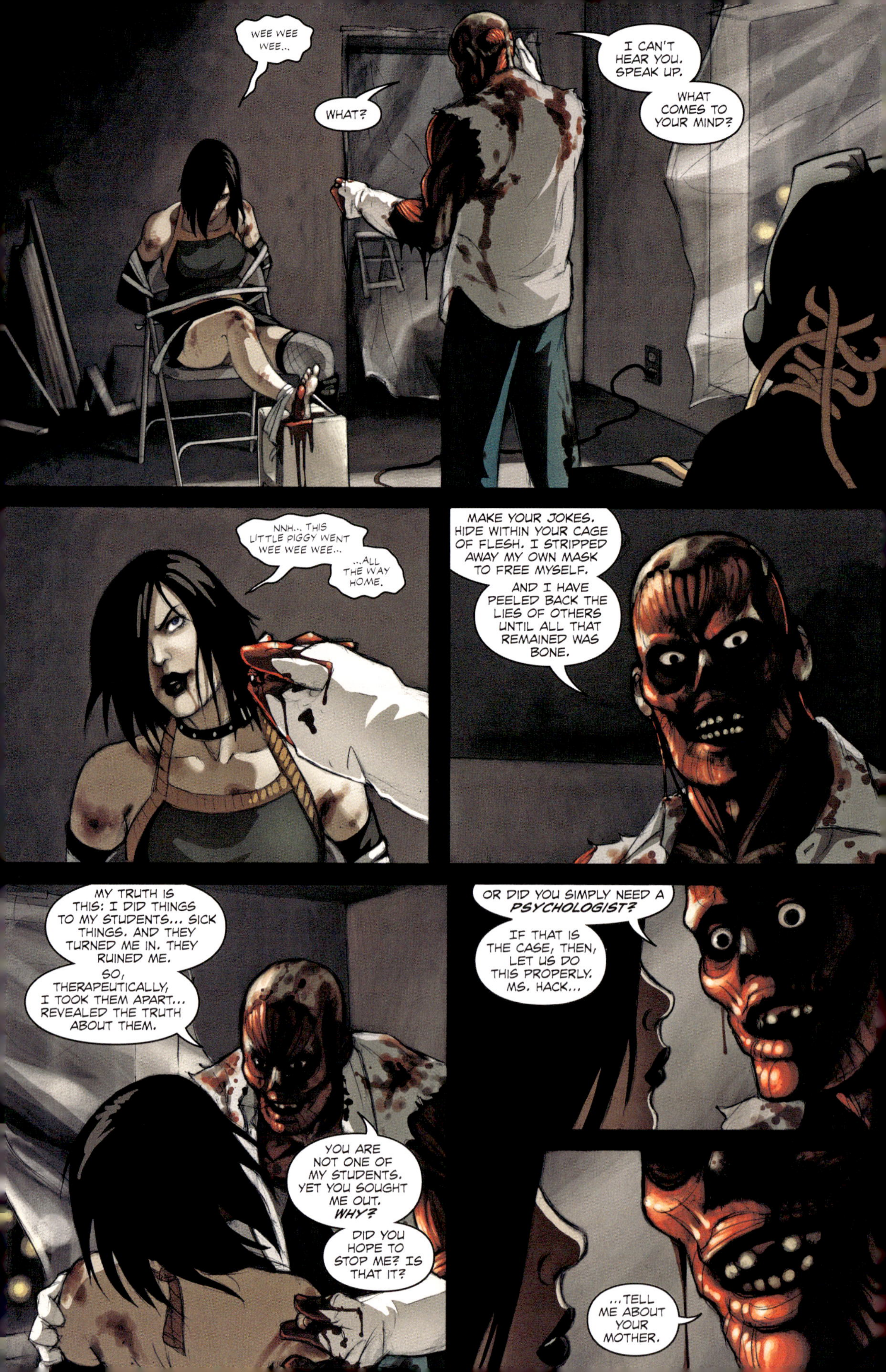
WEE WEE WEE...
WHAT?
I CAN'T HEAR YOU. SPEAK UP.
WHAT COMES TO YOUR MIND?
NNH... THIS LITTLE PIGGY WENT WEE WEE WEE...
...ALL THE WAY HOME.
MAKE YOUR JOKES. HIDE WITHIN YOUR CAGE OF FLESH. I STRIPPED AWAY MY OWN MASK TO FREE MYSELF.
AND I HAVE PEELED BACK THE LIES OF OTHERS UNTIL ALL THAT REMAINED WAS BONE.
MY TRUTH IS THIS: I DID THINGS TO MY STUDENTS... SICK THINGS. AND THEY TURNED ME IN. THEY RUINED ME.
SO, THERAPEUTICALLY, I TOOK THEM APART... REVEALED THE TRUTH ABOUT THEM.
YOU ARE NOT ONE OF MY STUDENTS. YET YOU SOUGHT ME OUT. *WHY?*
DID YOU HOPE TO STOP ME? IS THAT IT?
OR DID YOU SIMPLY NEED A *PSYCHOLOGIST?*
IF THAT IS THE CASE, THEN, LET US DO THIS PROPERLY. MS. HACK...
...TELL ME ABOUT YOUR MOTHER.

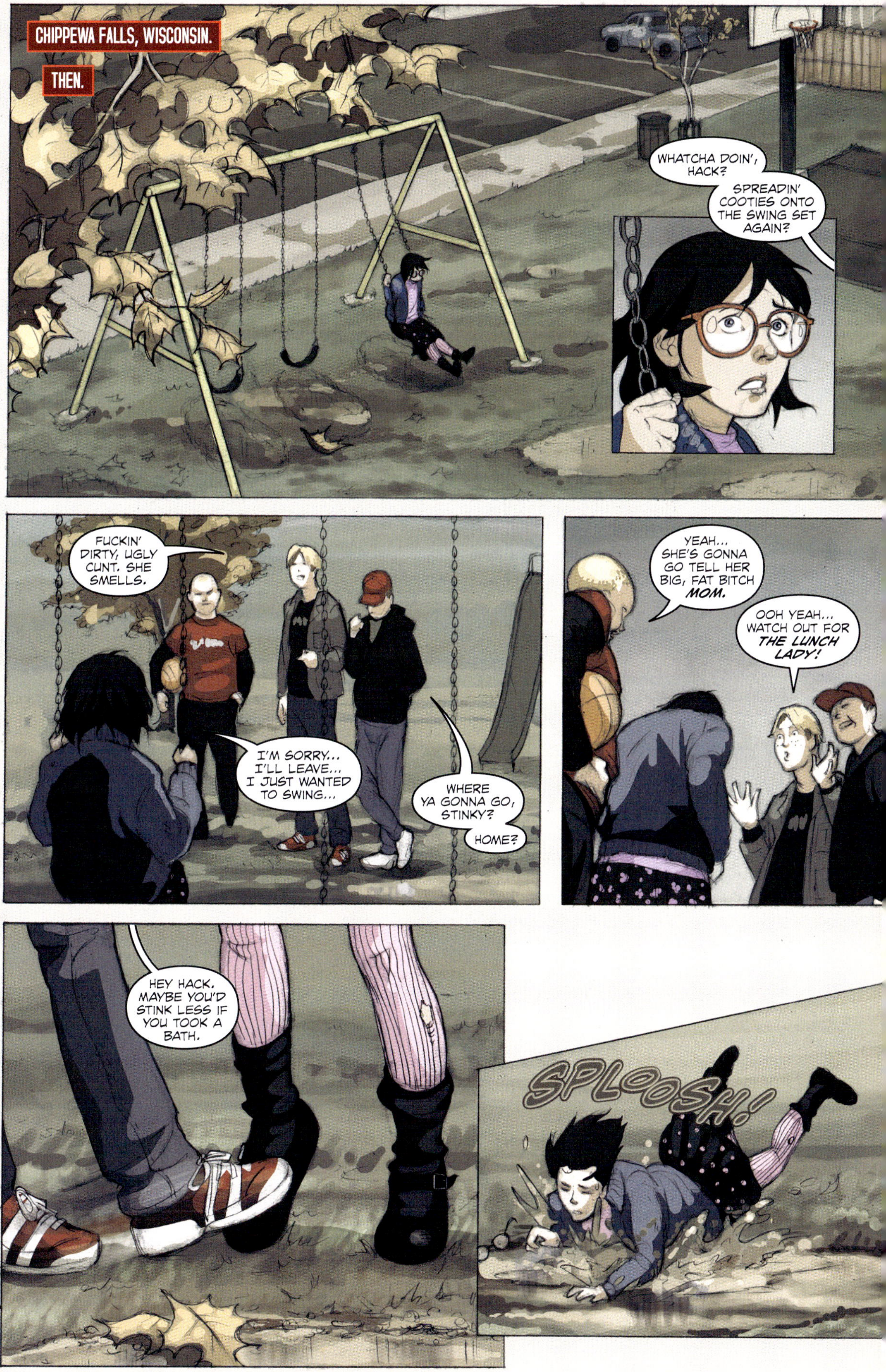
CHIPPEWA FALLS, WISCONSIN.
THEN.
WHATCHA DOIN', HACK?
SPREADIN' COOTIES ONTO THE SWING SET AGAIN?
FUCKIN' DIRTY, UGLY CUNT. SHE SMELLS.
I'M SORRY... I'LL LEAVE... I JUST WANTED TO SWING...
WHERE YA GONNA GO, STINKY?
HOME?
YEAH... SHE'S GONNA GO TELL HER BIG, FAT BITCH MOM.
OOH YEAH... WATCH OUT FOR THE LUNCH LADY!
HEY HACK. MAYBE YOU'D STINK LESS IF YOU TOOK A BATH.
SPLOOSH!

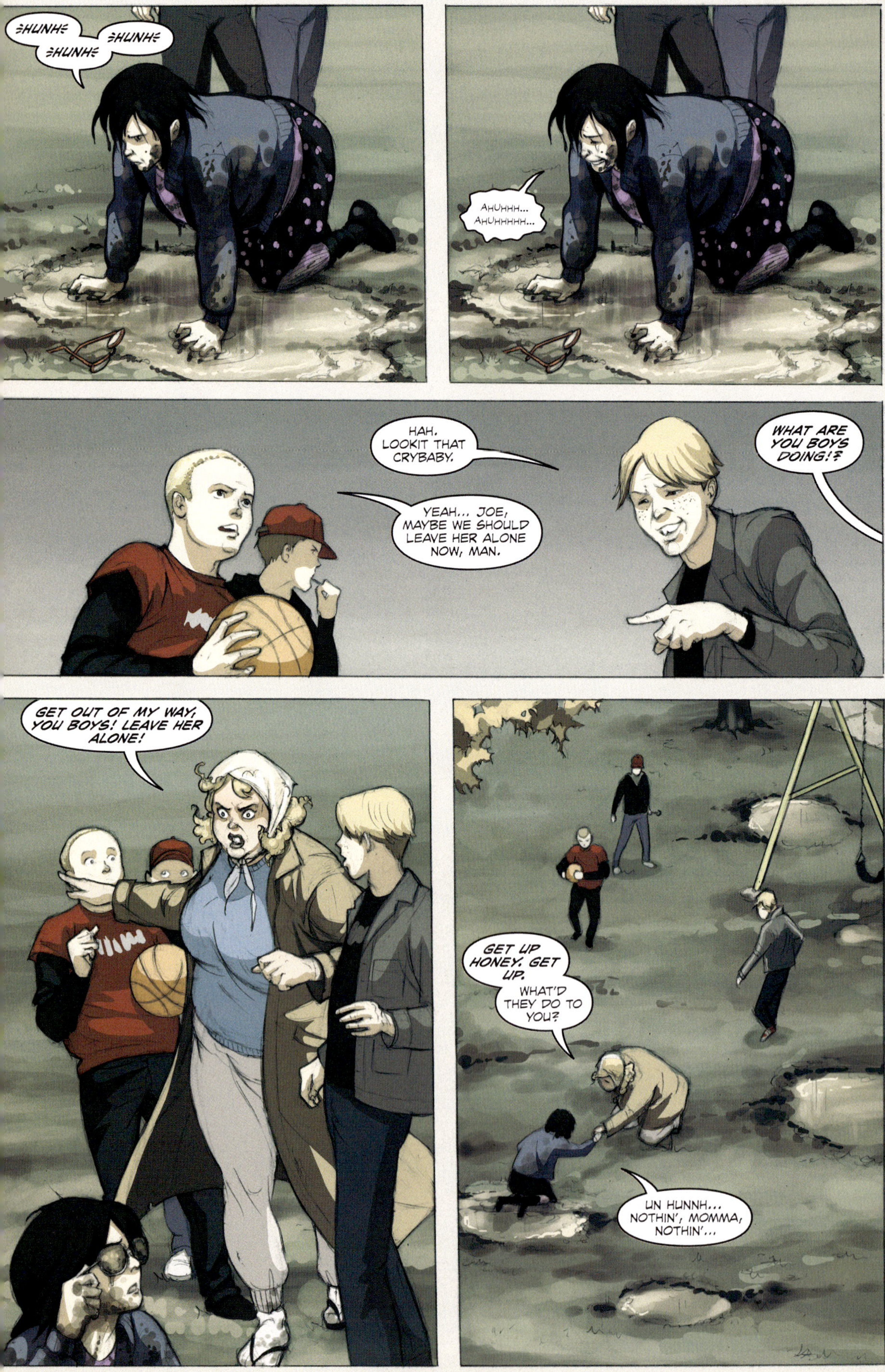

≷HUNH≶
≷HUNH≶
≷HUNH≶
AHUHHH...
AHUHHHHH...
HAH. LOOKIT THAT CRYBABY.
YEAH... JOE, MAYBE WE SHOULD LEAVE HER ALONE NOW, MAN.
WHAT ARE YOU BOYS DOING!?
GET OUT OF MY WAY, YOU BOYS! LEAVE HER ALONE!
GET UP HONEY. GET UP.
WHAT'D THEY DO TO YOU?
UN HUNNH... NOTHIN', MOMMA, NOTHIN'...

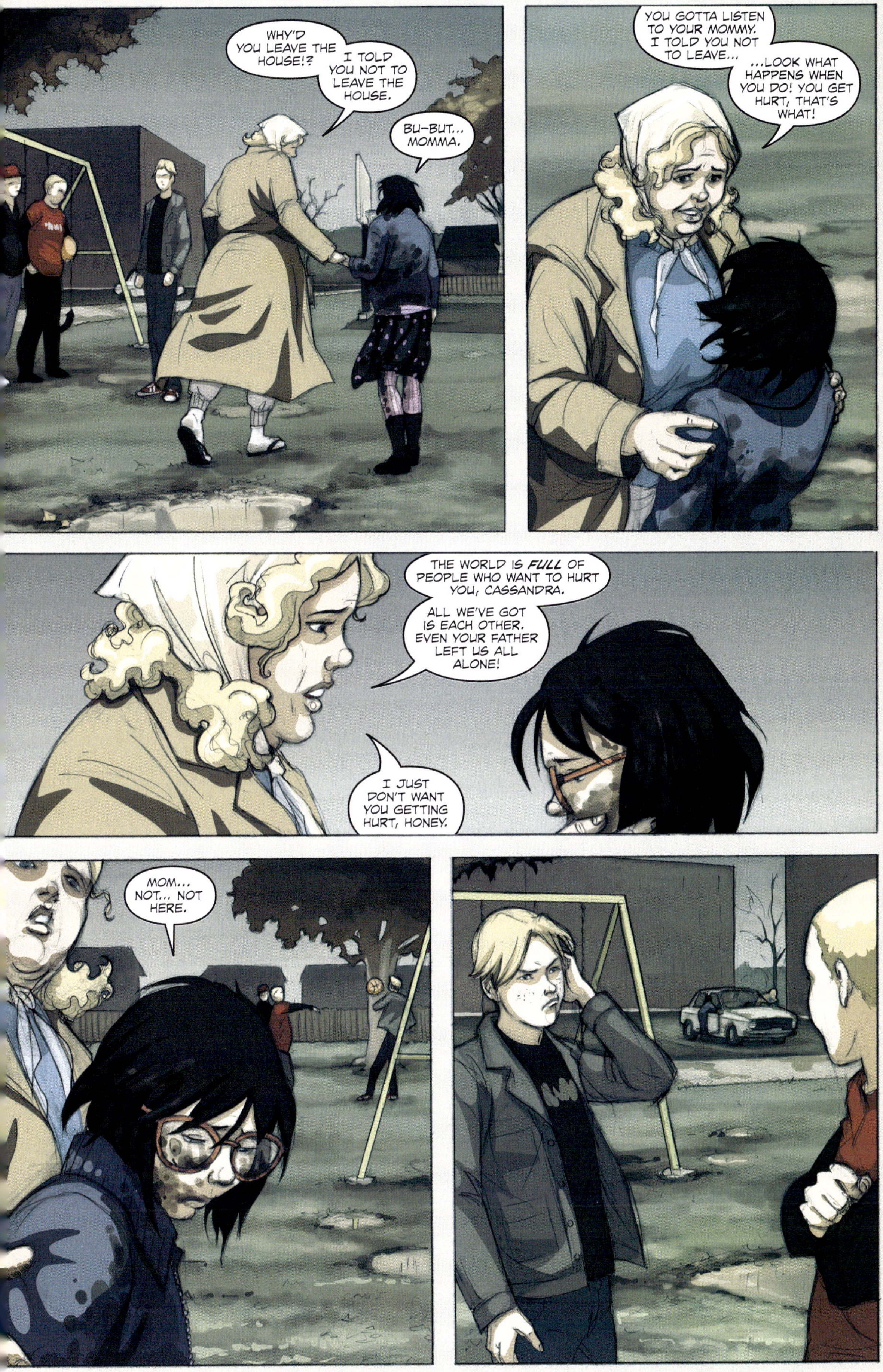
WHY'D YOU LEAVE THE HOUSE!?
I TOLD YOU NOT TO LEAVE THE HOUSE.
BU-BUT... MOMMA.
YOU GOTTA LISTEN TO YOUR MOMMY. I TOLD YOU NOT TO LEAVE...
...LOOK WHAT HAPPENS WHEN YOU DO! YOU GET HURT, THAT'S WHAT!
THE WORLD IS *FULL* OF PEOPLE WHO WANT TO HURT YOU, CASSANDRA.
ALL WE'VE GOT IS EACH OTHER. EVEN YOUR FATHER LEFT US ALL ALONE!
I JUST DON'T WANT YOU GETTING HURT, HONEY.
MOM... NOT... NOT HERE.

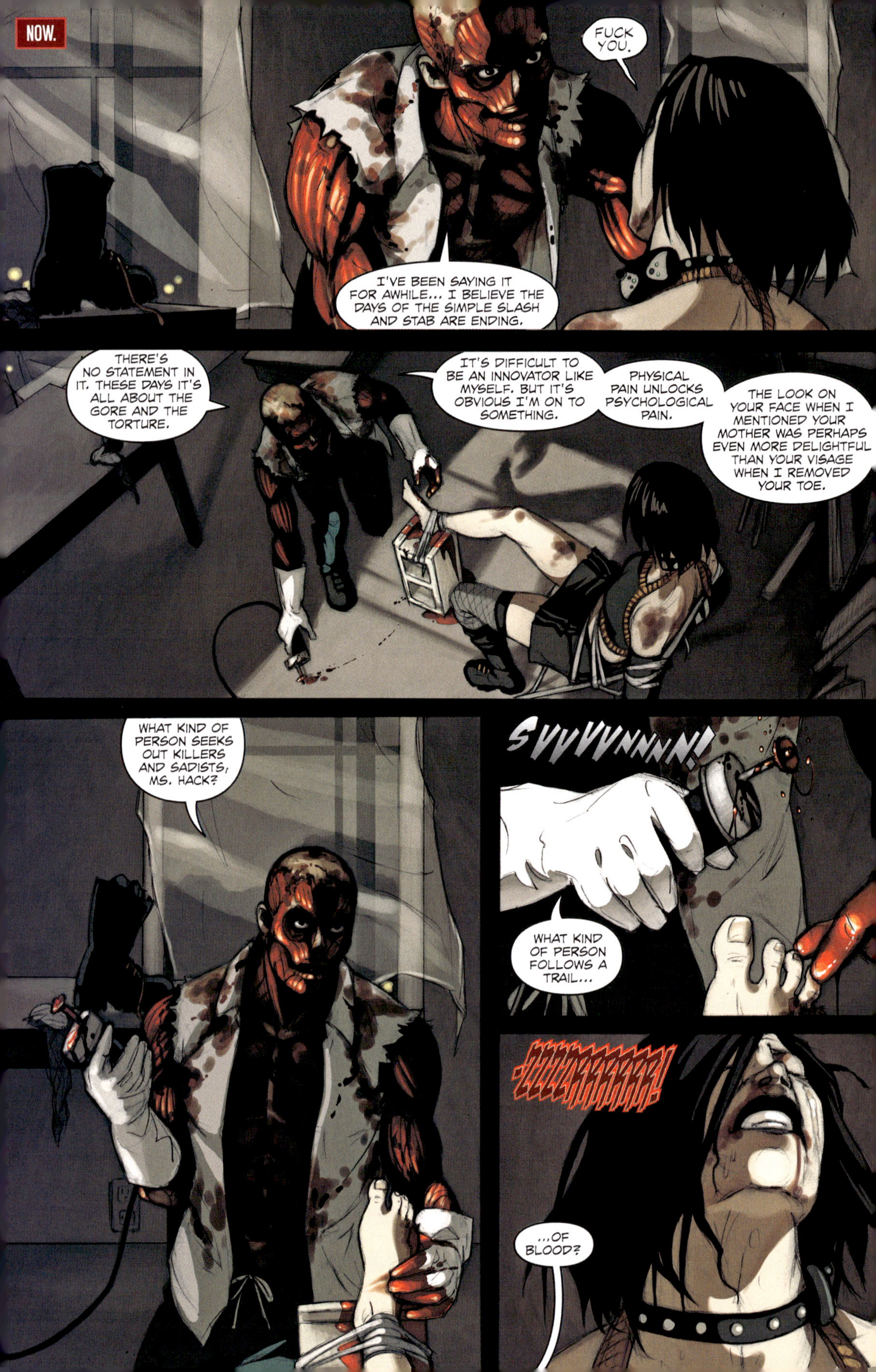
NOW.
FUCK YOU.
I'VE BEEN SAYING IT FOR AWHILE... I BELIEVE THE DAYS OF THE SIMPLE SLASH AND STAB ARE ENDING.
THERE'S NO STATEMENT IN IT. THESE DAYS IT'S ALL ABOUT THE GORE AND THE TORTURE.
IT'S DIFFICULT TO BE AN INNOVATOR LIKE MYSELF. BUT IT'S OBVIOUS I'M ON TO SOMETHING.
PHYSICAL PAIN UNLOCKS PSYCHOLOGICAL PAIN.
THE LOOK ON YOUR FACE WHEN I MENTIONED YOUR MOTHER WAS PERHAPS EVEN MORE DELIGHTFUL THAN YOUR VISAGE WHEN I REMOVED YOUR TOE.
WHAT KIND OF PERSON SEEKS OUT KILLERS AND SADISTS, MS. HACK?
SVVVVNNNN!
WHAT KIND OF PERSON FOLLOWS A TRAIL...
-ZZZZRRRRRRR!
...OF BLOOD?

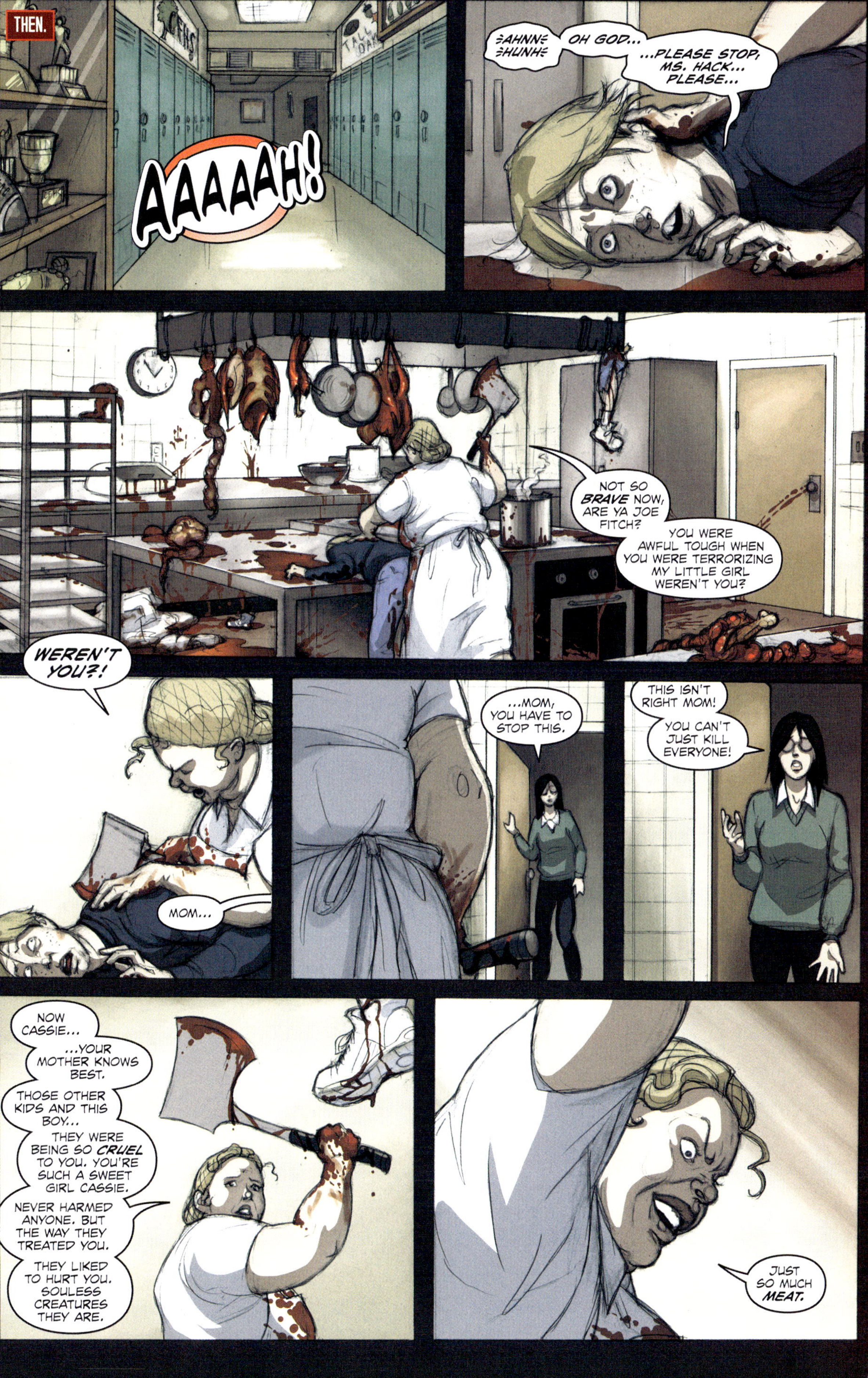
THEN.
AAAAAH!
AHNN HUNH
OH GOD...
...PLEASE STOP, MS. HACK... PLEASE...
NOT SO BRAVE NOW, ARE YA JOE FITCH?
YOU WERE AWFUL TOUGH WHEN YOU WERE TERRORIZING MY LITTLE GIRL WEREN'T YOU?
WEREN'T YOU?!
MOM...
...MOM, YOU HAVE TO STOP THIS.
THIS ISN'T RIGHT MOM!
YOU CAN'T JUST KILL EVERYONE!
NOW CASSIE...
...YOUR MOTHER KNOWS BEST.
THOSE OTHER KIDS AND THIS BOY...
THEY WERE BEING SO CRUEL TO YOU. YOU'RE SUCH A SWEET GIRL CASSIE.
NEVER HARMED ANYONE. BUT THE WAY THEY TREATED YOU.
THEY LIKED TO HURT YOU. SOULESS CREATURES THEY ARE.
JUST SO MUCH MEAT.

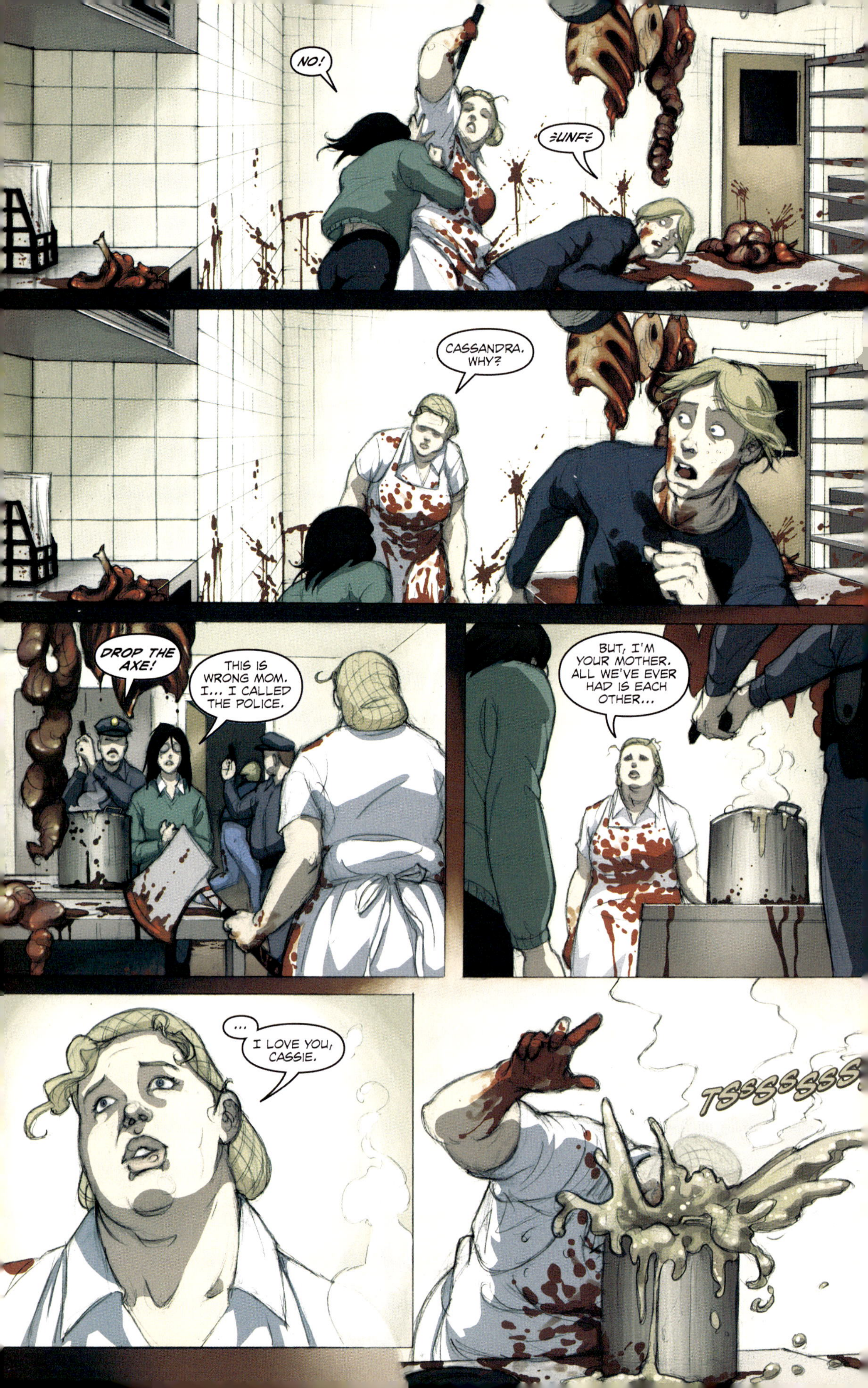
NO!
UNF
CASSANDRA. WHY?
DROP THE AXE!
THIS IS WRONG MOM. I... I CALLED THE POLICE.
BUT, I'M YOUR MOTHER. ALL WE'VE EVER HAD IS EACH OTHER...
...
I LOVE YOU, CASSIE.
TSSSSSSS

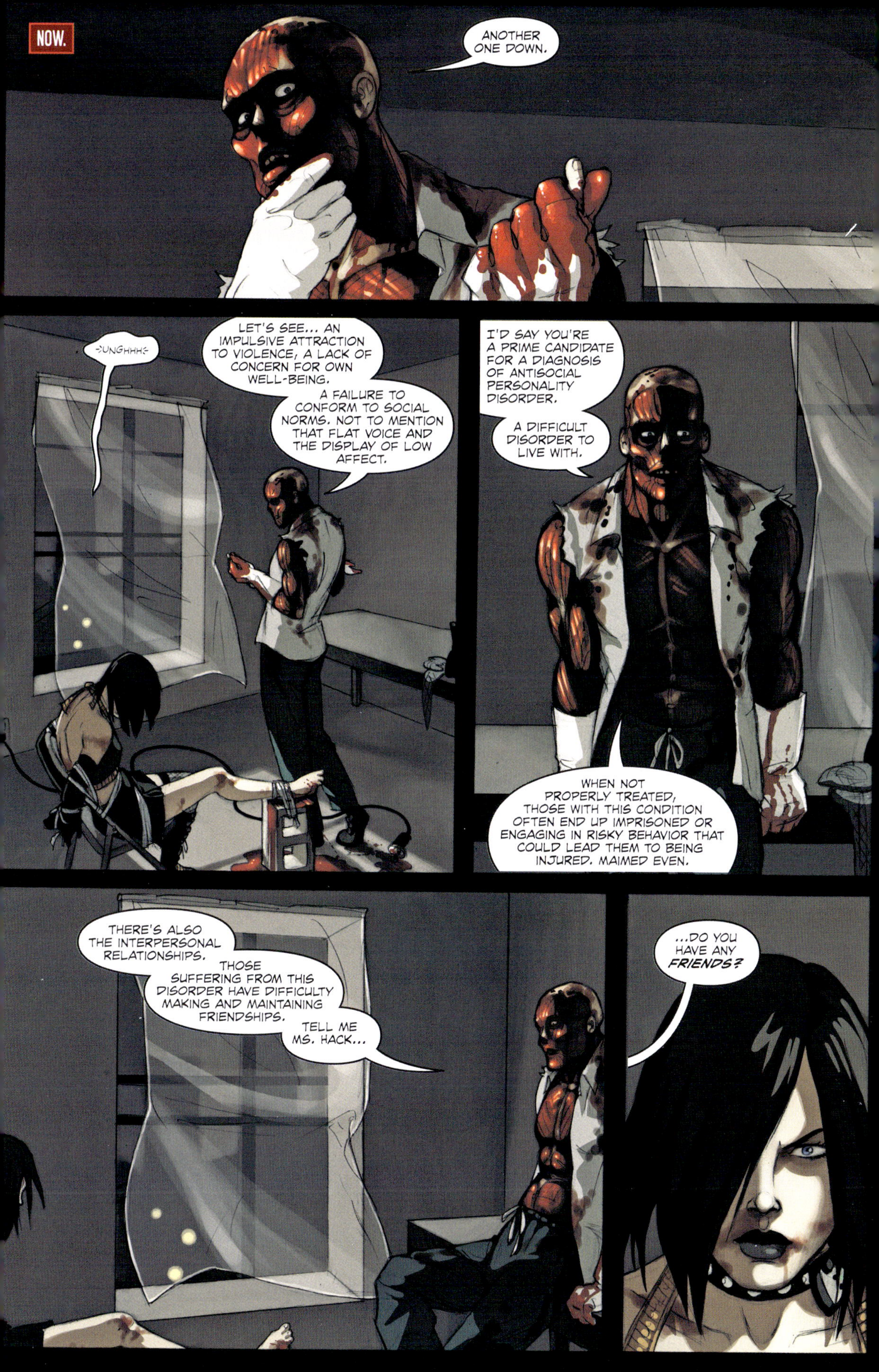
NOW.
ANOTHER ONE DOWN.
-UNGHHH-
LET'S SEE... AN IMPULSIVE ATTRACTION TO VIOLENCE, A LACK OF CONCERN FOR OWN WELL-BEING.
A FAILURE TO CONFORM TO SOCIAL NORMS. NOT TO MENTION THAT FLAT VOICE AND THE DISPLAY OF LOW AFFECT.
I'D SAY YOU'RE A PRIME CANDIDATE FOR A DIAGNOSIS OF ANTISOCIAL PERSONALITY DISORDER.
A DIFFICULT DISORDER TO LIVE WITH.
WHEN NOT PROPERLY TREATED, THOSE WITH THIS CONDITION OFTEN END UP IMPRISONED OR ENGAGING IN RISKY BEHAVIOR THAT COULD LEAD THEM TO BEING INJURED. MAIMED EVEN.
THERE'S ALSO THE INTERPERSONAL RELATIONSHIPS.
THOSE SUFFERING FROM THIS DISORDER HAVE DIFFICULTY MAKING AND MAINTAINING FRIENDSHIPS.
TELL ME MS. HACK...
...DO YOU HAVE ANY *FRIENDS?*

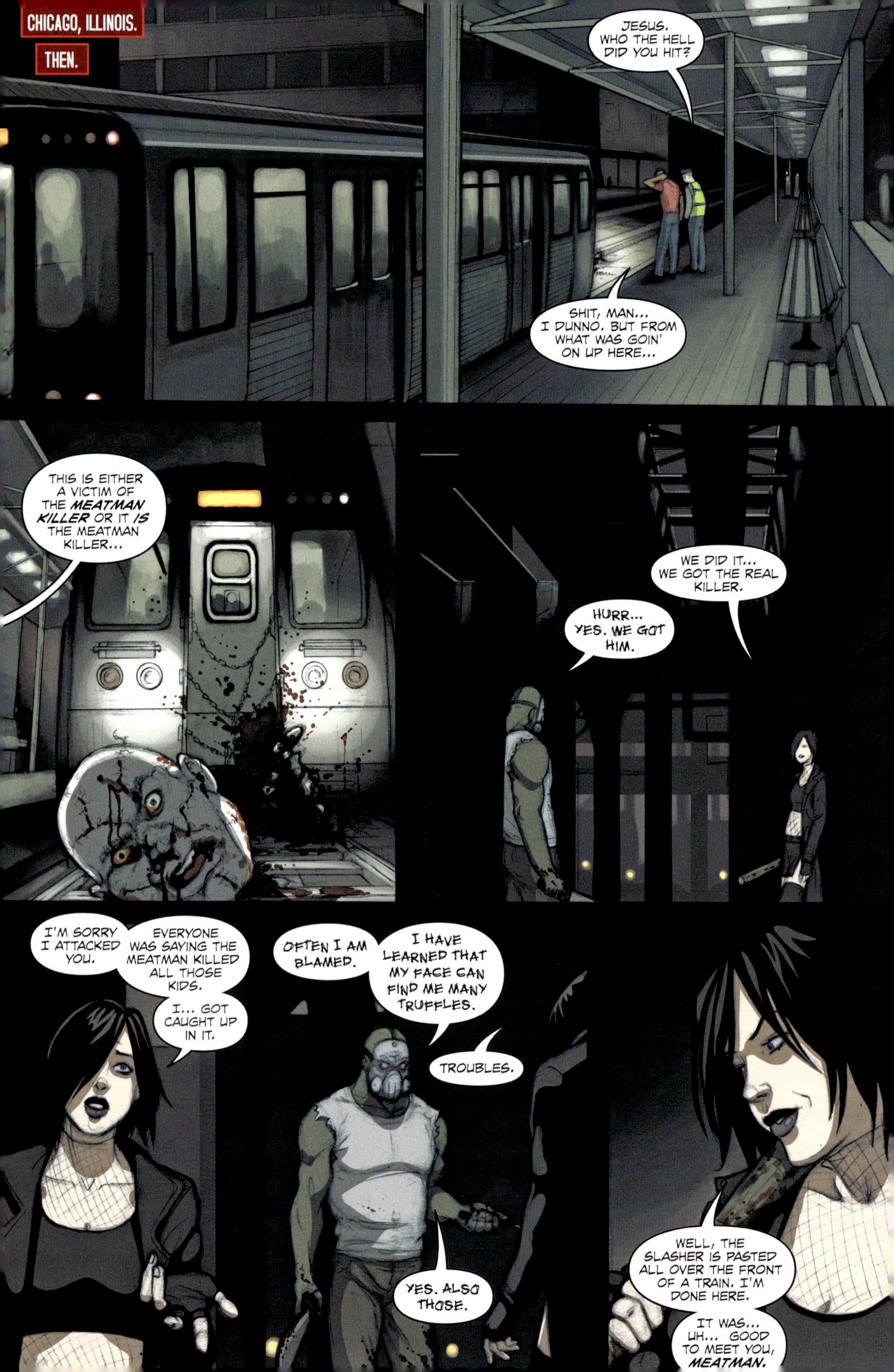
CHICAGO, ILLINOIS.
THEN.
JESUS. WHO THE HELL DID YOU HIT?
SHIT, MAN... I DUNNO. BUT FROM WHAT WAS GOIN' ON UP HERE...
THIS IS EITHER A VICTIM OF THE MEATMAN KILLER OR IT IS THE MEATMAN KILLER...
WE DID IT... WE GOT THE REAL KILLER.
HURR... YES. WE GOT HIM.
I'M SORRY I ATTACKED YOU.
EVERYONE WAS SAYING THE MEATMAN KILLED ALL THOSE KIDS.
I... GOT CAUGHT UP IN IT.
OFTEN I AM BLAMED.
I HAVE LEARNED THAT MY FACE CAN FIND ME MANY TRUFFLES.
TROUBLES.
YES. ALSO THOSE.
WELL, THE SLASHER IS PASTED ALL OVER THE FRONT OF A TRAIN. I'M DONE HERE.
IT WAS... UH... GOOD TO MEET YOU, MEATMAN.

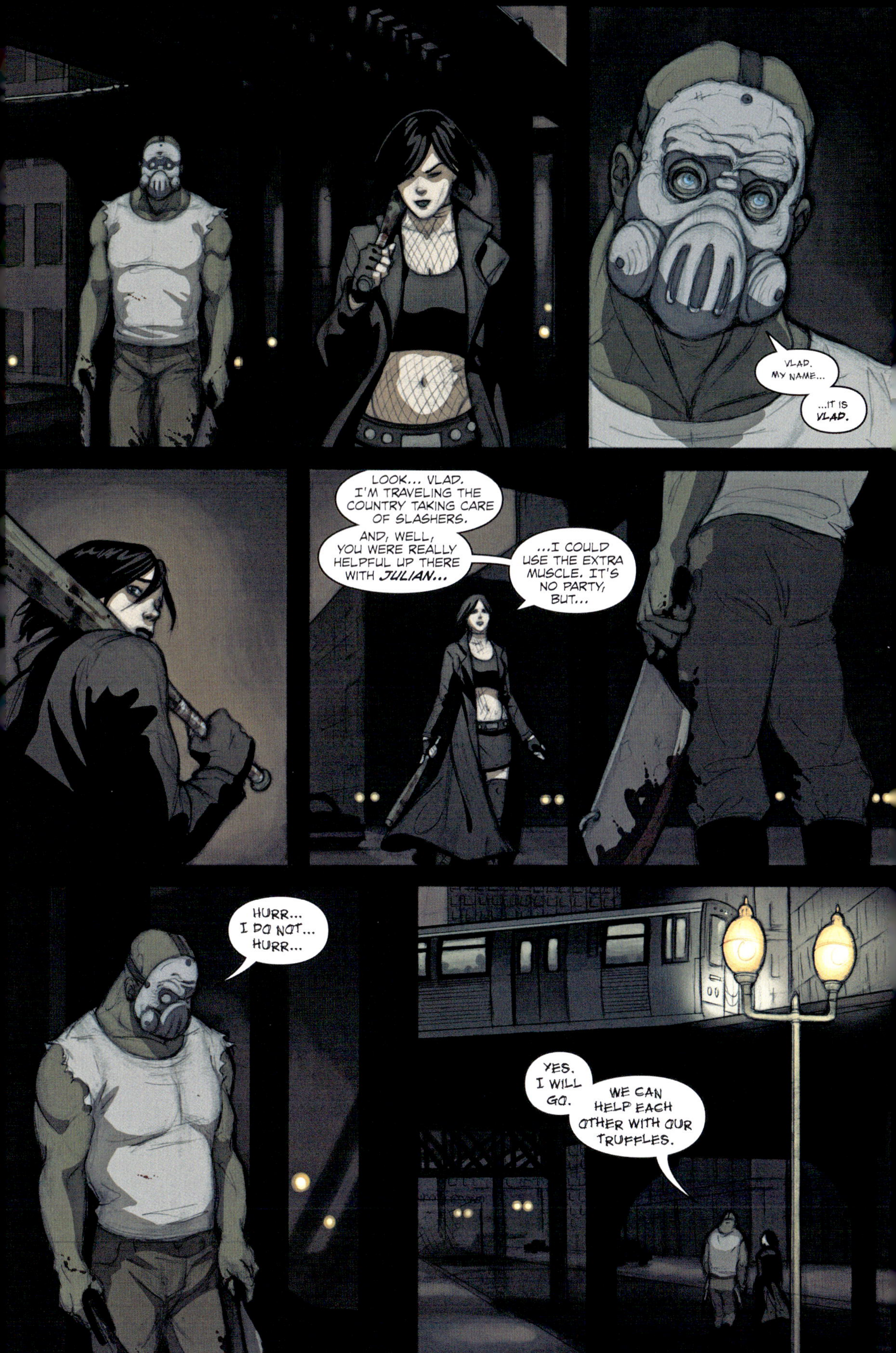
VLAD. MY NAME...
...IT IS VLAD.
LOOK... VLAD. I'M TRAVELING THE COUNTRY TAKING CARE OF SLASHERS.
AND, WELL, YOU WERE REALLY HELPFUL UP THERE WITH JULIAN...
...I COULD USE THE EXTRA MUSCLE. IT'S NO PARTY, BUT...
HURR... I DO NOT... HURR...
YES. I WILL GO.
WE CAN HELP EACH OTHER WITH OUR TRUFFLES.

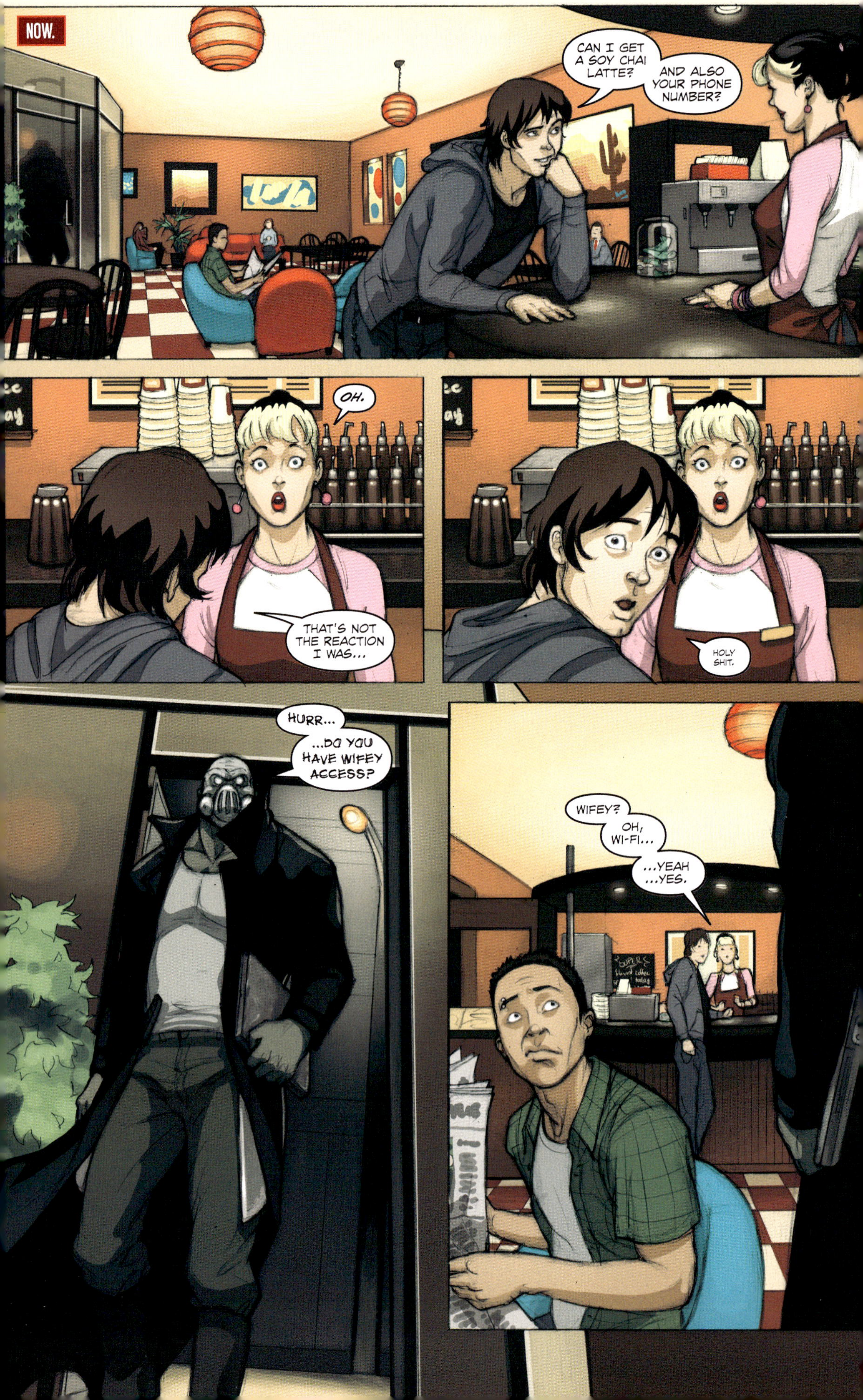
NOW.
CAN I GET A SOY CHAI LATTE?
AND ALSO YOUR PHONE NUMBER?
OH.
THAT'S NOT THE REACTION I WAS...
HOLY SHIT.
HURR...
...DO YOU HAVE WIFEY ACCESS?
WIFEY?
OH, WI-FI...
...YEAH ...YES.

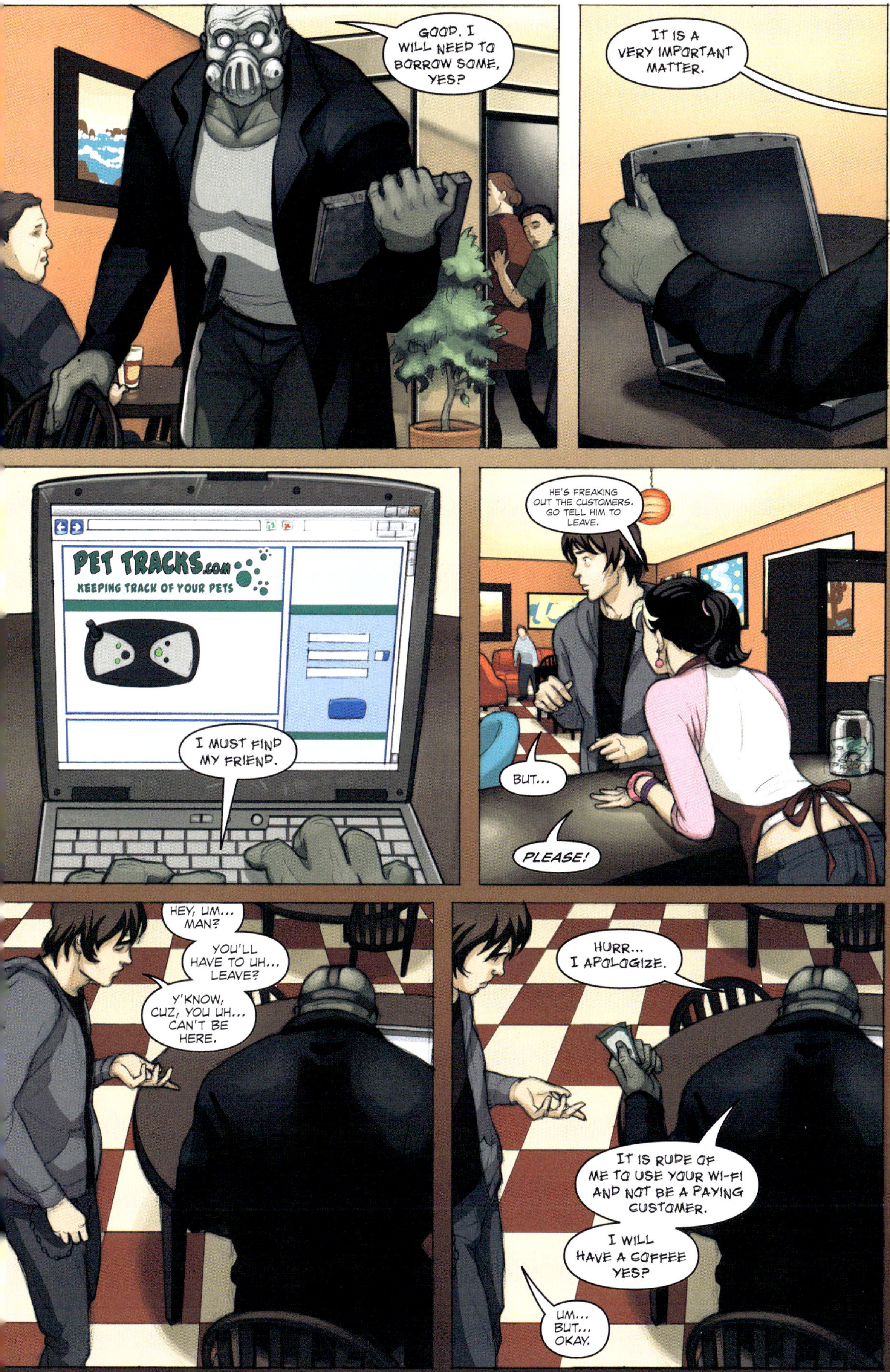
GOOD. I WILL NEED TO BORROW SOME, YES?
IT IS A VERY IMPORTANT MATTER.
PET TRACKS.com
KEEPING TRACK OF YOUR PETS
I MUST FIND MY FRIEND.
HE'S FREAKING OUT THE CUSTOMERS. GO TELL HIM TO LEAVE.
BUT...
PLEASE!
HEY, UM... MAN?
YOU'LL HAVE TO UH... LEAVE?
Y'KNOW, CUZ, YOU UH... CAN'T BE HERE.
HURR... I APOLOGIZE.
IT IS RUDE OF ME TO USE YOUR WI-FI AND NOT BE A PAYING CUSTOMER.
I WILL HAVE A COFFEE YES?
UM... BUT... OKAY.

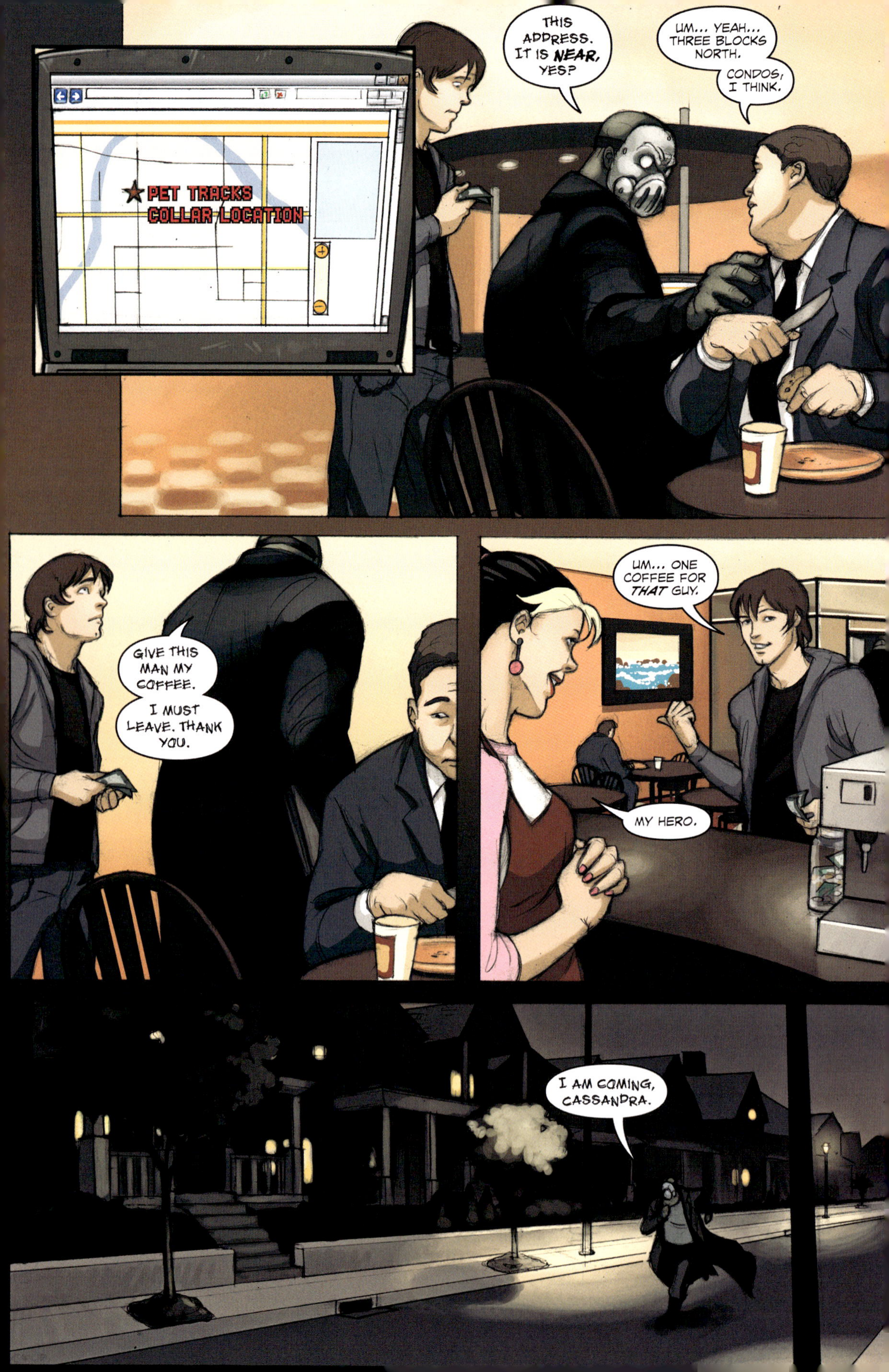
PET TRACKS COLLAR LOCATION
THIS ADDRESS. IT IS NEAR, YES?
UM... YEAH... THREE BLOCKS NORTH.
CONDOS, I THINK.
GIVE THIS MAN MY COFFEE.
I MUST LEAVE. THANK YOU.
UM... ONE COFFEE FOR THAT GUY.
MY HERO.
I AM COMING, CASSANDRA.

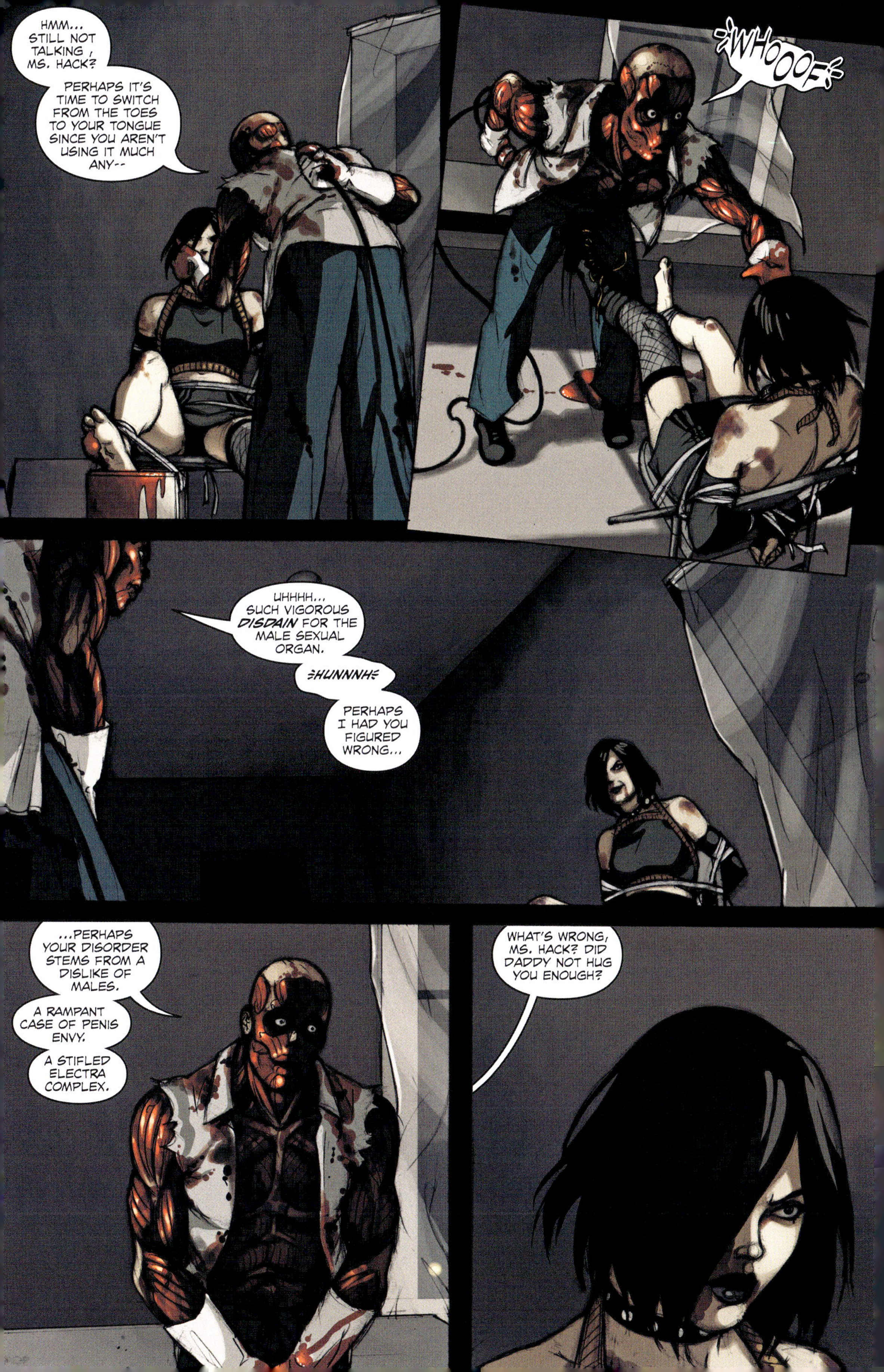
HMM... STILL NOT TALKING , MS. HACK?
PERHAPS IT'S TIME TO SWITCH FROM THE TOES TO YOUR TONGUE SINCE YOU AREN'T USING IT MUCH ANY--
WHOOOF
UHHHH... SUCH VIGOROUS DISDAIN FOR THE MALE SEXUAL ORGAN.
HUNNNH
PERHAPS I HAD YOU FIGURED WRONG...
...PERHAPS YOUR DISORDER STEMS FROM A DISLIKE OF MALES.
A RAMPANT CASE OF PENIS ENVY.
A STIFLED ELECTRA COMPLEX.
WHAT'S WRONG, MS. HACK? DID DADDY NOT HUG YOU ENOUGH?

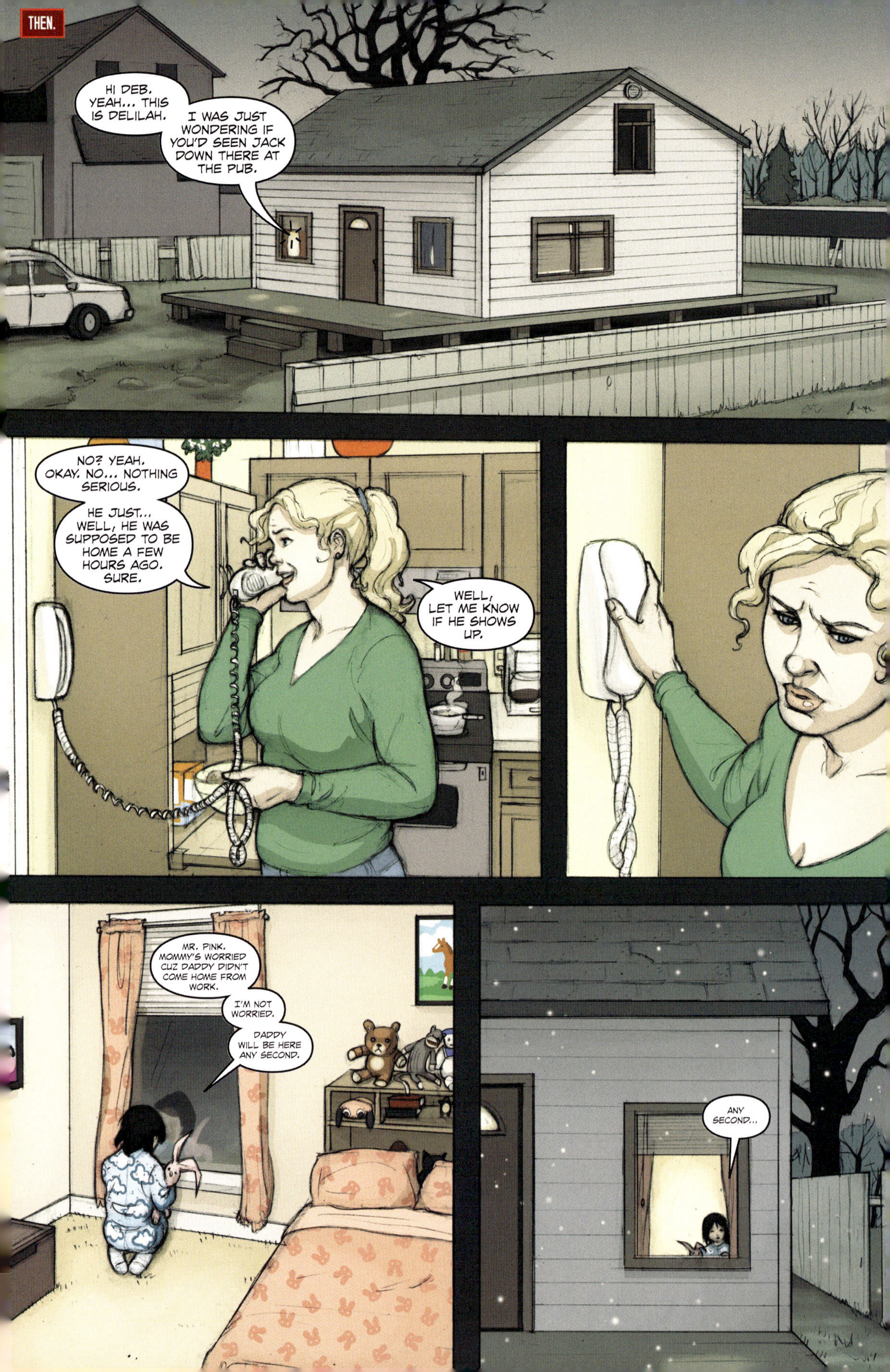
THEN.
HI DEB. YEAH... THIS IS DELILAH.
I WAS JUST WONDERING IF YOU'D SEEN JACK DOWN THERE AT THE PUB.
NO? YEAH. OKAY. NO... NOTHING SERIOUS.
HE JUST... WELL, HE WAS SUPPOSED TO BE HOME A FEW HOURS AGO. SURE.
WELL, LET ME KNOW IF HE SHOWS UP.
MR. PINK. MOMMY'S WORRIED CUZ DADDY DIDN'T COME HOME FROM WORK.
I'M NOT WORRIED.
DADDY WILL BE HERE ANY SECOND.
ANY SECOND...

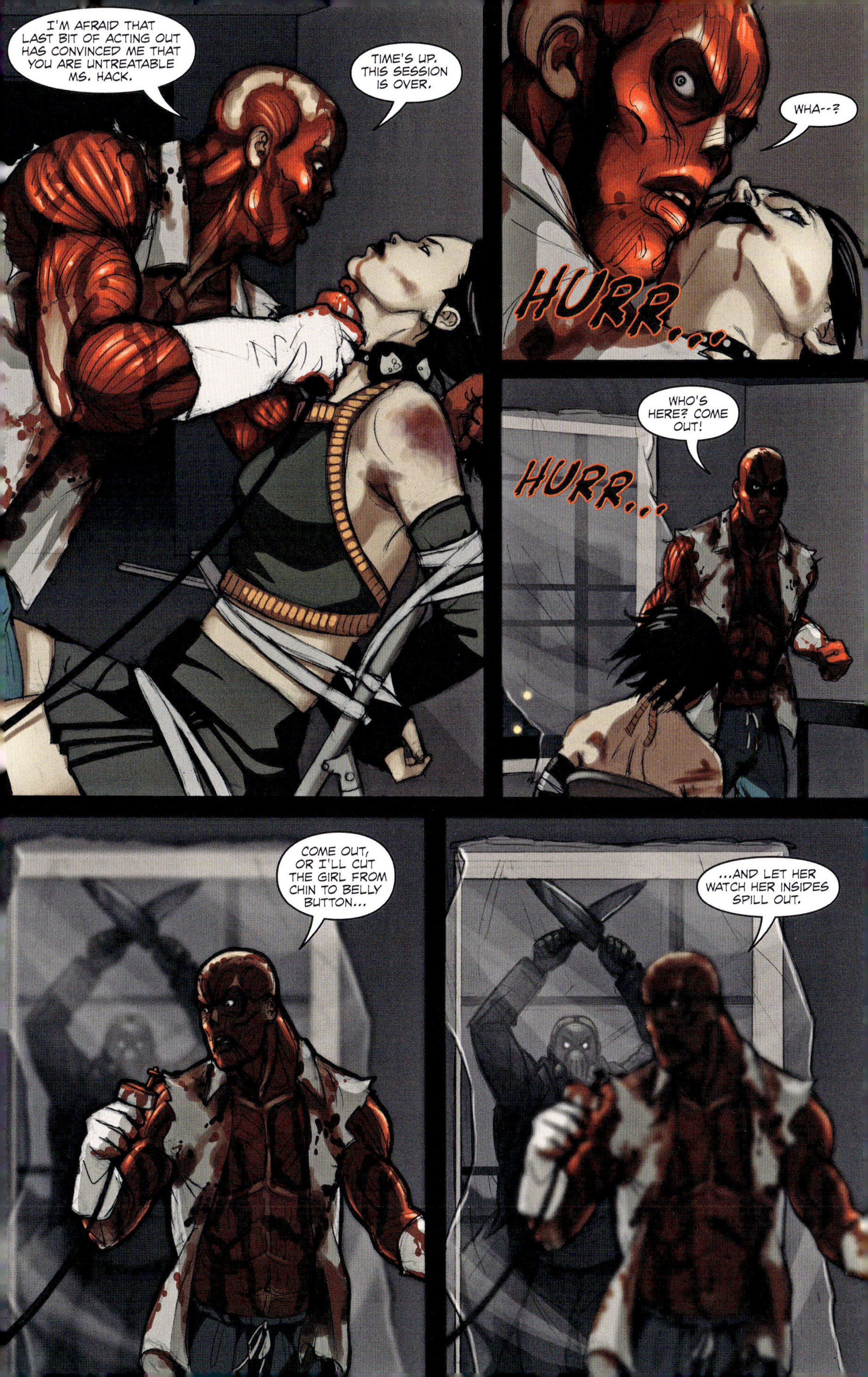
I'M AFRAID THAT LAST BIT OF ACTING OUT HAS CONVINCED ME THAT YOU ARE UNTREATABLE MS. HACK.
TIME'S UP. THIS SESSION IS OVER.
WHA--?
HURR...
WHO'S HERE? COME OUT!
HURR...
COME OUT, OR I'LL CUT THE GIRL FROM CHIN TO BELLY BUTTON...
...AND LET HER WATCH HER INSIDES SPILL OUT.

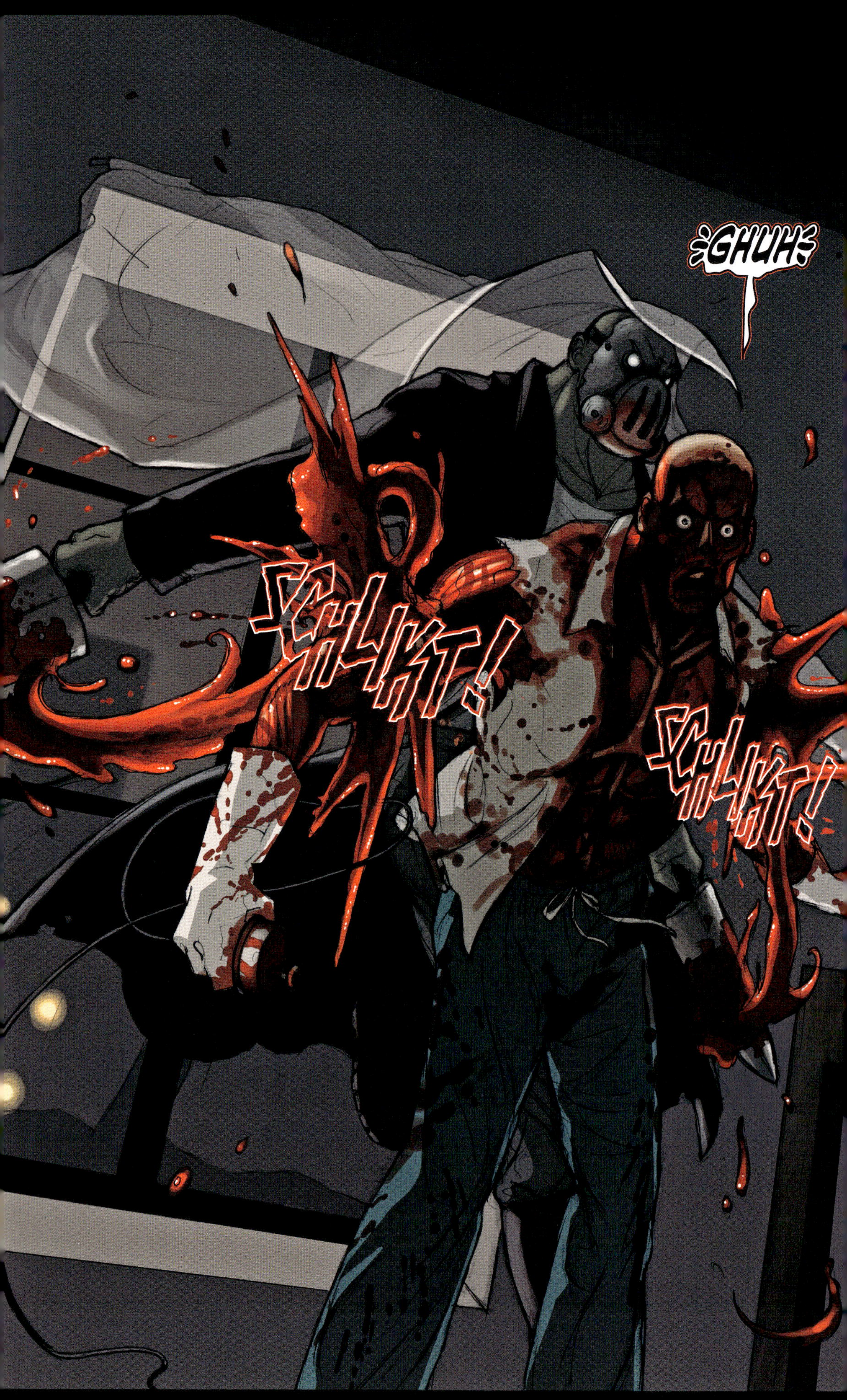
GHUH
SCHLIKT!
SCHLIKT!

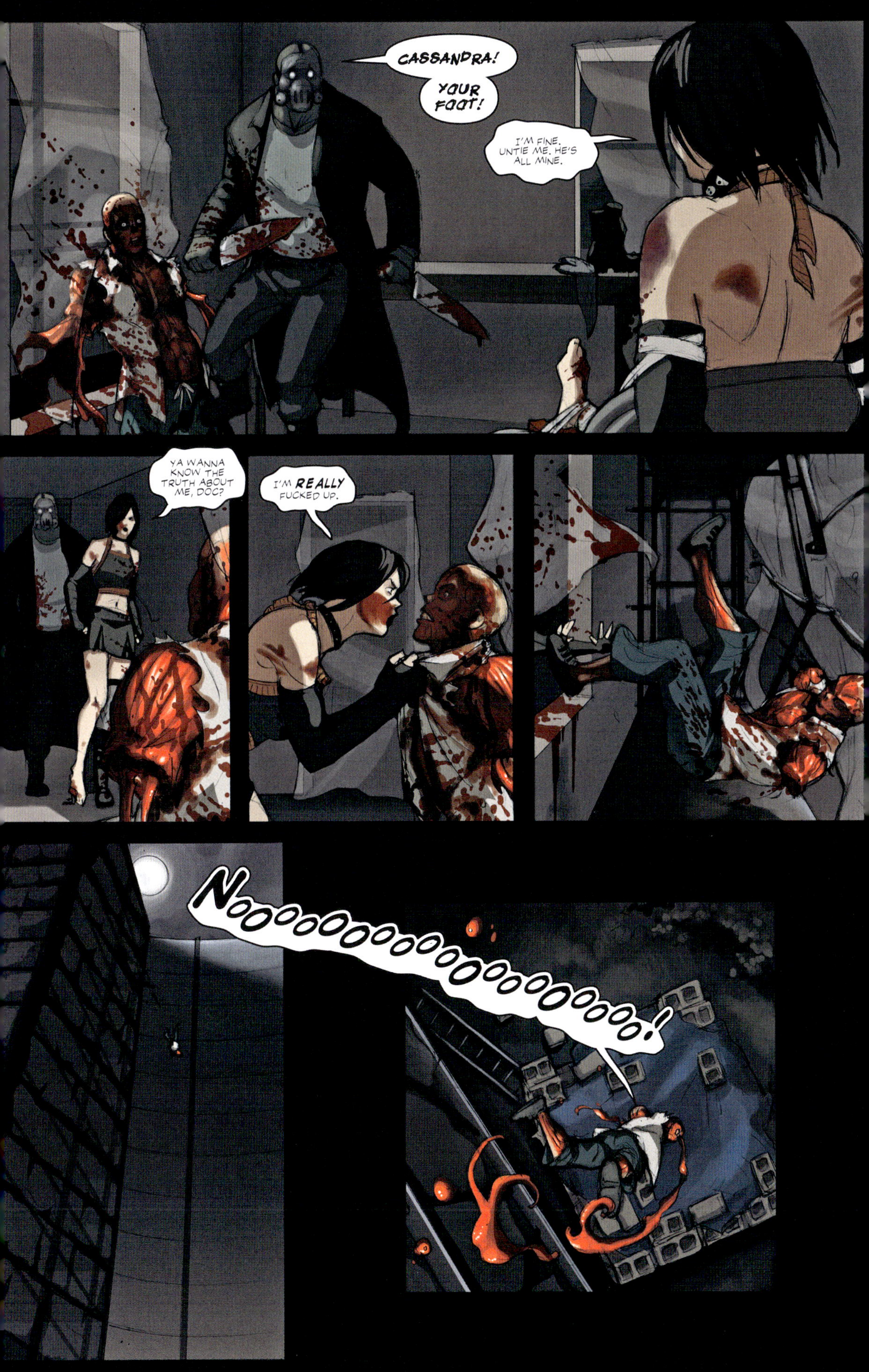
CASSANDRA!
YOUR FOOT!
I'M FINE. UNTIE ME. HE'S ALL MINE.
YA WANNA KNOW THE TRUTH ABOUT ME, DOC?
I'M **REALLY** FUCKED UP.
NOooooooooooooooooooooo!

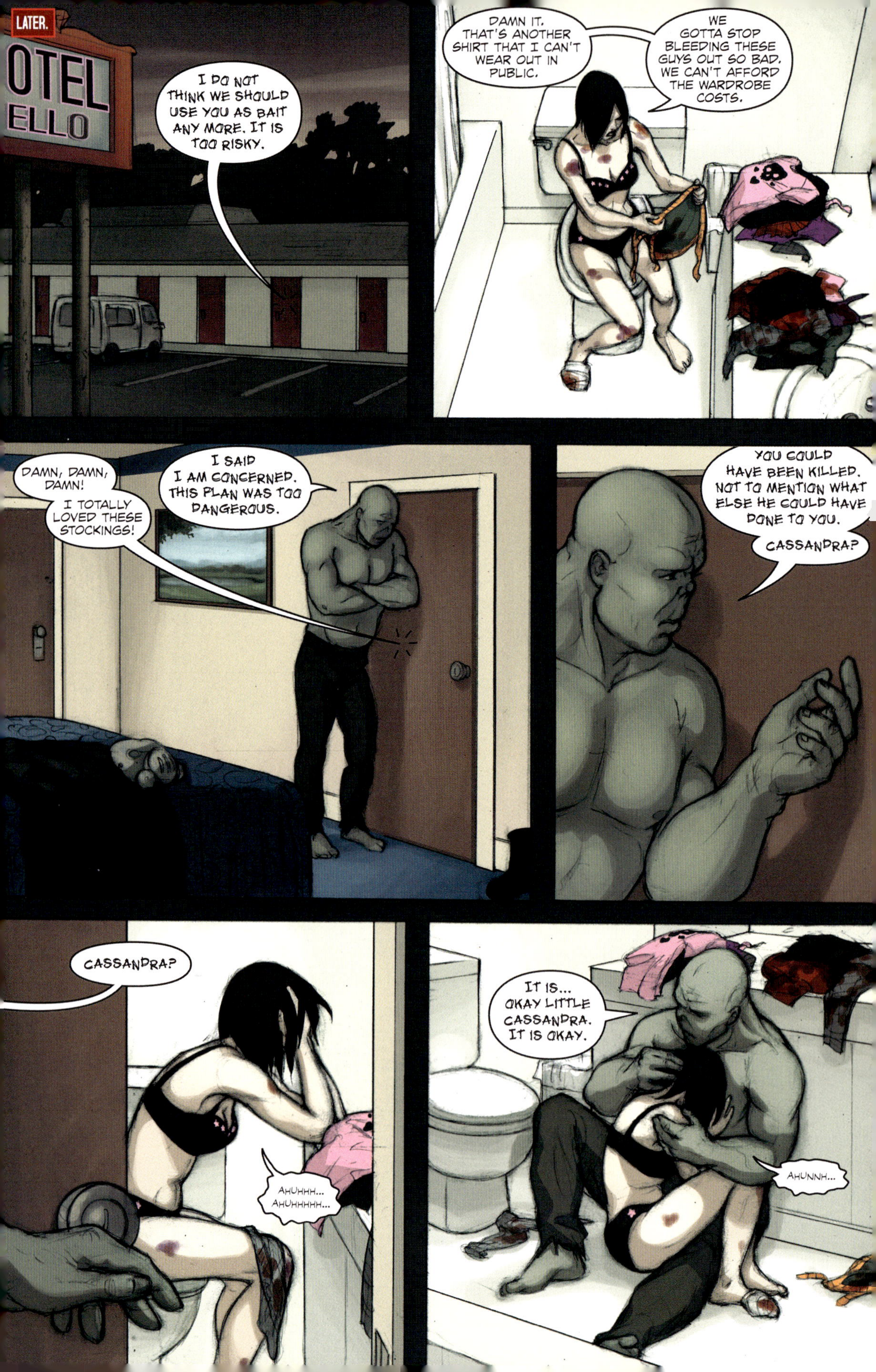
LATER.
OTEL
ELLO
I DO NOT THINK WE SHOULD USE YOU AS BAIT ANY MORE. IT IS TOO RISKY.
DAMN IT. THAT'S ANOTHER SHIRT THAT I CAN'T WEAR OUT IN PUBLIC.
WE GOTTA STOP BLEEDING THESE GUYS OUT SO BAD. WE CAN'T AFFORD THE WARDROBE COSTS.
DAMN, DAMN, DAMN!
I TOTALLY LOVED THESE STOCKINGS!
I SAID I AM CONCERNED. THIS PLAN WAS TOO DANGEROUS.
YOU COULD HAVE BEEN KILLED. NOT TO MENTION WHAT ELSE HE COULD HAVE DONE TO YOU.
CASSANDRA?
CASSANDRA?
AHUHHH... AHUHHHHH...
IT IS... OKAY LITTLE CASSANDRA. IT IS OKAY.
AHUNNH...

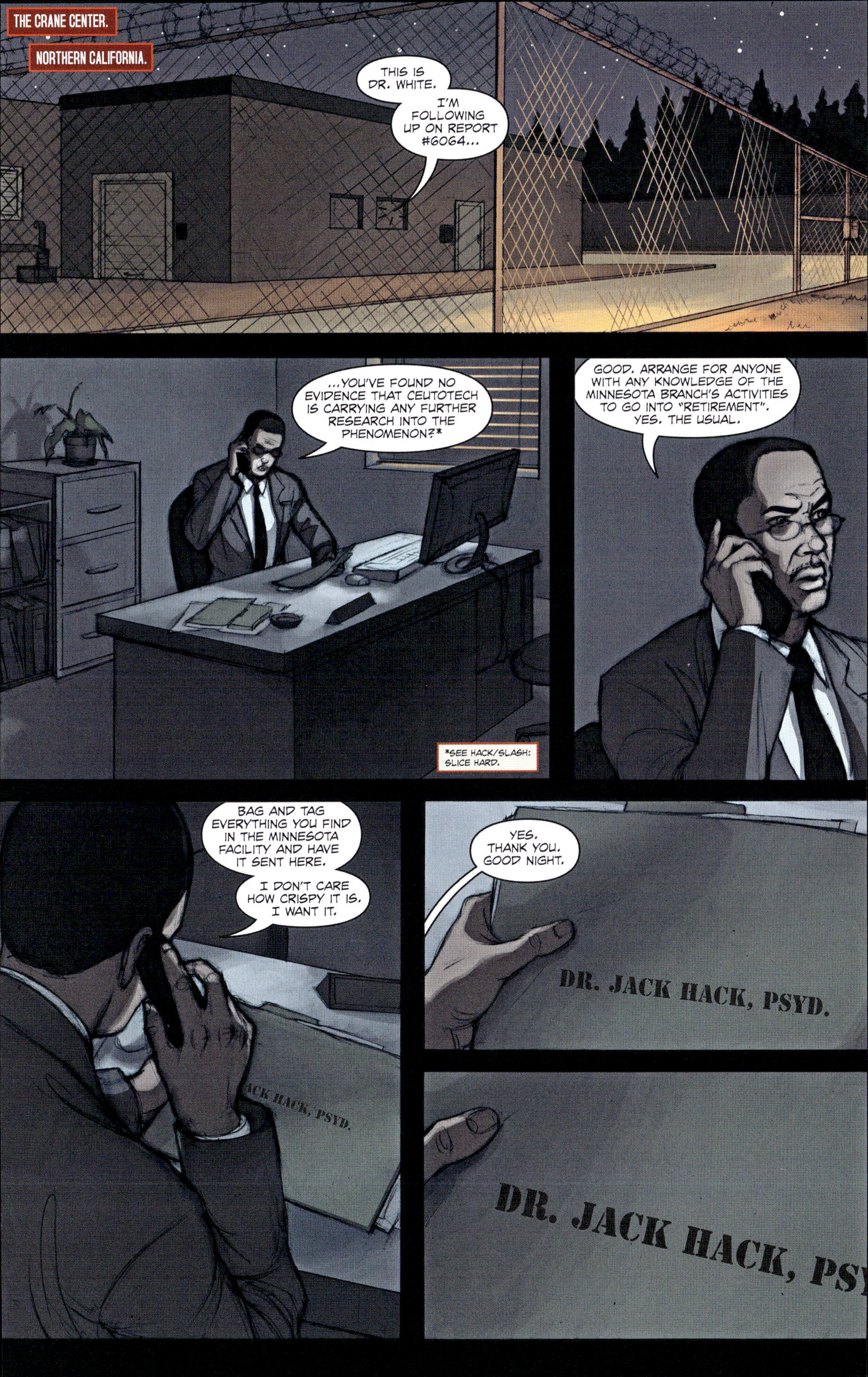
THE CRANE CENTER.
NORTHERN CALIFORNIA.
THIS IS DR. WHITE.
I'M FOLLOWING UP ON REPORT #6064...
...YOU'VE FOUND NO EVIDENCE THAT CEUTOTECH IS CARRYING ANY FURTHER RESEARCH INTO THE PHENOMENON?*
*SEE HACK/SLASH: SLICE HARD.
GOOD. ARRANGE FOR ANYONE WITH ANY KNOWLEDGE OF THE MINNESOTA BRANCH'S ACTIVITIES TO GO INTO "RETIREMENT". YES. THE USUAL.
BAG AND TAG EVERYTHING YOU FIND IN THE MINNESOTA FACILITY AND HAVE IT SENT HERE.
I DON'T CARE HOW CRISPY IT IS. I WANT IT.
YES. THANK YOU. GOOD NIGHT.
DR. JACK HACK, PSYD.

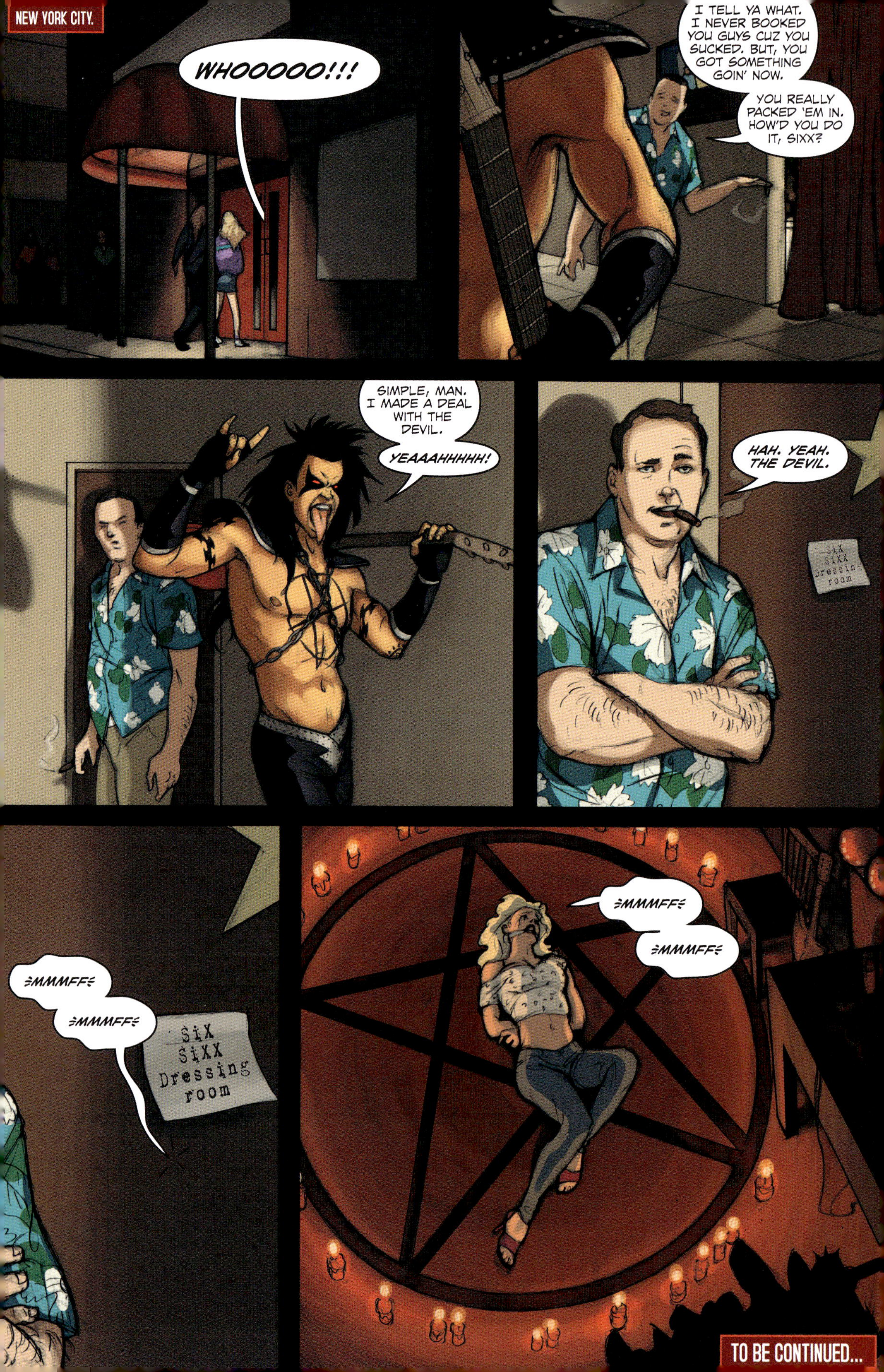
NEW YORK CITY.
WHOOOOO!!!
I TELL YA WHAT. I NEVER BOOKED YOU GUYS CUZ YOU SUCKED. BUT, YOU GOT SOMETHING GOIN' NOW.
YOU REALLY PACKED 'EM IN. HOW'D YOU DO IT, SIXX?
SIMPLE, MAN. I MADE A DEAL WITH THE DEVIL.
YEAAAHHHHH!
HAH. YEAH. THE DEVIL.
SIX SIXX Dressing room
MMMFF
MMMFF
MMMFF
MMMFF
SIX SIXX Dressing room
TO BE CONTINUED...

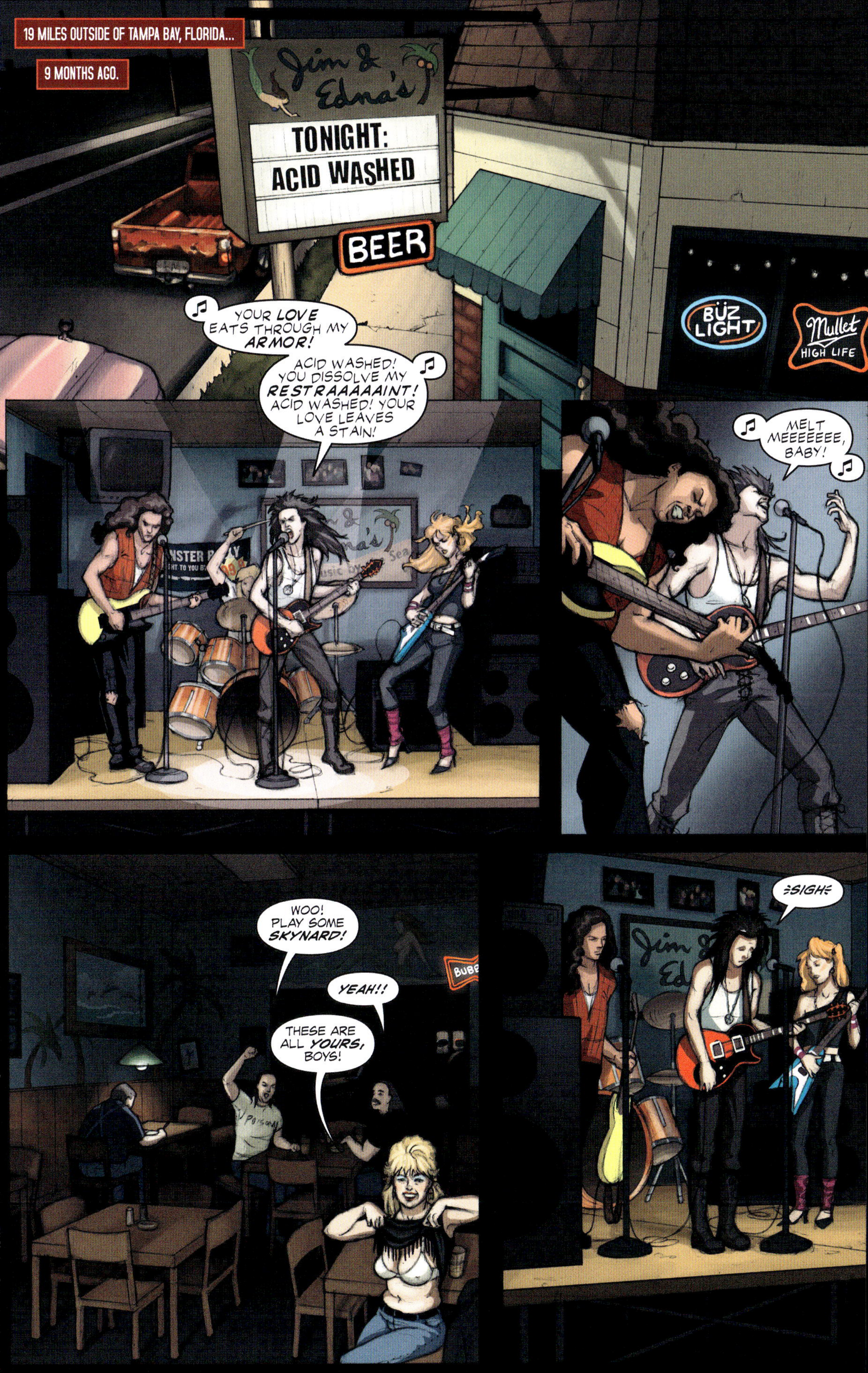

19 MILES OUTSIDE OF TAMPA BAY, FLORIDA...
9 MONTHS AGO.
Jim & Edna's
TONIGHT:
ACID WASHED
BEER
BÜZ LIGHT
Mullet HIGH LIFE
YOUR LOVE EATS THROUGH MY ARMOR!
ACID WASHED! YOU DISSOLVE MY RESTRAAAAAINT! ACID WASHED! YOUR LOVE LEAVES A STAIN!
MELT MEEEEEEE, BABY!
WOO! PLAY SOME SKYNARD!
YEAH!!
THESE ARE ALL YOURS, BOYS!
SIGH

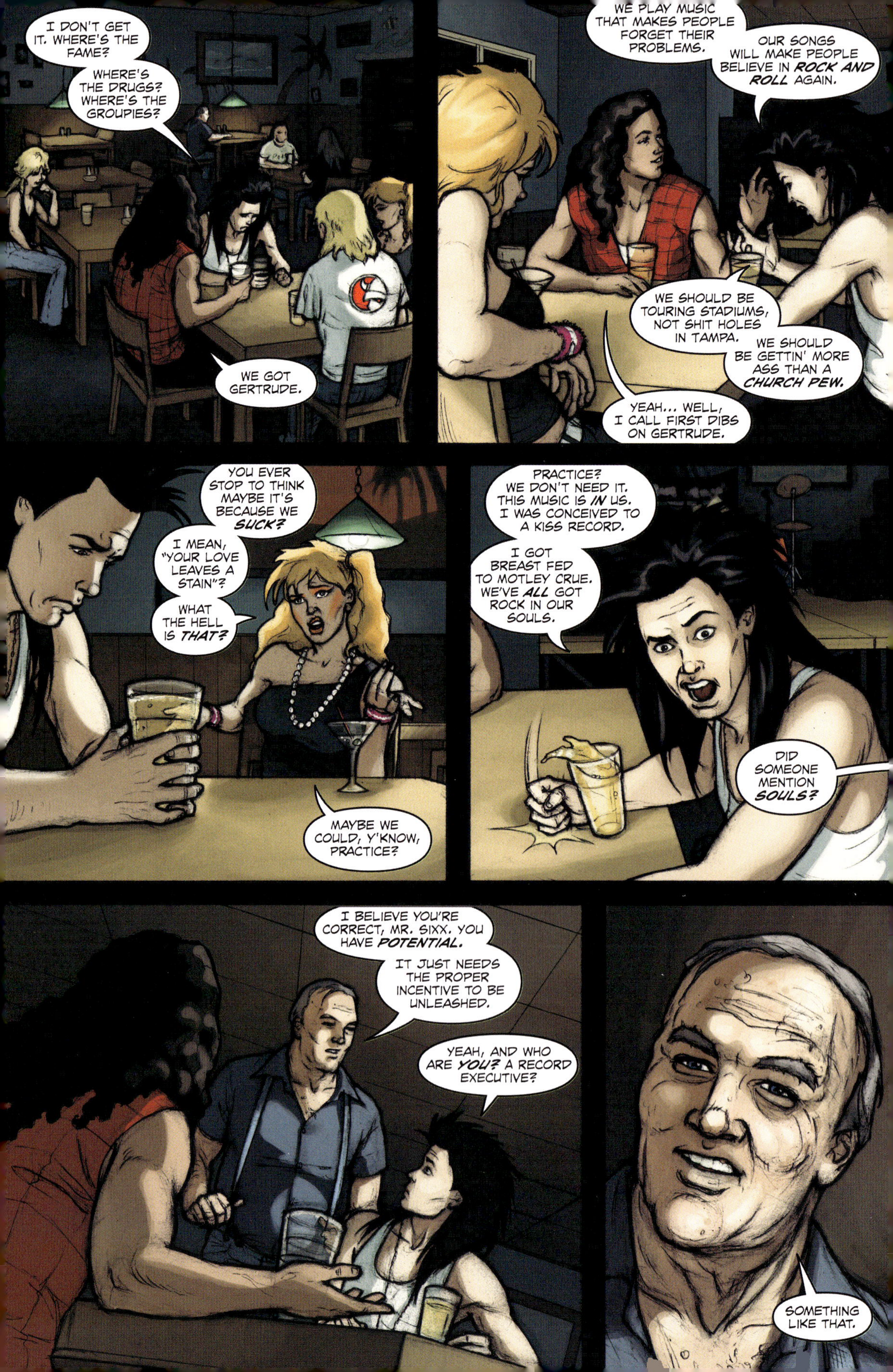
I DON'T GET IT. WHERE'S THE FAME?
WHERE'S THE DRUGS? WHERE'S THE GROUPIES?
WE GOT GERTRUDE.
WE PLAY MUSIC THAT MAKES PEOPLE FORGET THEIR PROBLEMS.
OUR SONGS WILL MAKE PEOPLE BELIEVE IN ROCK AND ROLL AGAIN.
WE SHOULD BE TOURING STADIUMS, NOT SHIT HOLES IN TAMPA.
WE SHOULD BE GETTIN' MORE ASS THAN A CHURCH PEW.
YEAH... WELL, I CALL FIRST DIBS ON GERTRUDE.
YOU EVER STOP TO THINK MAYBE IT'S BECAUSE WE SUCK?
I MEAN, "YOUR LOVE LEAVES A STAIN"?
WHAT THE HELL IS THAT?
MAYBE WE COULD, Y'KNOW, PRACTICE?
PRACTICE? WE DON'T NEED IT. THIS MUSIC IS IN US. I WAS CONCEIVED TO A KISS RECORD.
I GOT BREAST FED TO MOTLEY CRUE. WE'VE ALL GOT ROCK IN OUR SOULS.
DID SOMEONE MENTION SOULS?
I BELIEVE YOU'RE CORRECT, MR. SIXX. YOU HAVE POTENTIAL.
IT JUST NEEDS THE PROPER INCENTIVE TO BE UNLEASHED.
YEAH, AND WHO ARE YOU? A RECORD EXECUTIVE?
SOMETHING LIKE THAT.

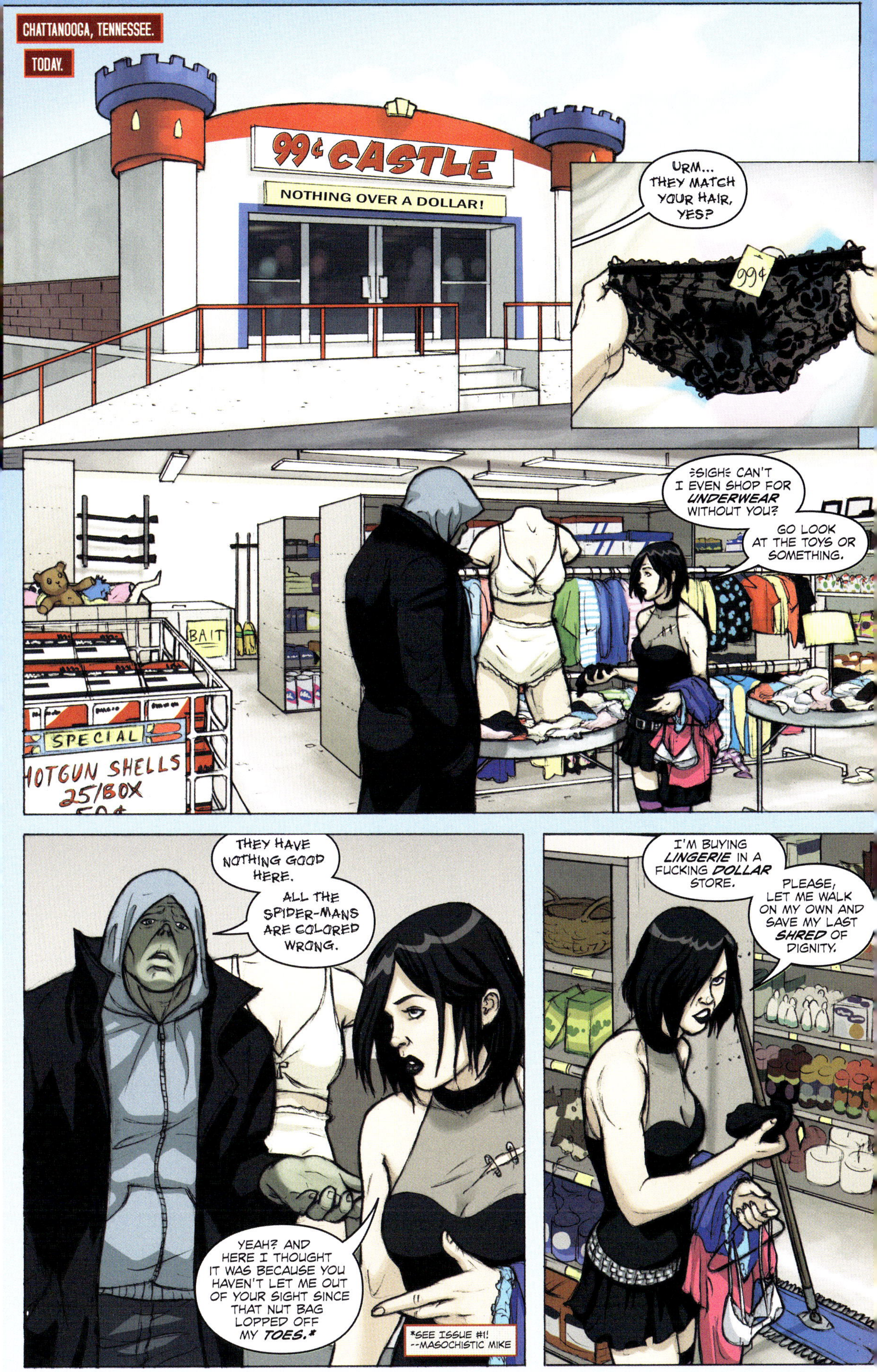

CHATTANOOGA, TENNESSEE.
TODAY.
99¢ CASTLE
NOTHING OVER A DOLLAR!
URM... THEY MATCH YOUR HAIR, YES?
99¢
=SIGH= CAN'T I EVEN SHOP FOR *UNDERWEAR* WITHOUT YOU?
GO LOOK AT THE TOYS OR SOMETHING.
BAIT
SPECIAL
HOTGUN SHELLS
25/BOX
THEY HAVE NOTHING GOOD HERE.
ALL THE SPIDER-MANS ARE COLORED WRONG.
YEAH? AND HERE I THOUGHT IT WAS BECAUSE YOU HAVEN'T LET ME OUT OF YOUR SIGHT SINCE THAT NUT BAG LOPPED OFF MY *TOES.**
*SEE ISSUE #1! --MASOCHISTIC MIKE
I'M BUYING *LINGERIE* IN A FUCKING *DOLLAR* STORE.
PLEASE, LET ME WALK ON MY OWN AND SAVE MY LAST *SHRED* OF DIGNITY.

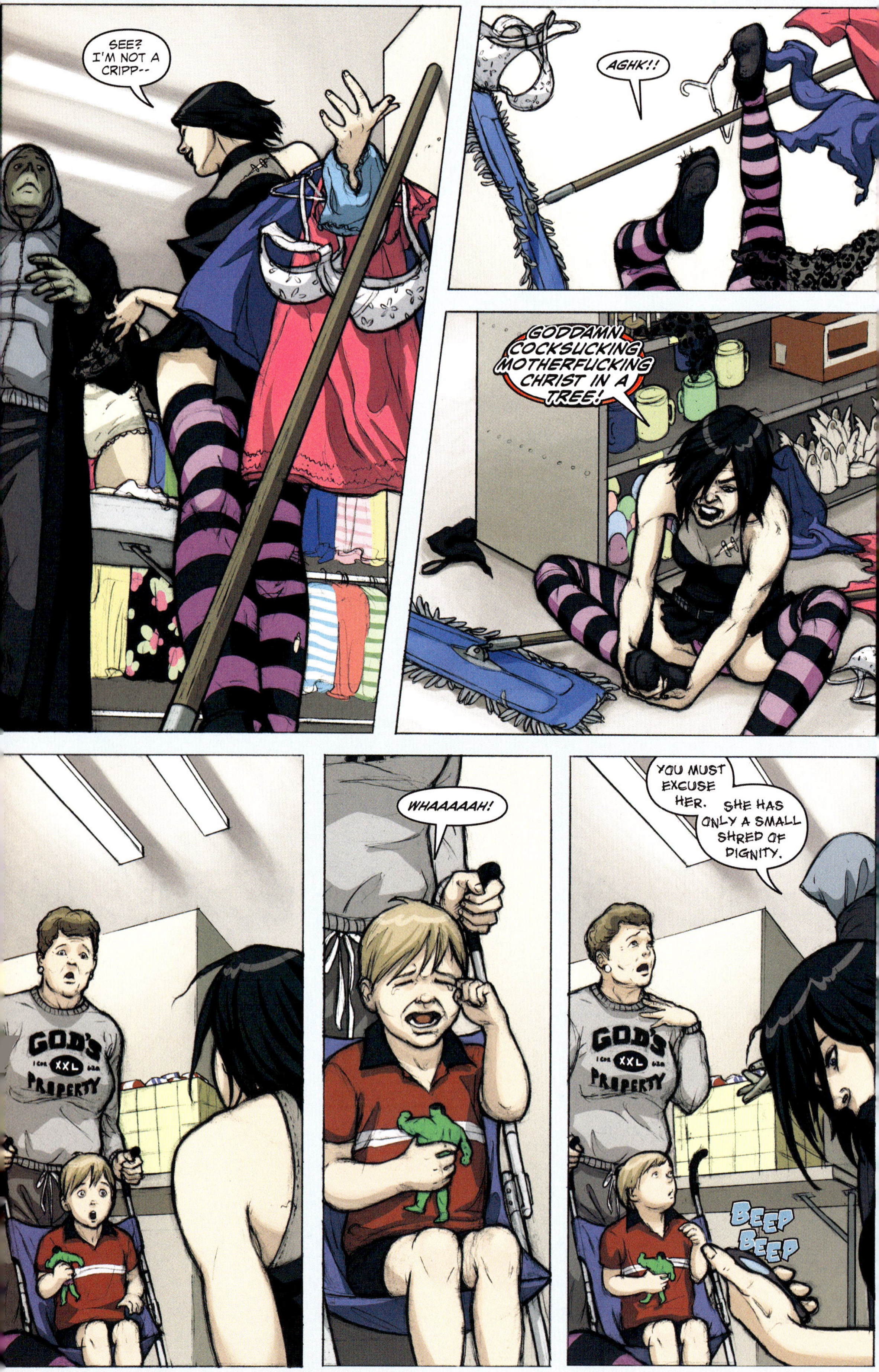
SEE? I'M NOT A CRIPP--
AGHK!!
GODDAMN COCKSUCKING MOTHERFUCKING CHRIST IN A TREE!
GOD'S XXL PROPERTY
WHAAAAAAH!
YOU MUST EXCUSE HER.
SHE HAS ONLY A SMALL SHRED OF DIGNITY.
GOD'S XXL PROPERTY
BEEP BEEP

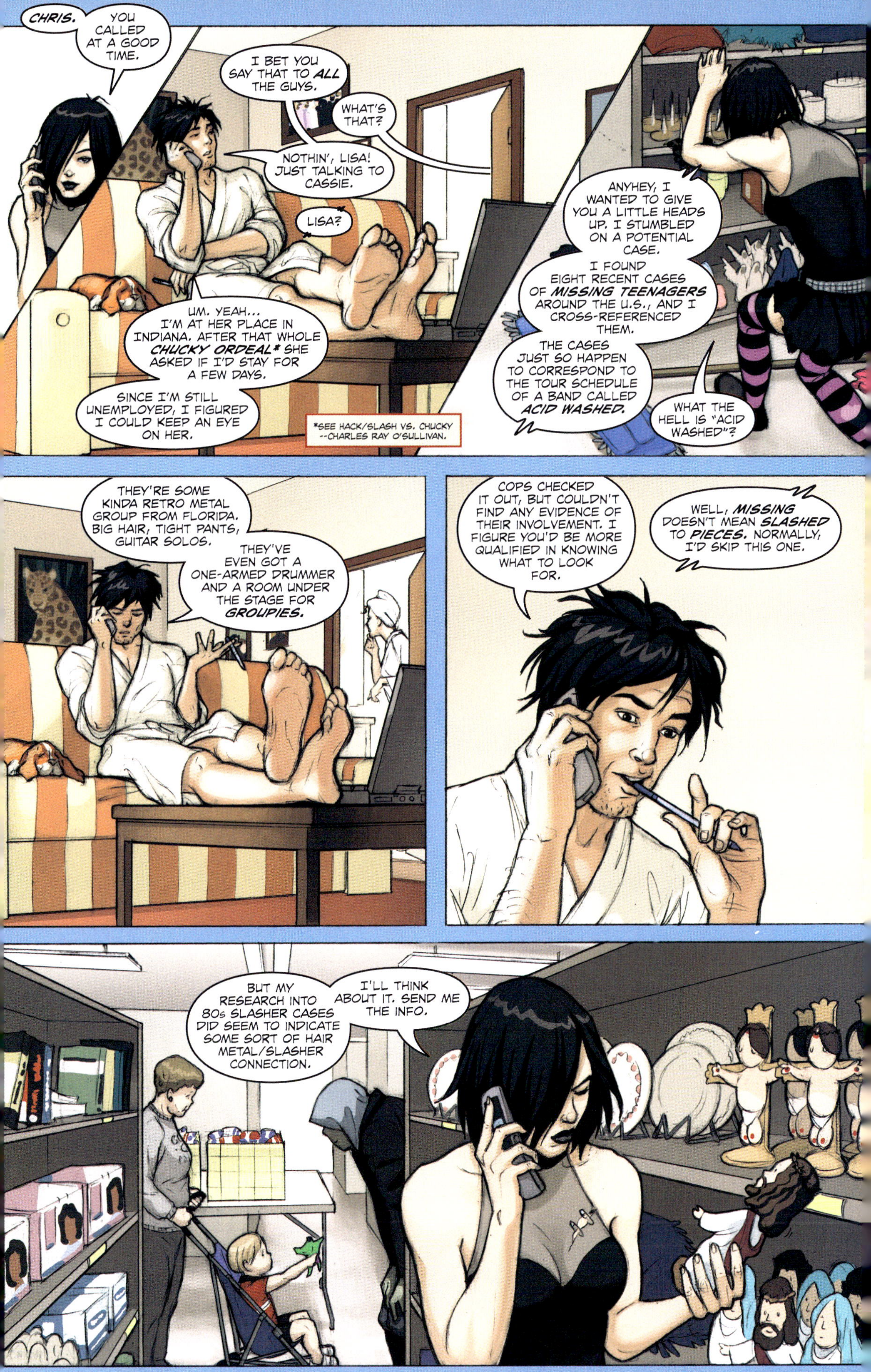
CHRIS.
YOU CALLED AT A GOOD TIME.
I BET YOU SAY THAT TO ALL THE GUYS.
WHAT'S THAT?
NOTHIN', LISA! JUST TALKING TO CASSIE.
LISA?
UM. YEAH... I'M AT HER PLACE IN INDIANA. AFTER THAT WHOLE CHUCKY ORDEAL* SHE ASKED IF I'D STAY FOR A FEW DAYS.
SINCE I'M STILL UNEMPLOYED, I FIGURED I COULD KEEP AN EYE ON HER.
*SEE HACK/SLASH VS. CHUCKY --CHARLES RAY O'SULLIVAN.
ANYHEY, I WANTED TO GIVE YOU A LITTLE HEADS UP. I STUMBLED ON A POTENTIAL CASE.
I FOUND EIGHT RECENT CASES OF MISSING TEENAGERS AROUND THE U.S., AND I CROSS-REFERENCED THEM.
THE CASES JUST SO HAPPEN TO CORRESPOND TO THE TOUR SCHEDULE OF A BAND CALLED ACID WASHED.
WHAT THE HELL IS "ACID WASHED"?
THEY'RE SOME KINDA RETRO METAL GROUP FROM FLORIDA. BIG HAIR, TIGHT PANTS, GUITAR SOLOS.
THEY'VE EVEN GOT A ONE-ARMED DRUMMER AND A ROOM UNDER THE STAGE FOR GROUPIES.
COPS CHECKED IT OUT, BUT COULDN'T FIND ANY EVIDENCE OF THEIR INVOLVEMENT. I FIGURE YOU'D BE MORE QUALIFIED IN KNOWING WHAT TO LOOK FOR.
WELL, MISSING DOESN'T MEAN SLASHED TO PIECES. NORMALLY, I'D SKIP THIS ONE.
BUT MY RESEARCH INTO 80s SLASHER CASES DID SEEM TO INDICATE SOME SORT OF HAIR METAL/SLASHER CONNECTION.
I'LL THINK ABOUT IT. SEND ME THE INFO.

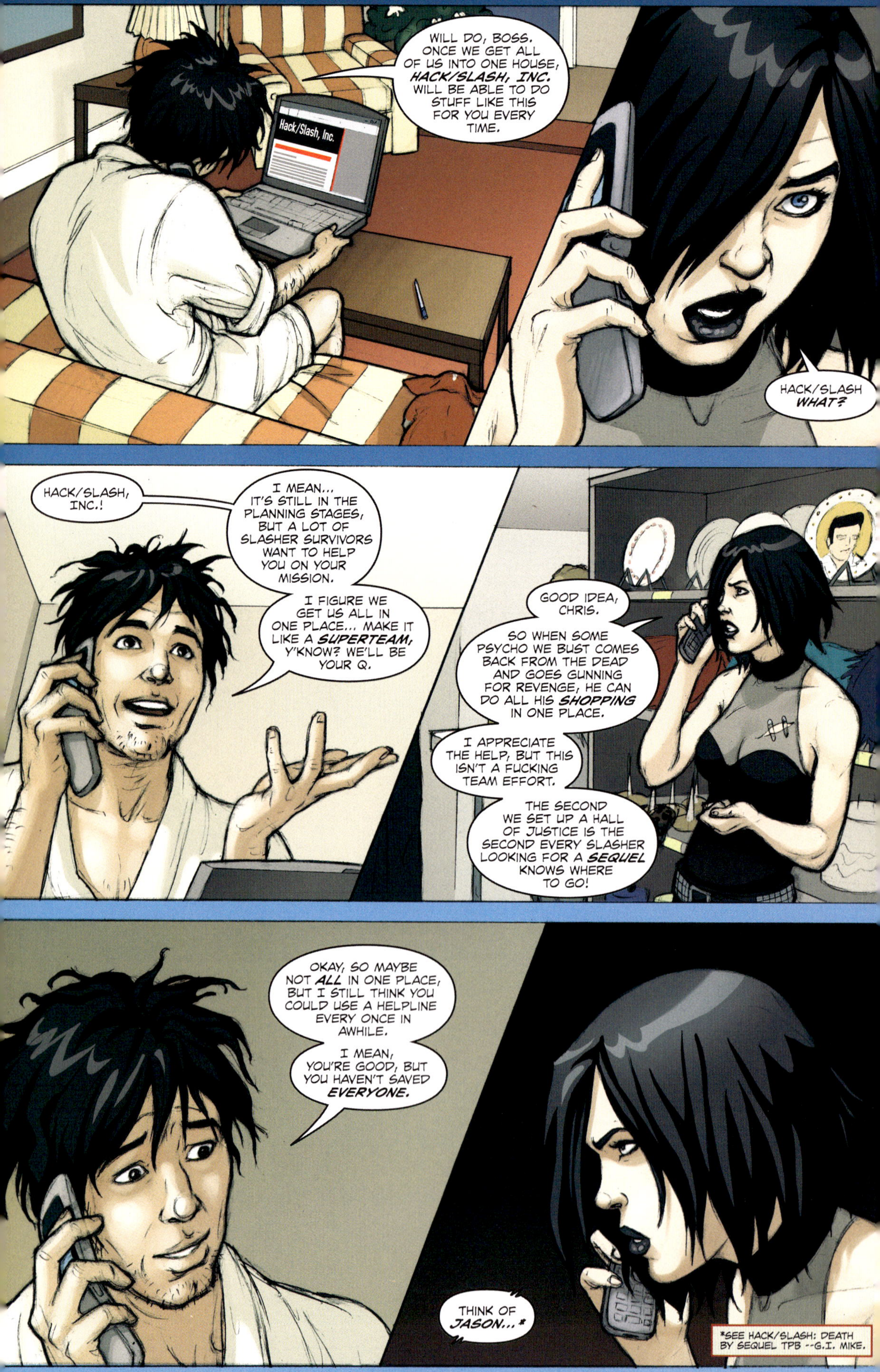
WILL DO, BOSS. ONCE WE GET ALL OF US INTO ONE HOUSE, HACK/SLASH, INC. WILL BE ABLE TO DO STUFF LIKE THIS FOR YOU EVERY TIME.
Hack/Slash, Inc.
HACK/SLASH WHAT?
HACK/SLASH, INC.!
I MEAN... IT'S STILL IN THE PLANNING STAGES, BUT A LOT OF SLASHER SURVIVORS WANT TO HELP YOU ON YOUR MISSION.
I FIGURE WE GET US ALL IN ONE PLACE... MAKE IT LIKE A SUPERTEAM, Y'KNOW? WE'LL BE YOUR Q.
GOOD IDEA, CHRIS.
SO WHEN SOME PSYCHO WE BUST COMES BACK FROM THE DEAD AND GOES GUNNING FOR REVENGE, HE CAN DO ALL HIS SHOPPING IN ONE PLACE.
I APPRECIATE THE HELP, BUT THIS ISN'T A FUCKING TEAM EFFORT.
THE SECOND WE SET UP A HALL OF JUSTICE IS THE SECOND EVERY SLASHER LOOKING FOR A SEQUEL KNOWS WHERE TO GO!
OKAY, SO MAYBE NOT ALL IN ONE PLACE, BUT I STILL THINK YOU COULD USE A HELPLINE EVERY ONCE IN AWHILE.
I MEAN, YOU'RE GOOD, BUT YOU HAVEN'T SAVED EVERYONE.
THINK OF JASON...*
*SEE HACK/SLASH: DEATH BY SEQUEL TPB --G.I. MIKE.

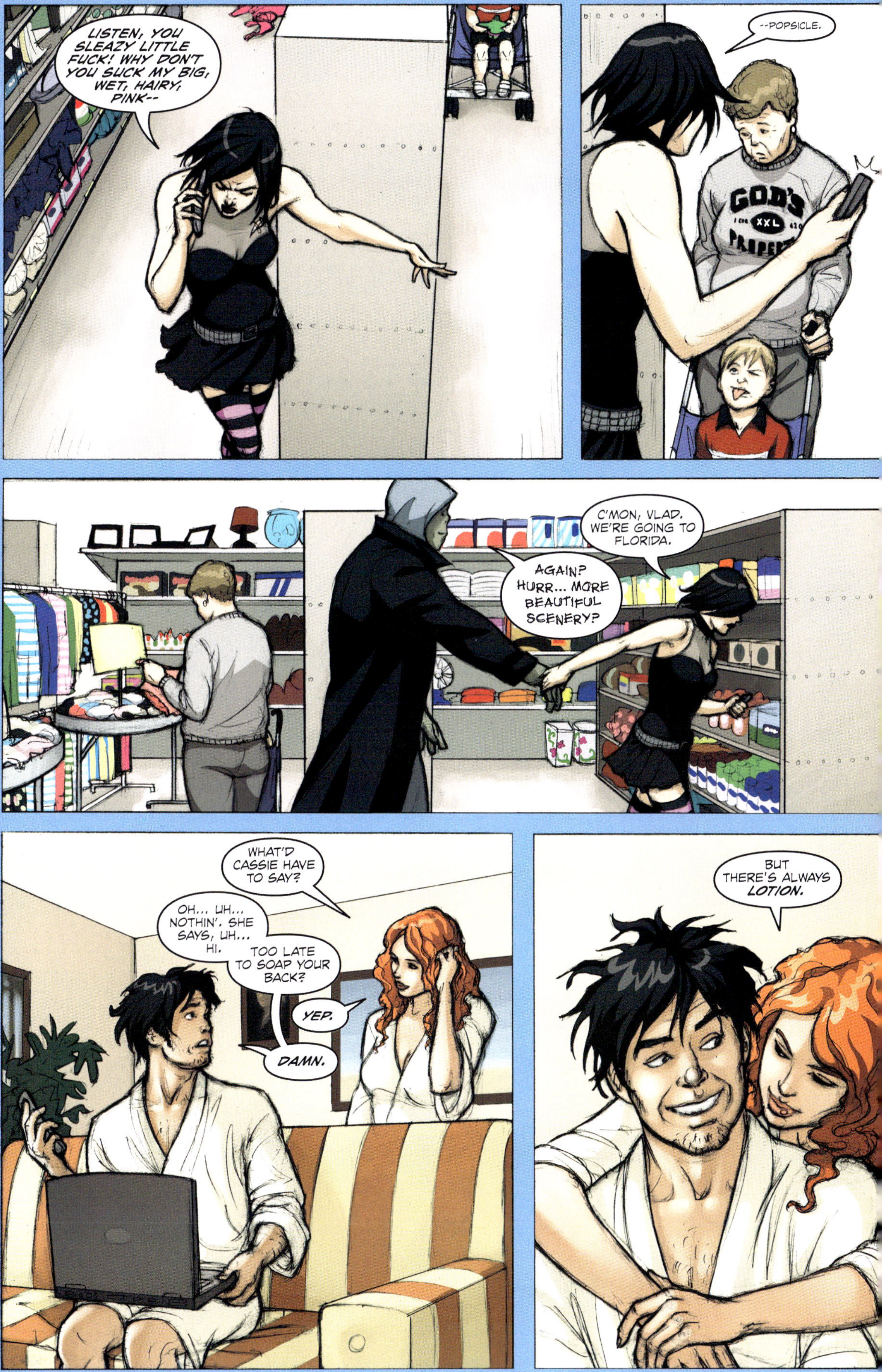

LISTEN, YOU SLEAZY LITTLE FUCK! WHY DON'T YOU SUCK MY BIG, WET, HAIRY, PINK--
--POPSICLE.
GOD'S XXL PROPERTY
C'MON, VLAD. WE'RE GOING TO FLORIDA.
AGAIN? HURR... MORE BEAUTIFUL SCENERY?
WHAT'D CASSIE HAVE TO SAY?
OH... UH... NOTHIN'. SHE SAYS, UH... HI.
TOO LATE TO SOAP YOUR BACK?
YEP.
DAMN.
BUT THERE'S ALWAYS LOTION.

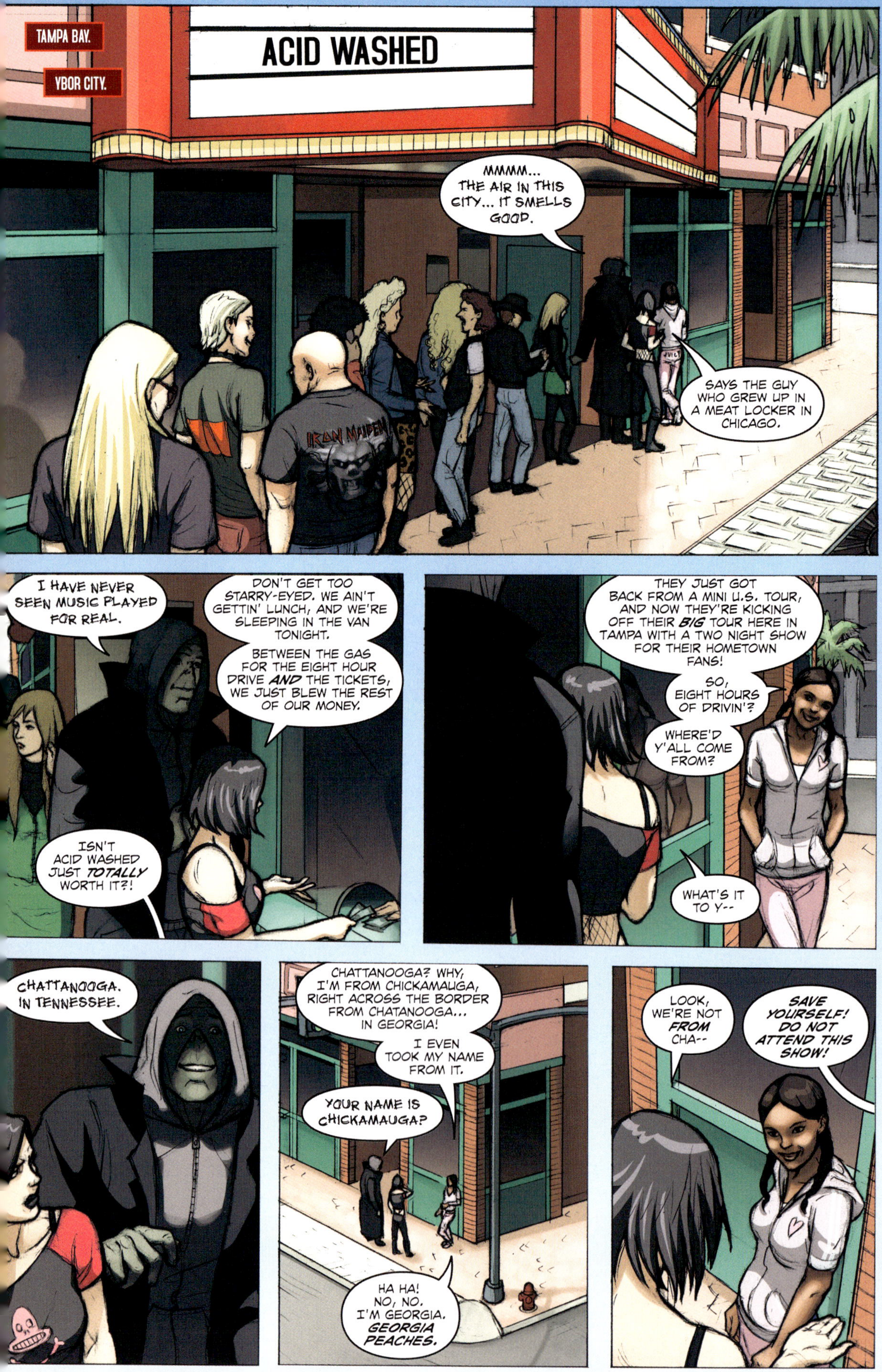
TAMPA BAY.
YBOR CITY.
ACID WASHED
MMMM... THE AIR IN THIS CITY... IT SMELLS GOOD.
SAYS THE GUY WHO GREW UP IN A MEAT LOCKER IN CHICAGO.
IRON MAIDEN
I HAVE NEVER SEEN MUSIC PLAYED FOR REAL.
DON'T GET TOO STARRY-EYED. WE AIN'T GETTIN' LUNCH, AND WE'RE SLEEPING IN THE VAN TONIGHT.
BETWEEN THE GAS FOR THE EIGHT HOUR DRIVE AND THE TICKETS, WE JUST BLEW THE REST OF OUR MONEY.
ISN'T ACID WASHED JUST TOTALLY WORTH IT?!
THEY JUST GOT BACK FROM A MINI U.S. TOUR, AND NOW THEY'RE KICKING OFF THEIR BIG TOUR HERE IN TAMPA WITH A TWO NIGHT SHOW FOR THEIR HOMETOWN FANS!
SO, EIGHT HOURS OF DRIVIN'?
WHERE'D Y'ALL COME FROM?
WHAT'S IT TO Y--
CHATTANOOGA. IN TENNESSEE.
CHATTANOOGA? WHY, I'M FROM CHICKAMAUGA, RIGHT ACROSS THE BORDER FROM CHATANOOGA... IN GEORGIA!
I EVEN TOOK MY NAME FROM IT.
YOUR NAME IS CHICKAMAUGA?
HA HA! NO, NO. I'M GEORGIA. GEORGIA PEACHES.
LOOK, WE'RE NOT FROM CHA--
SAVE YOURSELF! DO NOT ATTEND THIS SHOW!

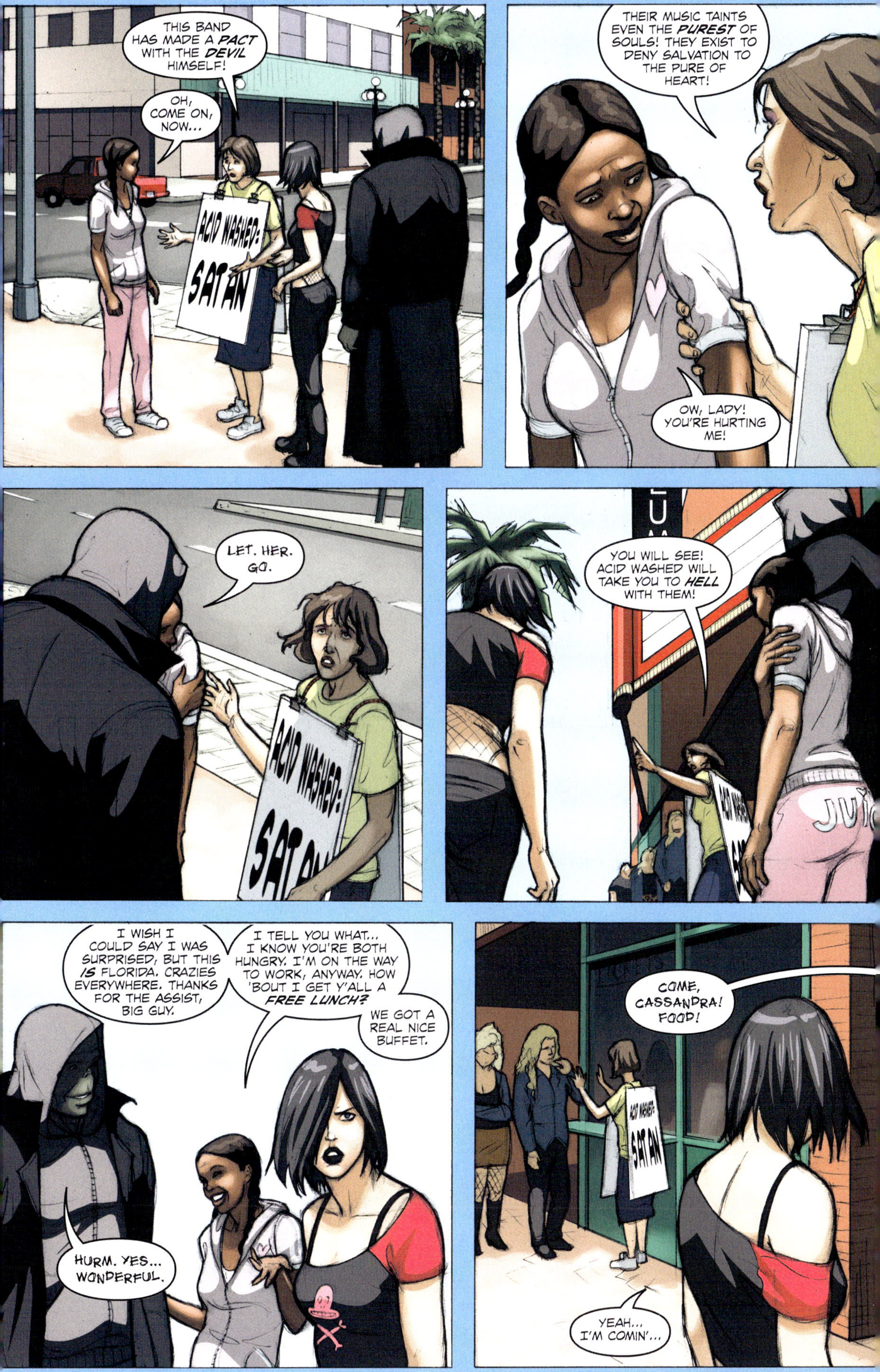
THIS BAND HAS MADE A *PACT* WITH THE *DEVIL* HIMSELF!
OH, COME ON, NOW...
ACID WASHED: SATAN
THEIR MUSIC TAINTS EVEN THE *PUREST* OF SOULS! THEY EXIST TO DENY SALVATION TO THE PURE OF HEART!
OW, LADY! YOU'RE HURTING ME!
LET. HER. GO.
ACID WASHED: SATAN
YOU WILL SEE! ACID WASHED WILL TAKE YOU TO *HELL* WITH THEM!
I WISH I COULD SAY I WAS SURPRISED, BUT THIS *IS* FLORIDA. CRAZIES EVERYWHERE. THANKS FOR THE ASSIST, BIG GUY.
I TELL YOU WHAT... I KNOW YOU'RE BOTH HUNGRY. I'M ON THE WAY TO WORK, ANYWAY. HOW 'BOUT I GET Y'ALL A *FREE LUNCH?*
WE GOT A REAL NICE BUFFET.
HURM. YES... WONDERFUL.
COME, CASSANDRA! FOOD!
ACID WASHED: SATAN
YEAH... I'M COMIN'...

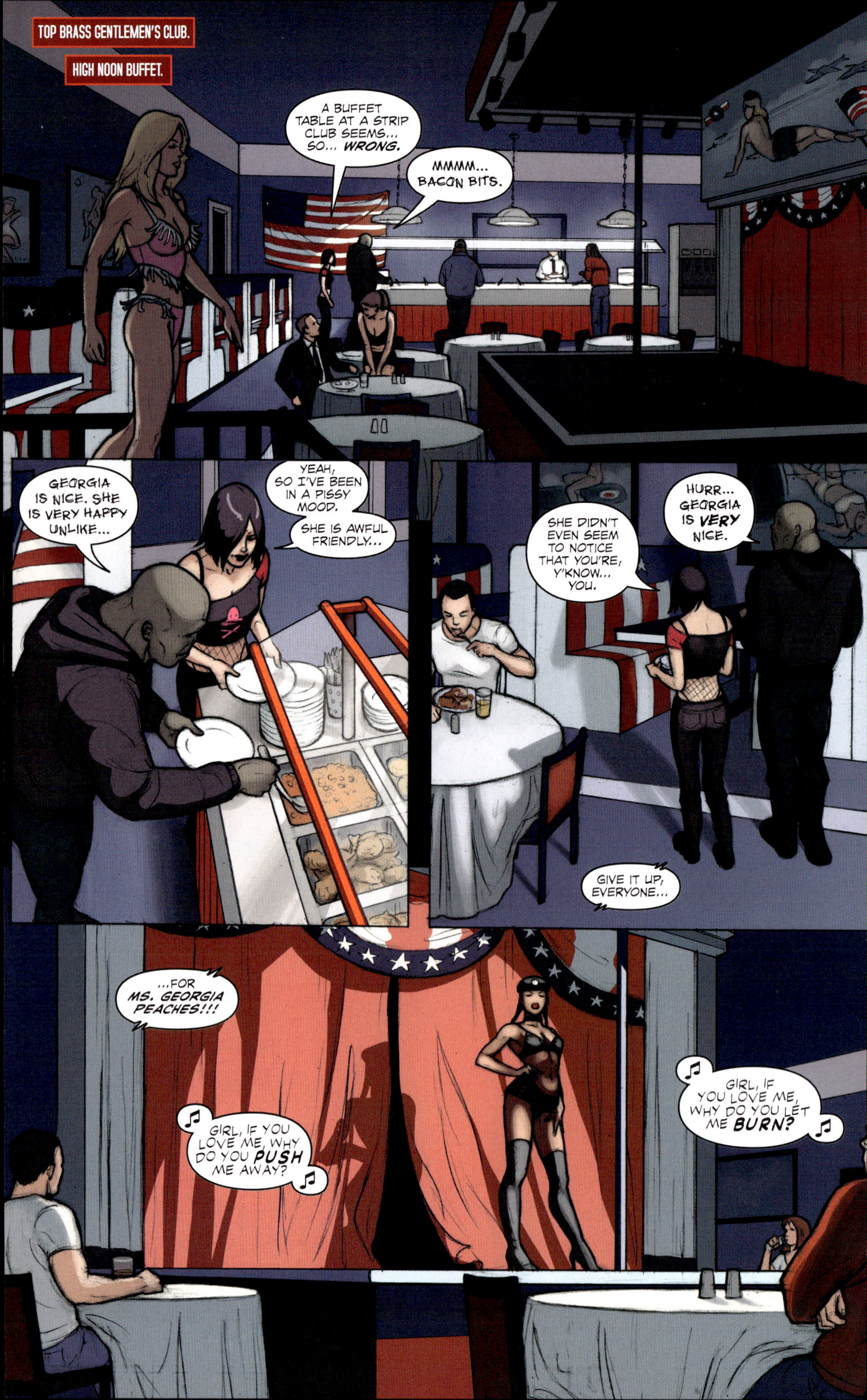
TOP BRASS GENTLEMEN'S CLUB.
HIGH NOON BUFFET.
A BUFFET TABLE AT A STRIP CLUB SEEMS... SO... WRONG.
MMMM... BACON BITS.
GEORGIA IS NICE. SHE IS VERY HAPPY UNLIKE...
YEAH, SO I'VE BEEN IN A PISSY MOOD.
SHE IS AWFUL FRIENDLY...
SHE DIDN'T EVEN SEEM TO NOTICE THAT YOU'RE, Y'KNOW... YOU.
HURR... GEORGIA IS VERY NICE.
GIVE IT UP, EVERYONE...
...FOR MS. GEORGIA PEACHES!!!
GIRL, IF YOU LOVE ME, WHY DO YOU PUSH ME AWAY?
GIRL, IF YOU LOVE ME, WHY DO YOU LET ME BURN?

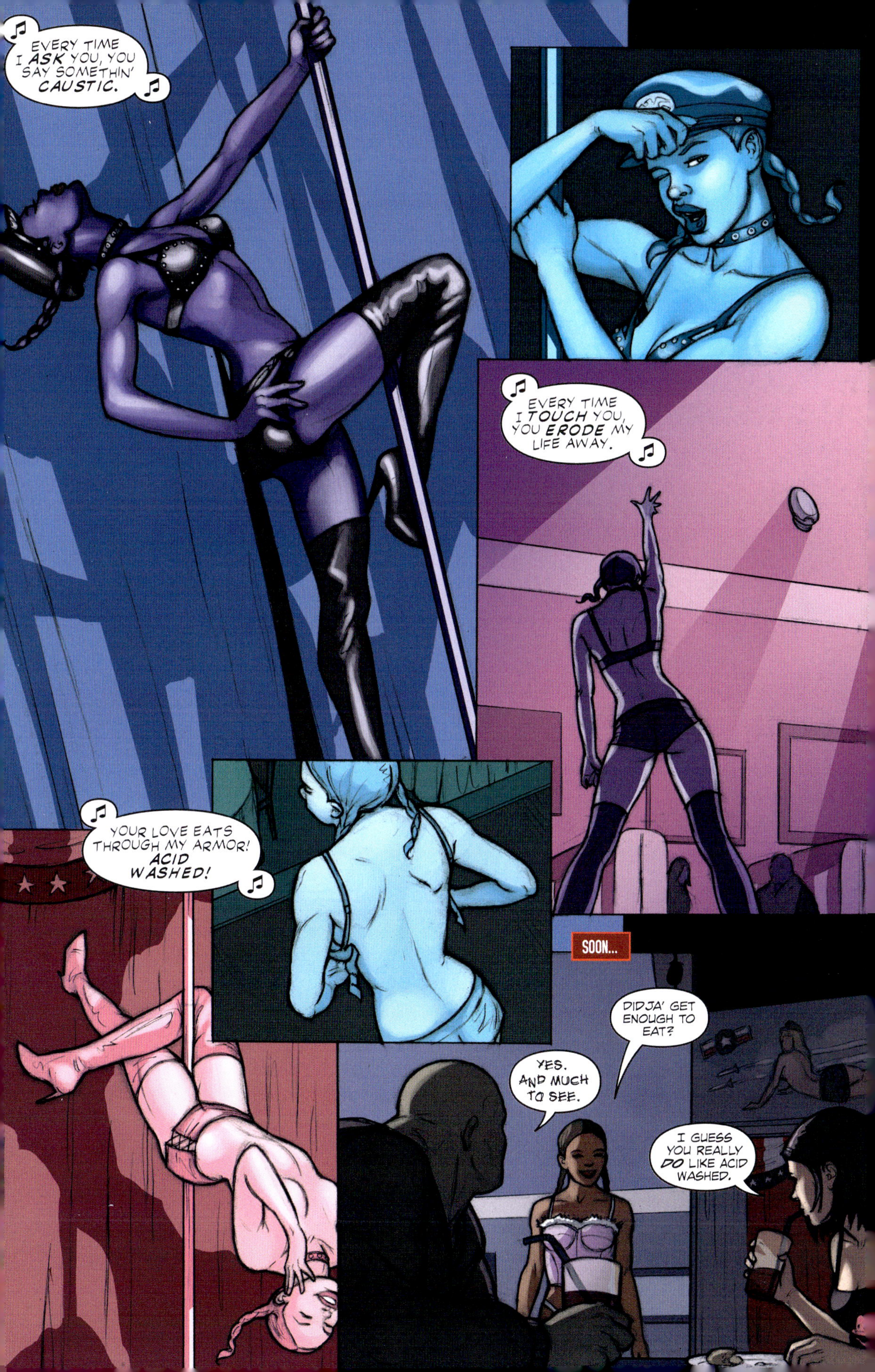
♫ EVERY TIME I ASK YOU, YOU SAY SOMETHIN' CAUSTIC. ♫
♫ EVERY TIME I TOUCH YOU, YOU ERODE MY LIFE AWAY. ♫
♫ YOUR LOVE EATS THROUGH MY ARMOR! ACID WASHED! ♫
SOON...
DIDJA' GET ENOUGH TO EAT?
YES. AND MUCH TO SEE.
I GUESS YOU REALLY DO LIKE ACID WASHED.

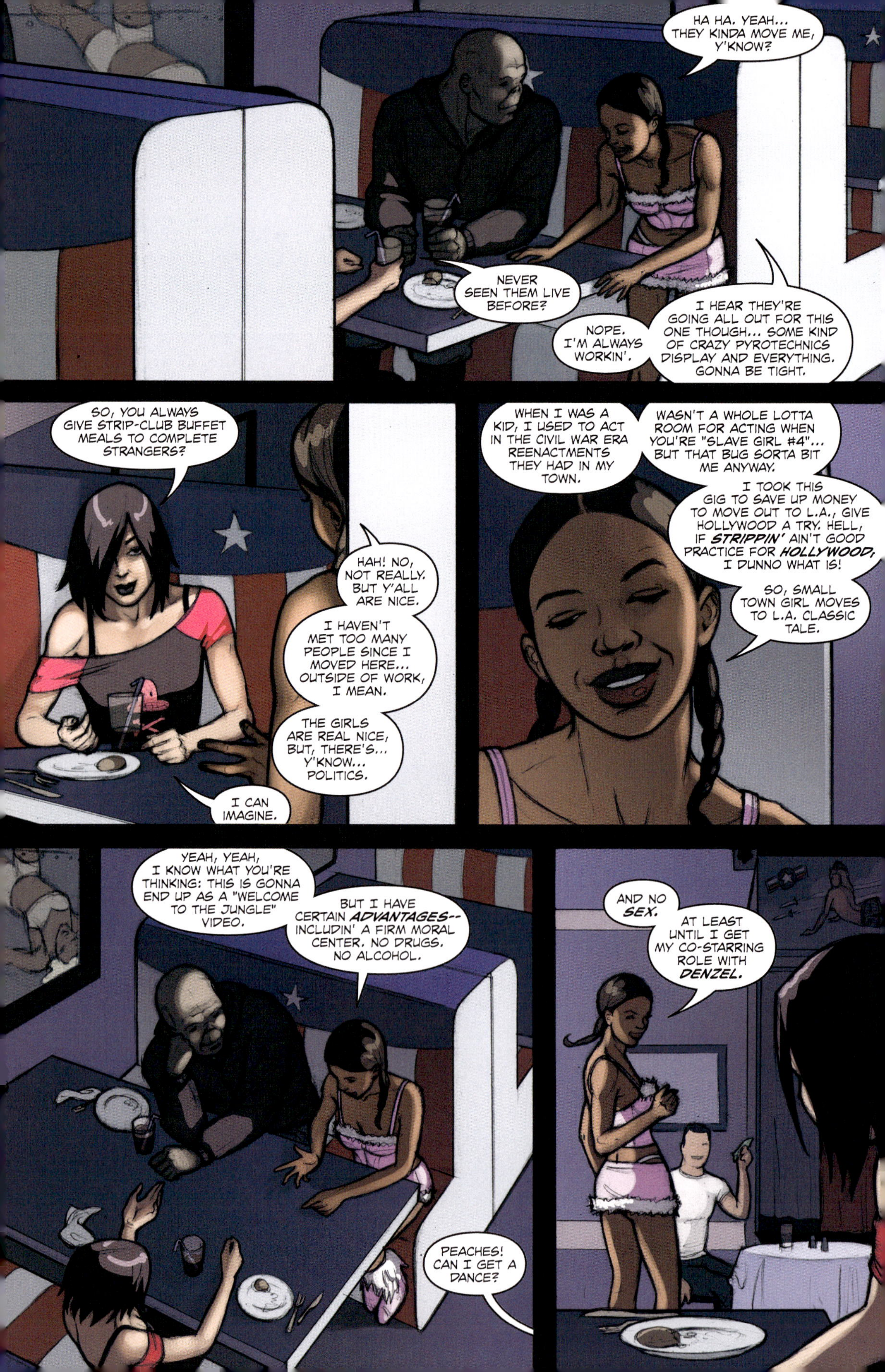
HA HA. YEAH... THEY KINDA MOVE ME, Y'KNOW?
NEVER SEEN THEM LIVE BEFORE?
NOPE. I'M ALWAYS WORKIN'.
I HEAR THEY'RE GOING ALL OUT FOR THIS ONE THOUGH... SOME KIND OF CRAZY PYROTECHNICS DISPLAY AND EVERYTHING. GONNA BE TIGHT.
SO, YOU ALWAYS GIVE STRIP-CLUB BUFFET MEALS TO COMPLETE STRANGERS?
HAH! NO, NOT REALLY. BUT Y'ALL ARE NICE.
I HAVEN'T MET TOO MANY PEOPLE SINCE I MOVED HERE... OUTSIDE OF WORK, I MEAN.
THE GIRLS ARE REAL NICE, BUT, THERE'S... Y'KNOW... POLITICS.
I CAN IMAGINE.
WHEN I WAS A KID, I USED TO ACT IN THE CIVIL WAR ERA REENACTMENTS THEY HAD IN MY TOWN.
WASN'T A WHOLE LOTTA ROOM FOR ACTING WHEN YOU'RE "SLAVE GIRL #4"... BUT THAT BUG SORTA BIT ME ANYWAY.
I TOOK THIS GIG TO SAVE UP MONEY TO MOVE OUT TO L.A., GIVE HOLLYWOOD A TRY. HELL, IF ***STRIPPIN'*** AIN'T GOOD PRACTICE FOR ***HOLLYWOOD,*** I DUNNO WHAT IS!
SO, SMALL TOWN GIRL MOVES TO L.A. CLASSIC TALE.
YEAH, YEAH, I KNOW WHAT YOU'RE THINKING: THIS IS GONNA END UP AS A "WELCOME TO THE JUNGLE" VIDEO.
BUT I HAVE CERTAIN ***ADVANTAGES--*** INCLUDIN' A FIRM MORAL CENTER. NO DRUGS. NO ALCOHOL.
PEACHES! CAN I GET A DANCE?
AND NO ***SEX.***
AT LEAST UNTIL I GET MY CO-STARRING ROLE WITH ***DENZEL.***

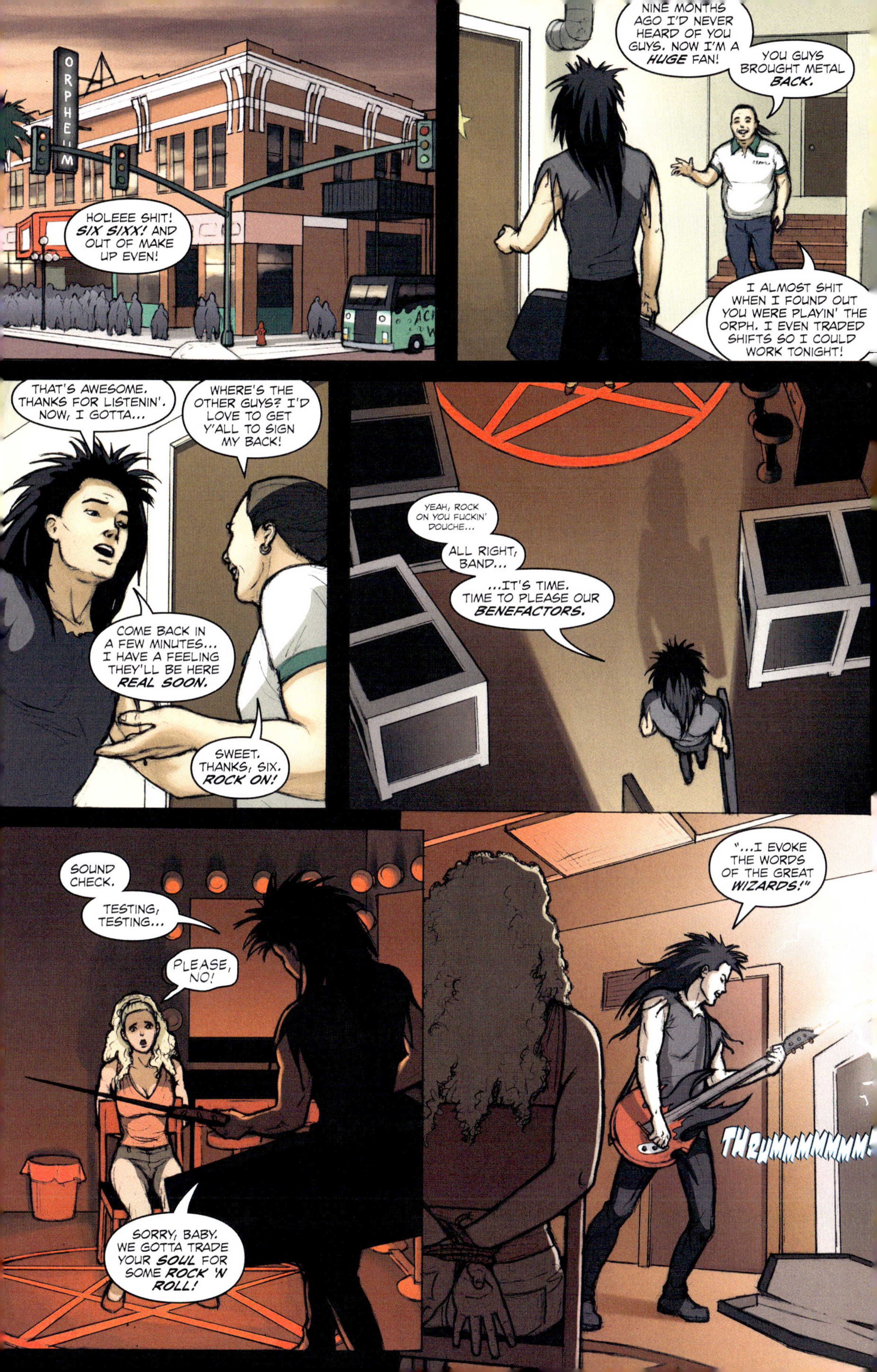

ORPHEUM
HOLEEE SHIT! SIX SIXX! AND OUT OF MAKE UP EVEN!
NINE MONTHS AGO I'D NEVER HEARD OF YOU GUYS. NOW I'M A HUGE FAN!
YOU GUYS BROUGHT METAL BACK.
I ALMOST SHIT WHEN I FOUND OUT YOU WERE PLAYIN' THE ORPH. I EVEN TRADED SHIFTS SO I COULD WORK TONIGHT!
THAT'S AWESOME. THANKS FOR LISTENIN'. NOW, I GOTTA...
WHERE'S THE OTHER GUYS? I'D LOVE TO GET Y'ALL TO SIGN MY BACK!
COME BACK IN A FEW MINUTES... I HAVE A FEELING THEY'LL BE HERE REAL SOON.
SWEET. THANKS, SIX. ROCK ON!
YEAH, ROCK ON YOU FUCKIN' DOUCHE...
ALL RIGHT, BAND...
...IT'S TIME. TIME TO PLEASE OUR BENEFACTORS.
SOUND CHECK.
TESTING, TESTING...
PLEASE, NO!
SORRY, BABY. WE GOTTA TRADE YOUR SOUL FOR SOME ROCK 'N ROLL!
"...I EVOKE THE WORDS OF THE GREAT WIZARDS!"
THRUMMMMMMM!

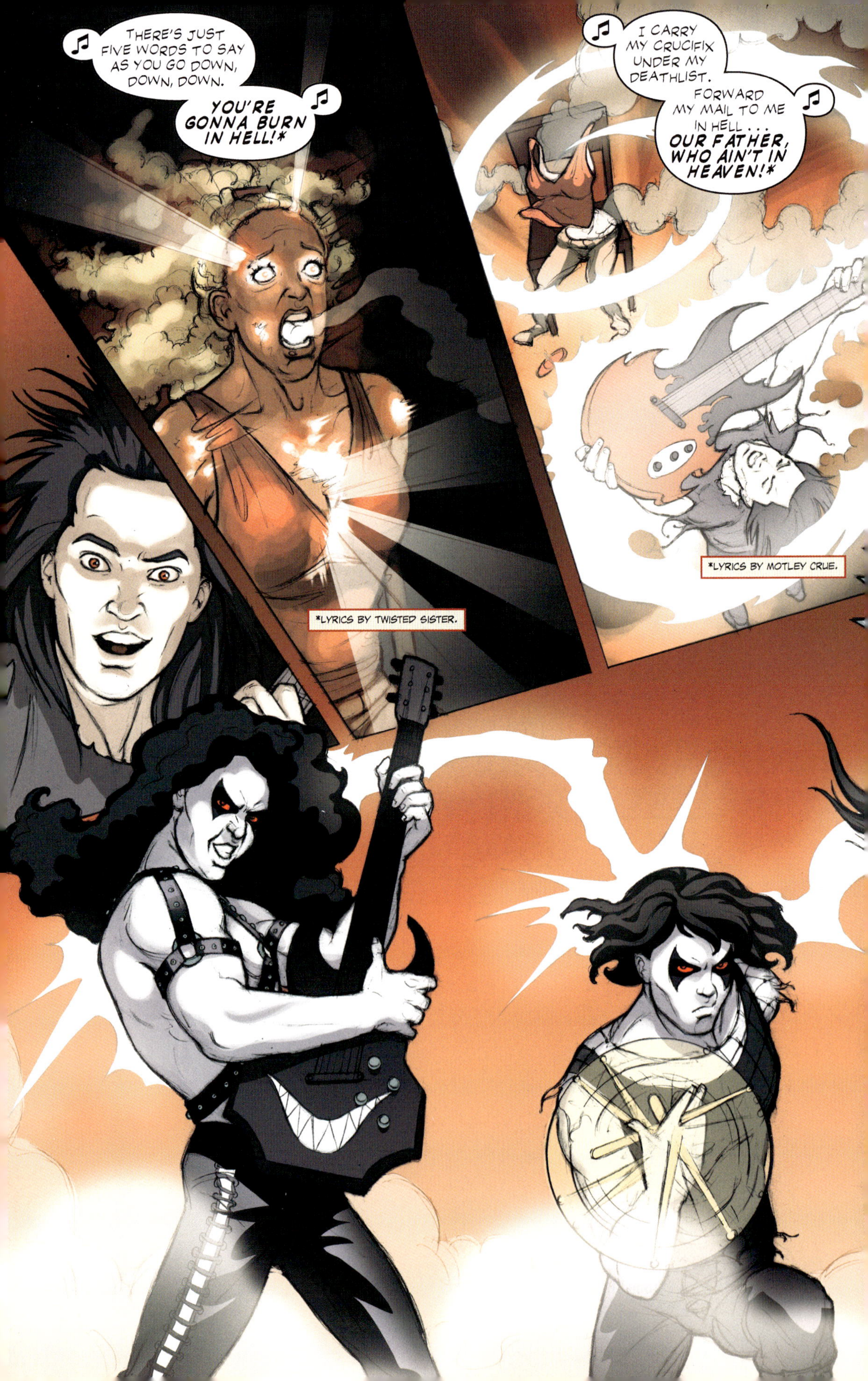
THERE'S JUST FIVE WORDS TO SAY AS YOU GO DOWN, DOWN, DOWN.
YOU'RE GONNA BURN IN HELL!*
*LYRICS BY TWISTED SISTER.
I CARRY MY CRUCIFIX UNDER MY DEATHLIST.
FORWARD MY MAIL TO ME IN HELL . . . OUR FATHER, WHO AIN'T IN HEAVEN!*
*LYRICS BY MOTLEY CRUE.

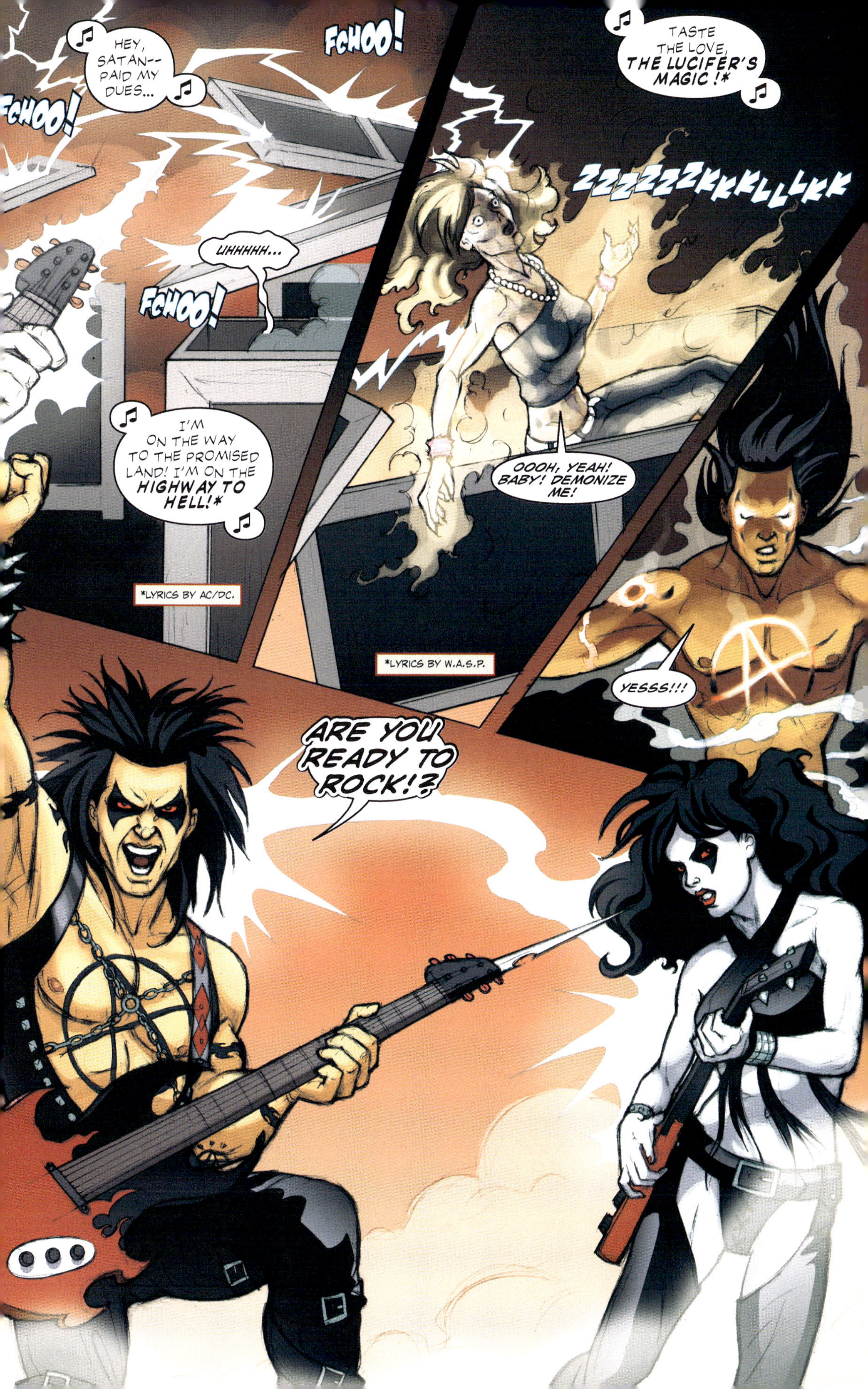
HEY, SATAN-- PAID MY DUES...
FCHOO!
FCHOO!
UHHHHH...
FCHOO!
I'M ON THE WAY TO THE PROMISED LAND! I'M ON THE HIGHWAY TO HELL!*
*LYRICS BY AC/DC.
TASTE THE LOVE, THE LUCIFER'S MAGIC!*
ZZZZZZKKKLLLKK
OOOH, YEAH! BABY! DEMONIZE ME!
*LYRICS BY W.A.S.P.
YESSS!!!
ARE YOU READY TO ROCK!?

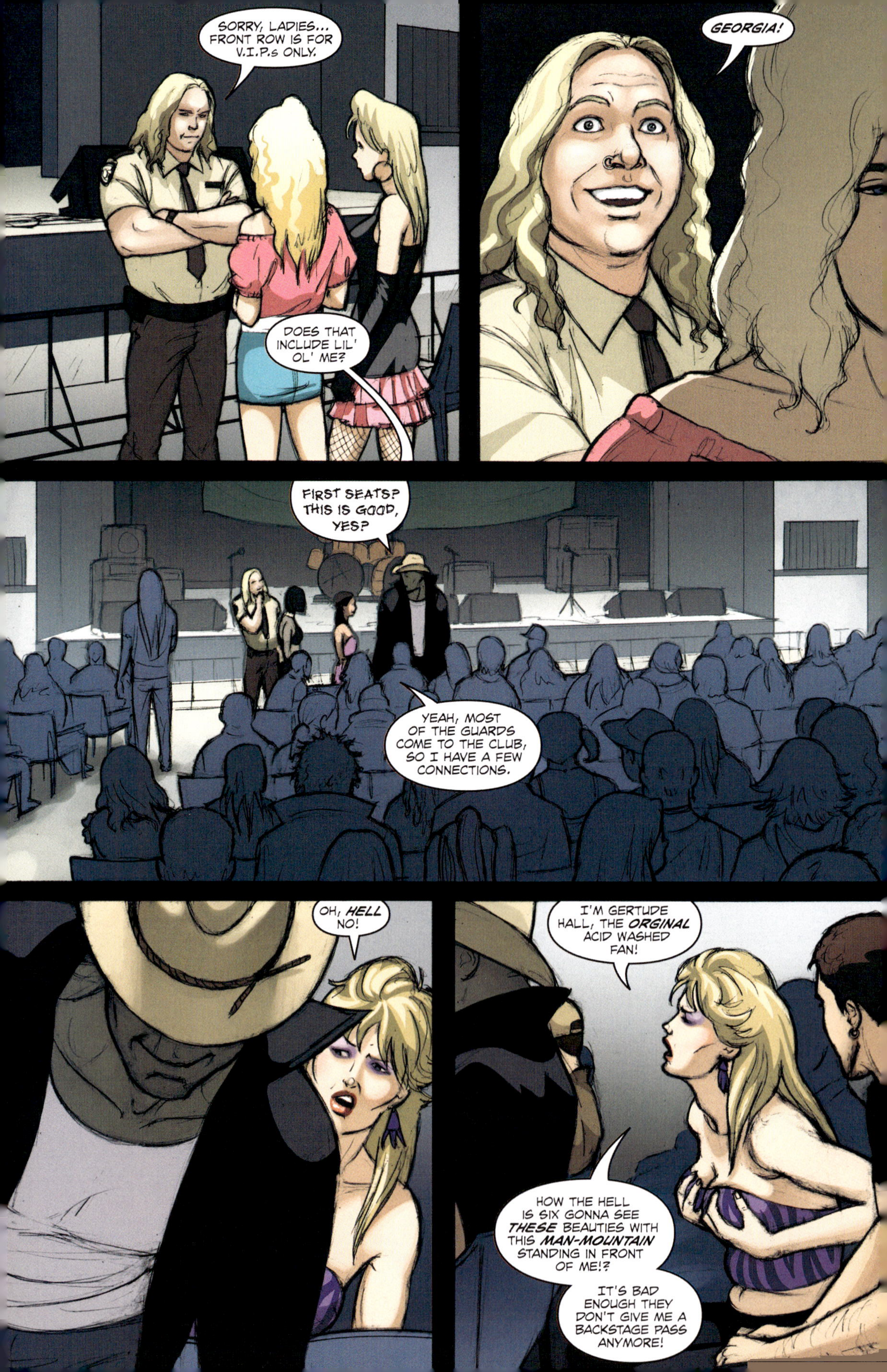
SORRY, LADIES... FRONT ROW IS FOR V.I.P.s ONLY.
DOES THAT INCLUDE LIL' OL' ME?
GEORGIA!
FIRST SEATS? THIS IS GOOD, YES?
YEAH, MOST OF THE GUARDS COME TO THE CLUB, SO I HAVE A FEW CONNECTIONS.
OH, HELL NO!
I'M GERTUDE HALL, THE ORGINAL ACID WASHED FAN!
HOW THE HELL IS SIX GONNA SEE THESE BEAUTIES WITH THIS MAN-MOUNTAIN STANDING IN FRONT OF ME!?
IT'S BAD ENOUGH THEY DON'T GIVE ME A BACKSTAGE PASS ANYMORE!

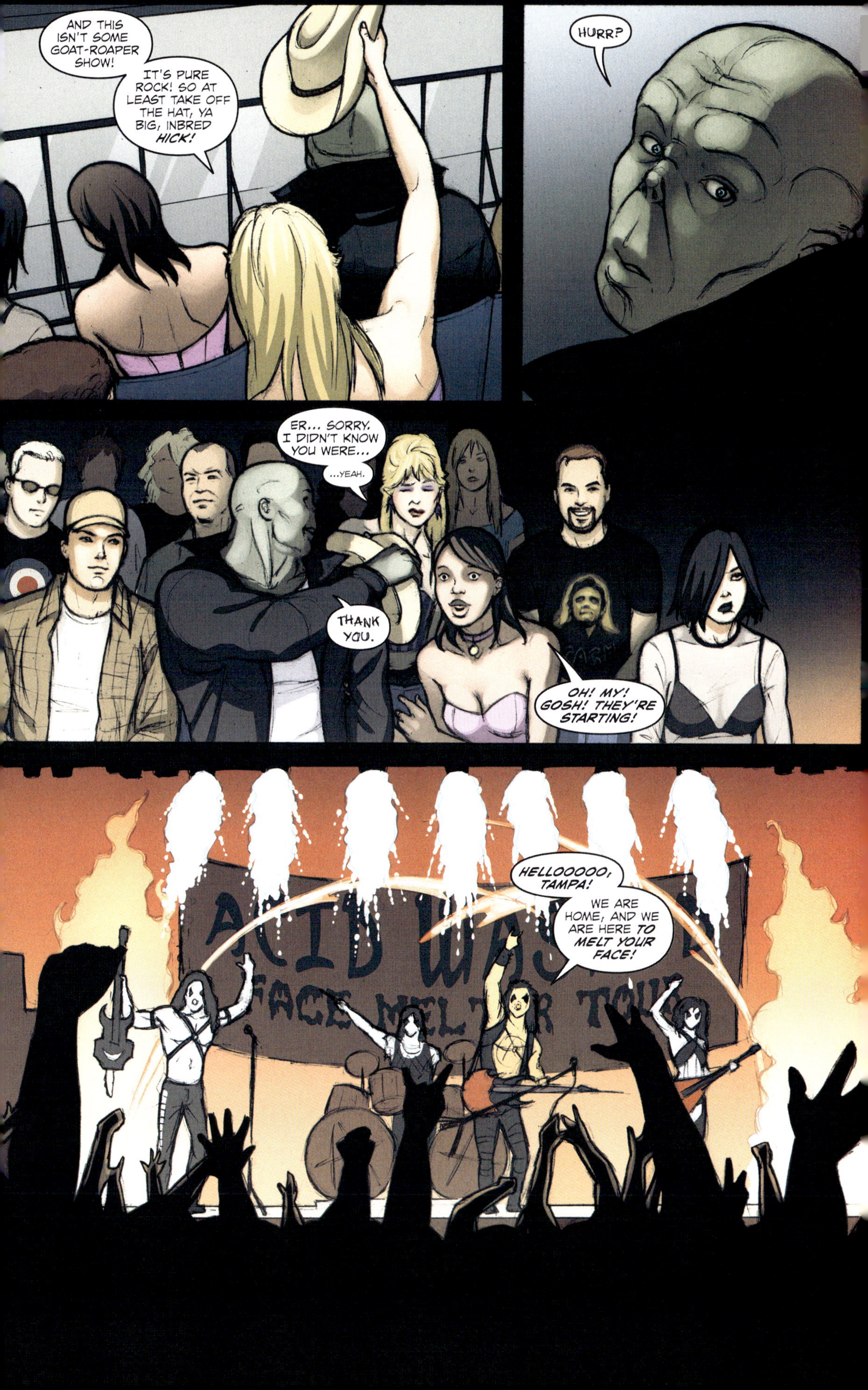
AND THIS ISN'T SOME GOAT-ROAPER SHOW!
IT'S PURE ROCK! SO AT LEAST TAKE OFF THE HAT, YA BIG, INBRED HICK!
HURR?
ER... SORRY. I DIDN'T KNOW YOU WERE...
...YEAH.
THANK YOU.
OH! MY! GOSH! THEY'RE STARTING!
ACID WAS
FACE MELTER TOUR
HELLOOOOO, TAMPA!
WE ARE HOME, AND WE ARE HERE TO MELT YOUR FACE!

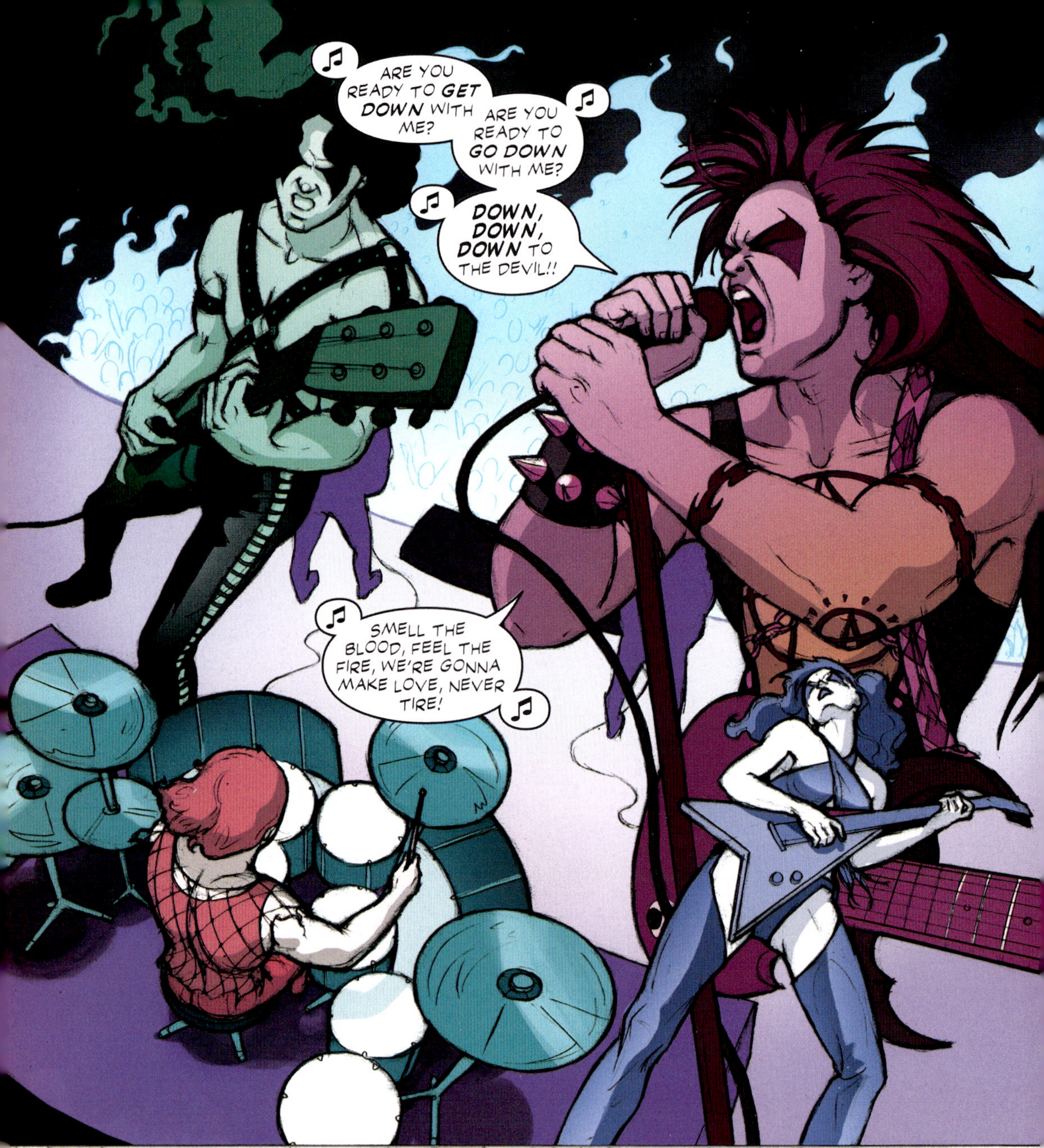
♫ ARE YOU READY TO **GET DOWN** WITH ME?
♫ ARE YOU READY TO **GO DOWN** WITH ME?
♫ **DOWN, DOWN, DOWN** TO THE DEVIL!!
♫ SMELL THE BLOOD, FEEL THE FIRE, WE'RE GONNA MAKE LOVE, NEVER TIRE! ♫

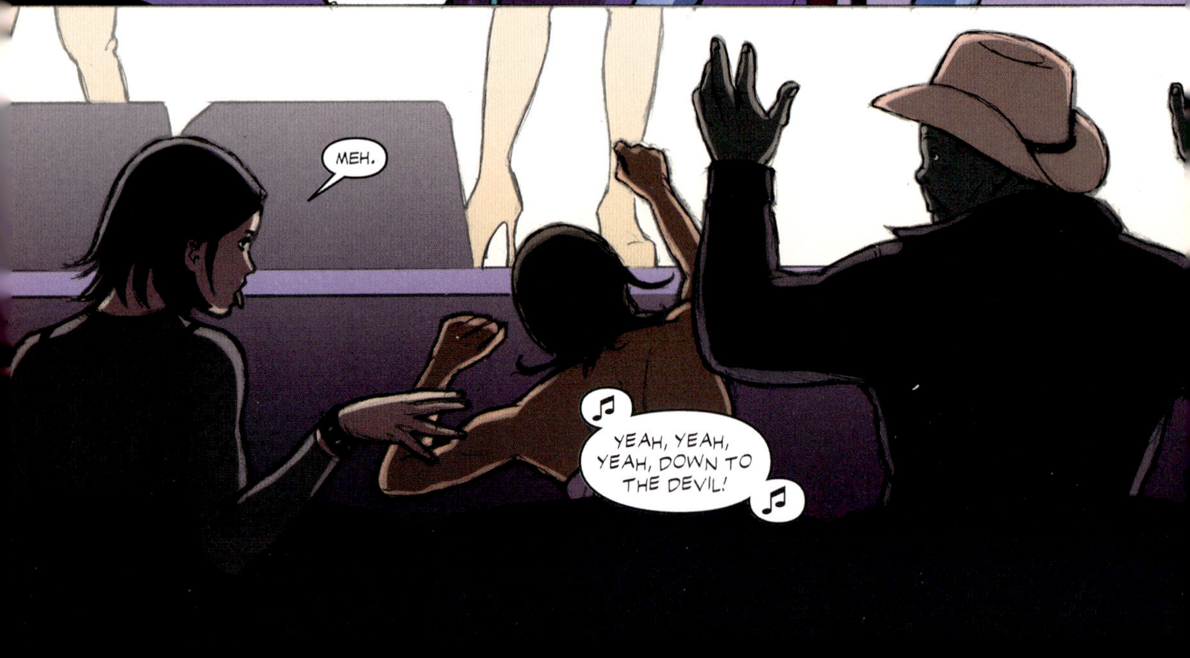
MEH.
♫ YEAH, YEAH, YEAH, DOWN TO THE DEVIL! ♫

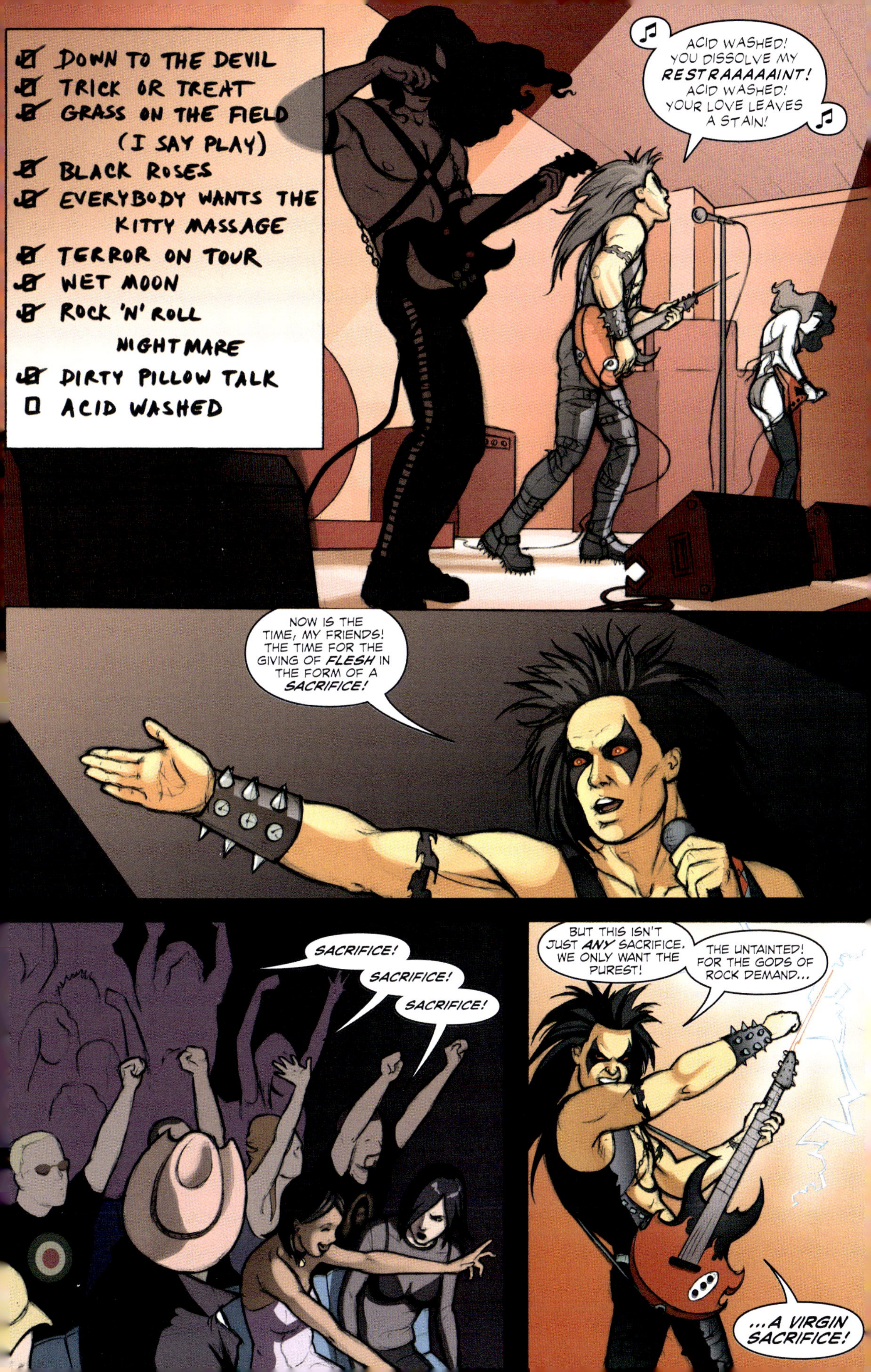
☑ DOWN TO THE DEVIL
☑ TRICK OR TREAT
☑ GRASS ON THE FIELD (I SAY PLAY)
☑ BLACK ROSES
☑ EVERYBODY WANTS THE KITTY MASSAGE
☑ TERROR ON TOUR
☑ WET MOON
☑ ROCK 'N' ROLL NIGHTMARE
☑ DIRTY PILLOW TALK
☐ ACID WASHED
♫ ACID WASHED! YOU DISSOLVE MY RESTRAAAAAINT! ACID WASHED! YOUR LOVE LEAVES A STAIN! ♫
NOW IS THE TIME, MY FRIENDS! THE TIME FOR THE GIVING OF FLESH IN THE FORM OF A SACRIFICE!
SACRIFICE!
SACRIFICE!
SACRIFICE!
BUT THIS ISN'T JUST ANY SACRIFICE. WE ONLY WANT THE PUREST!
THE UNTAINTED! FOR THE GODS OF ROCK DEMAND...
...A VIRGIN SACRIFICE!

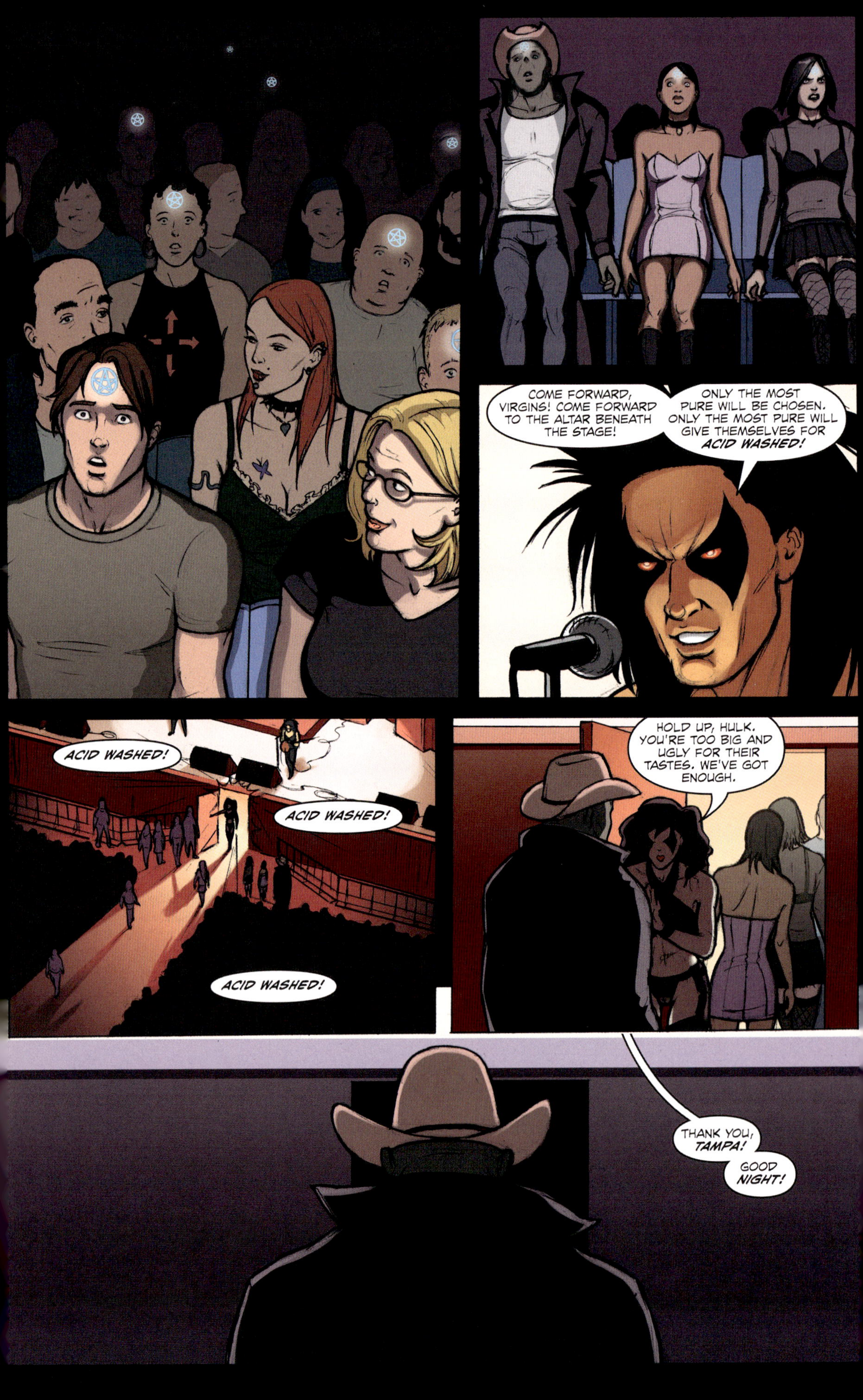
COME FORWARD, VIRGINS! COME FORWARD TO THE ALTAR BENEATH THE STAGE!
ONLY THE MOST PURE WILL BE CHOSEN. ONLY THE MOST PURE WILL GIVE THEMSELVES FOR ACID WASHED!
ACID WASHED!
ACID WASHED!
ACID WASHED!
HOLD UP, HULK. YOU'RE TOO BIG AND UGLY FOR THEIR TASTES. WE'VE GOT ENOUGH.
THANK YOU, TAMPA!
GOOD NIGHT!

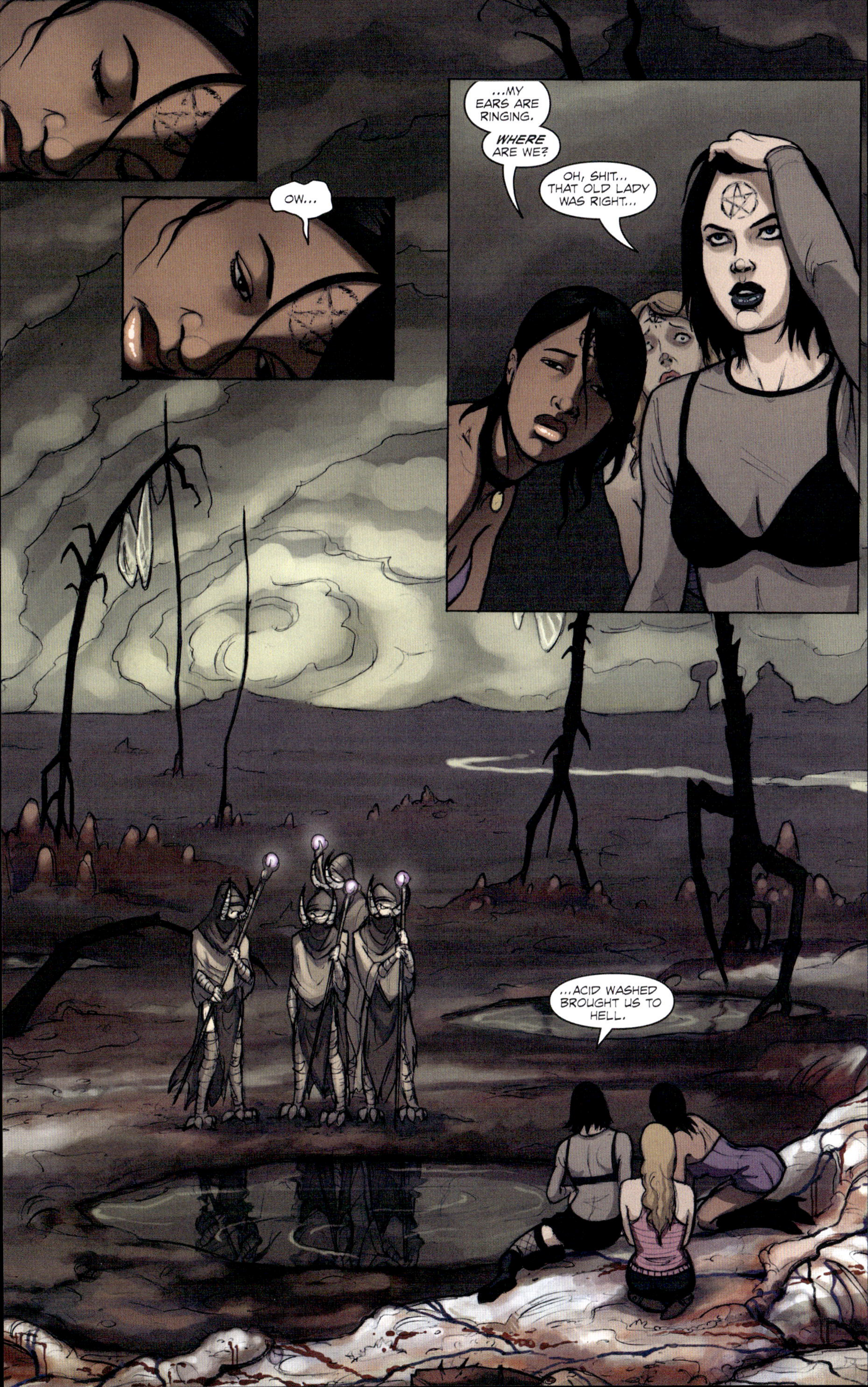
OW...
...MY EARS ARE RINGING. WHERE ARE WE?
OH, SHIT... THAT OLD LADY WAS RIGHT...
...ACID WASHED BROUGHT US TO HELL.

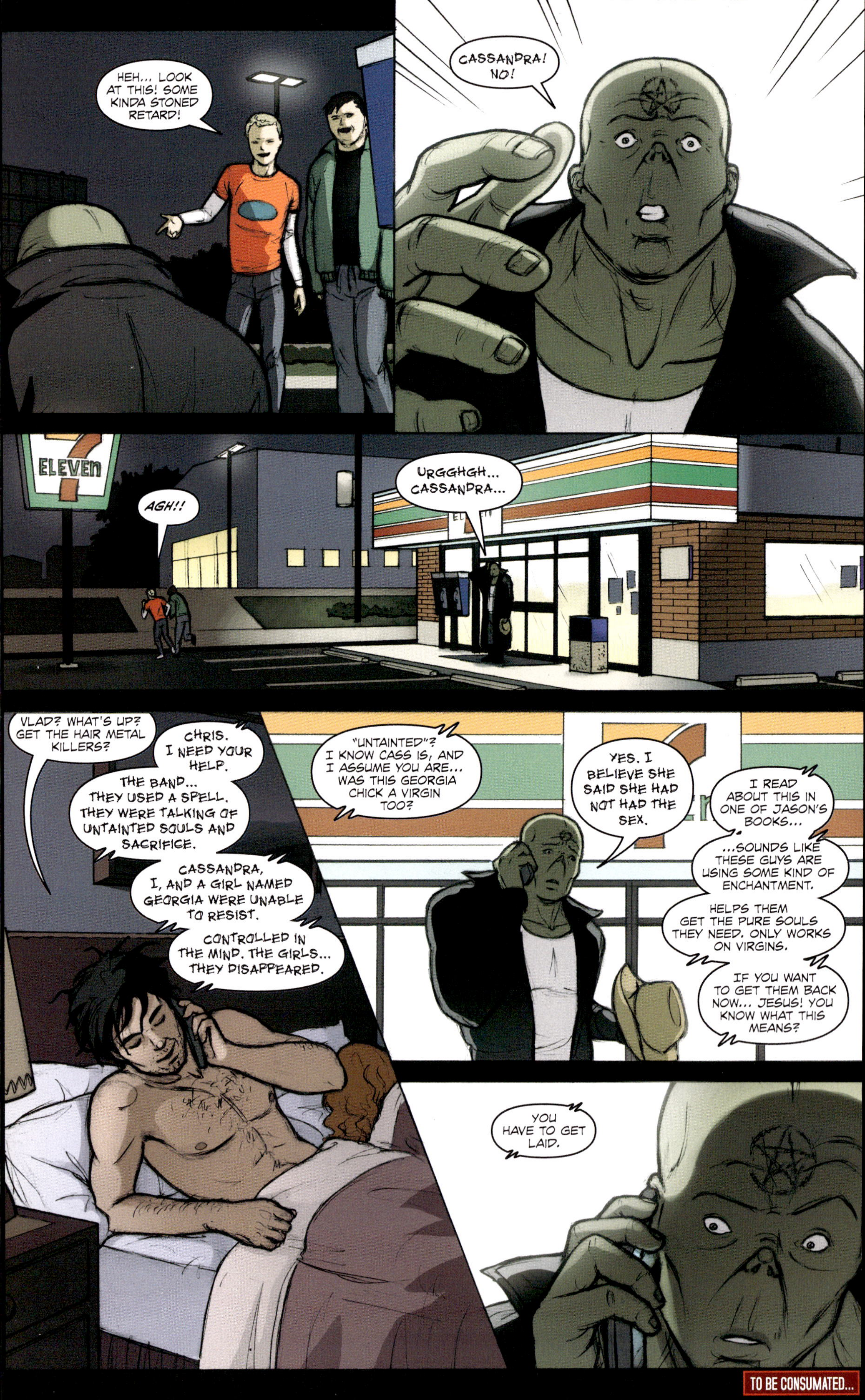
HEH... LOOK AT THIS! SOME KINDA STONED RETARD!
CASSANDRA! NO!
ELEVEN
AGH!!
URGGHGH... CASSANDRA...
VLAD? WHAT'S UP? GET THE HAIR METAL KILLERS?
CHRIS. I NEED YOUR HELP.
THE BAND... THEY USED A SPELL. THEY WERE TALKING OF UNTAINTED SOULS AND SACRIFICE.
CASSANDRA, I, AND A GIRL NAMED GEORGIA WERE UNABLE TO RESIST.
CONTROLLED IN THE MIND. THE GIRLS... THEY DISAPPEARED.
"UNTAINTED"? I KNOW CASS IS, AND I ASSUME YOU ARE... WAS THIS GEORGIA CHICK A VIRGIN TOO?
YES. I BELIEVE SHE SAID SHE HAD NOT HAD THE SEX.
I READ ABOUT THIS IN ONE OF JASON'S BOOKS...
...SOUNDS LIKE THESE GUYS ARE USING SOME KIND OF ENCHANTMENT.
HELPS THEM GET THE PURE SOULS THEY NEED. ONLY WORKS ON VIRGINS.
IF YOU WANT TO GET THEM BACK NOW... JESUS! YOU KNOW WHAT THIS MEANS?
YOU HAVE TO GET LAID.
TO BE CONSUMATED...

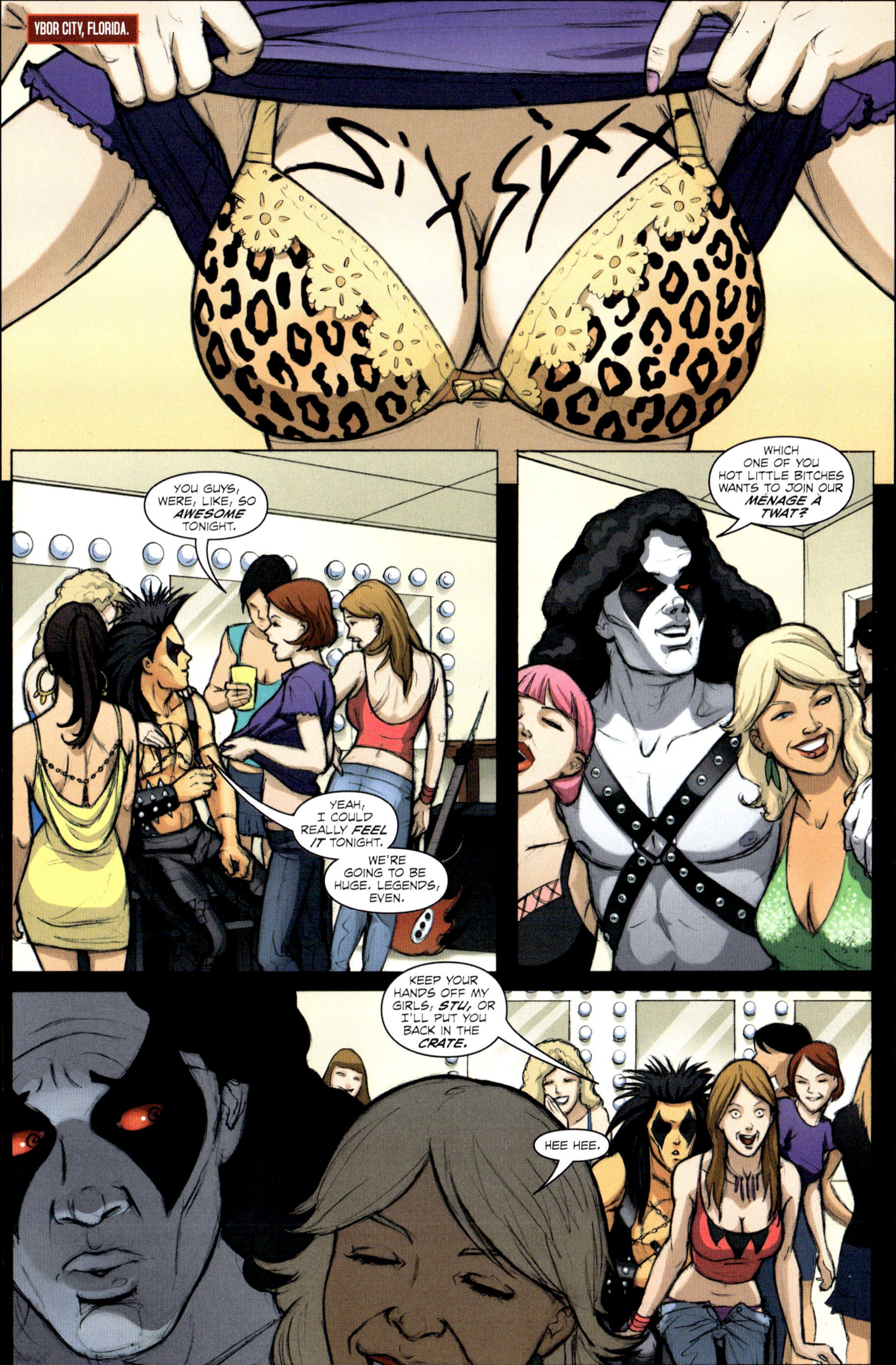
YBOR CITY, FLORIDA.
SIXX SIXX
YOU GUYS, WERE, LIKE, SO *AWESOME* TONIGHT.
YEAH, I COULD REALLY *FEEL IT* TONIGHT.
WE'RE GOING TO BE HUGE. LEGENDS, EVEN.
WHICH ONE OF YOU HOT LITTLE BITCHES WANTS TO JOIN OUR *MÉNAGE À TWAT?*
KEEP YOUR HANDS OFF MY GIRLS, *STU,* OR I'LL PUT YOU BACK IN THE *CRATE.*
HEE HEE.

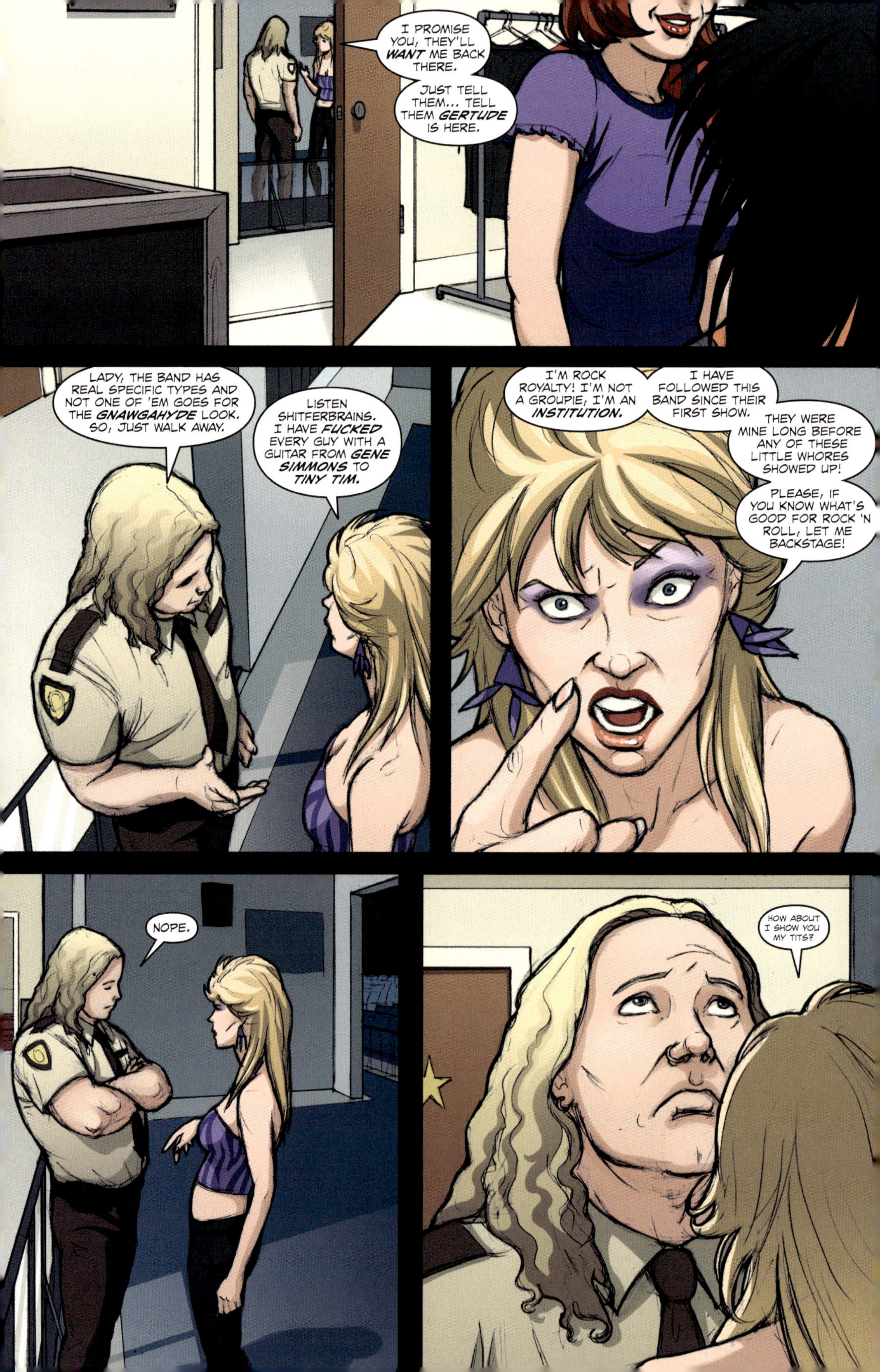
I PROMISE YOU, THEY'LL *WANT* ME BACK THERE.
JUST TELL THEM... TELL THEM *GERTUDE* IS HERE.
LADY, THE BAND HAS REAL SPECIFIC TYPES AND NOT ONE OF 'EM GOES FOR THE *GNAWGAHYDE* LOOK. SO, JUST WALK AWAY.
LISTEN SHITFERBRAINS. I HAVE *FUCKED* EVERY GUY WITH A GUITAR FROM *GENE SIMMONS* TO *TINY TIM.*
I'M ROCK ROYALTY! I'M NOT A GROUPIE, I'M AN *INSTITUTION.*
I HAVE FOLLOWED THIS BAND SINCE THEIR FIRST SHOW.
THEY WERE MINE LONG BEFORE ANY OF THESE LITTLE WHORES SHOWED UP!
PLEASE, IF YOU KNOW WHAT'S GOOD FOR ROCK 'N ROLL, LET ME BACKSTAGE!
NOPE.
HOW ABOUT I SHOW YOU MY TITS?

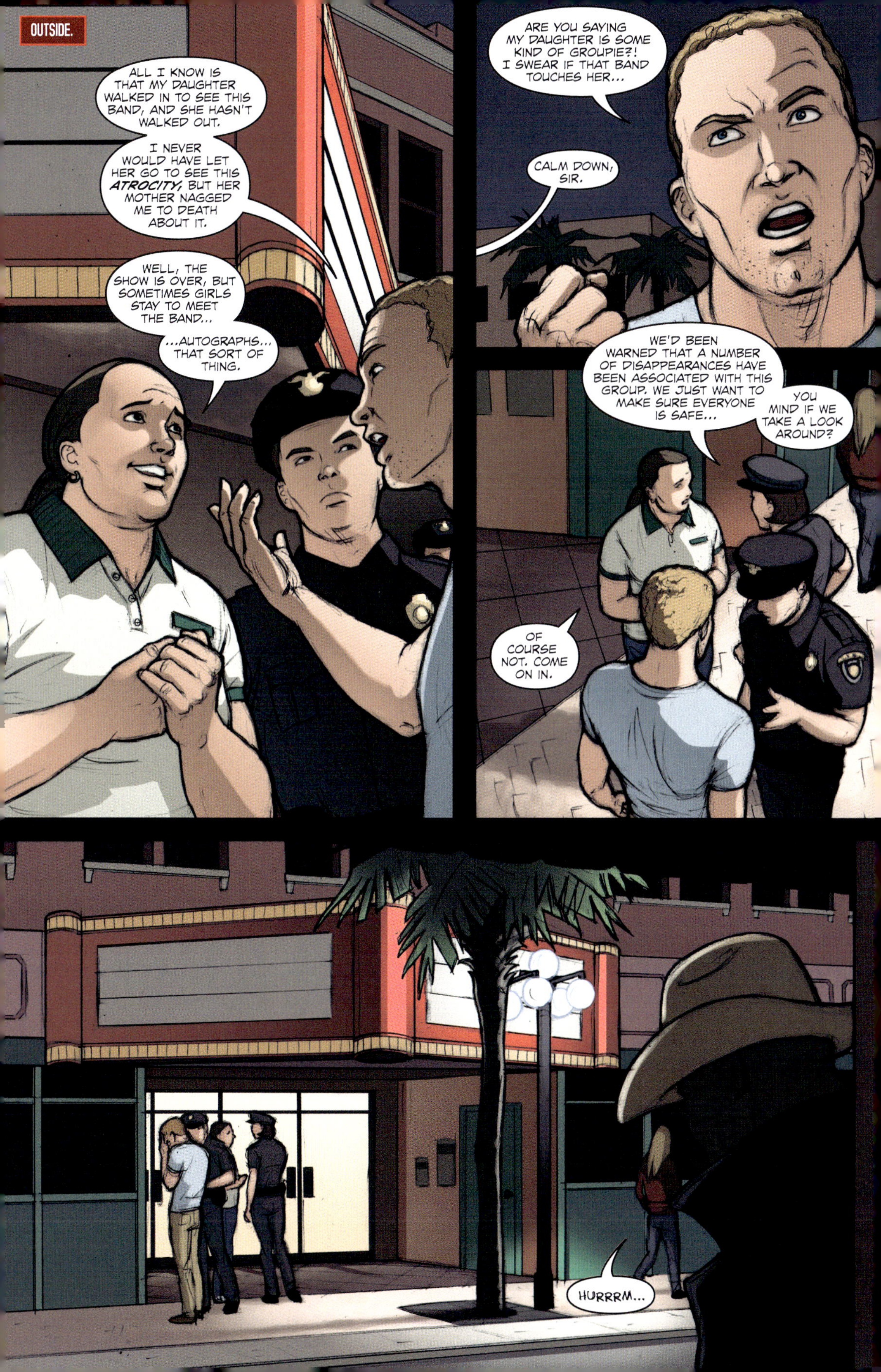
OUTSIDE.
ALL I KNOW IS THAT MY DAUGHTER WALKED IN TO SEE THIS BAND, AND SHE HASN'T WALKED OUT.
I NEVER WOULD HAVE LET HER GO TO SEE THIS ATROCITY, BUT HER MOTHER NAGGED ME TO DEATH ABOUT IT.
WELL, THE SHOW IS OVER, BUT SOMETIMES GIRLS STAY TO MEET THE BAND...
...AUTOGRAPHS... THAT SORT OF THING.
ARE YOU SAYING MY DAUGHTER IS SOME KIND OF GROUPIE?! I SWEAR IF THAT BAND TOUCHES HER...
CALM DOWN, SIR.
WE'D BEEN WARNED THAT A NUMBER OF DISAPPEARANCES HAVE BEEN ASSOCIATED WITH THIS GROUP. WE JUST WANT TO MAKE SURE EVERYONE IS SAFE...
YOU MIND IF WE TAKE A LOOK AROUND?
OF COURSE NOT. COME ON IN.
HURRRM...

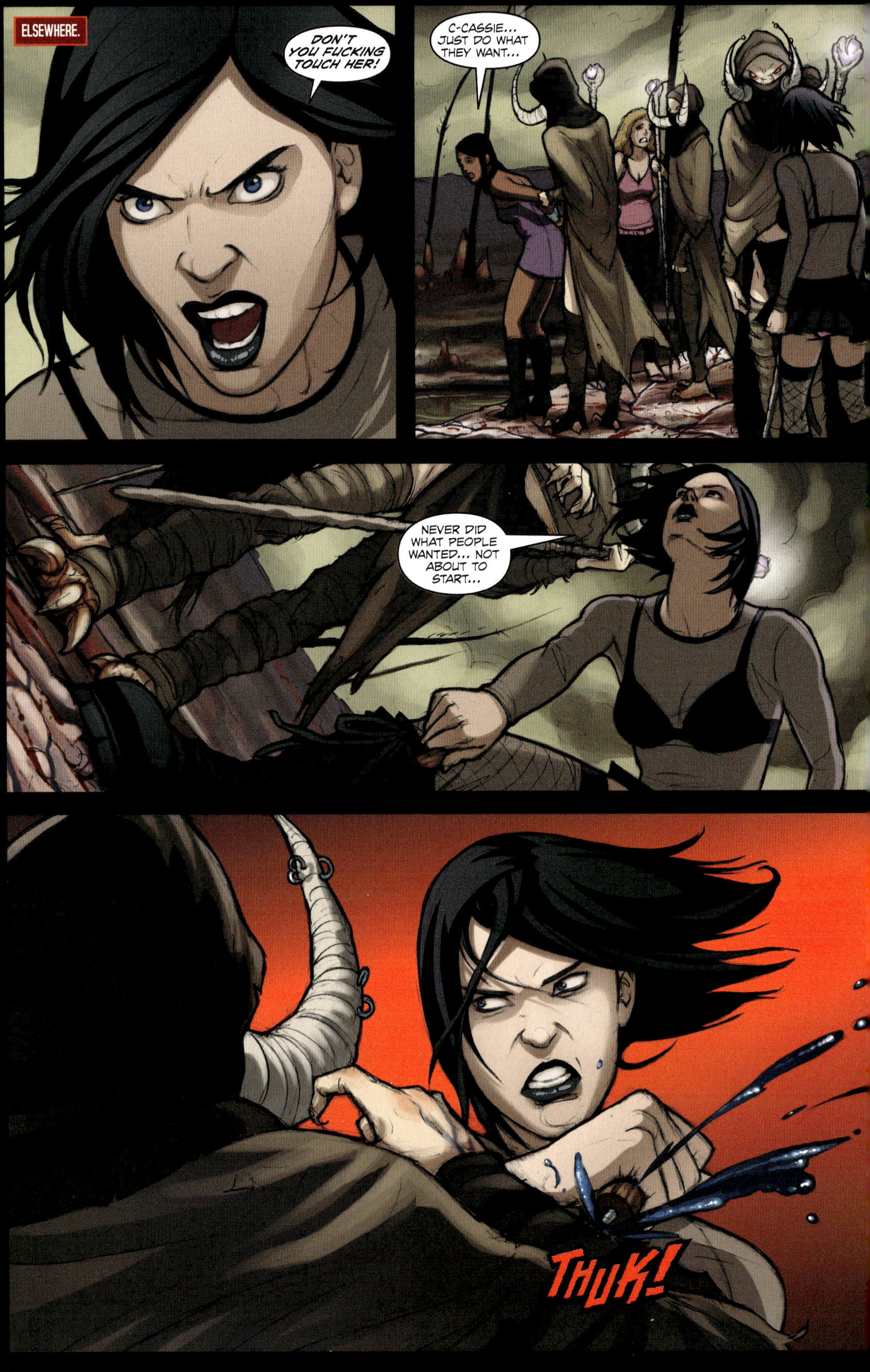
ELSEWHERE.
DON'T YOU FUCKING TOUCH HER!
C-CASSIE... JUST DO WHAT THEY WANT...
NEVER DID WHAT PEOPLE WANTED... NOT ABOUT TO START...
THUK!

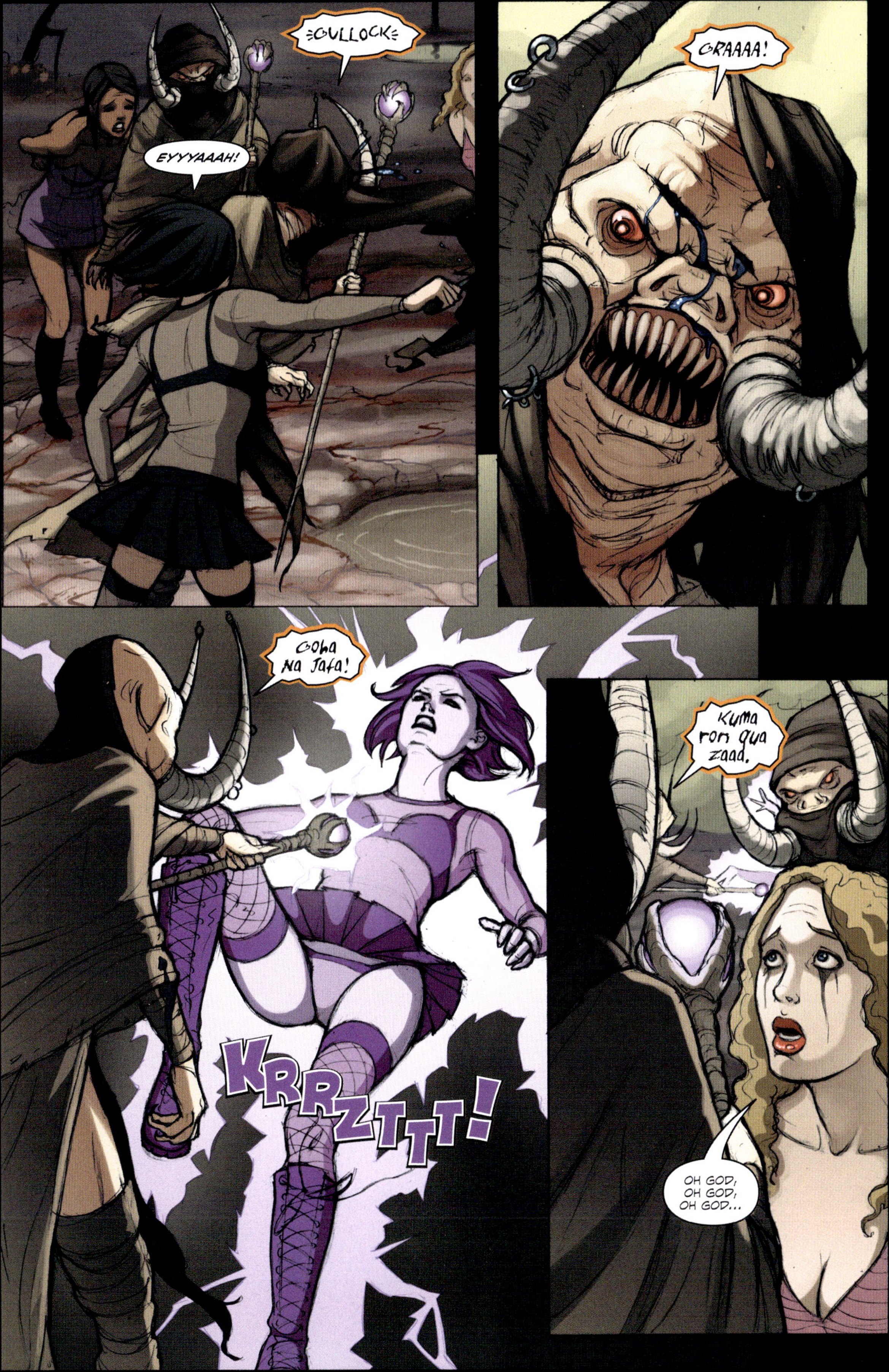
GULLOCK
EYYYAAAH!
GRAAAA!
Goha Na Jafa!
KRRZTTTT!
Kuma ron qua zaad.
OH GOD, OH GOD, OH GOD...

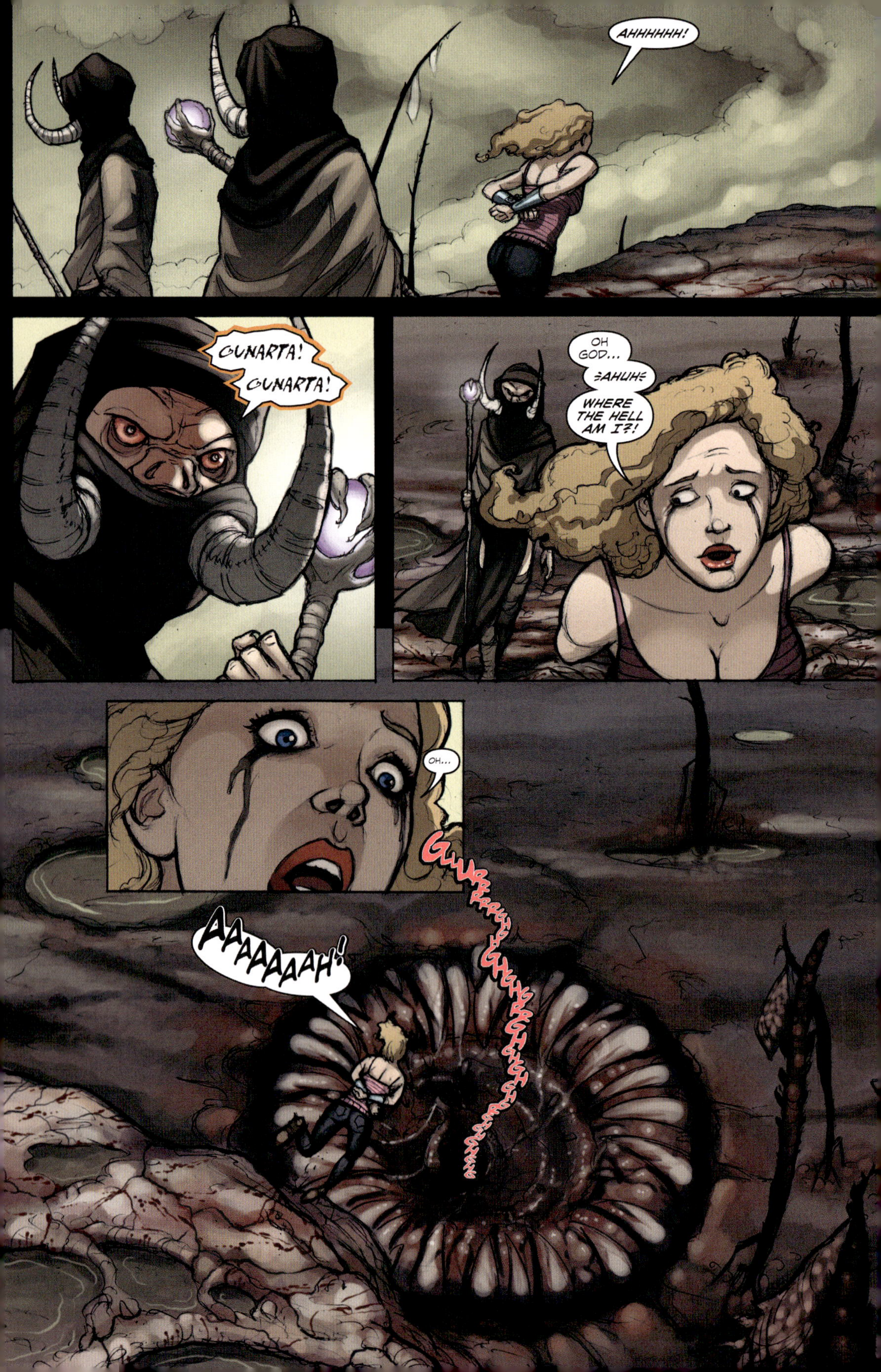

AHHHHHHH!
GUNARTA! GUNARTA!
OH GOD...
≥AHUH≤
WHERE THE HELL AM I?!
OH...
AAAAAAAH!

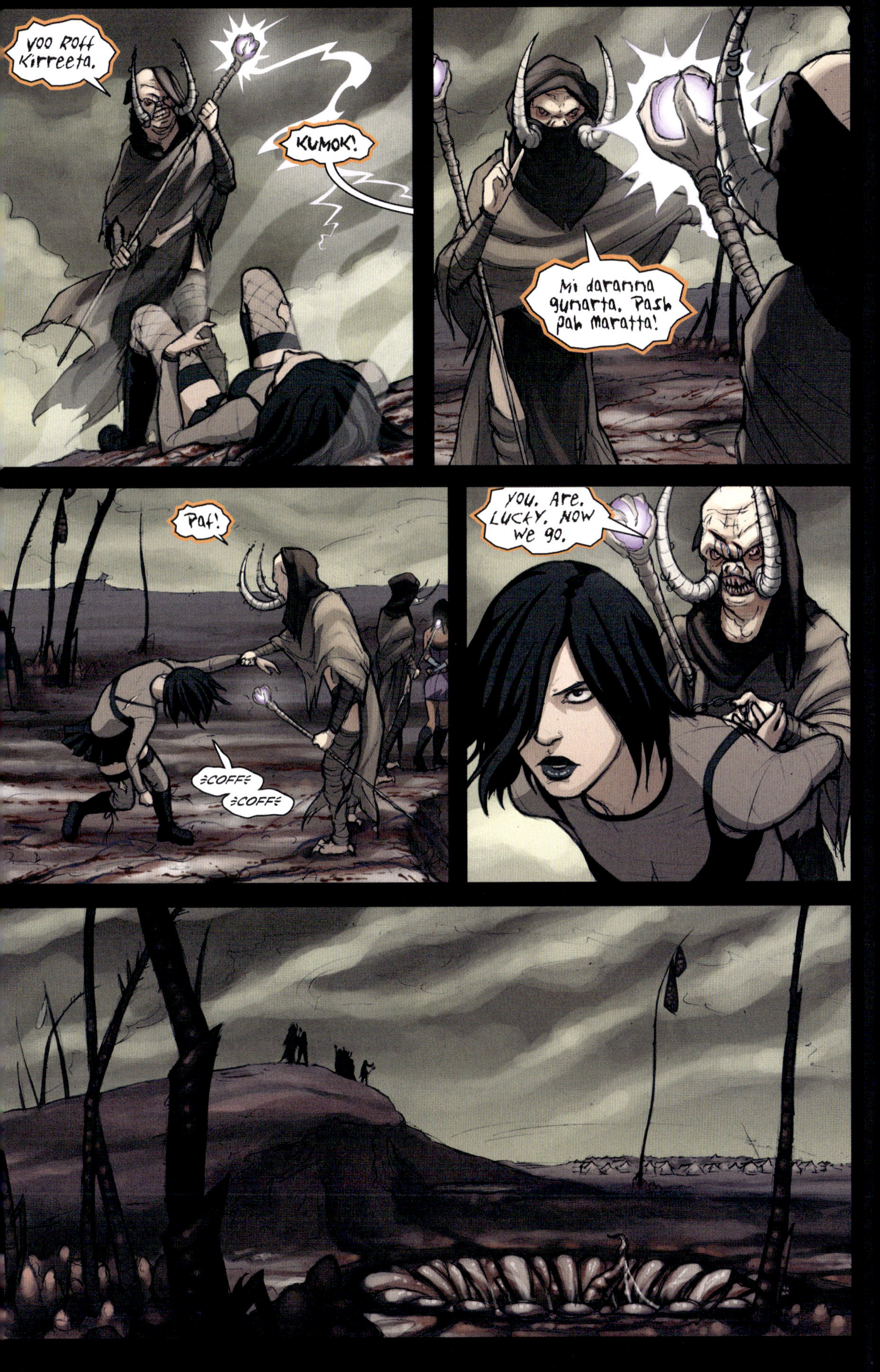

Voo Roff Kirreeta.
KUMOK!
Mi daranna gunarta. Pash pah Maratta!
Paf!
COFF
COFF
You. Are. Lucky. Now we go.

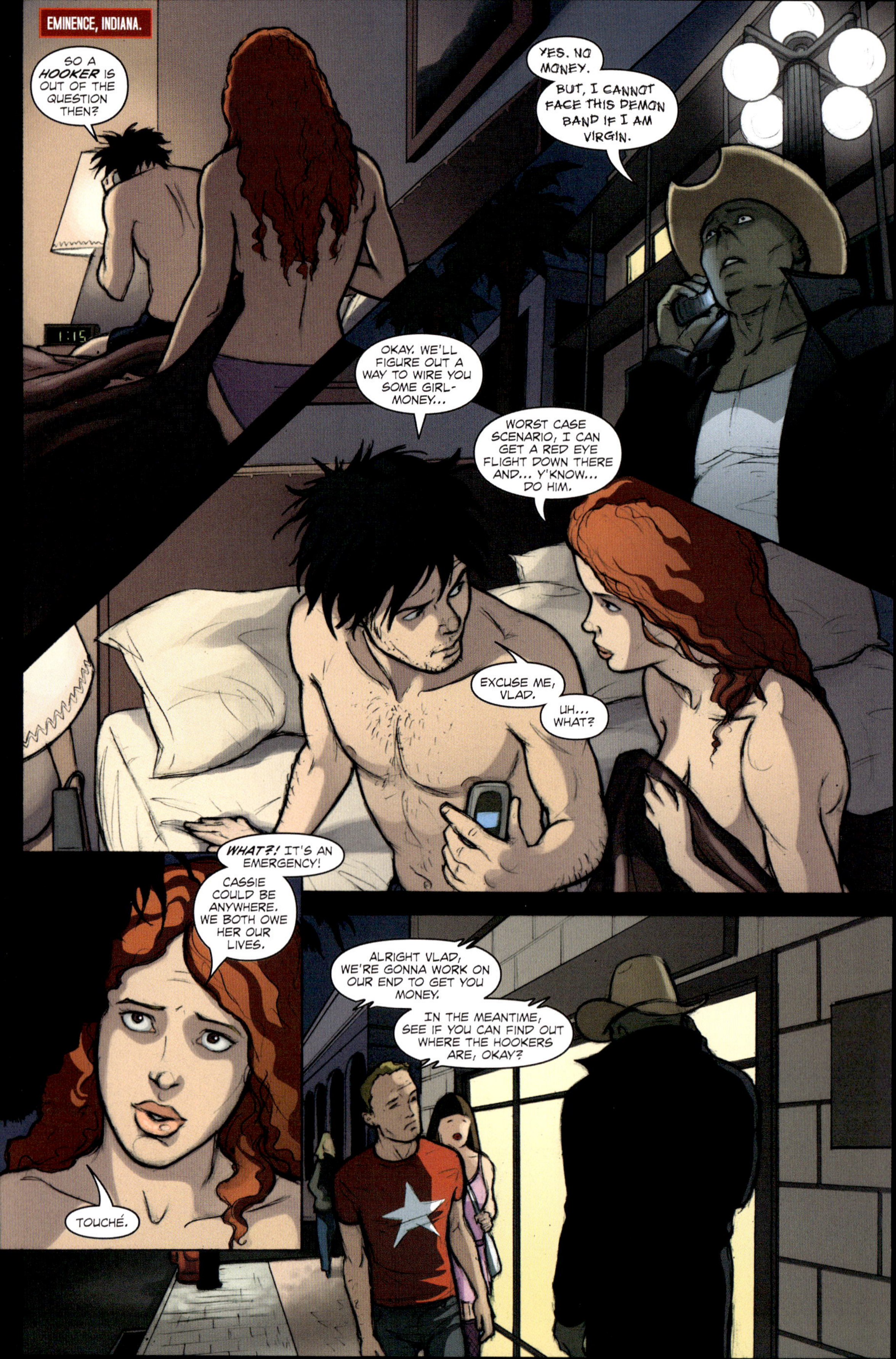
EMINENCE, INDIANA.
SO A HOOKER IS OUT OF THE QUESTION THEN?
YES. NO MONEY.
BUT, I CANNOT FACE THIS DEMON BAND IF I AM VIRGIN.
OKAY. WE'LL FIGURE OUT A WAY TO WIRE YOU SOME GIRL-MONEY...
WORST CASE SCENARIO, I CAN GET A RED EYE FLIGHT DOWN THERE AND... Y'KNOW... DO HIM.
EXCUSE ME, VLAD.
UH... WHAT?
WHAT?! IT'S AN EMERGENCY!
CASSIE COULD BE ANYWHERE. WE BOTH OWE HER OUR LIVES.
TOUCHÉ.
ALRIGHT VLAD, WE'RE GONNA WORK ON OUR END TO GET YOU MONEY.
IN THE MEANTIME, SEE IF YOU CAN FIND OUT WHERE THE HOOKERS ARE, OKAY?

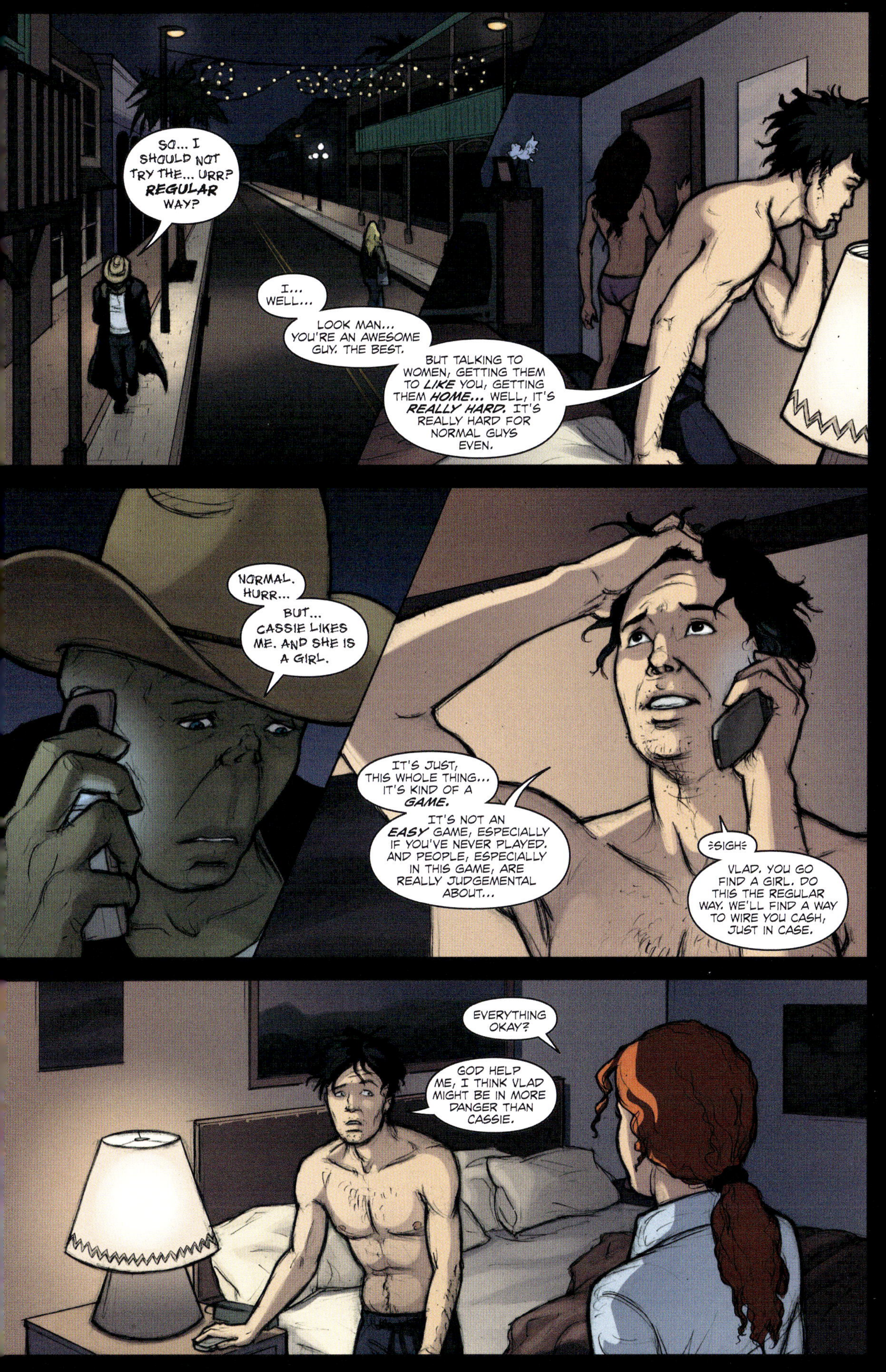

SO... I SHOULD NOT TRY THE... URR? **REGULAR** WAY?
I... WELL...
LOOK MAN... YOU'RE AN AWESOME GUY. THE BEST.
BUT TALKING TO WOMEN, GETTING THEM TO **LIKE** YOU, GETTING THEM **HOME...** WELL, IT'S **REALLY HARD.** IT'S REALLY HARD FOR NORMAL GUYS EVEN.
NORMAL. HURR...
BUT... CASSIE LIKES ME. AND SHE IS A GIRL.
IT'S JUST, THIS WHOLE THING... IT'S KIND OF A **GAME.**
IT'S NOT AN **EASY** GAME, ESPECIALLY IF YOU'VE NEVER PLAYED. AND PEOPLE, ESPECIALLY IN THIS GAME, ARE REALLY JUDGEMENTAL ABOUT...
=SIGH=
VLAD. YOU GO FIND A GIRL. DO THIS THE REGULAR WAY. WE'LL FIND A WAY TO WIRE YOU CASH, JUST IN CASE.
EVERYTHING OKAY?
GOD HELP ME, I THINK VLAD MIGHT BE IN MORE DANGER THAN CASSIE.

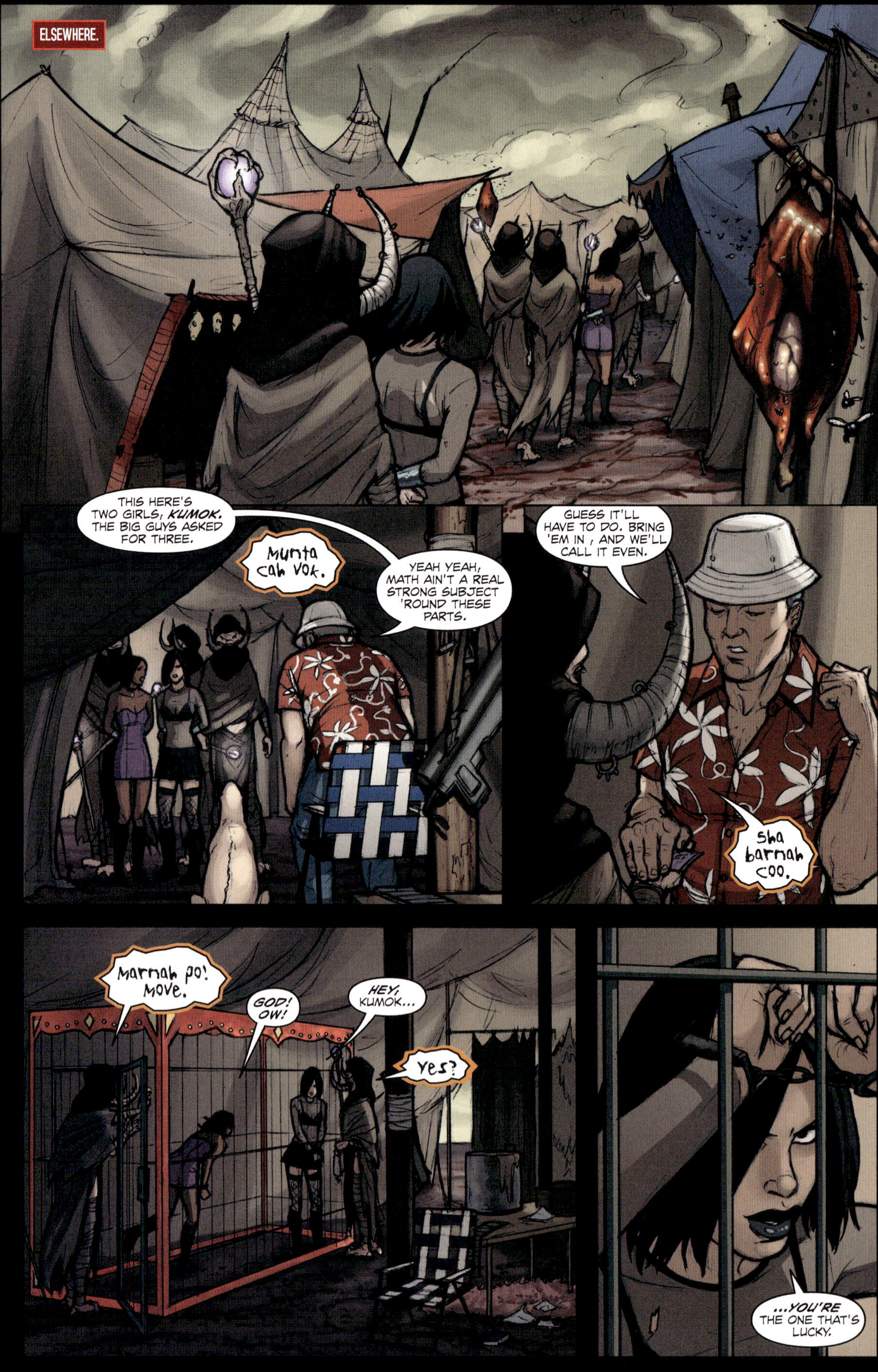
ELSEWHERE.
THIS HERE'S TWO GIRLS, KUMOK. THE BIG GUYS ASKED FOR THREE.
Munta cah vok.
YEAH YEAH, MATH AIN'T A REAL STRONG SUBJECT 'ROUND THESE PARTS.
GUESS IT'LL HAVE TO DO. BRING 'EM IN , AND WE'LL CALL IT EVEN.
Sha barnah coo.
Marnah po! Move.
GOD! OW!
HEY, KUMOK...
Yes?
...YOU'RE THE ONE THAT'S LUCKY.

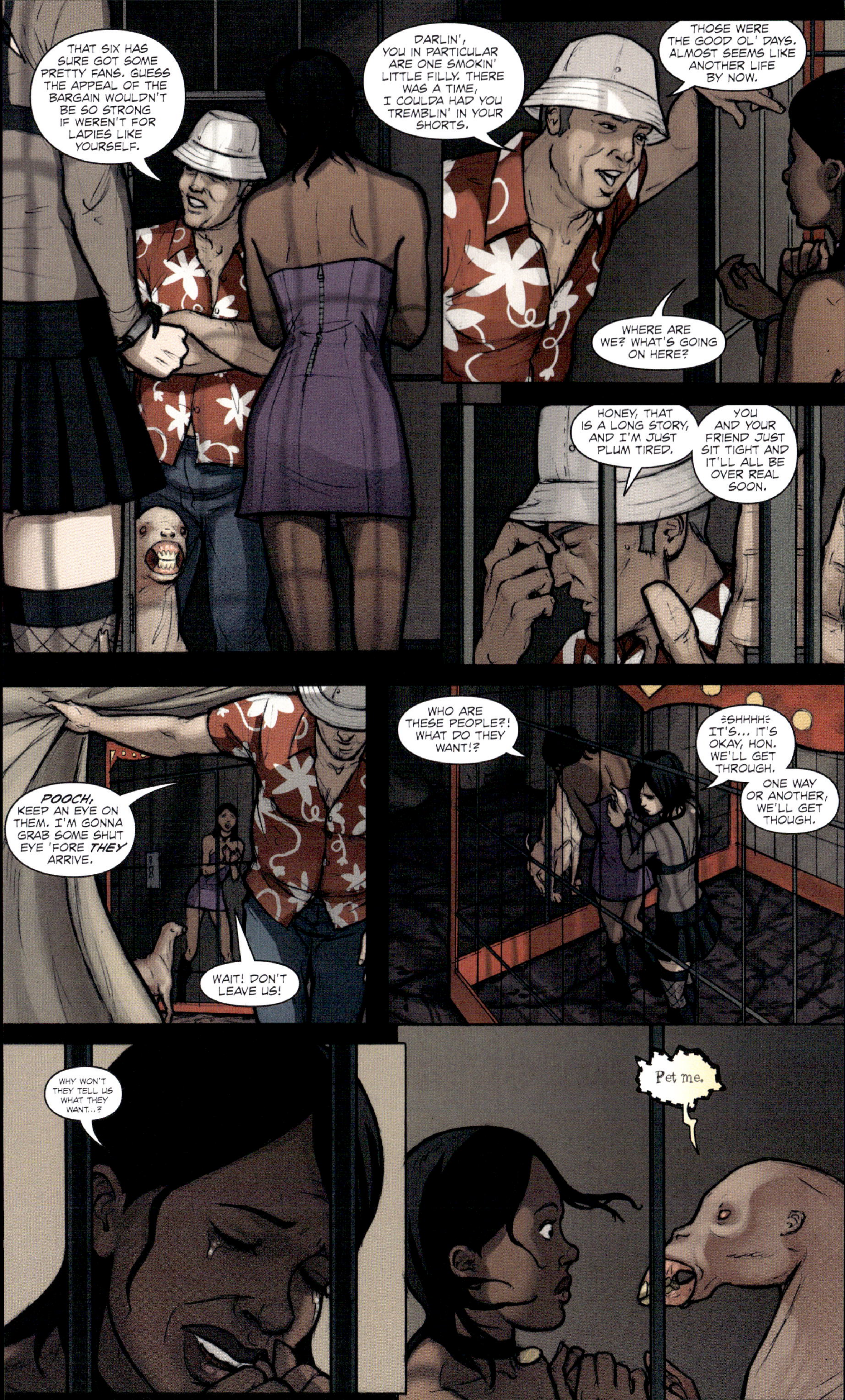
THAT SIX HAS SURE GOT SOME PRETTY FANS. GUESS THE APPEAL OF THE BARGAIN WOULDN'T BE SO STRONG IF WEREN'T FOR LADIES LIKE YOURSELF.
DARLIN', YOU IN PARTICULAR ARE ONE SMOKIN' LITTLE FILLY. THERE WAS A TIME, I COULDA HAD YOU TREMBLIN' IN YOUR SHORTS.
THOSE WERE THE GOOD OL' DAYS. ALMOST SEEMS LIKE ANOTHER LIFE BY NOW.
WHERE ARE WE? WHAT'S GOING ON HERE?
HONEY, THAT IS A LONG STORY, AND I'M JUST PLUM TIRED.
YOU AND YOUR FRIEND JUST SIT TIGHT AND IT'LL ALL BE OVER REAL SOON.
POOCH, KEEP AN EYE ON THEM. I'M GONNA GRAB SOME SHUT EYE 'FORE THEY ARRIVE.
WAIT! DON'T LEAVE US!
WHO ARE THESE PEOPLE?! WHAT DO THEY WANT!?
SHHHH IT'S... IT'S OKAY, HON. WE'LL GET THROUGH.
ONE WAY OR ANOTHER, WE'LL GET THOUGH.
WHY WON'T THEY TELL US WHAT THEY WANT...?
Pet me.

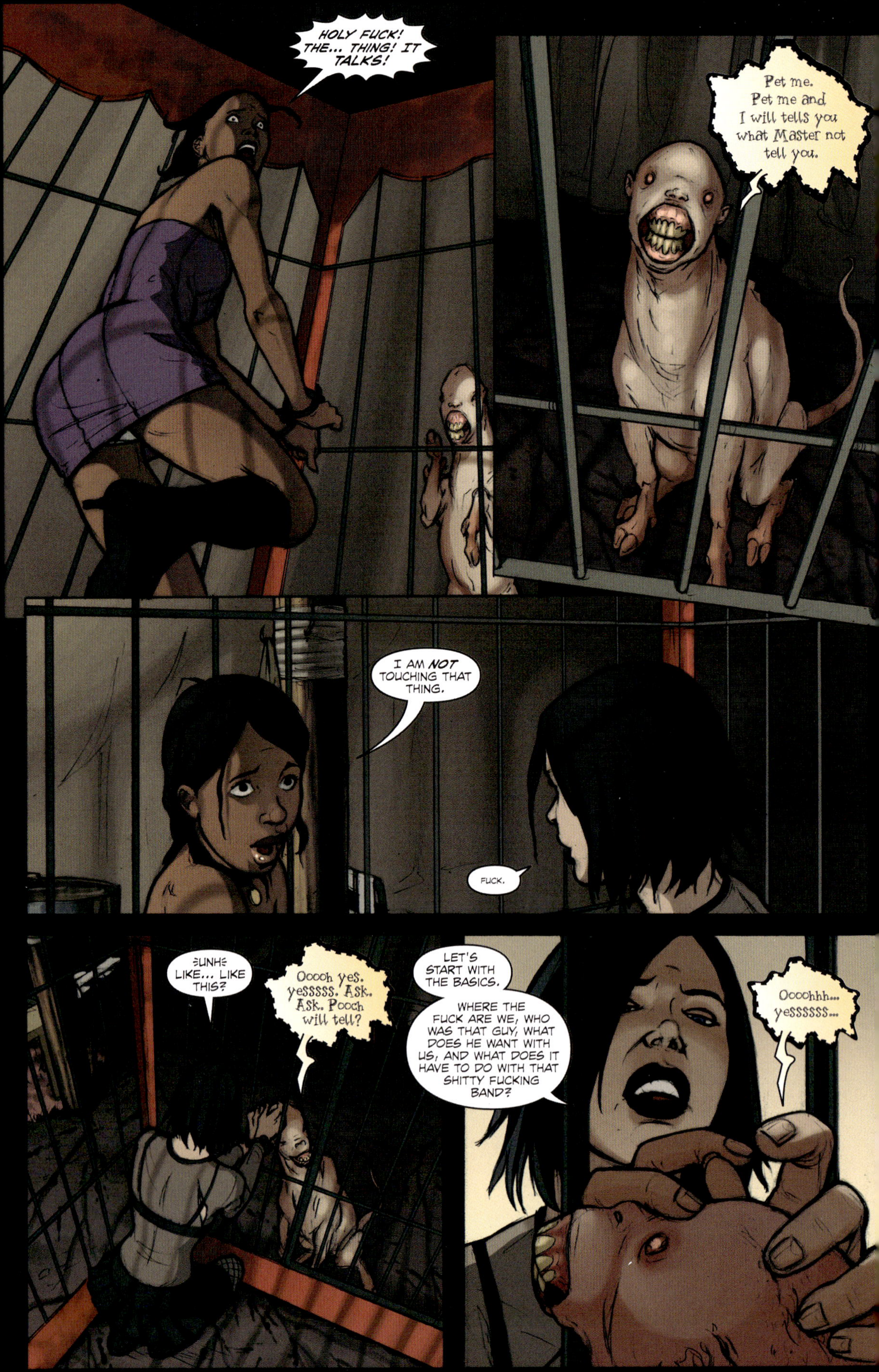
HOLY FUCK! THE... THING! IT TALKS!
Pet me. Pet me and I will tells you what Master not tell you.
I AM NOT TOUCHING THAT THING.
FUCK.
=UNH= LIKE... LIKE THIS?
Ooooh yes. yessssss. Ask. Ask. Pooch will tell?
LET'S START WITH THE BASICS.
WHERE THE FUCK ARE WE, WHO WAS THAT GUY, WHAT DOES HE WANT WITH US, AND WHAT DOES IT HAVE TO DO WITH THAT SHITTY FUCKING BAND?
Oooohhh... yesssssss...

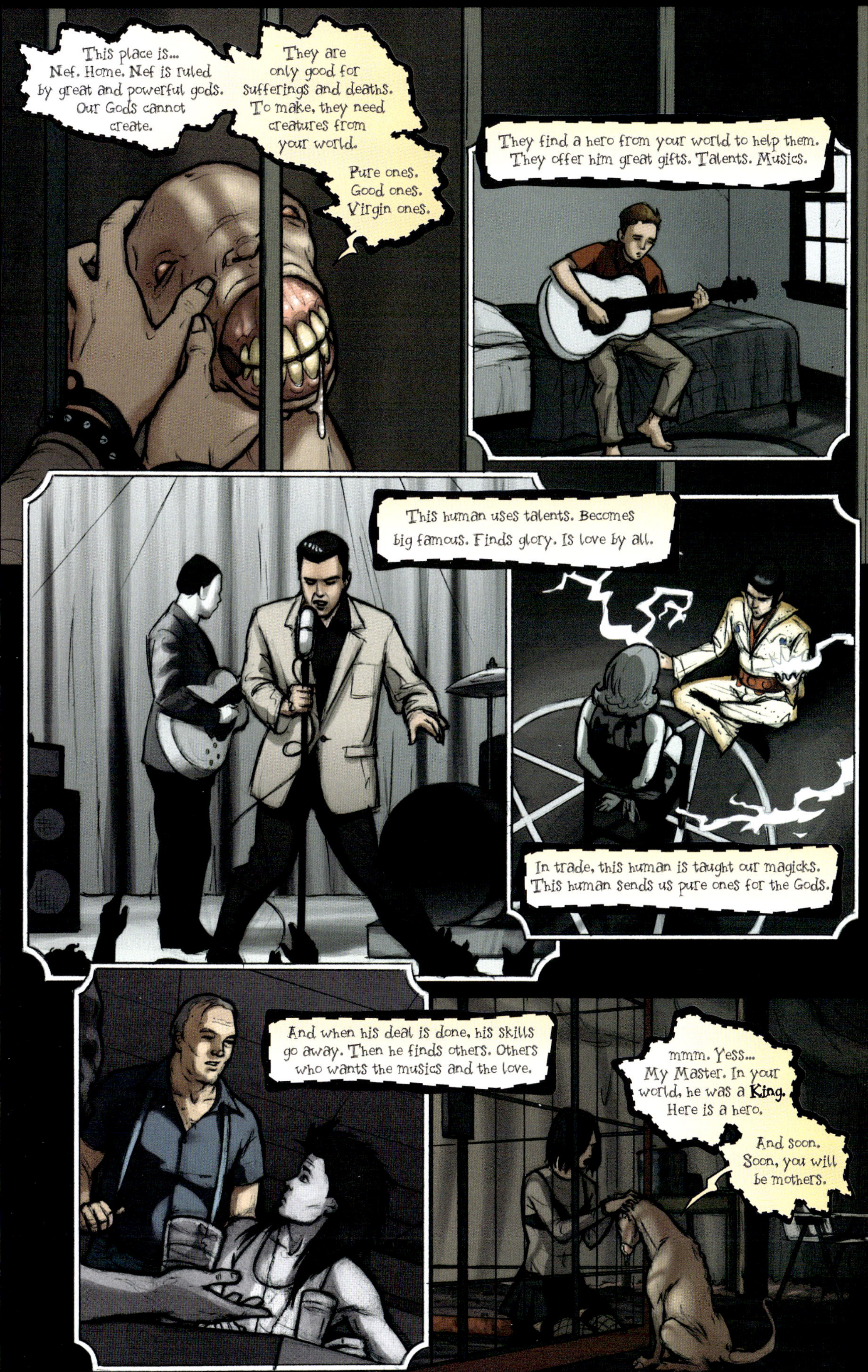

This place is... Nef. Home. Nef is ruled by great and powerful gods. Our Gods cannot create.
They are only good for sufferings and deaths. To make, they need creatures from your world.
Pure ones. Good ones. Virgin ones.
They find a hero from your world to help them. They offer him great gifts. Talents. Musics.
This human uses talents. Becomes big famous. Finds glory. Is love by all.
In trade, this human is taught our magicks. This human sends us pure ones for the Gods.
And when his deal is done, his skills go away. Then he finds others. Others who wants the musics and the love.
mmm. Yess... My Master. In your world, he was a King. Here is a hero.
And soon. Soon, you will be mothers.

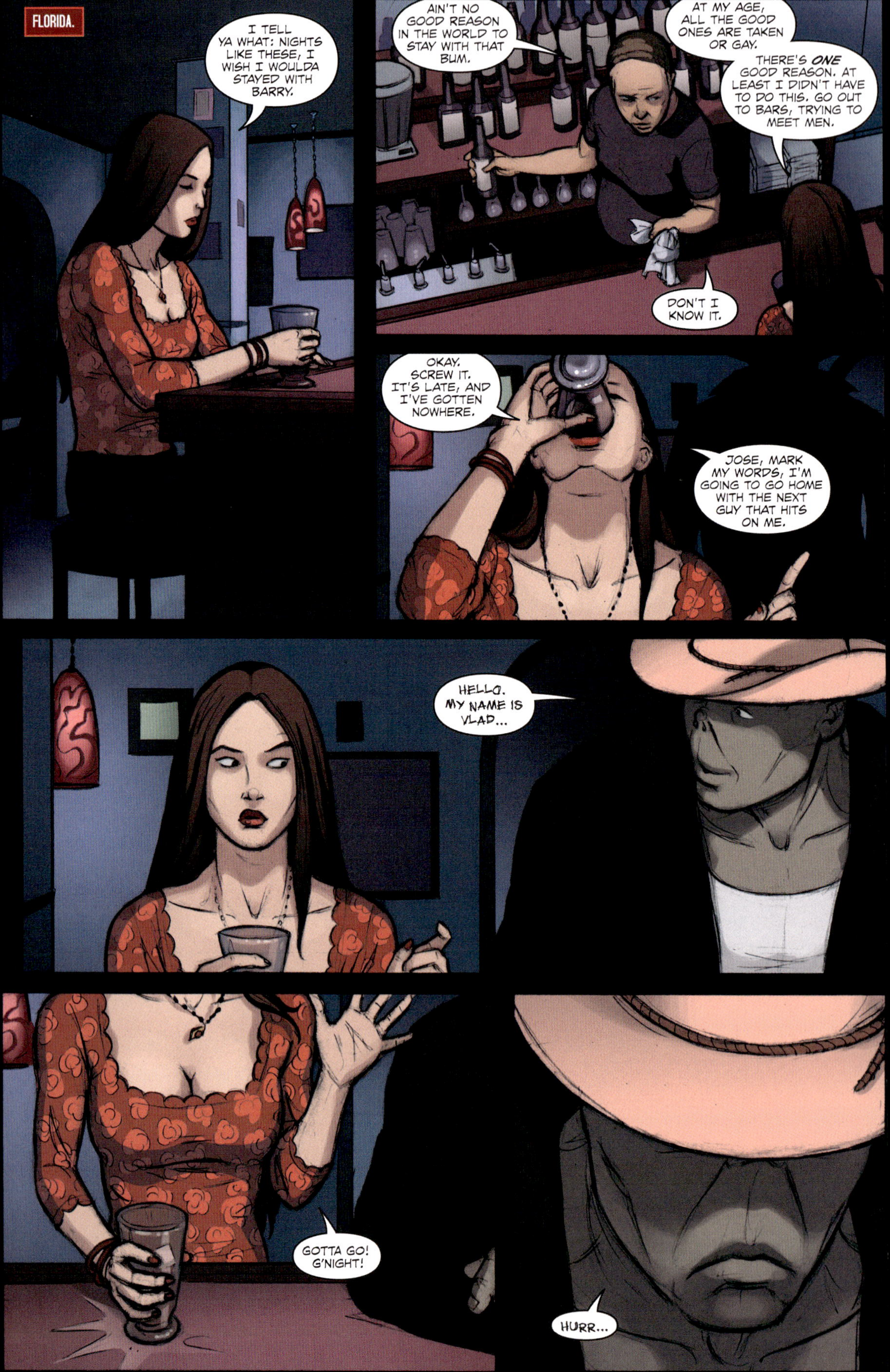
FLORIDA.
I TELL YA WHAT: NIGHTS LIKE THESE, I WISH I WOULDA STAYED WITH BARRY.
AIN'T NO GOOD REASON IN THE WORLD TO STAY WITH THAT BUM.
AT MY AGE, ALL THE GOOD ONES ARE TAKEN OR GAY.
THERE'S *ONE* GOOD REASON. AT LEAST I DIDN'T HAVE TO DO THIS. GO OUT TO BARS, TRYING TO MEET MEN.
DON'T I KNOW IT.
OKAY. SCREW IT. IT'S LATE, AND I'VE GOTTEN NOWHERE.
JOSE, MARK MY WORDS, I'M GOING TO GO HOME WITH THE NEXT GUY THAT HITS ON ME.
HELLO. MY NAME IS VLAD...
GOTTA GO! G'NIGHT!
HURR...

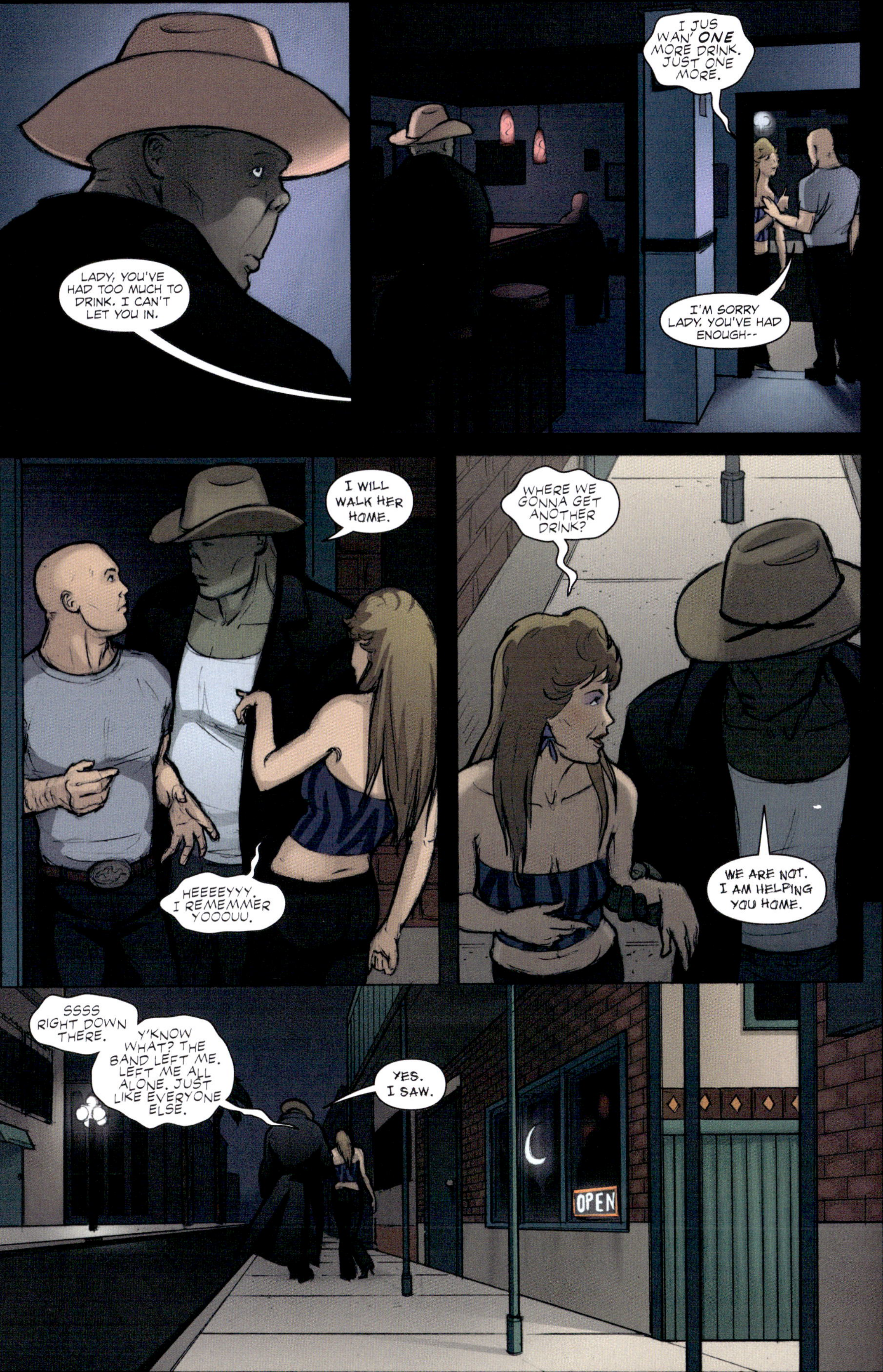
LADY, YOU'VE HAD TOO MUCH TO DRINK. I CAN'T LET YOU IN.
I JUS WAN' ONE MORE DRINK. JUST ONE MORE.
I'M SORRY LADY. YOU'VE HAD ENOUGH--
I WILL WALK HER HOME.
HEEEEYYY. I REMEMMER YOOOUU.
WHERE WE GONNA GET ANOTHER DRINK?
WE ARE NOT. I AM HELPING YOU HOME.
SSSS RIGHT DOWN THERE.
Y'KNOW WHAT? THE BAND LEFT ME. LEFT ME ALL ALONE. JUST LIKE EVERYONE ELSE.
YES. I SAW.
OPEN

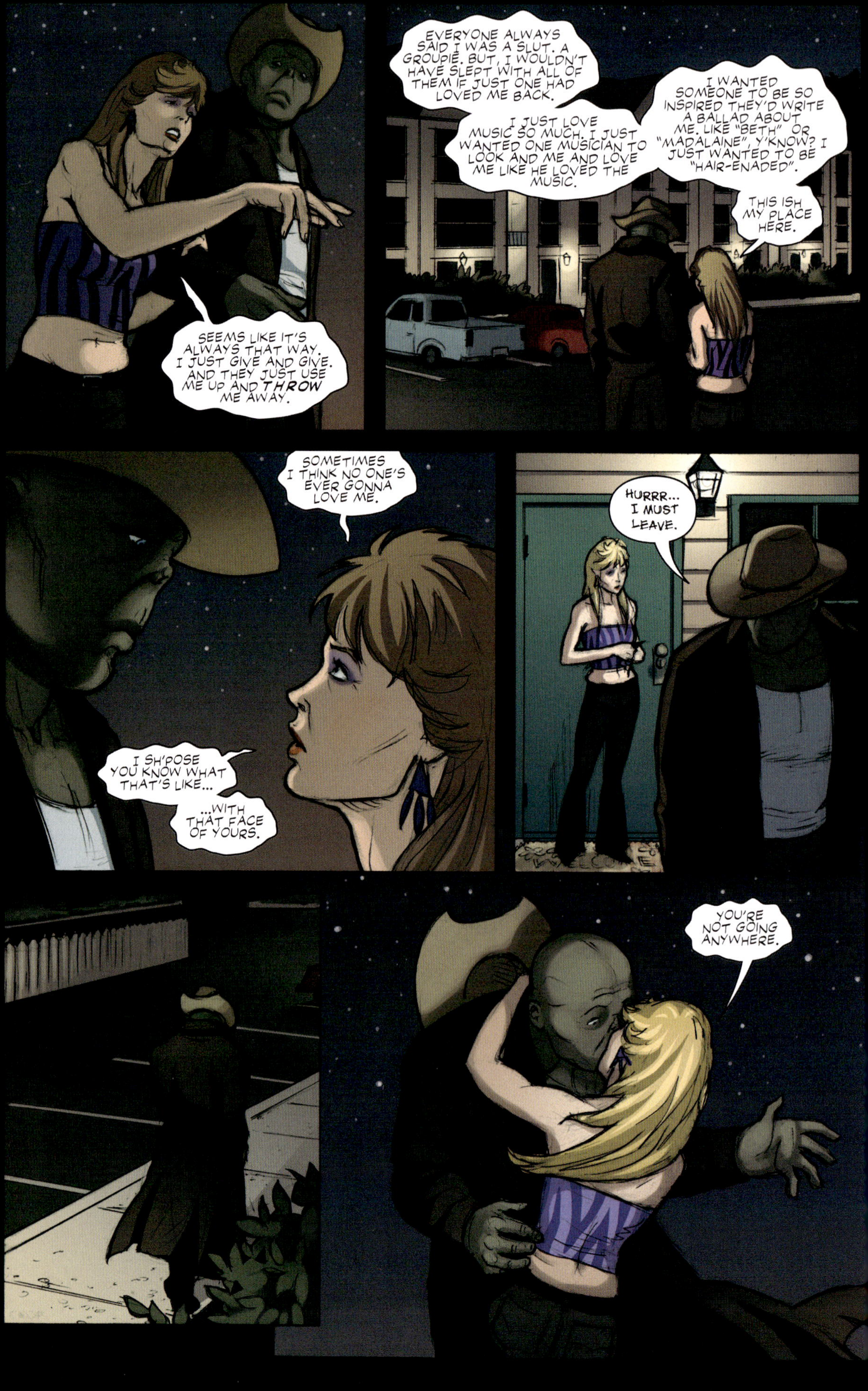
SEEMS LIKE IT'S ALWAYS THAT WAY. I JUST GIVE AND GIVE. AND THEY JUST USE ME UP AND THROW ME AWAY.
EVERYONE ALWAYS SAID I WAS A SLUT. A GROUPIE. BUT, I WOULDN'T HAVE SLEPT WITH ALL OF THEM IF JUST ONE HAD LOVED ME BACK.
I JUST LOVE MUSIC SO MUCH. I JUST WANTED ONE MUSICIAN TO LOOK AND ME AND LOVE ME LIKE HE LOVED THE MUSIC.
I WANTED SOMEONE TO BE SO INSPIRED THEY'D WRITE A BALLAD ABOUT ME. LIKE "BETH" OR "MADALAINE", Y'KNOW? I JUST WANTED TO BE "HAIR-ENADED".
THIS ISH MY PLACE HERE.
SOMETIMES I THINK NO ONE'S EVER GONNA LOVE ME.
I SH'POSE YOU KNOW WHAT THAT'S LIKE...
...WITH THAT FACE OF YOURS.
HURRR... I MUST LEAVE.
YOU'RE NOT GOING ANYWHERE.

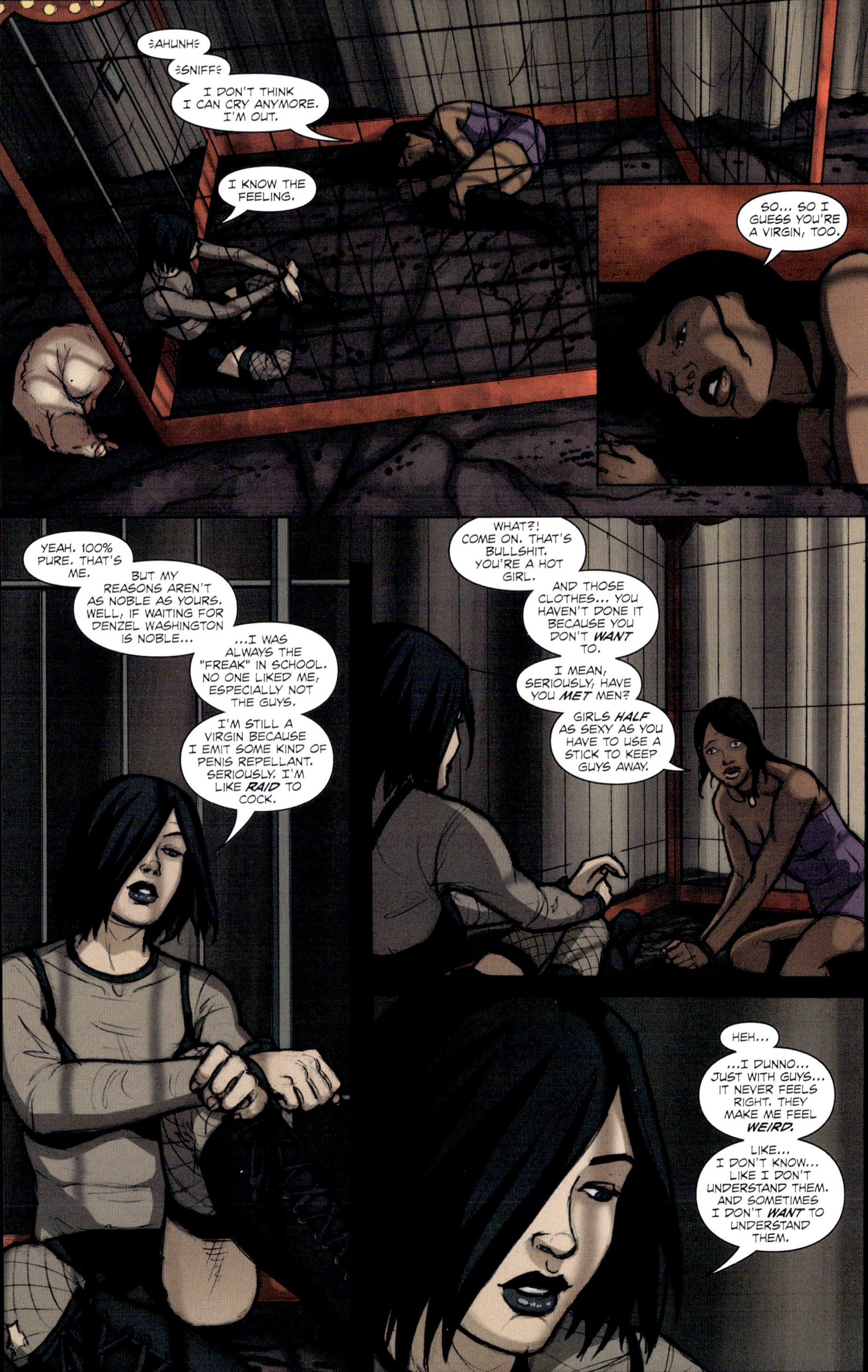

AHUNH
SNIFF
I DON'T THINK I CAN CRY ANYMORE. I'M OUT.
I KNOW THE FEELING.
SO... SO I GUESS YOU'RE A VIRGIN, TOO.
YEAH. 100% PURE. THAT'S ME.
BUT MY REASONS AREN'T AS NOBLE AS YOURS. WELL, IF WAITING FOR DENZEL WASHINGTON IS NOBLE...
...I WAS ALWAYS THE "FREAK" IN SCHOOL. NO ONE LIKED ME, ESPECIALLY NOT THE GUYS.
I'M STILL A VIRGIN BECAUSE I EMIT SOME KIND OF PENIS REPELLANT. SERIOUSLY. I'M LIKE RAID TO COCK.
WHAT?! COME ON. THAT'S BULLSHIT. YOU'RE A HOT GIRL.
AND THOSE CLOTHES... YOU HAVEN'T DONE IT BECAUSE YOU DON'T WANT TO.
I MEAN, SERIOUSLY, HAVE YOU MET MEN?
GIRLS HALF AS SEXY AS YOU HAVE TO USE A STICK TO KEEP GUYS AWAY.
HEH...
...I DUNNO... JUST WITH GUYS... IT NEVER FEELS RIGHT. THEY MAKE ME FEEL WEIRD.
LIKE... I DON'T KNOW... LIKE I DON'T UNDERSTAND THEM. AND SOMETIMES I DON'T WANT TO UNDERSTAND THEM.

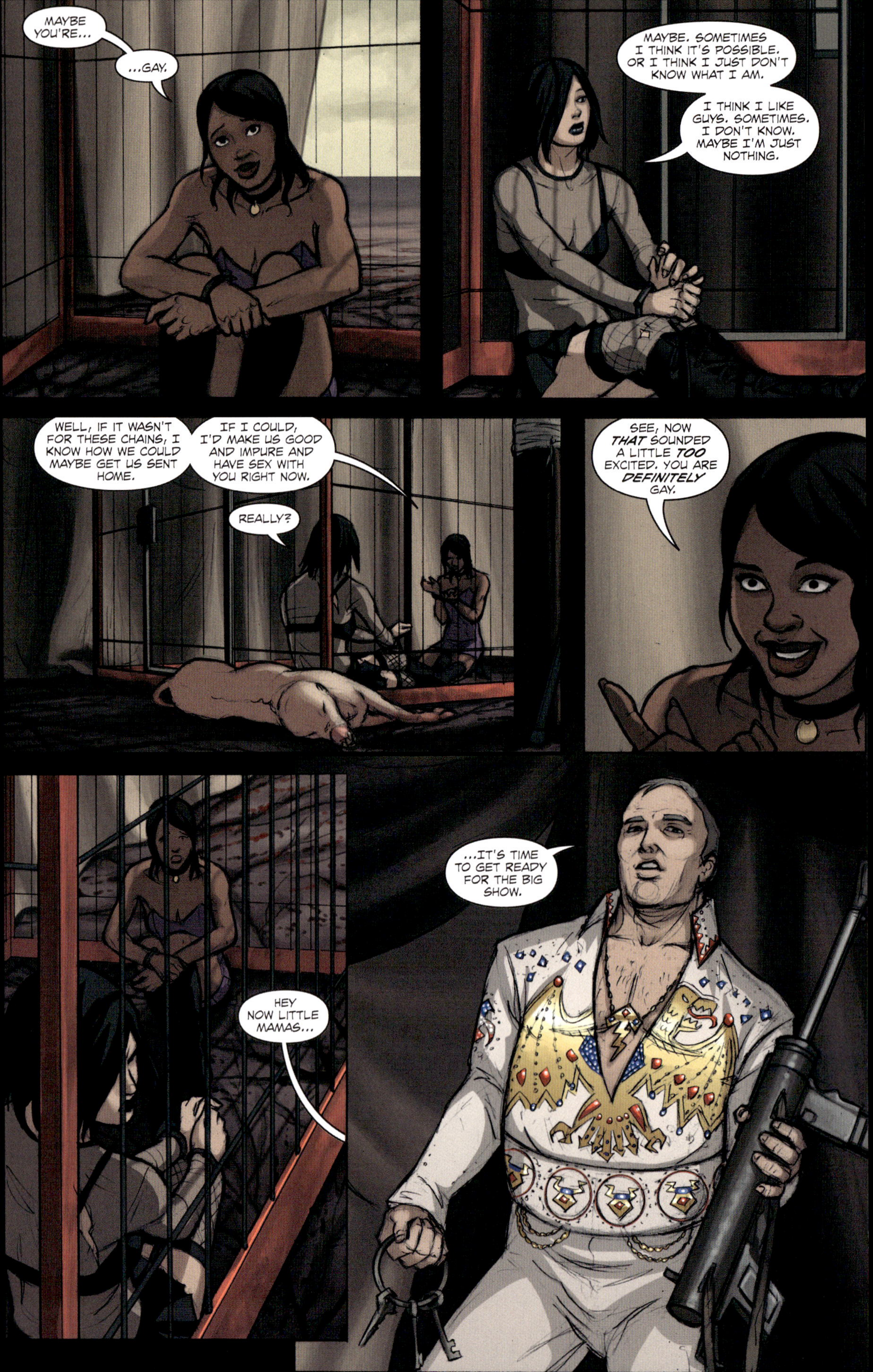
MAYBE YOU'RE...
...GAY.
MAYBE. SOMETIMES I THINK IT'S POSSIBLE. OR I THINK I JUST DON'T KNOW WHAT I AM.
I THINK I LIKE GUYS. SOMETIMES. I DON'T KNOW. MAYBE I'M JUST NOTHING.
WELL, IF IT WASN'T FOR THESE CHAINS, I KNOW HOW WE COULD MAYBE GET US SENT HOME.
IF I COULD, I'D MAKE US GOOD AND IMPURE AND HAVE SEX WITH YOU RIGHT NOW.
REALLY?
SEE, NOW *THAT* SOUNDED A LITTLE *TOO* EXCITED. YOU ARE *DEFINITELY* GAY.
HEY NOW LITTLE MAMAS...
...IT'S TIME TO GET READY FOR THE BIG SHOW.

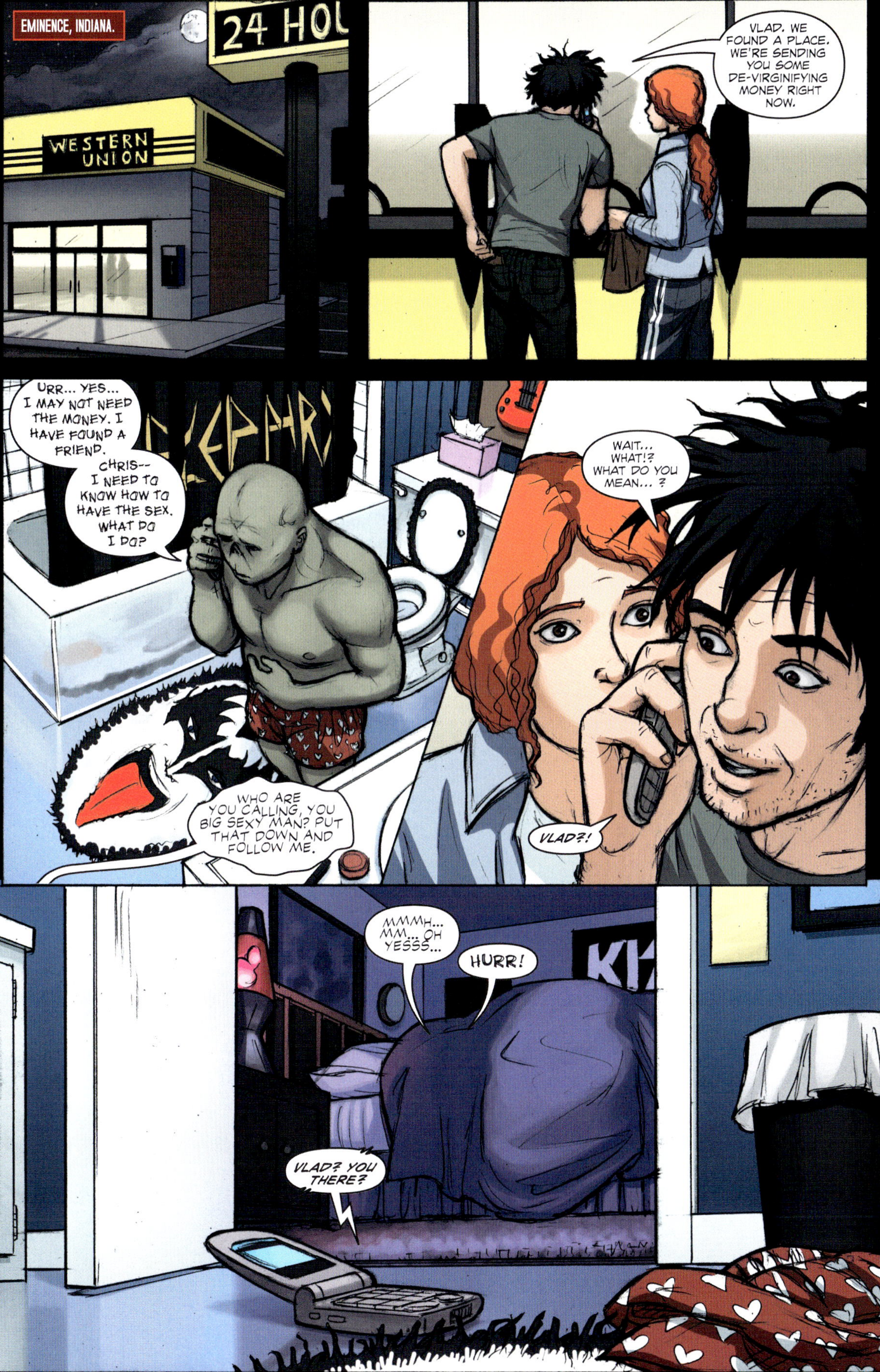
EMINENCE, INDIANA.
WESTERN UNION
24 HOU
VLAD. WE FOUND A PLACE. WE'RE SENDING YOU SOME DE-VIRGINIFYING MONEY RIGHT NOW.
URR... YES... I MAY NOT NEED THE MONEY. I HAVE FOUND A FRIEND.
CHRIS-- I NEED TO KNOW HOW TO HAVE THE SEX. WHAT DO I DO?
WHO ARE YOU CALLING, YOU BIG SEXY MAN? PUT THAT DOWN AND FOLLOW ME.
WAIT... WHAT!? WHAT DO YOU MEAN... ?
VLAD?!
MMMH... MM... OH YESSS...
HURR!
VLAD? YOU THERE?

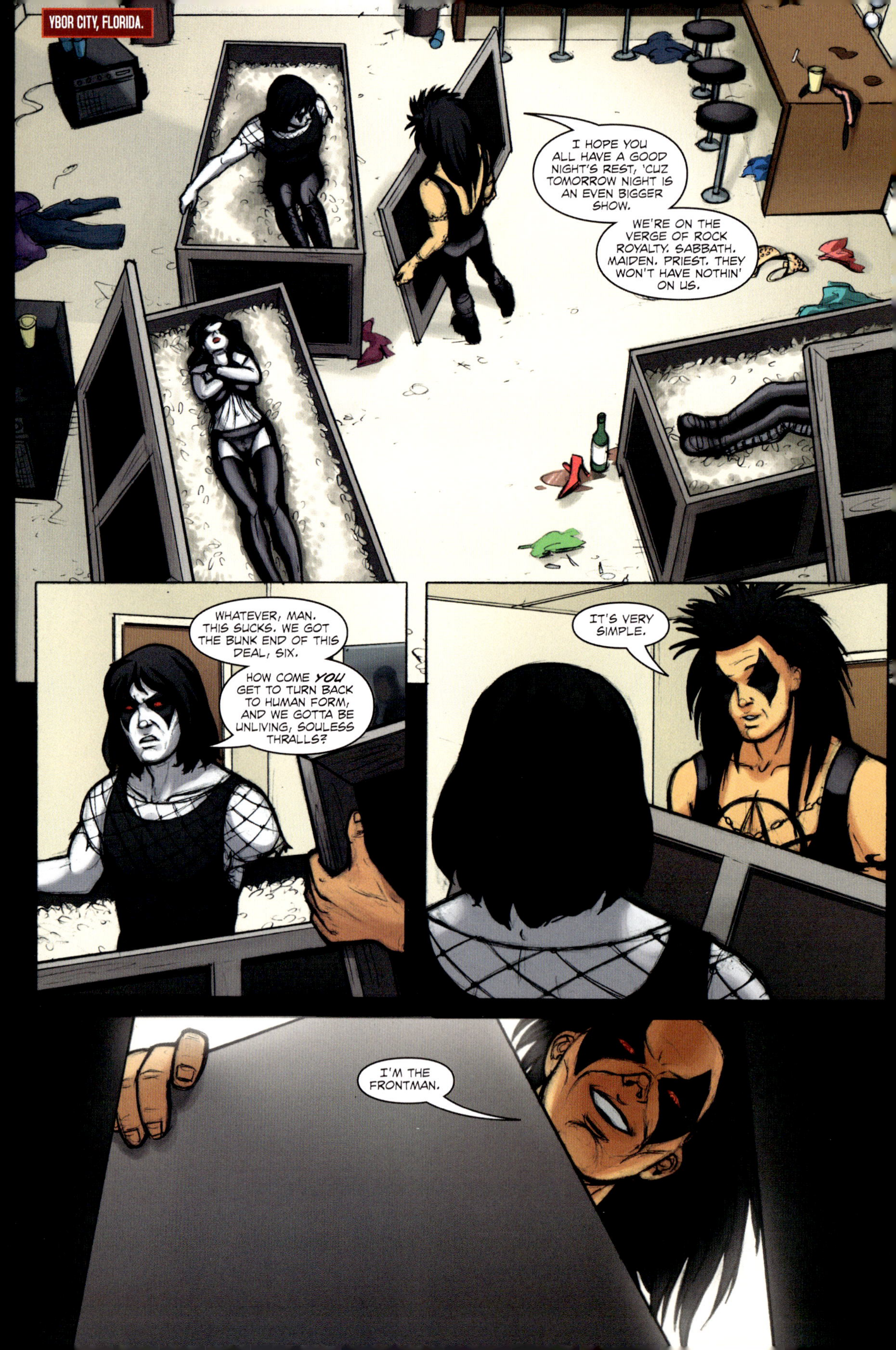
YBOR CITY, FLORIDA.
I HOPE YOU ALL HAVE A GOOD NIGHT'S REST, 'CUZ TOMORROW NIGHT IS AN EVEN BIGGER SHOW.
WE'RE ON THE VERGE OF ROCK ROYALTY. SABBATH. MAIDEN. PRIEST. THEY WON'T HAVE NOTHIN' ON US.
WHATEVER, MAN. THIS SUCKS. WE GOT THE BUNK END OF THIS DEAL, SIX.
HOW COME YOU GET TO TURN BACK TO HUMAN FORM, AND WE GOTTA BE UNLIVING, SOULESS THRALLS?
IT'S VERY SIMPLE.
I'M THE FRONTMAN.

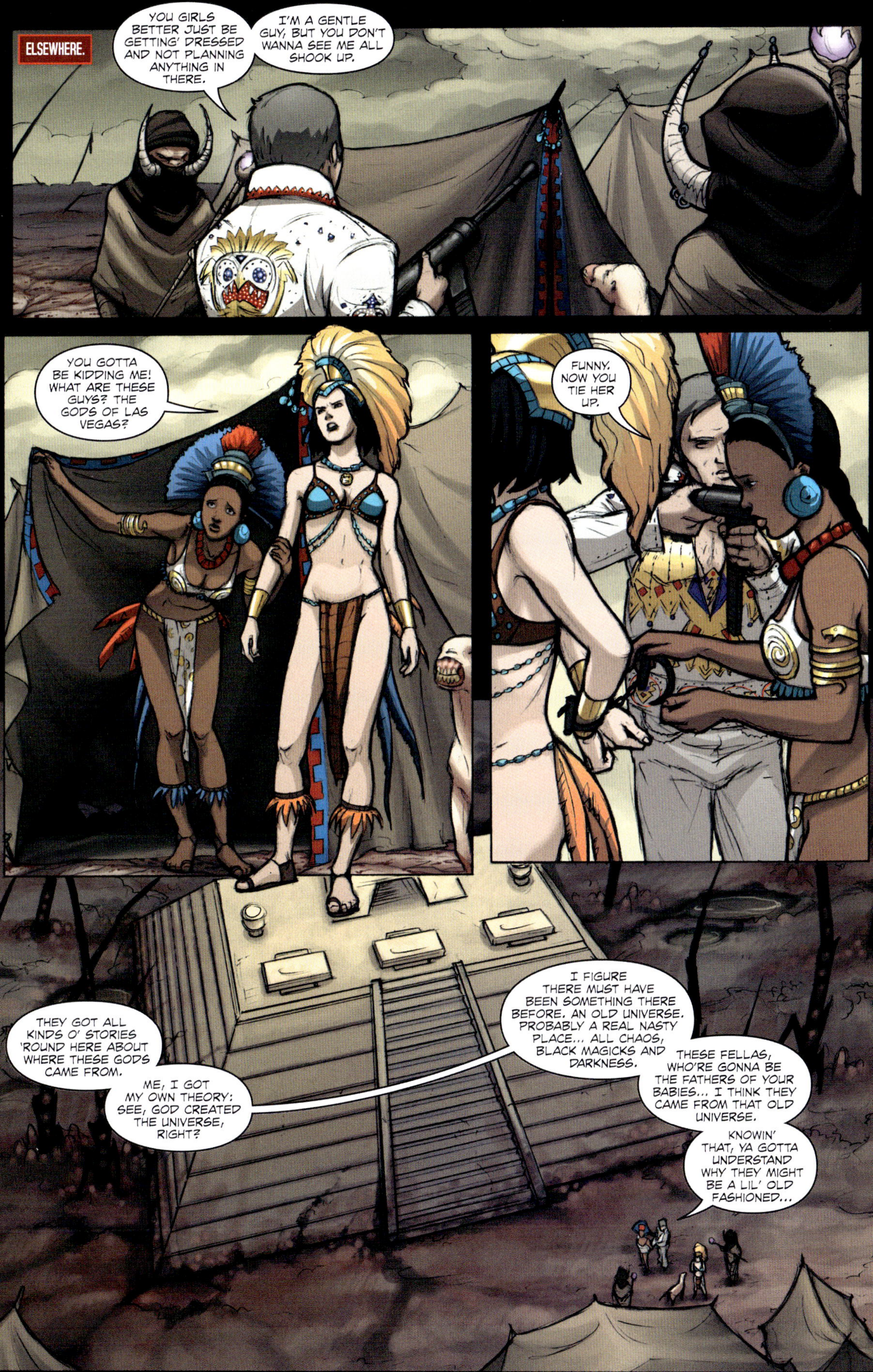
ELSEWHERE.
YOU GIRLS BETTER JUST BE GETTING' DRESSED AND NOT PLANNING ANYTHING IN THERE.
I'M A GENTLE GUY, BUT YOU DON'T WANNA SEE ME ALL SHOOK UP.
YOU GOTTA BE KIDDING ME! WHAT ARE THESE GUYS? THE GODS OF LAS VEGAS?
FUNNY. NOW YOU TIE HER UP.
THEY GOT ALL KINDS O' STORIES 'ROUND HERE ABOUT WHERE THESE GODS CAME FROM.
ME, I GOT MY OWN THEORY: SEE, GOD CREATED THE UNIVERSE, RIGHT?
I FIGURE THERE MUST HAVE BEEN SOMETHING THERE BEFORE. AN OLD UNIVERSE. PROBABLY A REAL NASTY PLACE... ALL CHAOS, BLACK MAGICKS AND DARKNESS.
THESE FELLAS, WHO'RE GONNA BE THE FATHERS OF YOUR BABIES... I THINK THEY CAME FROM THAT OLD UNIVERSE.
KNOWIN' THAT, YA GOTTA UNDERSTAND WHY THEY MIGHT BE A LIL' OLD FASHIONED...

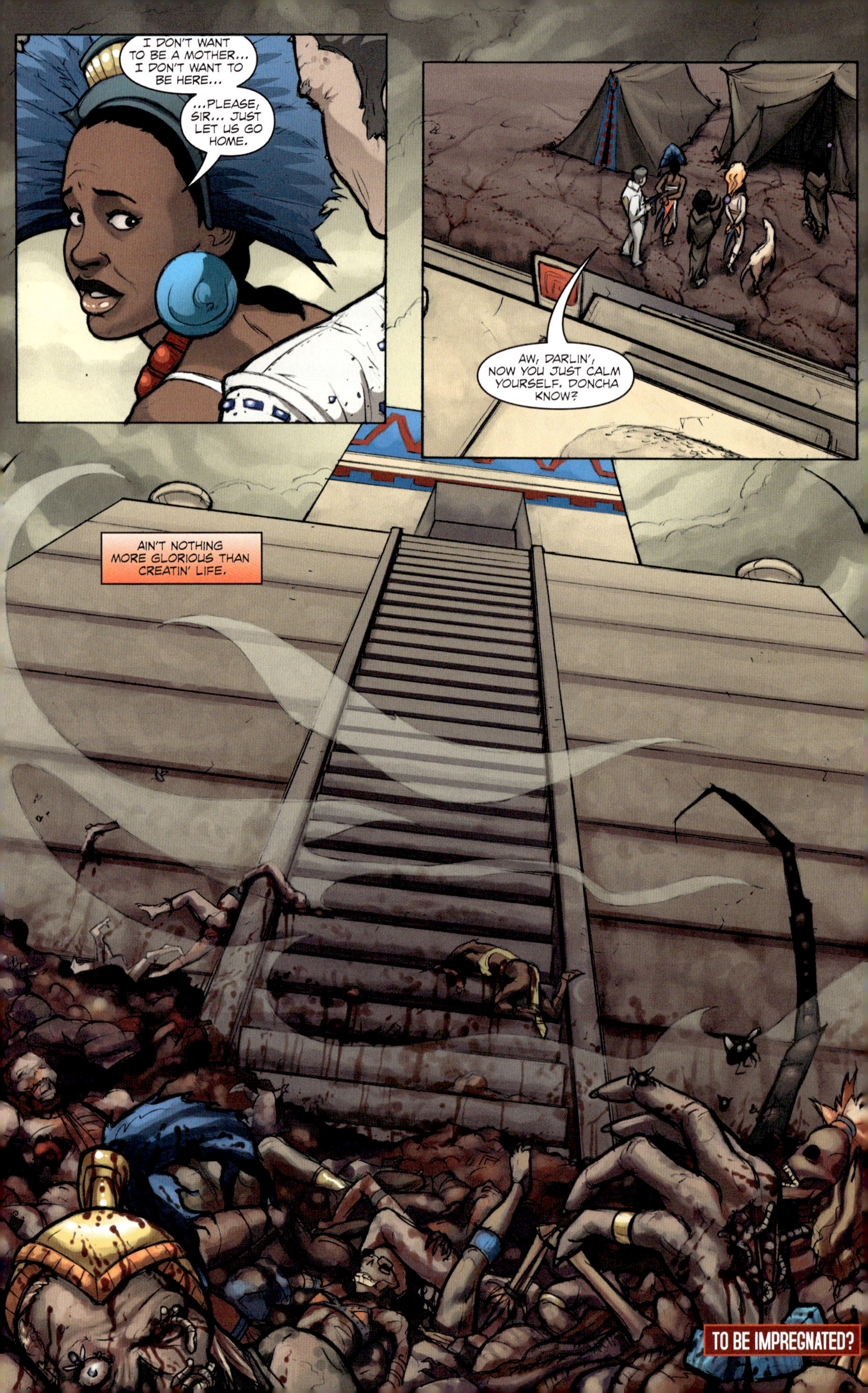
I DON'T WANT TO BE A MOTHER... I DON'T WANT TO BE HERE...
...PLEASE, SIR... JUST LET US GO HOME.
AW, DARLIN', NOW YOU JUST CALM YOURSELF, DONCHA KNOW?
AIN'T NOTHING MORE GLORIOUS THAN CREATIN' LIFE.
TO BE IMPREGNATED?

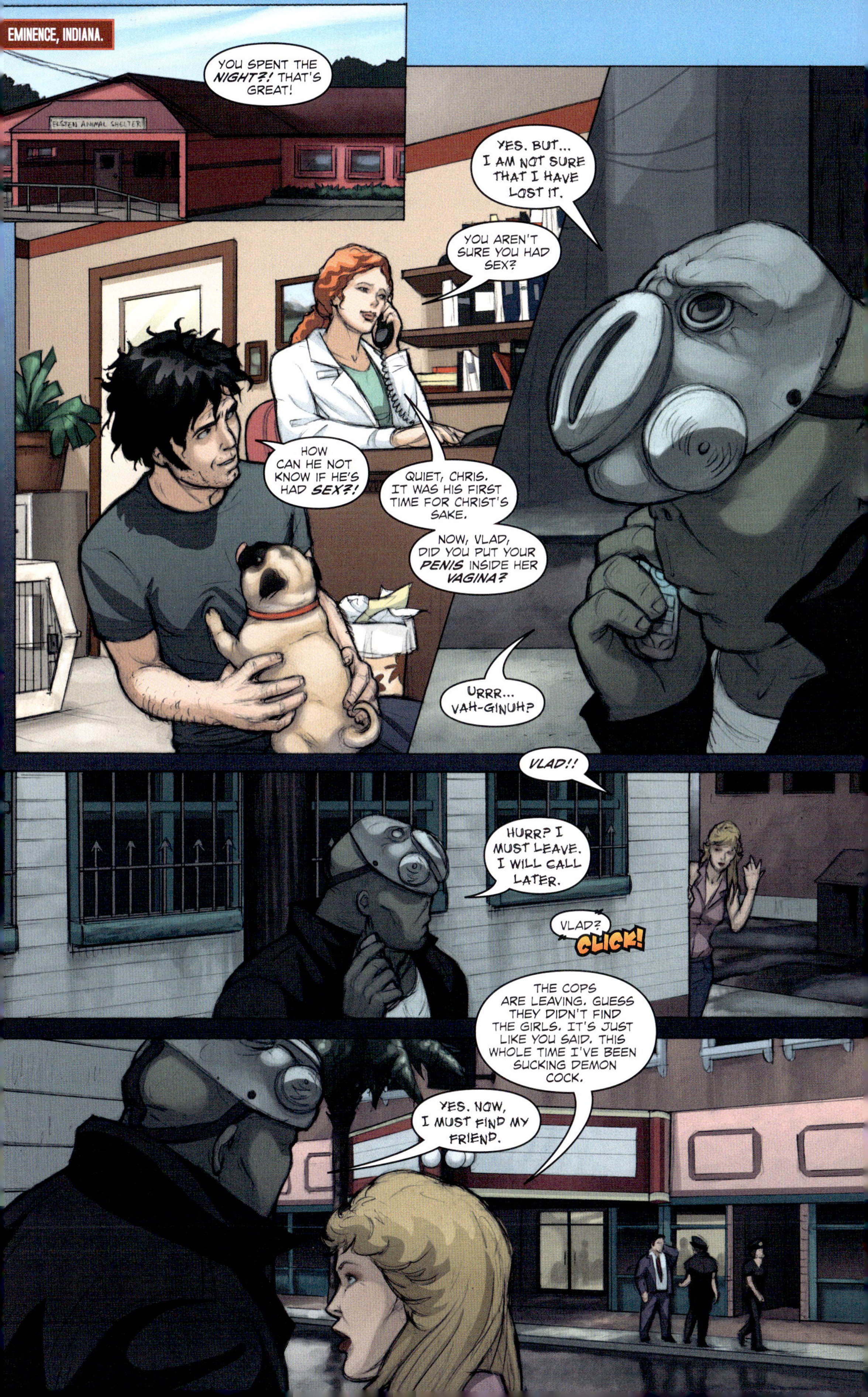

EMINENCE, INDIANA.
ELSTEN ANIMAL SHELTER
YOU SPENT THE NIGHT?! THAT'S GREAT!
YES. BUT... I AM NOT SURE THAT I HAVE LOST IT.
YOU AREN'T SURE YOU HAD SEX?
HOW CAN HE NOT KNOW IF HE'S HAD SEX?!
QUIET, CHRIS. IT WAS HIS FIRST TIME FOR CHRIST'S SAKE.
NOW, VLAD, DID YOU PUT YOUR PENIS INSIDE HER VAGINA?
URRR... VAH-GINUH?
VLAD!!
HURR? I MUST LEAVE. I WILL CALL LATER.
VLAD?
CLICK!
THE COPS ARE LEAVING. GUESS THEY DIDN'T FIND THE GIRLS. IT'S JUST LIKE YOU SAID. THIS WHOLE TIME I'VE BEEN SUCKING DEMON COCK.
YES. NOW, I MUST FIND MY FRIEND.

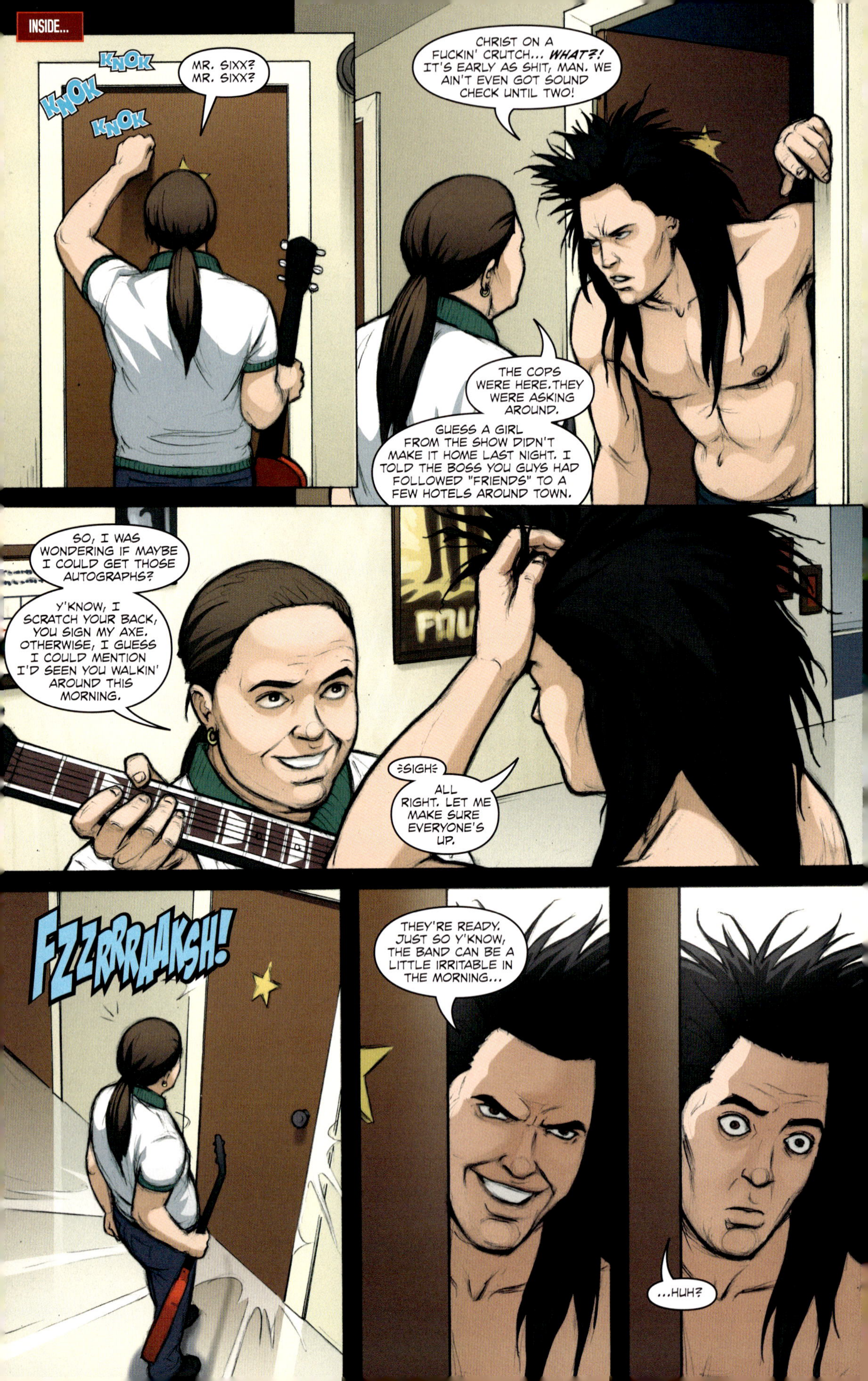

INSIDE...
KNOK
KNOK
KNOK
MR. SIXX? MR. SIXX?
CHRIST ON A FUCKIN' CRUTCH... WHAT?! IT'S EARLY AS SHIT, MAN. WE AIN'T EVEN GOT SOUND CHECK UNTIL TWO!
THE COPS WERE HERE. THEY WERE ASKING AROUND.
GUESS A GIRL FROM THE SHOW DIDN'T MAKE IT HOME LAST NIGHT. I TOLD THE BOSS YOU GUYS HAD FOLLOWED "FRIENDS" TO A FEW HOTELS AROUND TOWN.
SO, I WAS WONDERING IF MAYBE I COULD GET THOSE AUTOGRAPHS?
Y'KNOW, I SCRATCH YOUR BACK, YOU SIGN MY AXE. OTHERWISE, I GUESS I COULD MENTION I'D SEEN YOU WALKIN' AROUND THIS MORNING.
=SIGH=
ALL RIGHT. LET ME MAKE SURE EVERYONE'S UP.
FZZRRRAAKSH!
THEY'RE READY. JUST SO Y'KNOW, THE BAND CAN BE A LITTLE IRRITABLE IN THE MORNING...
...HUH?

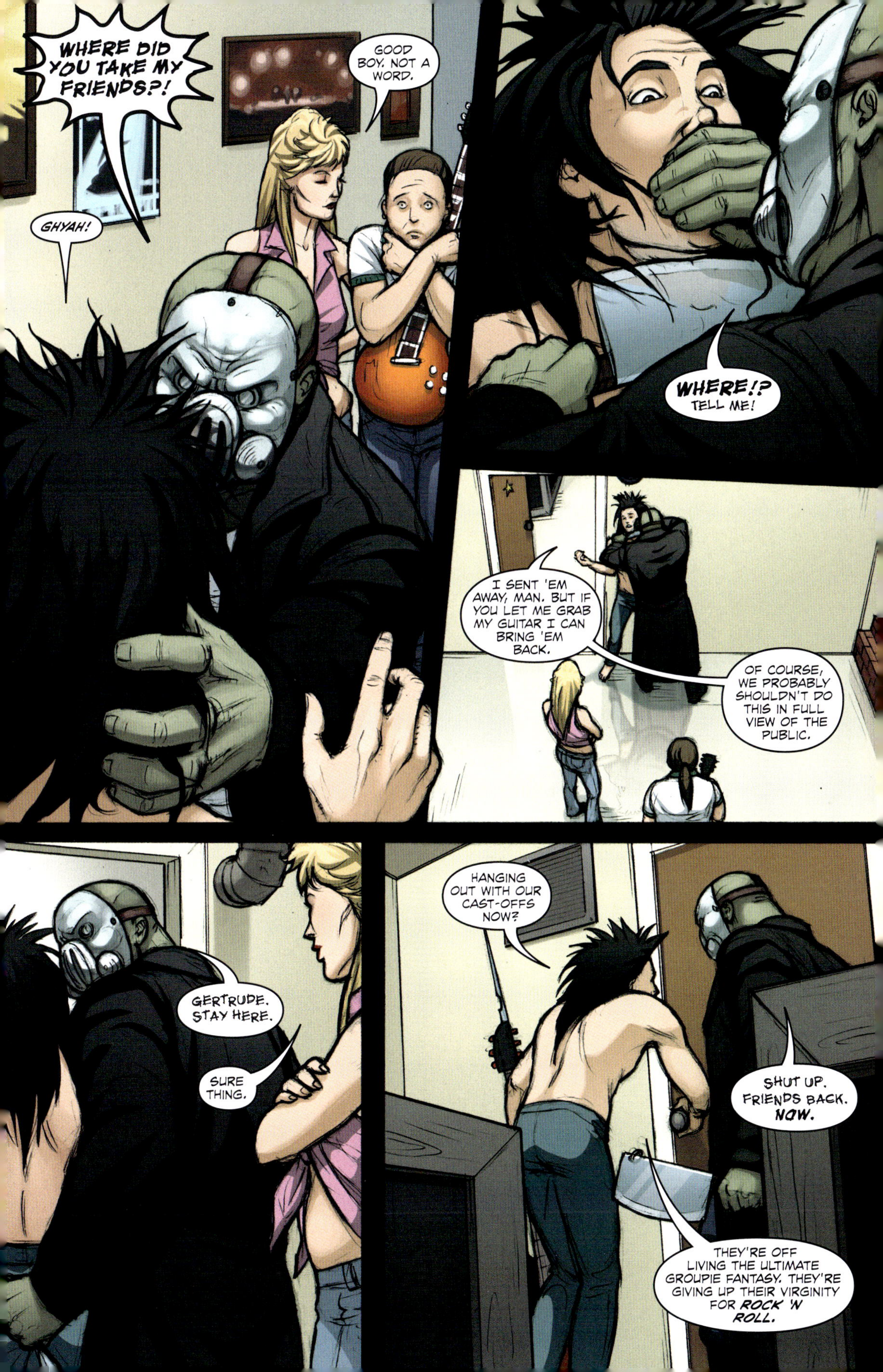
WHERE DID YOU TAKE MY FRIENDS?!
GHYAH!
GOOD BOY. NOT A WORD.
WHERE!? TELL ME!
I SENT 'EM AWAY, MAN. BUT IF YOU LET ME GRAB MY GUITAR I CAN BRING 'EM BACK.
OF COURSE, WE PROBABLY SHOULDN'T DO THIS IN FULL VIEW OF THE PUBLIC.
GERTRUDE. STAY HERE.
SURE THING.
HANGING OUT WITH OUR CAST-OFFS NOW?
SHUT UP. FRIENDS BACK. NOW.
THEY'RE OFF LIVING THE ULTIMATE GROUPIE FANTASY. THEY'RE GIVING UP THEIR VIRGINITY FOR ROCK 'N ROLL.

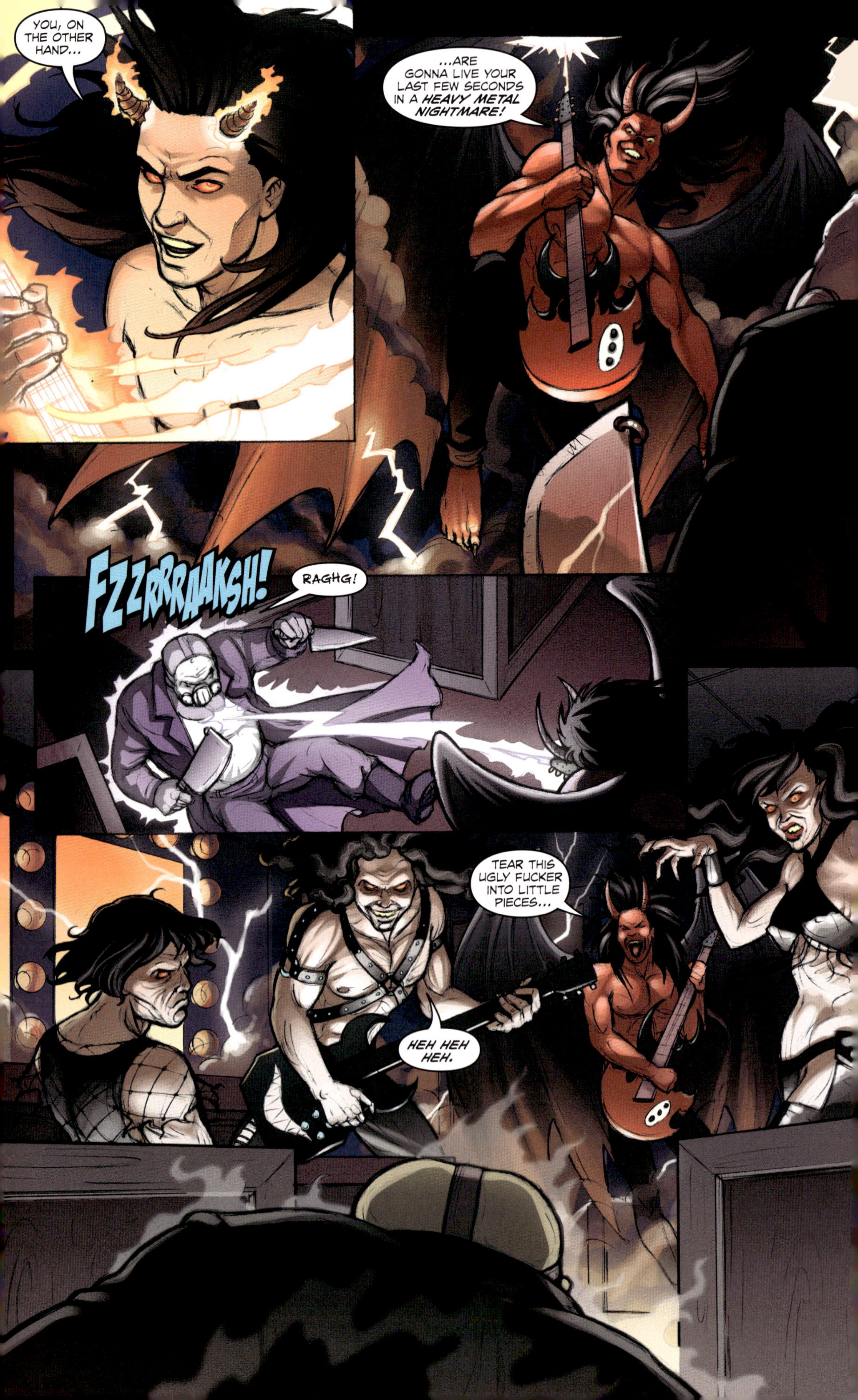

YOU, ON THE OTHER HAND...
...ARE GONNA LIVE YOUR LAST FEW SECONDS IN A HEAVY METAL NIGHTMARE!
FZZRRRAAKSH!
RAGHG!
TEAR THIS UGLY FUCKER INTO LITTLE PIECES...
HEH HEH HEH.

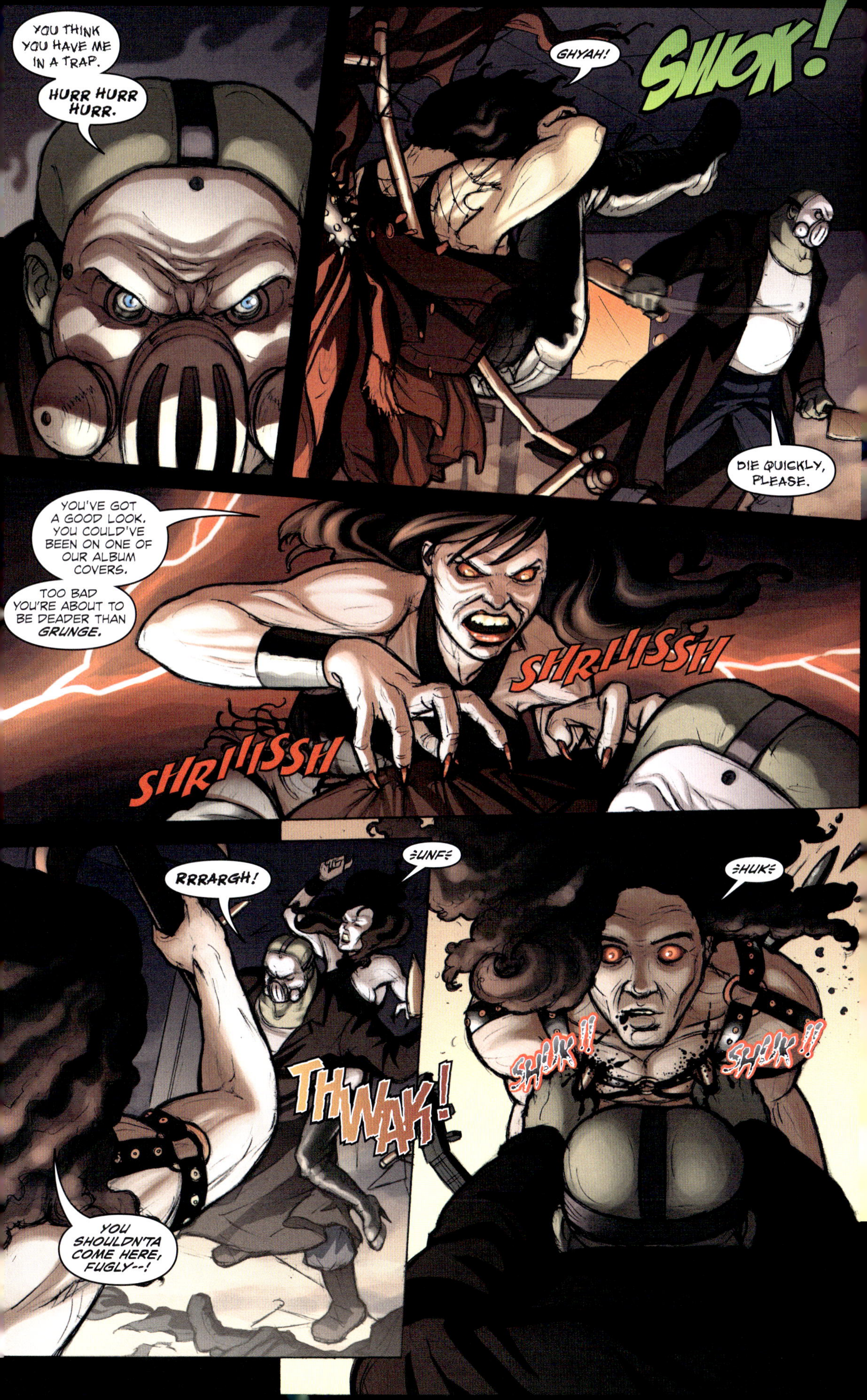

YOU THINK YOU HAVE ME IN A TRAP.
HURR HURR HURR.
GHYAH!
SHOK!
DIE QUICKLY, PLEASE.
YOU'VE GOT A GOOD LOOK. YOU COULD'VE BEEN ON ONE OF OUR ALBUM COVERS.
TOO BAD YOU'RE ABOUT TO BE DEADER THAN GRUNGE.
SHRIIISSH
SHRIIISSH
RRRARGH!
UNF
THWAK!
YOU SHOULDN'TA COME HERE, FUGLY--!
HUK
SHUK!!
SHUK!!

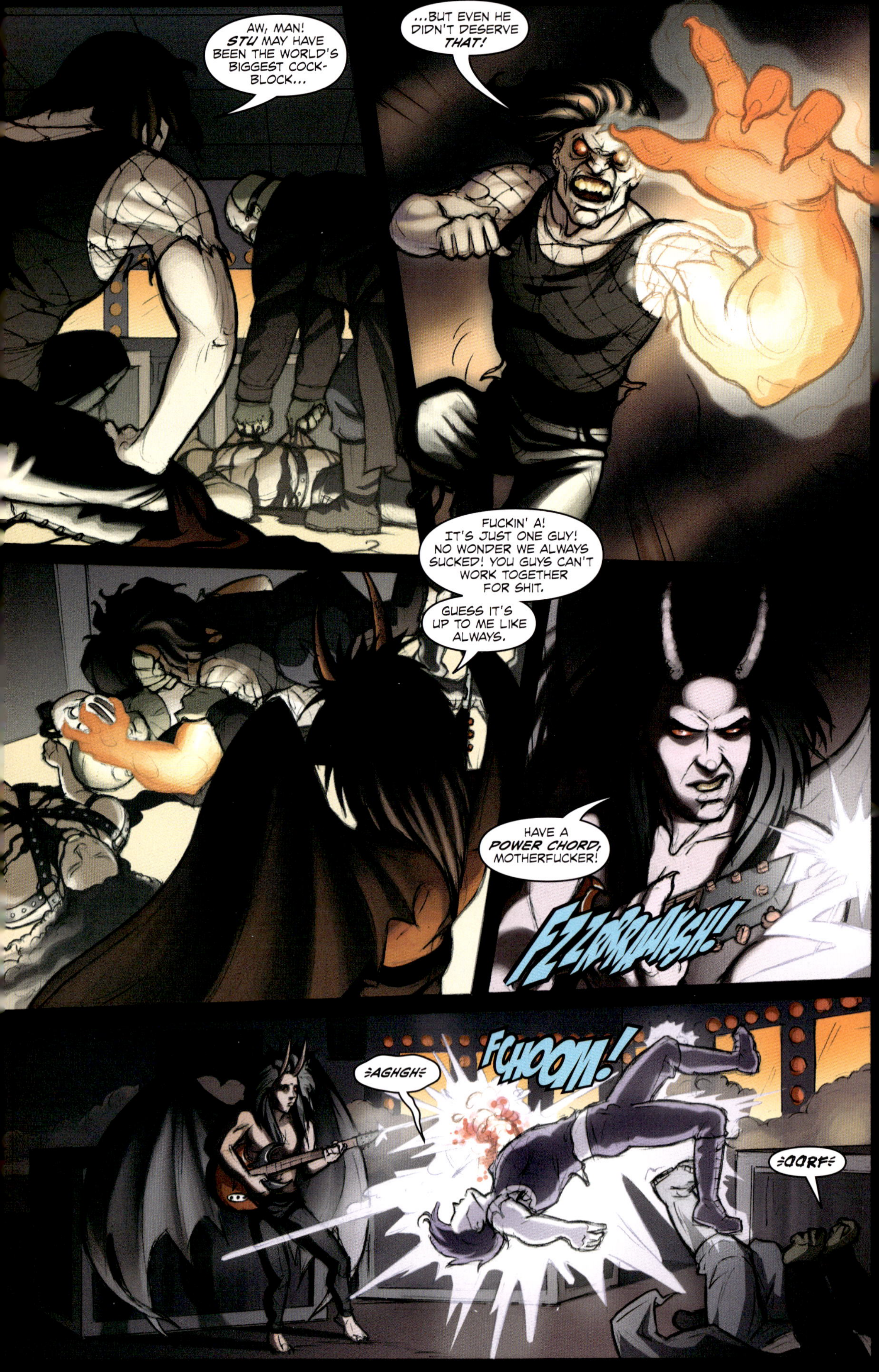
AW, MAN! STU MAY HAVE BEEN THE WORLD'S BIGGEST COCK-BLOCK...
...BUT EVEN HE DIDN'T DESERVE THAT!
FUCKIN' A! IT'S JUST ONE GUY! NO WONDER WE ALWAYS SUCKED! YOU GUYS CAN'T WORK TOGETHER FOR SHIT.
GUESS IT'S UP TO ME LIKE ALWAYS.
HAVE A POWER CHORD, MOTHERFUCKER!
FZZZRRRAASH!
FCHOOM!
AGHGH
OORF

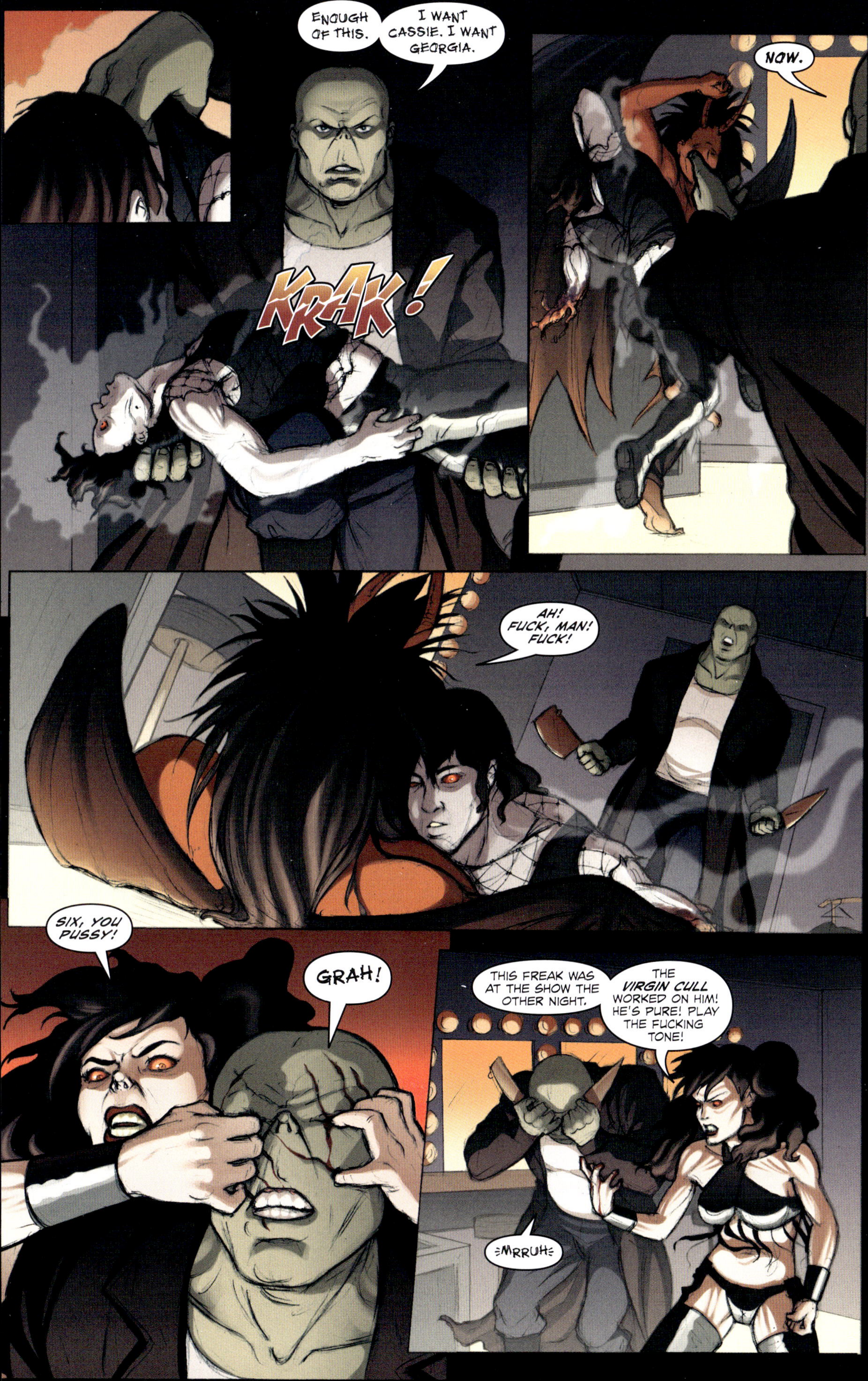

ENOUGH OF THIS.
I WANT CASSIE. I WANT GEORGIA.
KRAK!
NOW.
AH! FUCK, MAN! FUCK!
SIX, YOU PUSSY!
GRAH!
THIS FREAK WAS AT THE SHOW THE OTHER NIGHT.
THE *VIRGIN CULL* WORKED ON HIM! HE'S PURE! PLAY THE FUCKING TONE!
MRRUH

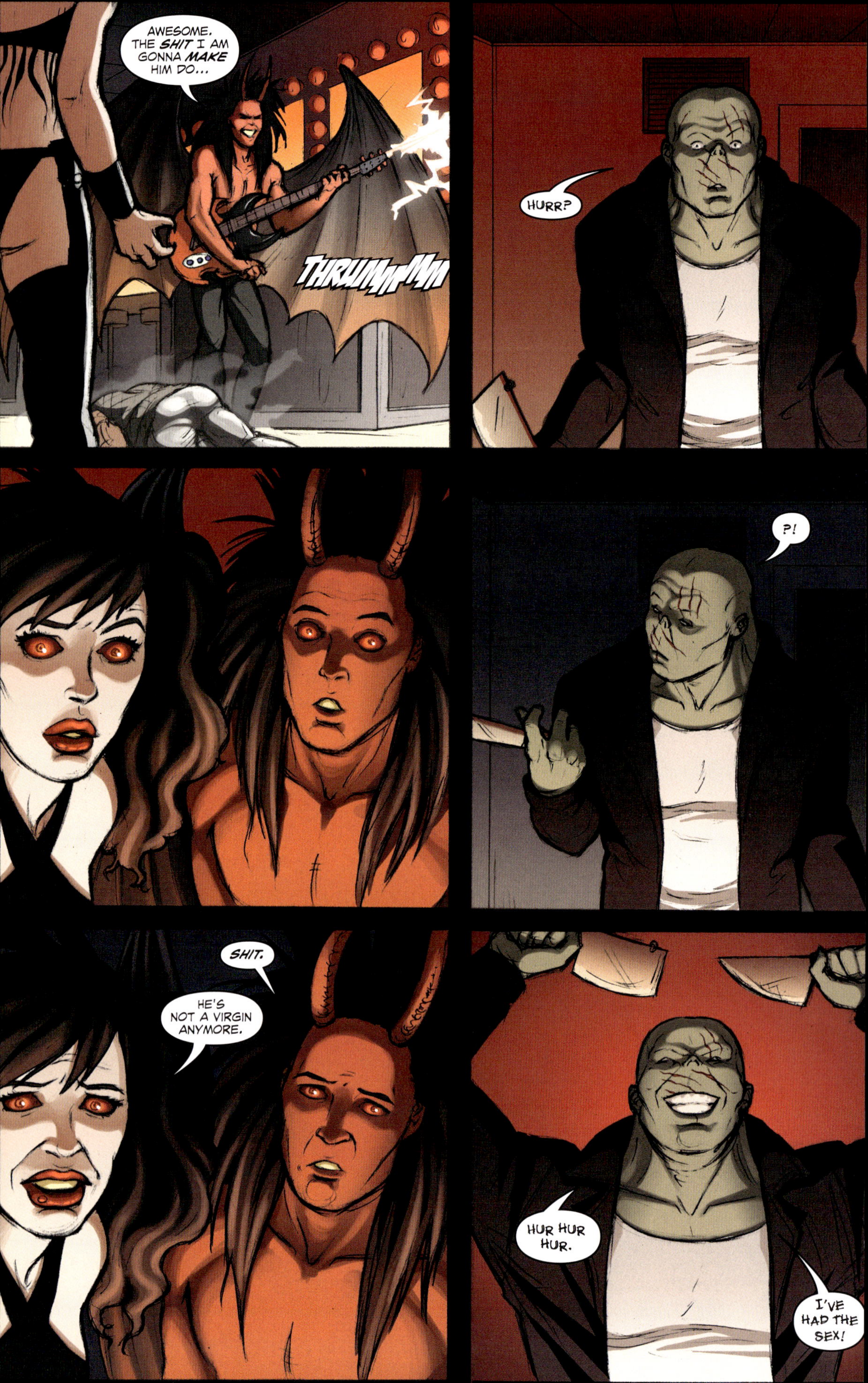
AWESOME. THE SHIT I AM GONNA MAKE HIM DO...
THRUMMMM
HURR?
?!
SHIT.
HE'S NOT A VIRGIN ANYMORE.
HUR HUR HUR.
I'VE HAD THE SEX!

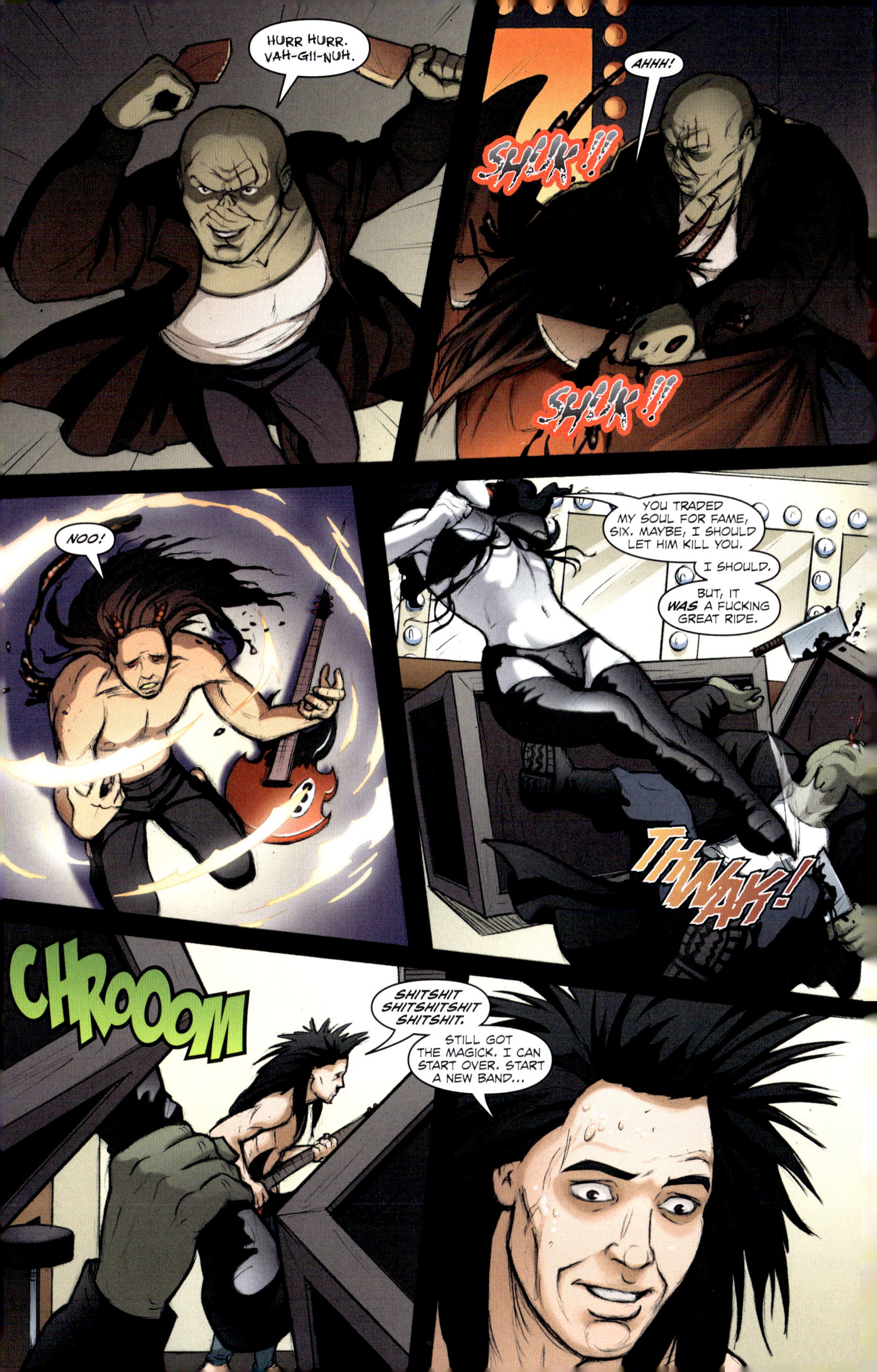
HURR HURR. VAH-GII-NUH.
AHHH!
SHUK!!
SHUK!!
NOO!
YOU TRADED MY SOUL FOR FAME, SIX. MAYBE, I SHOULD LET HIM KILL YOU.
I SHOULD.
BUT, IT WAS A FUCKING GREAT RIDE.
THWAK!
CHROOOM
SHITSHIT SHITSHITSHIT SHITSHIT.
STILL GOT THE MAGICK. I CAN START OVER. START A NEW BAND...

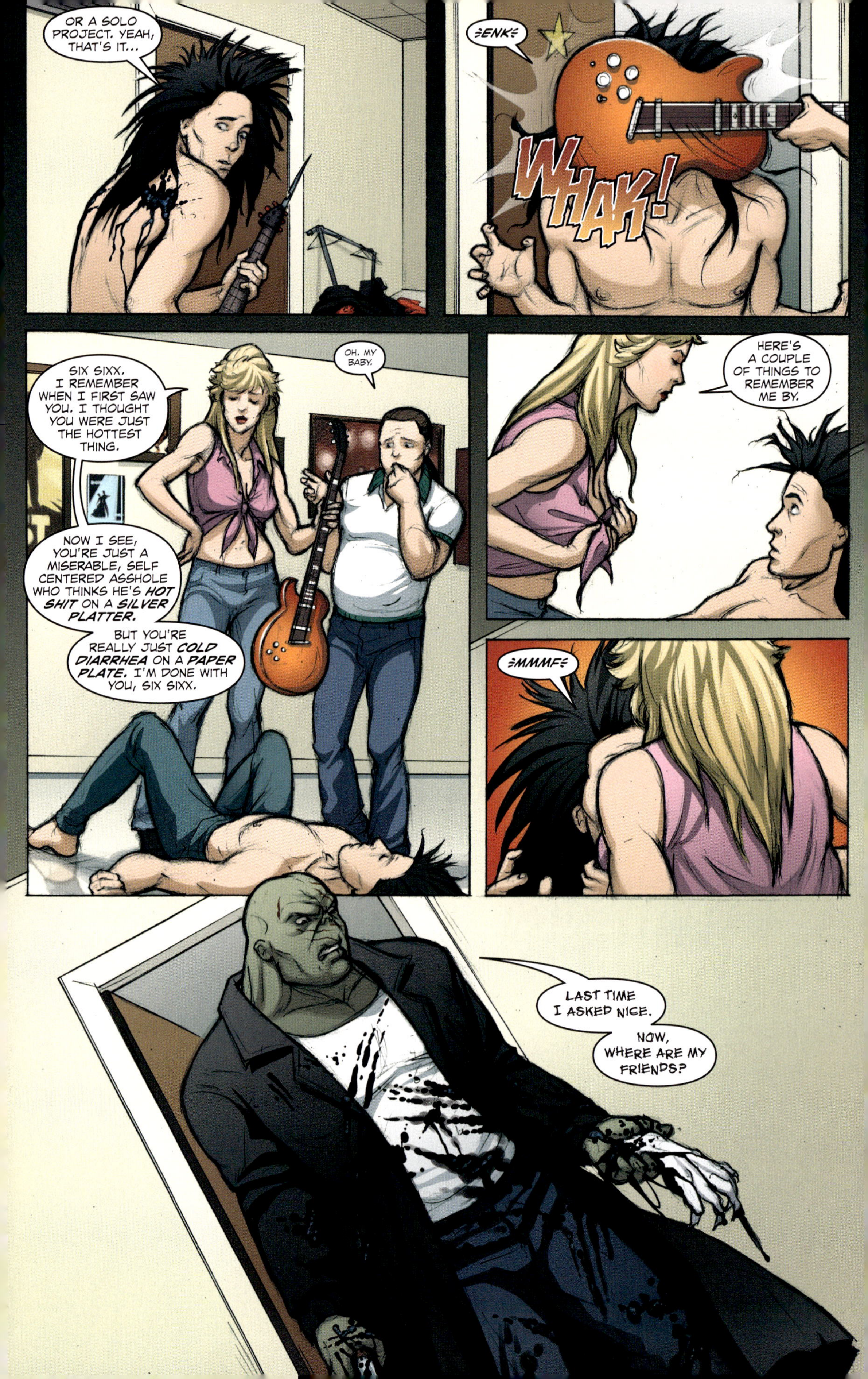

OR A SOLO PROJECT. YEAH, THAT'S IT...
ENK
WHAK!
SIX SIXX. I REMEMBER WHEN I FIRST SAW YOU. I THOUGHT YOU WERE JUST THE HOTTEST THING.
OH. MY BABY.
NOW I SEE, YOU'RE JUST A MISERABLE, SELF CENTERED ASSHOLE WHO THINKS HE'S HOT SHIT ON A SILVER PLATTER.
BUT YOU'RE REALLY JUST COLD DIARRHEA ON A PAPER PLATE. I'M DONE WITH YOU, SIX SIXX.
HERE'S A COUPLE OF THINGS TO REMEMBER ME BY.
MMMF
LAST TIME I ASKED NICE.
NOW, WHERE ARE MY FRIENDS?

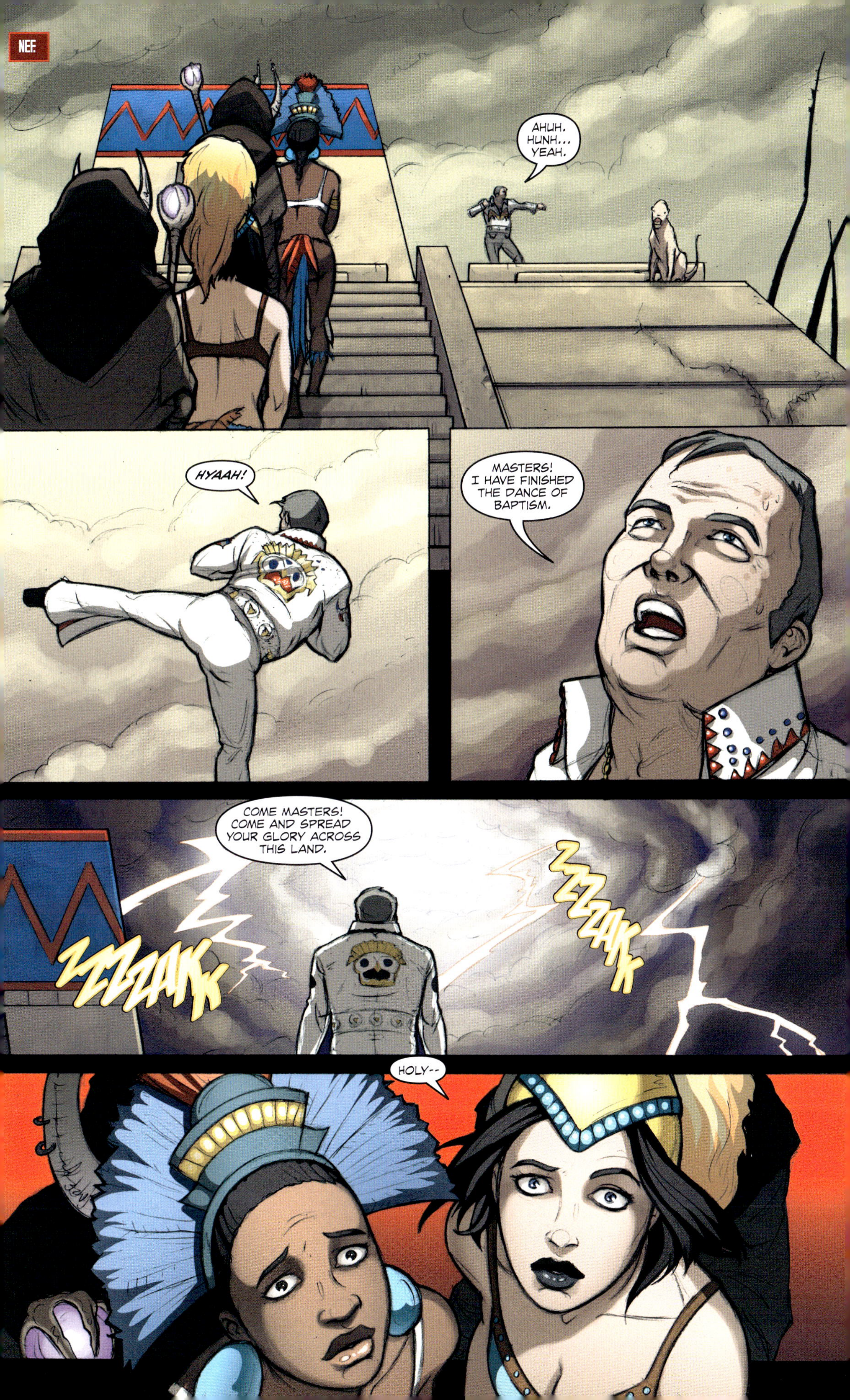
NEF.
AHUH. HUNH... YEAH.
HYAAH!
MASTERS! I HAVE FINISHED THE DANCE OF BAPTISM.
COME MASTERS! COME AND SPREAD YOUR GLORY ACROSS THIS LAND.
ZZZZAKK
ZZZZAKK
HOLY--

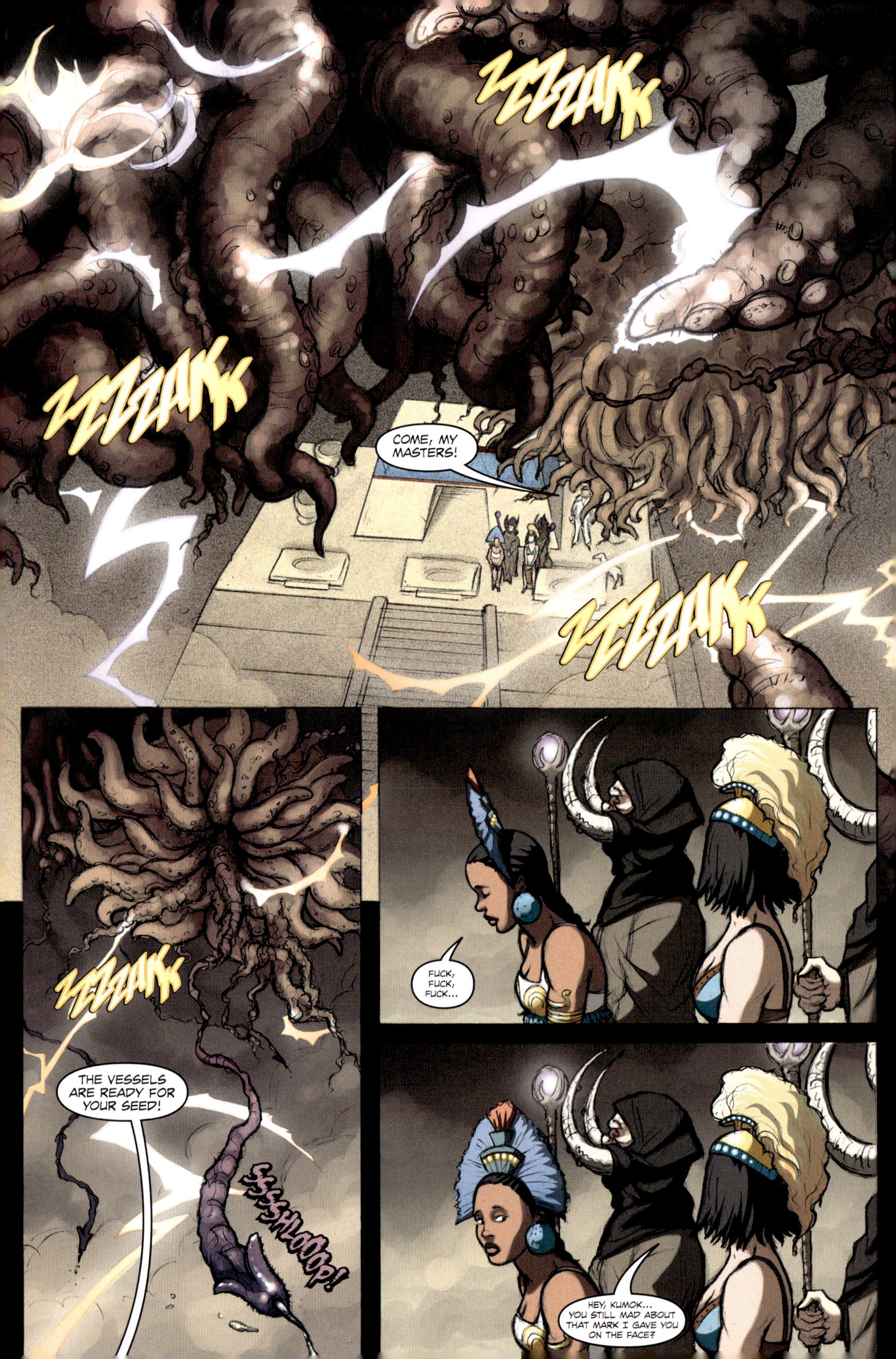
ZZZZAKK
ZZZZAKK
COME, MY MASTERS!
ZZZZAKK
ZZZZAKK
THE VESSELS ARE READY FOR YOUR SEED!
SSSSHLOOOP!
FUCK, FUCK, FUCK...
HEY, KUMOK... YOU STILL MAD ABOUT THAT MARK I GAVE YOU ON THE FACE?

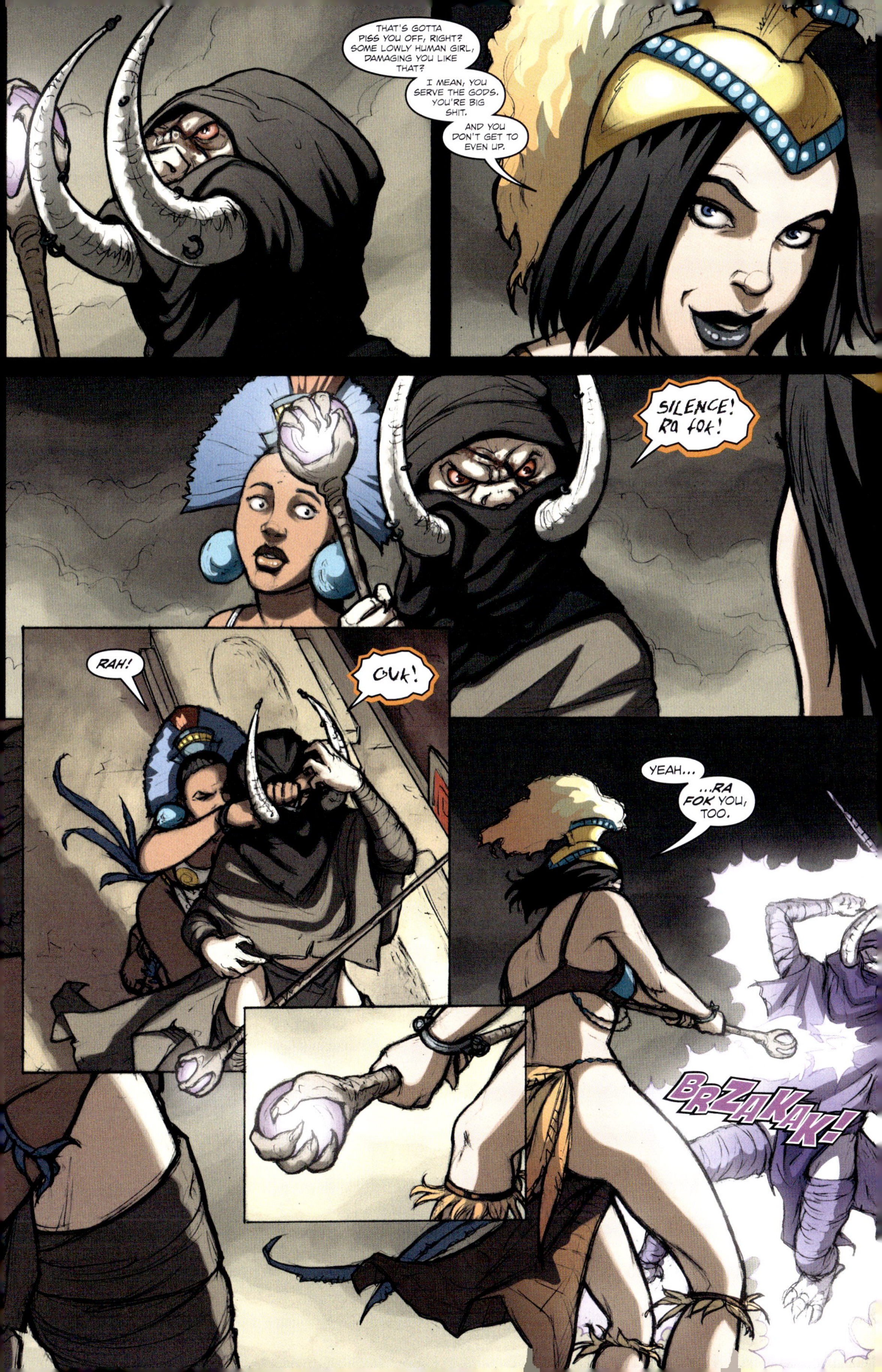
THAT'S GOTTA PISS YOU OFF, RIGHT? SOME LOWLY HUMAN GIRL, DAMAGING YOU LIKE THAT?
I MEAN, YOU SERVE THE GODS. YOU'RE BIG SHIT.
AND YOU DON'T GET TO EVEN UP.
SILENCE! RA FOK!
RAH!
OUK!
YEAH... ...RA FOK YOU, TOO.
BRZAKAK!

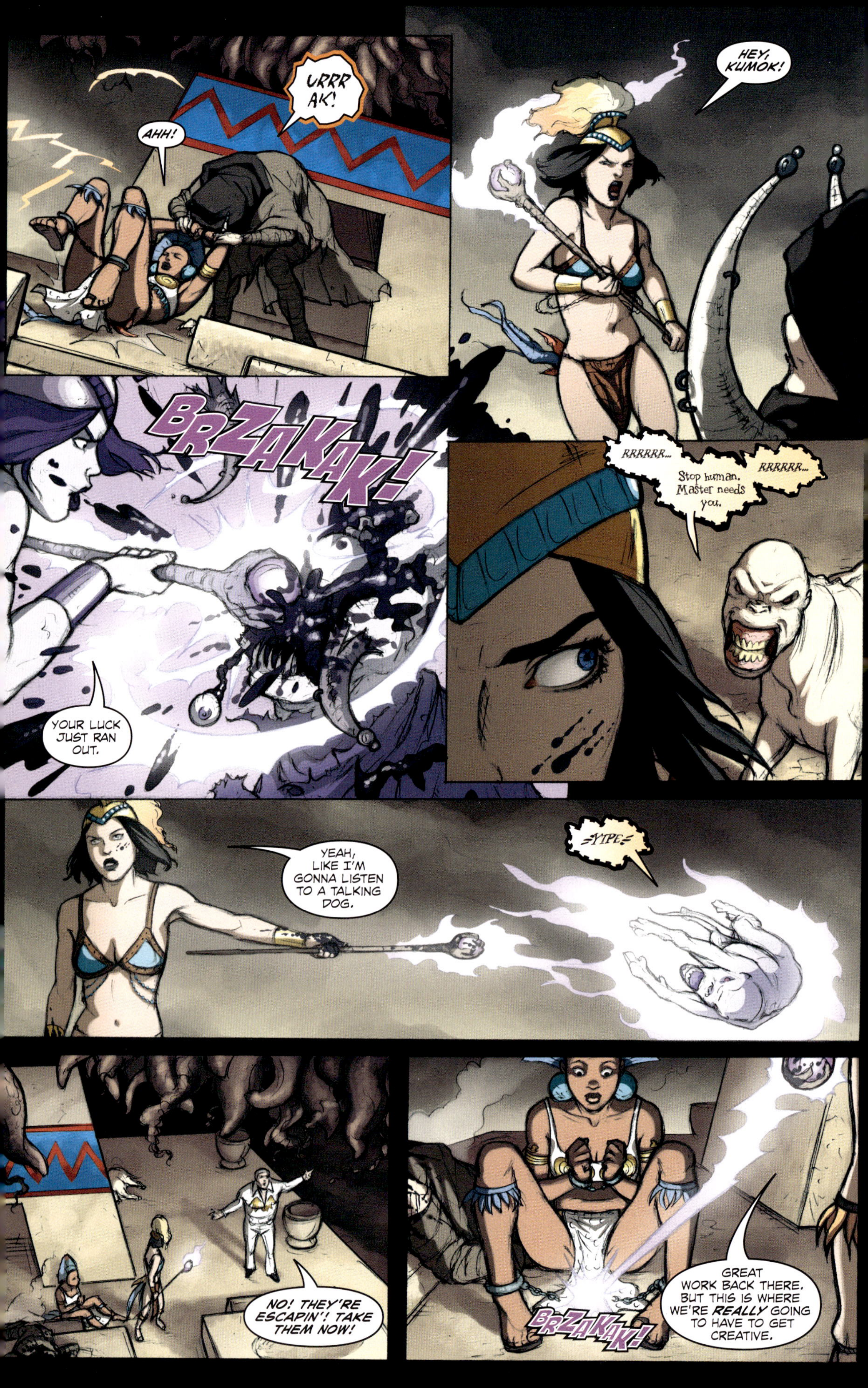
URRR AK!
AHH!
HEY, KUMOK!
BRZAKAK!
YOUR LUCK JUST RAN OUT.
RRRRRR...
Stop human. Master needs you.
RRRRRR...
YEAH, LIKE I'M GONNA LISTEN TO A TALKING DOG.
YIPE
NO! THEY'RE ESCAPIN'! TAKE THEM NOW!
GREAT WORK BACK THERE. BUT THIS IS WHERE WE'RE REALLY GOING TO HAVE TO GET CREATIVE.
BRZAKAK!

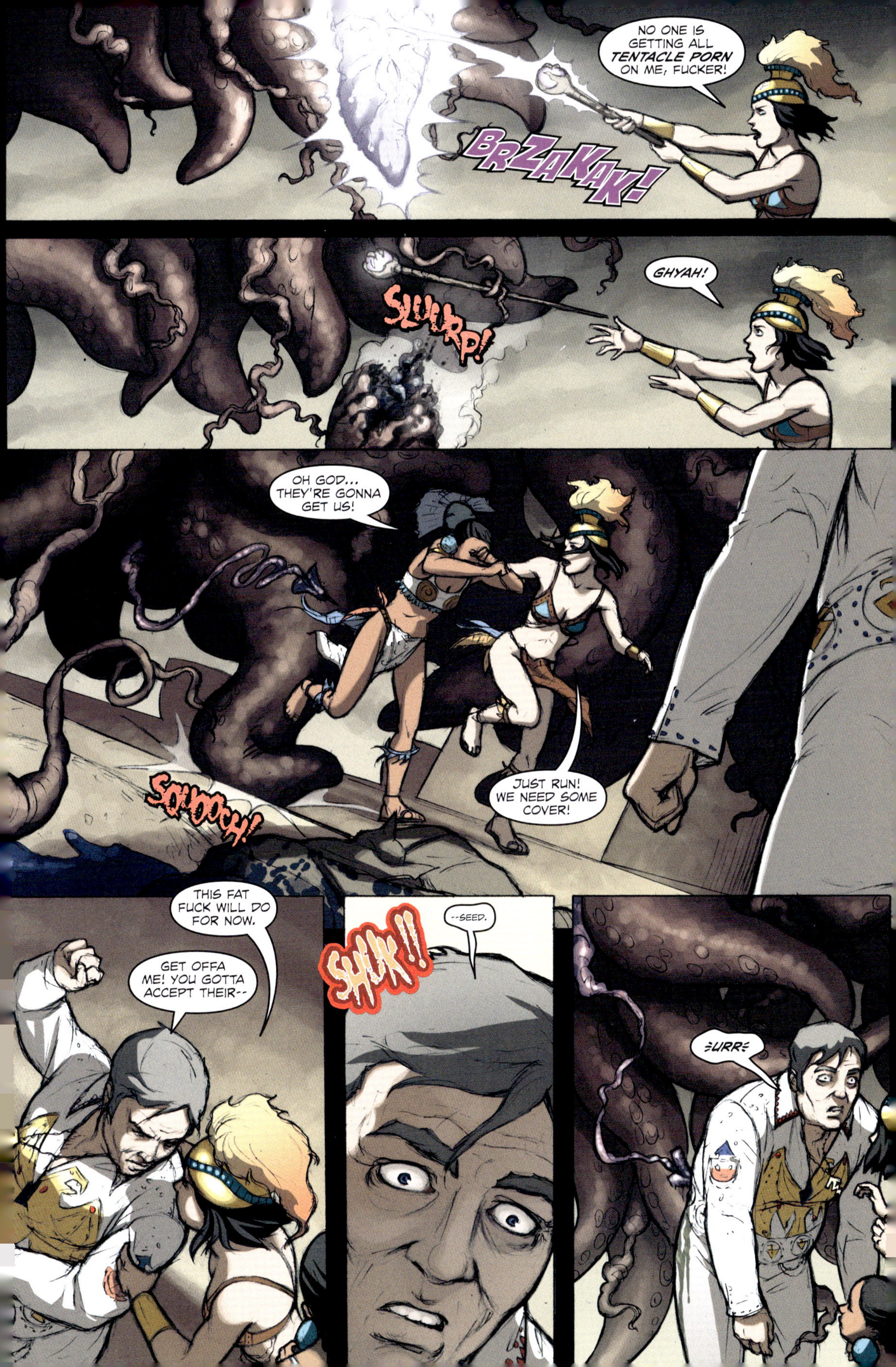
NO ONE IS GETTING ALL TENTACLE PORN ON ME, FUCKER!
BRZAKAK!
GHYAH!
SLUURP!
OH GOD... THEY'RE GONNA GET US!
JUST RUN! WE NEED SOME COVER!
SCHOOCH!
THIS FAT FUCK WILL DO FOR NOW.
GET OFFA ME! YOU GOTTA ACCEPT THEIR--
SHUK!!
--SEED.
URR

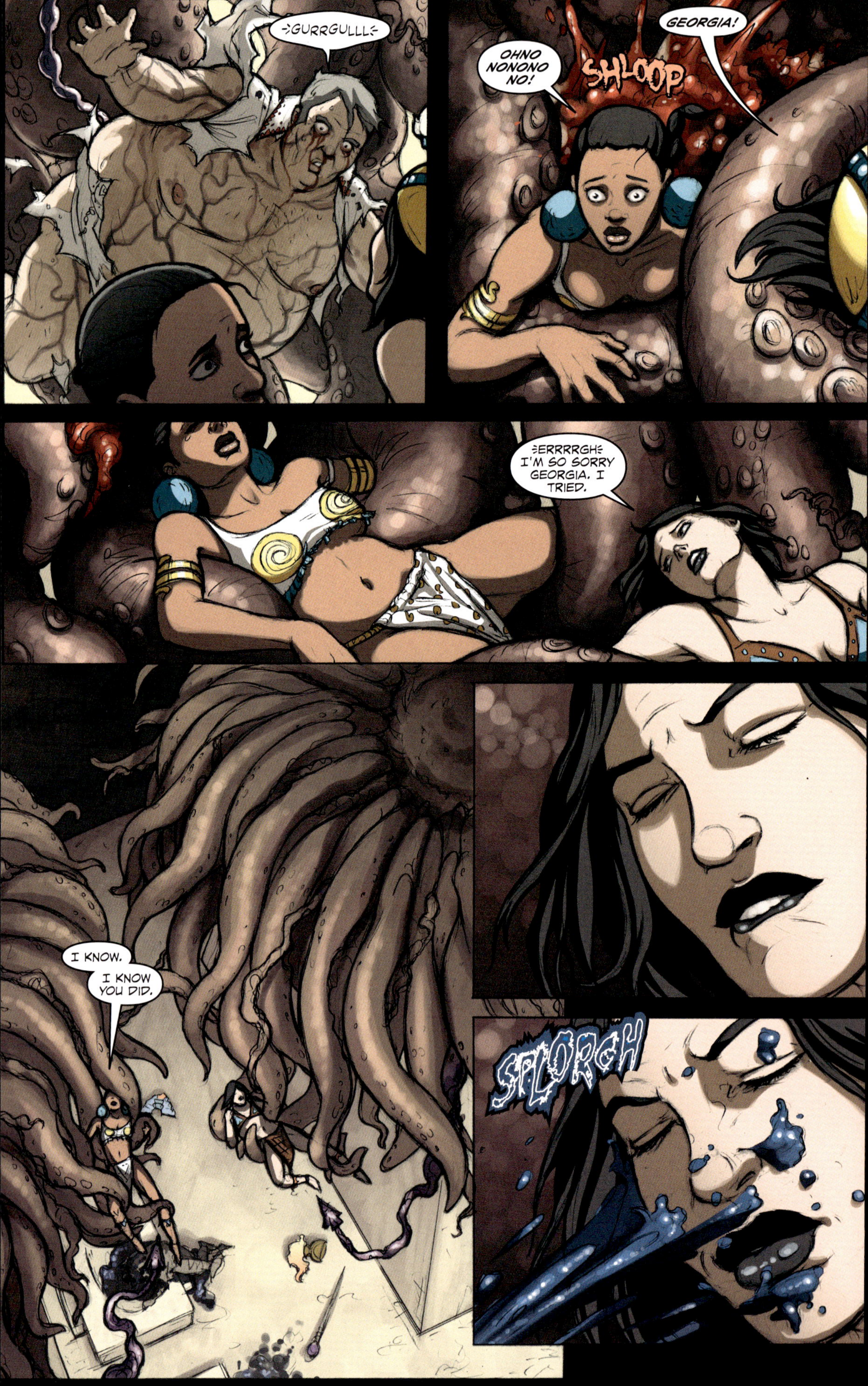

=GURRGULLL=
OHNO NONONO NO!
SHLOOP
GEORGIA!
=ERRRRGH= I'M SO SORRY GEORGIA. I TRIED.
I KNOW.
I KNOW YOU DID.
SPLORGH

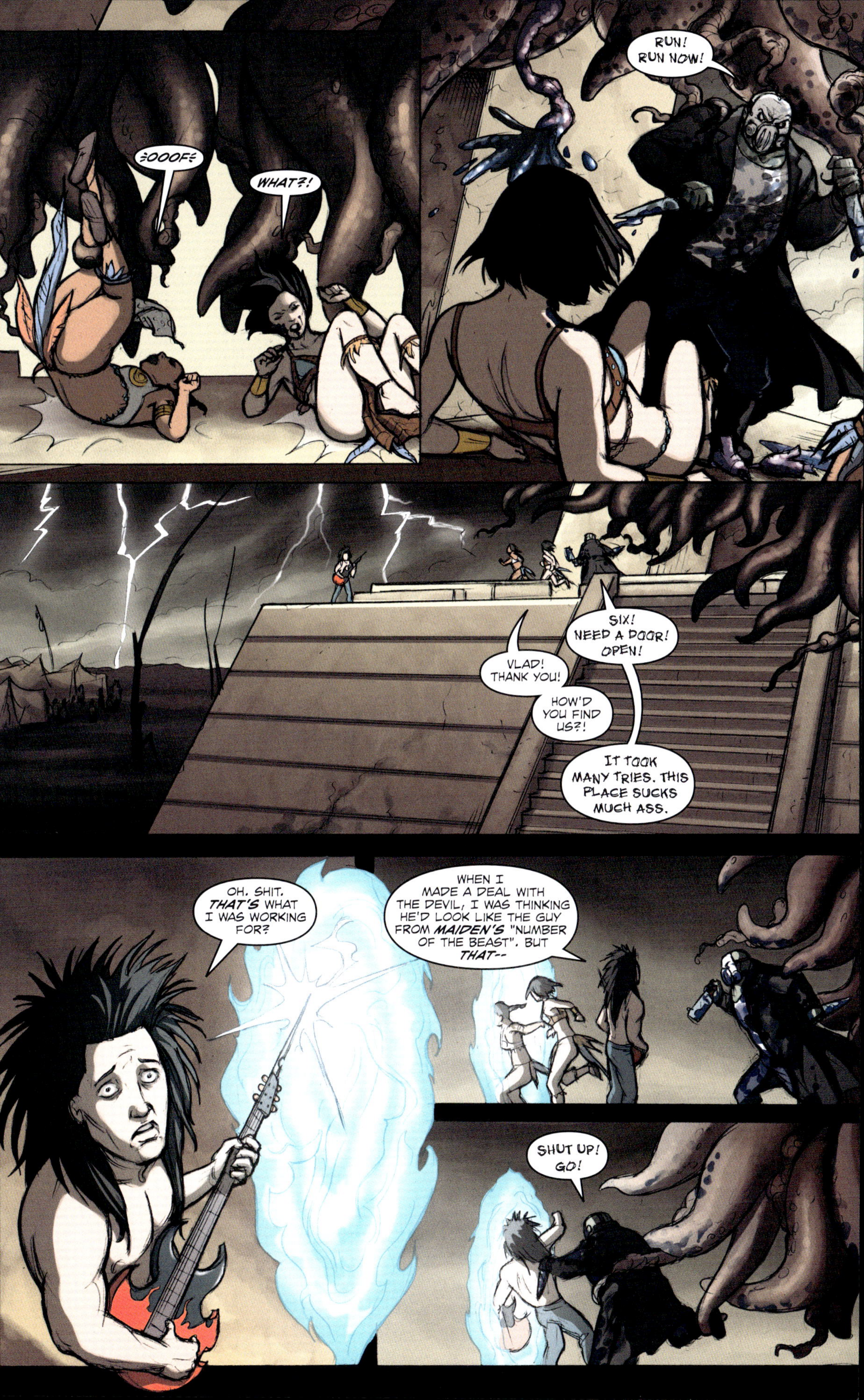
OOOF
WHAT?!
RUN! RUN NOW!
VLAD! THANK YOU!
SIX! NEED A DOOR! OPEN!
HOW'D YOU FIND US?!
IT TOOK MANY TRIES. THIS PLACE SUCKS MUCH ASS.
OH. SHIT. THAT'S WHAT I WAS WORKING FOR?
WHEN I MADE A DEAL WITH THE DEVIL, I WAS THINKING HE'D LOOK LIKE THE GUY FROM MAIDEN'S "NUMBER OF THE BEAST". BUT THAT--
SHUT UP! GO!

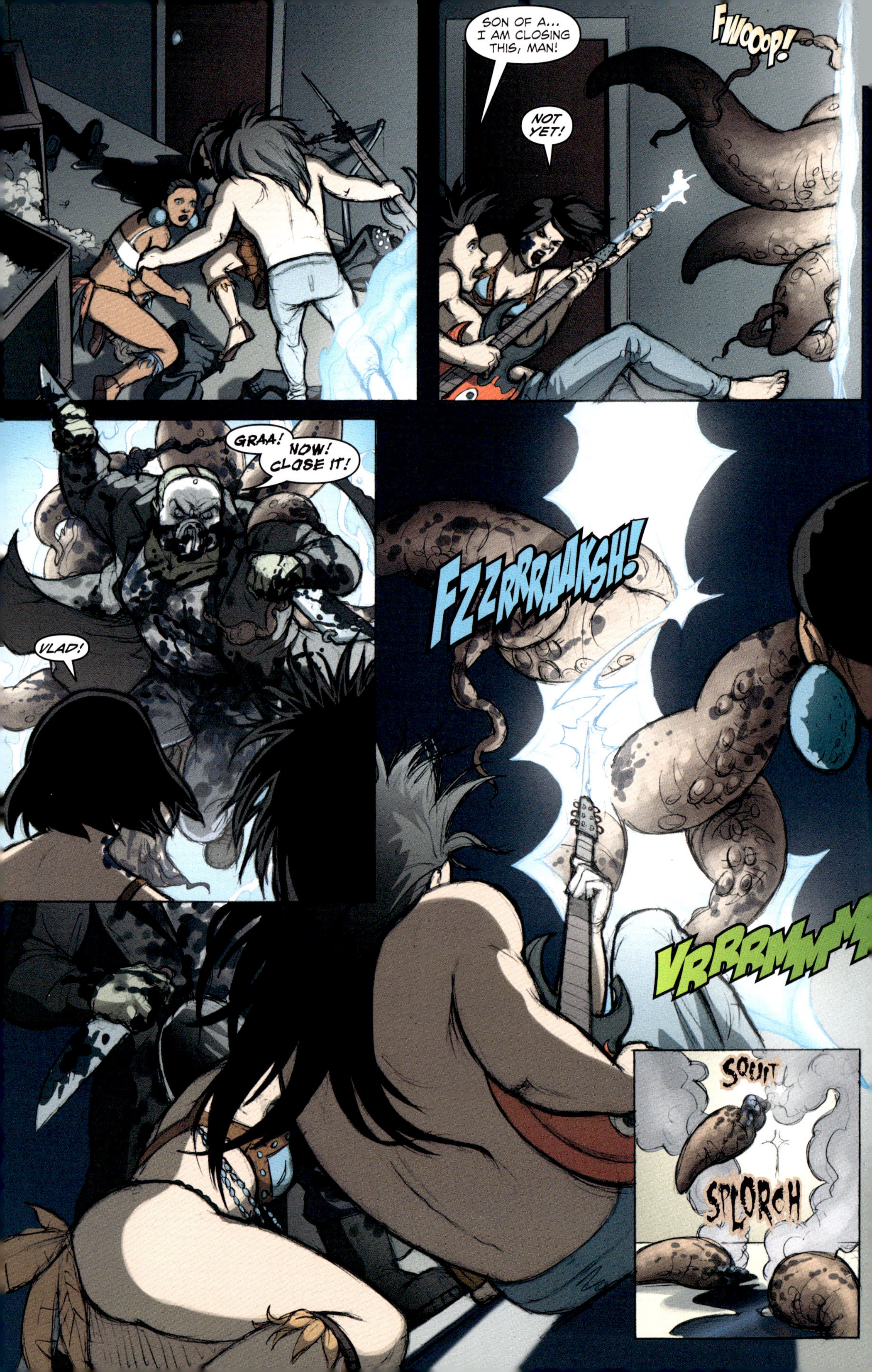
SON OF A... I AM CLOSING THIS, MAN!
FWOOOP!
NOT YET!
GRAA!
NOW! CLOSE IT!
VLAD!
FZZRRRAAKSH!
VRRRMMMM
SQUIT
SPLORCH

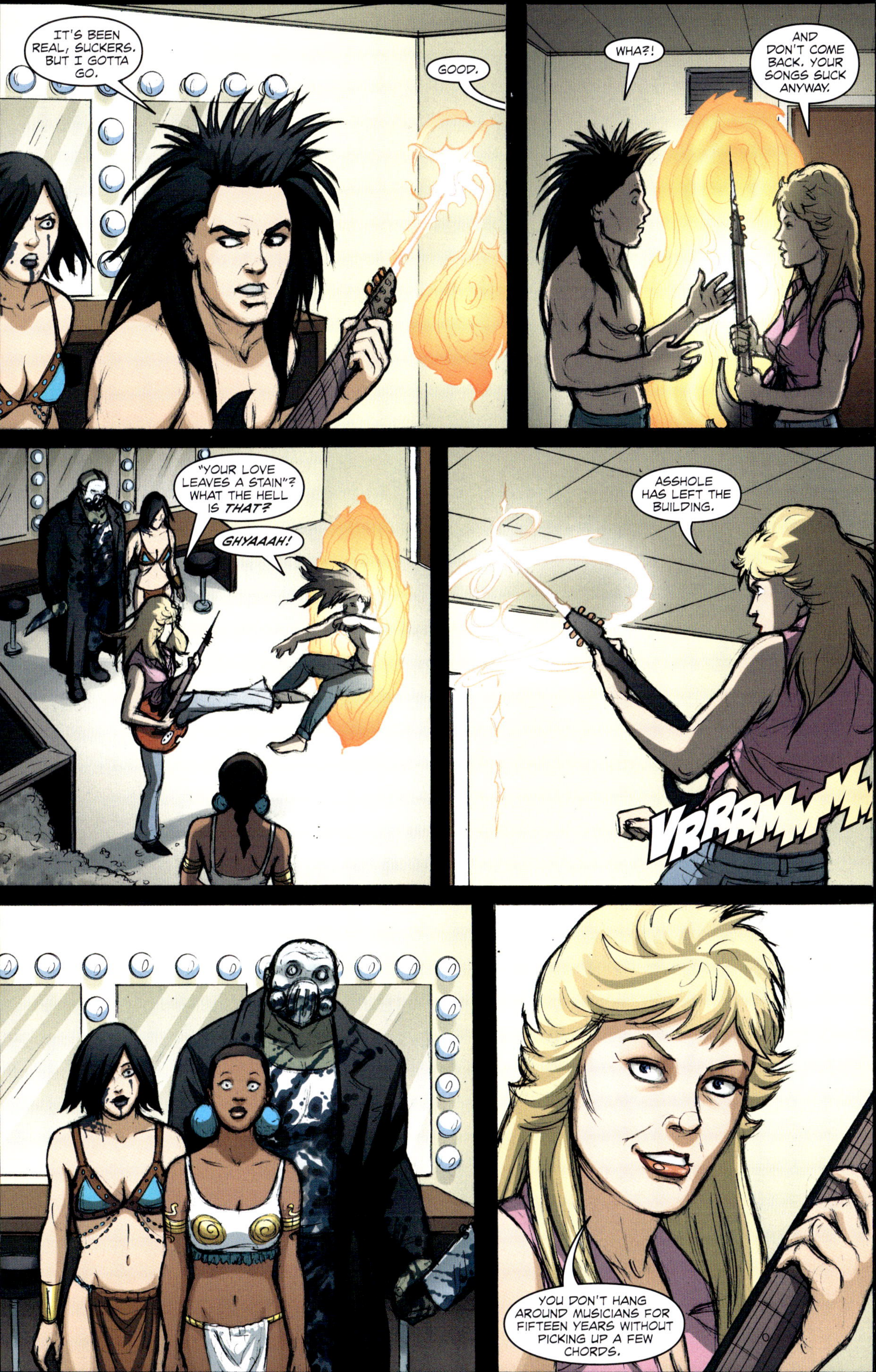

IT'S BEEN REAL, SUCKERS. BUT I GOTTA GO.
GOOD.
WHA?!
AND DON'T COME BACK. YOUR SONGS SUCK ANYWAY.
"YOUR LOVE LEAVES A STAIN"? WHAT THE HELL IS *THAT?*
GHYAAAH!
ASSHOLE HAS LEFT THE BUILDING.
VRRRMMMMM
YOU DON'T HANG AROUND MUSICIANS FOR FIFTEEN YEARS WITHOUT PICKING UP A FEW CHORDS.

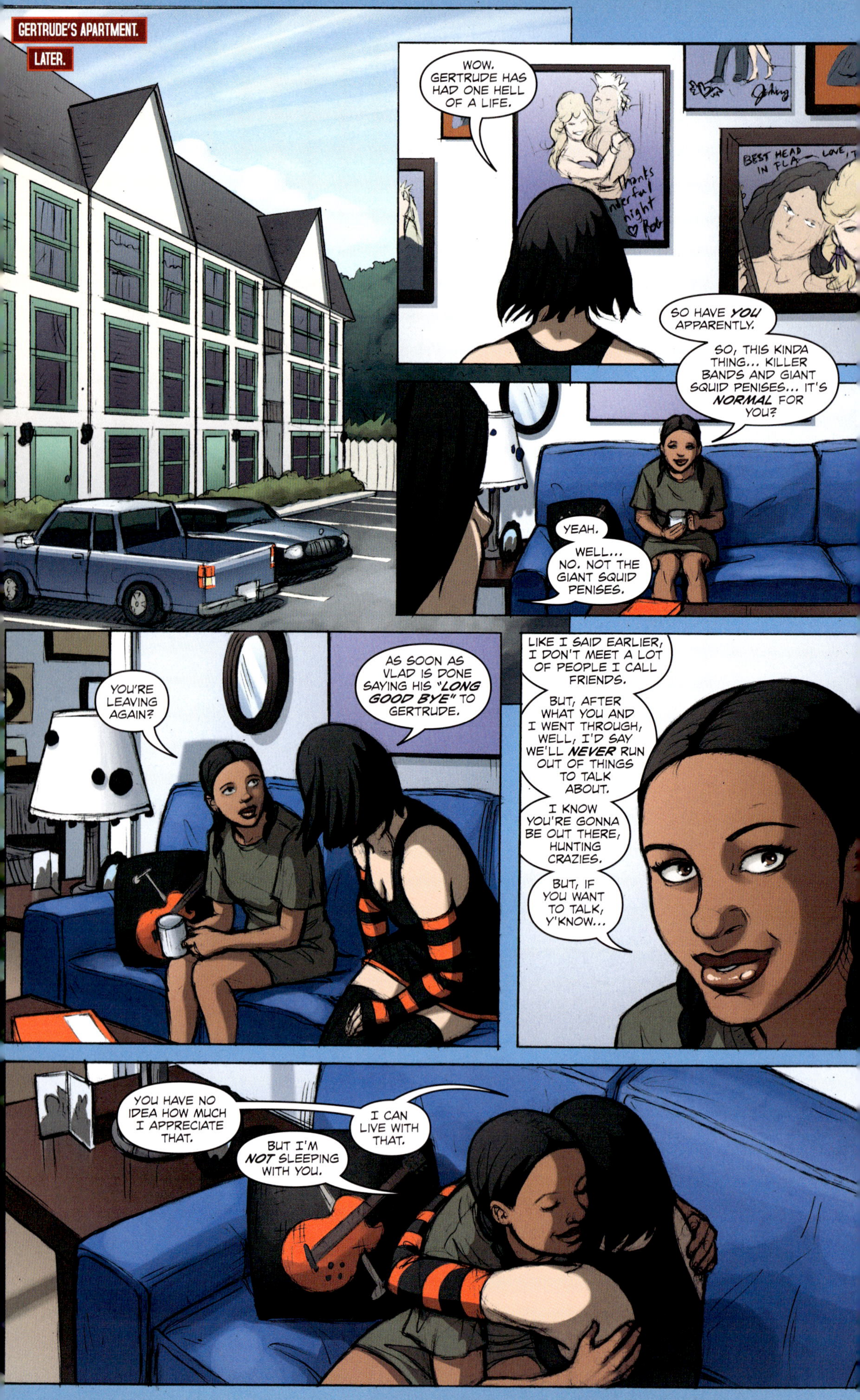
GERTRUDE'S APARTMENT.
LATER.
WOW. GERTRUDE HAS HAD ONE HELL OF A LIFE.
BEST HEAD IN FLA
SO HAVE *YOU* APPARENTLY.
SO, THIS KINDA THING... KILLER BANDS AND GIANT SQUID PENISES... IT'S *NORMAL* FOR YOU?
YEAH.
WELL... NO. NOT THE GIANT SQUID PENISES.
YOU'RE LEAVING AGAIN?
AS SOON AS VLAD IS DONE SAYING HIS "*LONG GOOD BYE*" TO GERTRUDE.
LIKE I SAID EARLIER, I DON'T MEET A LOT OF PEOPLE I CALL FRIENDS.
BUT, AFTER WHAT YOU AND I WENT THROUGH, WELL, I'D SAY WE'LL *NEVER* RUN OUT OF THINGS TO TALK ABOUT.
I KNOW YOU'RE GONNA BE OUT THERE, HUNTING CRAZIES.
BUT, IF YOU WANT TO TALK, Y'KNOW...
YOU HAVE NO IDEA HOW MUCH I APPRECIATE THAT.
BUT I'M *NOT* SLEEPING WITH YOU.
I CAN LIVE WITH THAT.

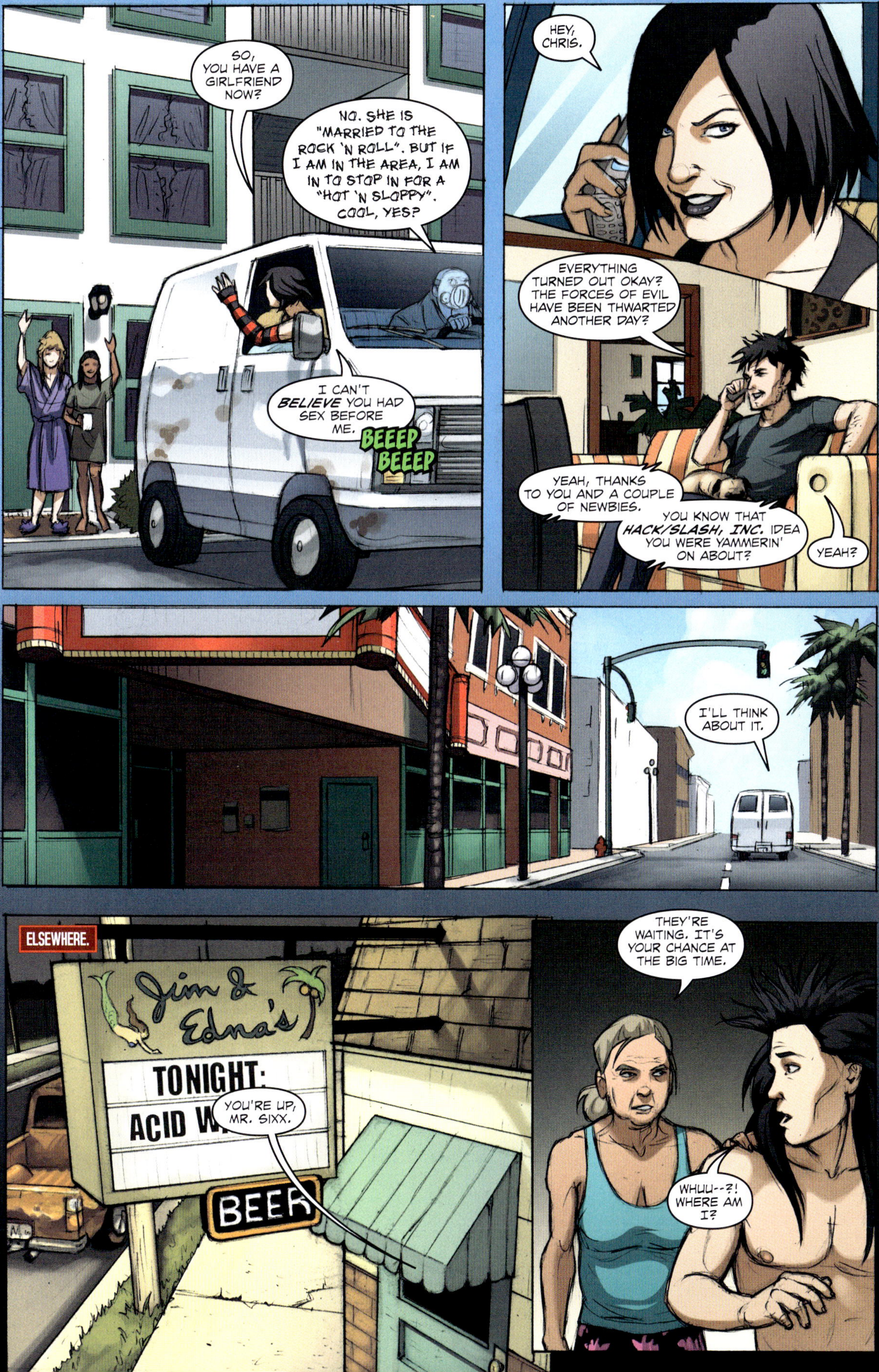
SO, YOU HAVE A GIRLFRIEND NOW?
NO. SHE IS "MARRIED TO THE ROCK 'N ROLL". BUT IF I AM IN THE AREA, I AM IN TO STOP IN FOR A "HOT 'N SLOPPY". COOL, YES?
I CAN'T BELIEVE YOU HAD SEX BEFORE ME.
BEEEP BEEEP
HEY, CHRIS.
EVERYTHING TURNED OUT OKAY? THE FORCES OF EVIL HAVE BEEN THWARTED ANOTHER DAY?
YEAH, THANKS TO YOU AND A COUPLE OF NEWBIES.
YOU KNOW THAT HACK/SLASH, INC. IDEA YOU WERE YAMMERIN' ON ABOUT?
YEAH?
I'LL THINK ABOUT IT.
ELSEWHERE.
Jim & Edna's
TONIGHT:
ACID W
YOU'RE UP, MR. SIXX.
BEER
THEY'RE WAITING. IT'S YOUR CHANCE AT THE BIG TIME.
WHUU--?! WHERE AM I?

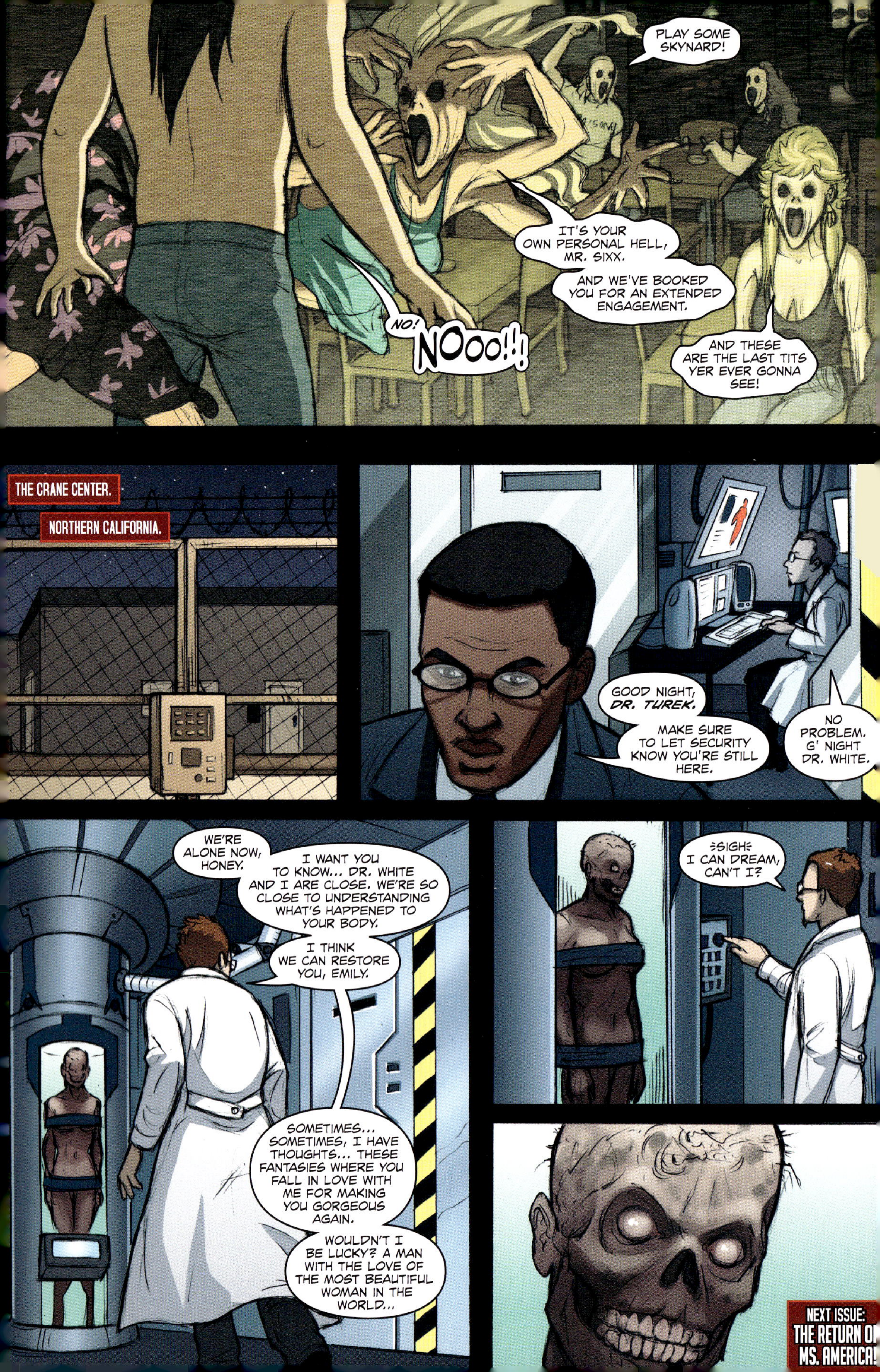
PLAY SOME SKYNARD!
IT'S YOUR OWN PERSONAL HELL, MR. SIXX.
AND WE'VE BOOKED YOU FOR AN EXTENDED ENGAGEMENT.
NO! NOOO!!!
AND THESE ARE THE LAST TITS YER EVER GONNA SEE!
THE CRANE CENTER.
NORTHERN CALIFORNIA.
GOOD NIGHT, DR. TUREK.
MAKE SURE TO LET SECURITY KNOW YOU'RE STILL HERE.
NO PROBLEM. G' NIGHT DR. WHITE.
WE'RE ALONE NOW, HONEY.
I WANT YOU TO KNOW... DR. WHITE AND I ARE CLOSE. WE'RE SO CLOSE TO UNDERSTANDING WHAT'S HAPPENED TO YOUR BODY.
I THINK WE CAN RESTORE YOU, EMILY.
SOMETIMES... SOMETIMES, I HAVE THOUGHTS... THESE FANTASIES WHERE YOU FALL IN LOVE WITH ME FOR MAKING YOU GORGEOUS AGAIN.
WOULDN'T I BE LUCKY? A MAN WITH THE LOVE OF THE MOST BEAUTIFUL WOMAN IN THE WORLD...
SIGH
I CAN DREAM, CAN'T I?
NEXT ISSUE: THE RETURN OF MS. AMERICA!

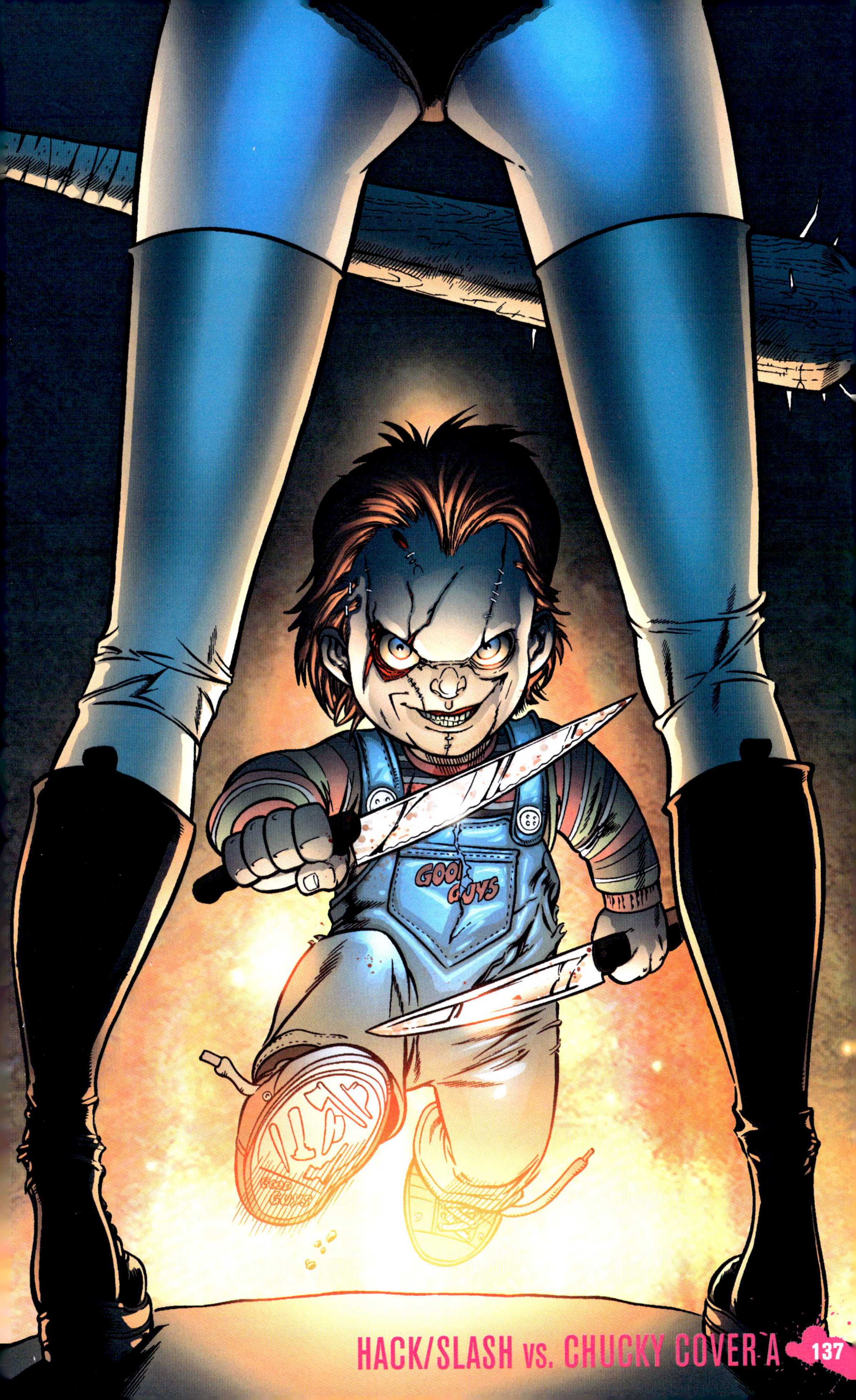
GOOD GUYS

HACK/SLASH vs. CHUCKY COVER A

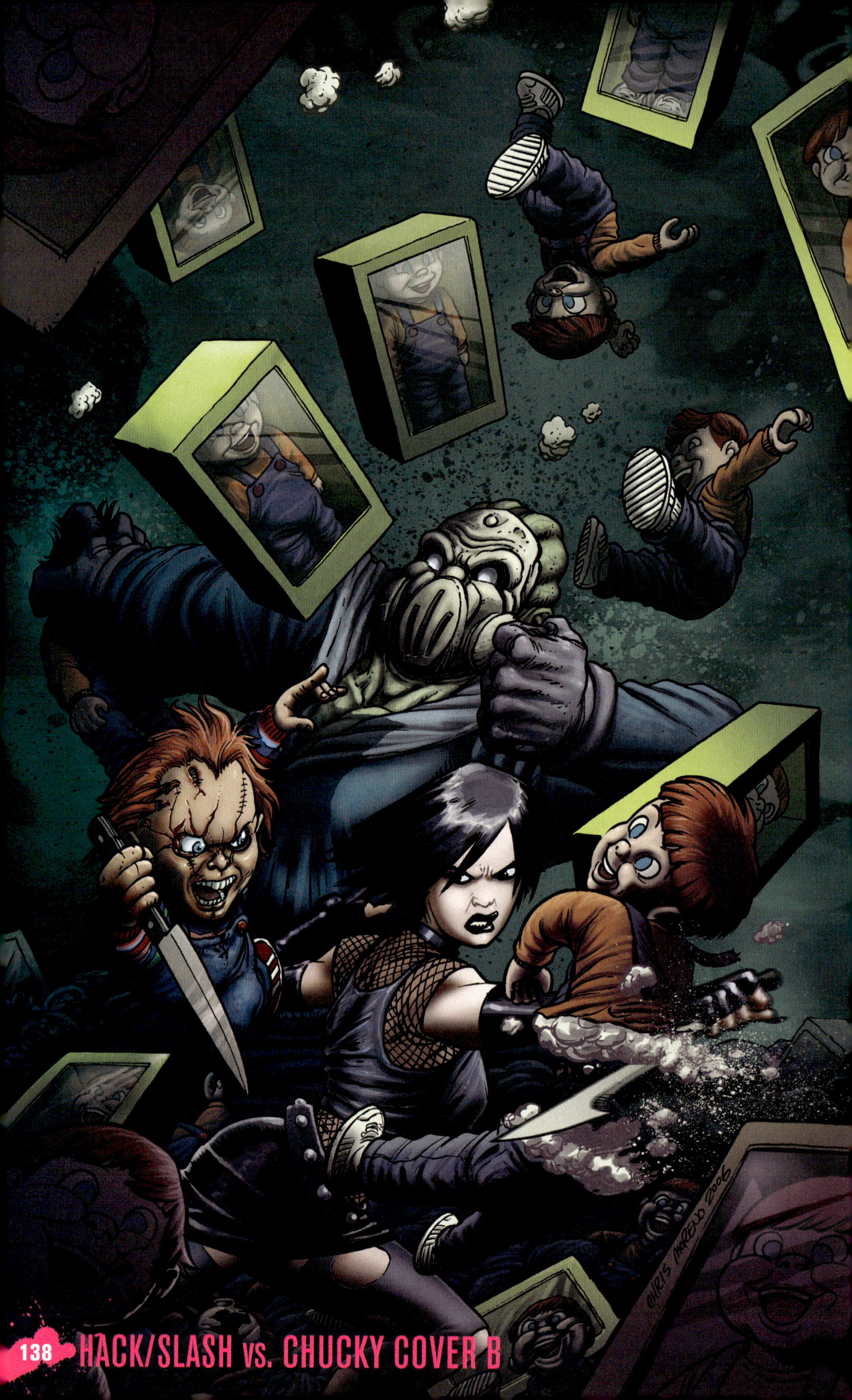
CHRIS MORENO 2006

HACK/SLASH vs. CHUCKY COVER B

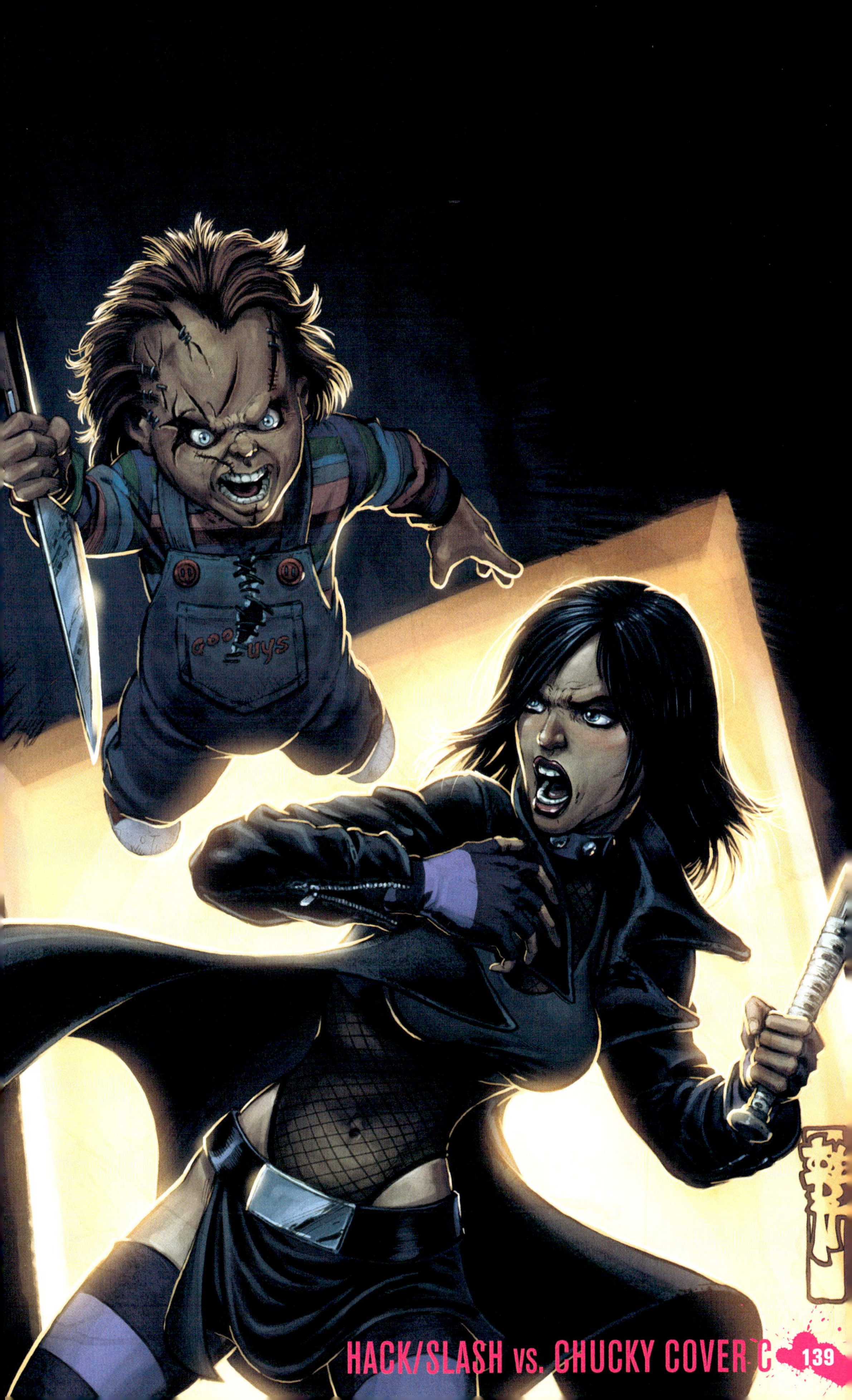

HACK/SLASH vs. CHUCKY COVER C

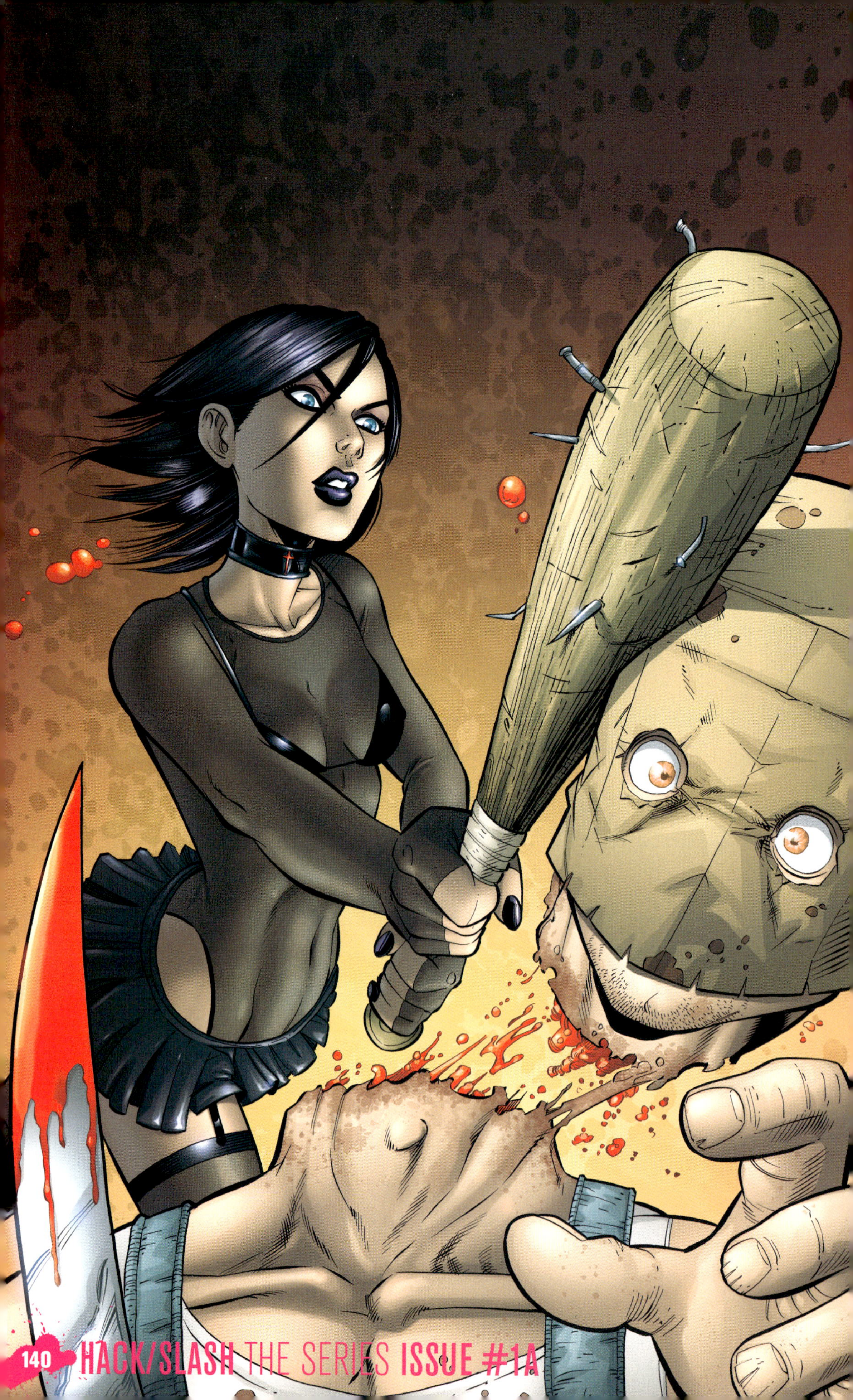

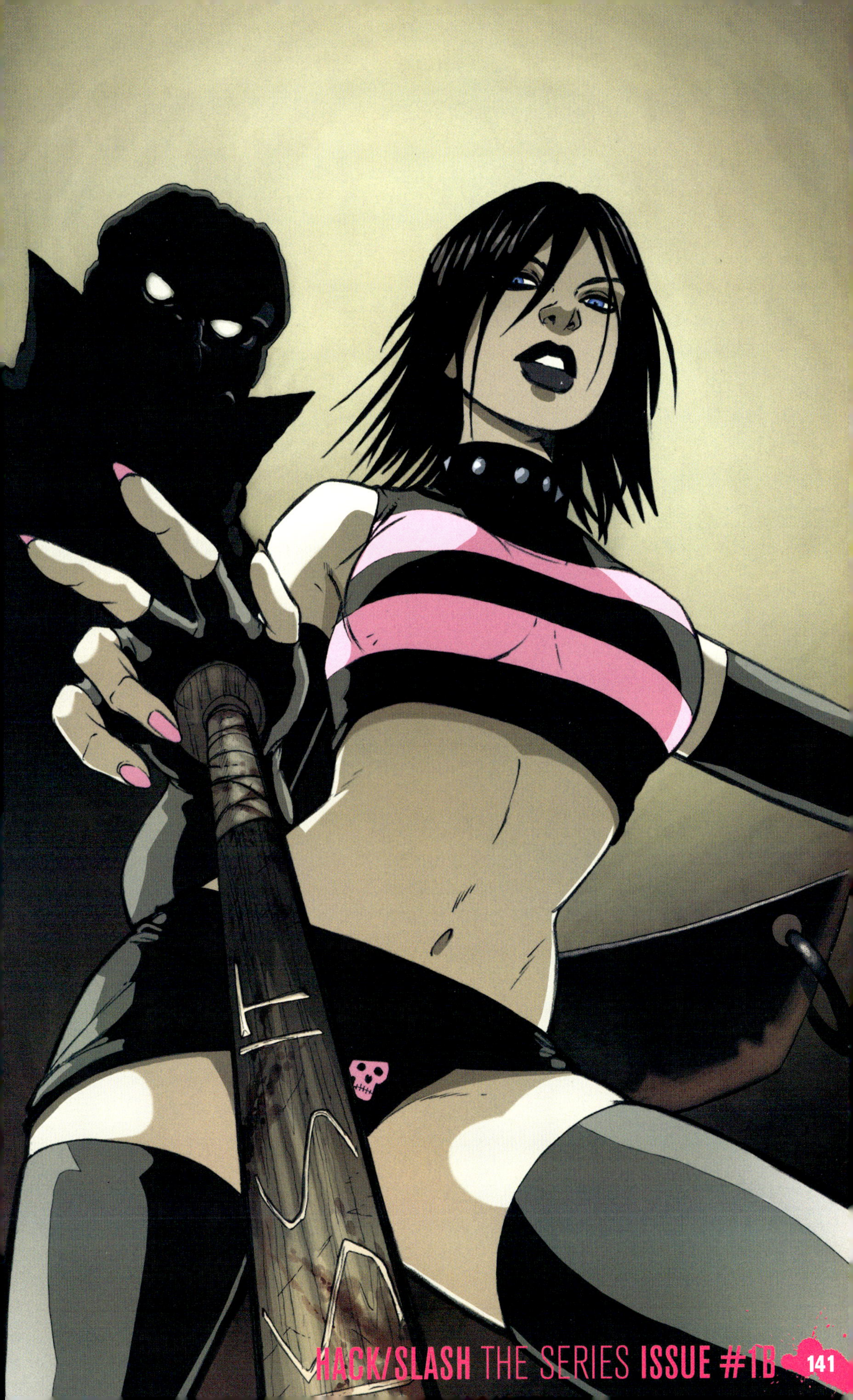

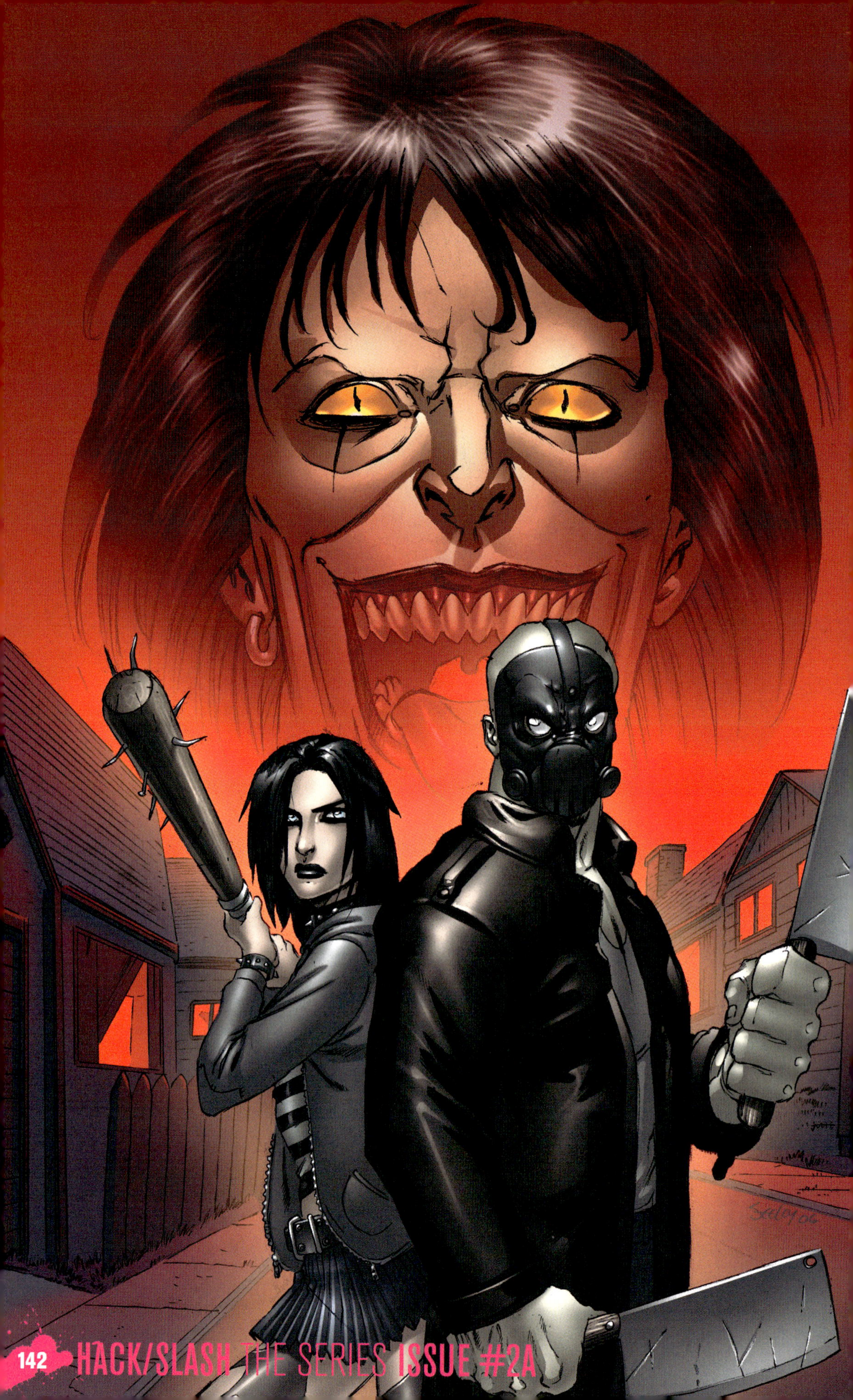

HACK/SLASH THE SERIES ISSUE #2A

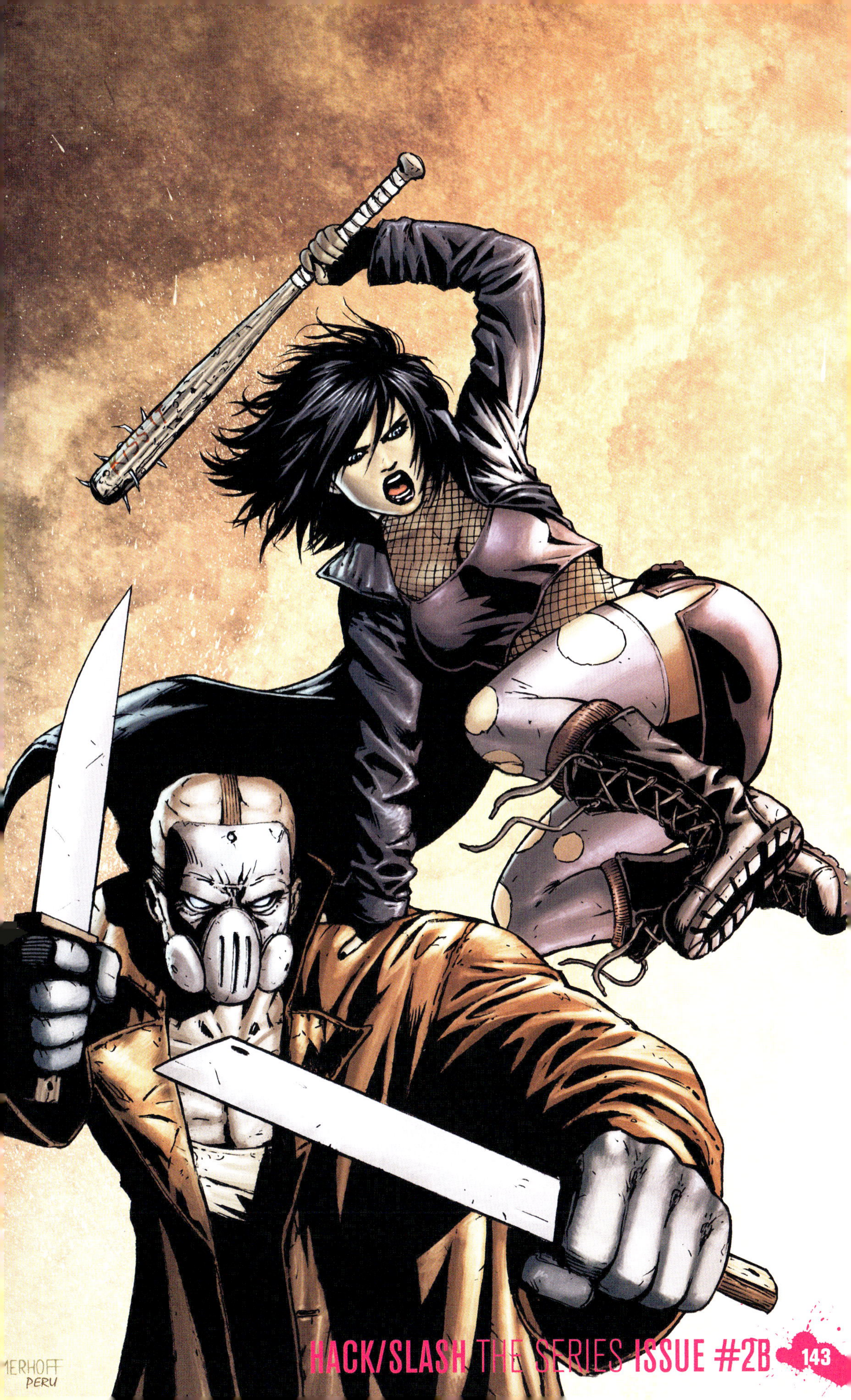
ERHOFF
PERU

HACK/SLASH THE SERIES ISSUE #2B

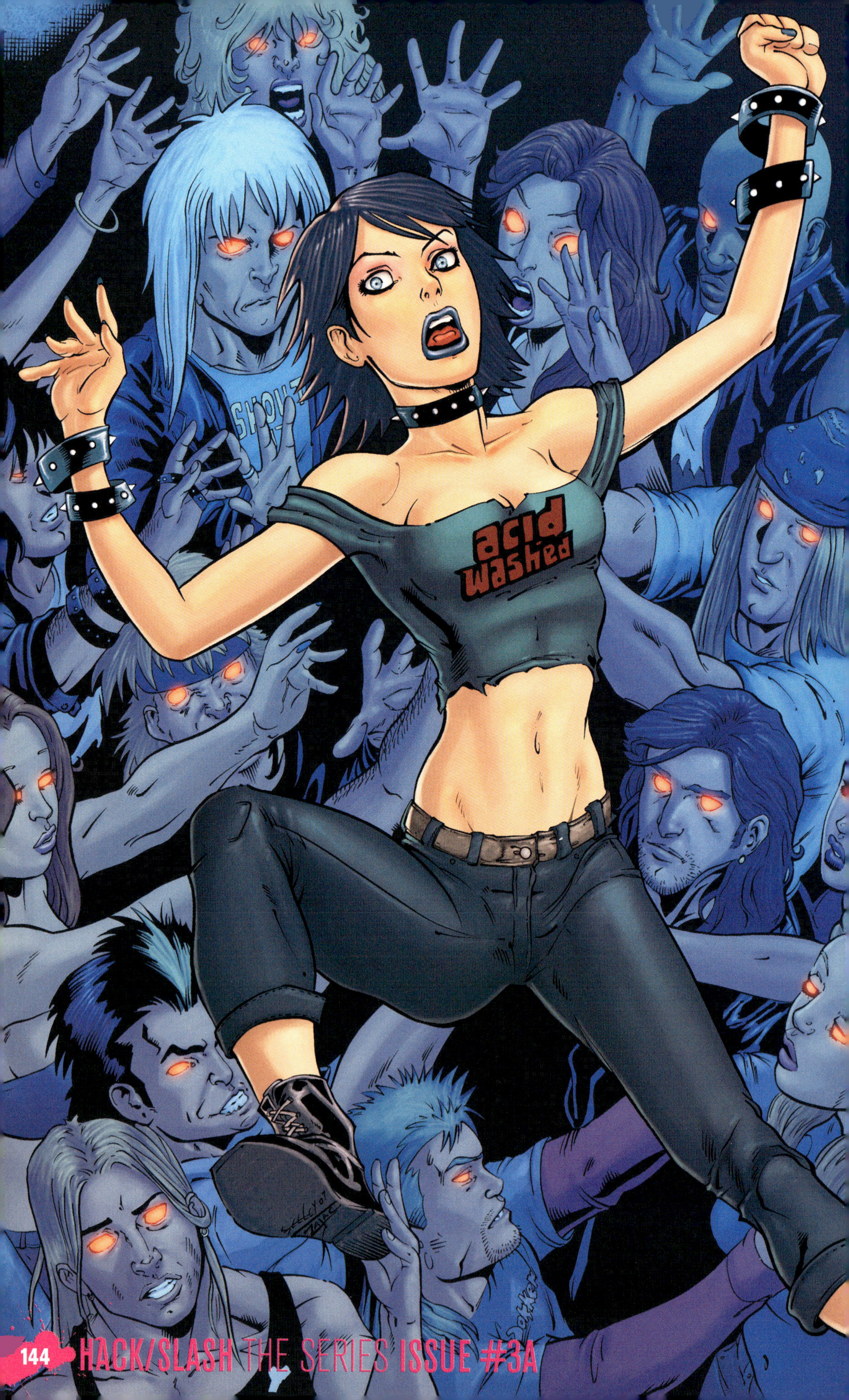
acid
washed

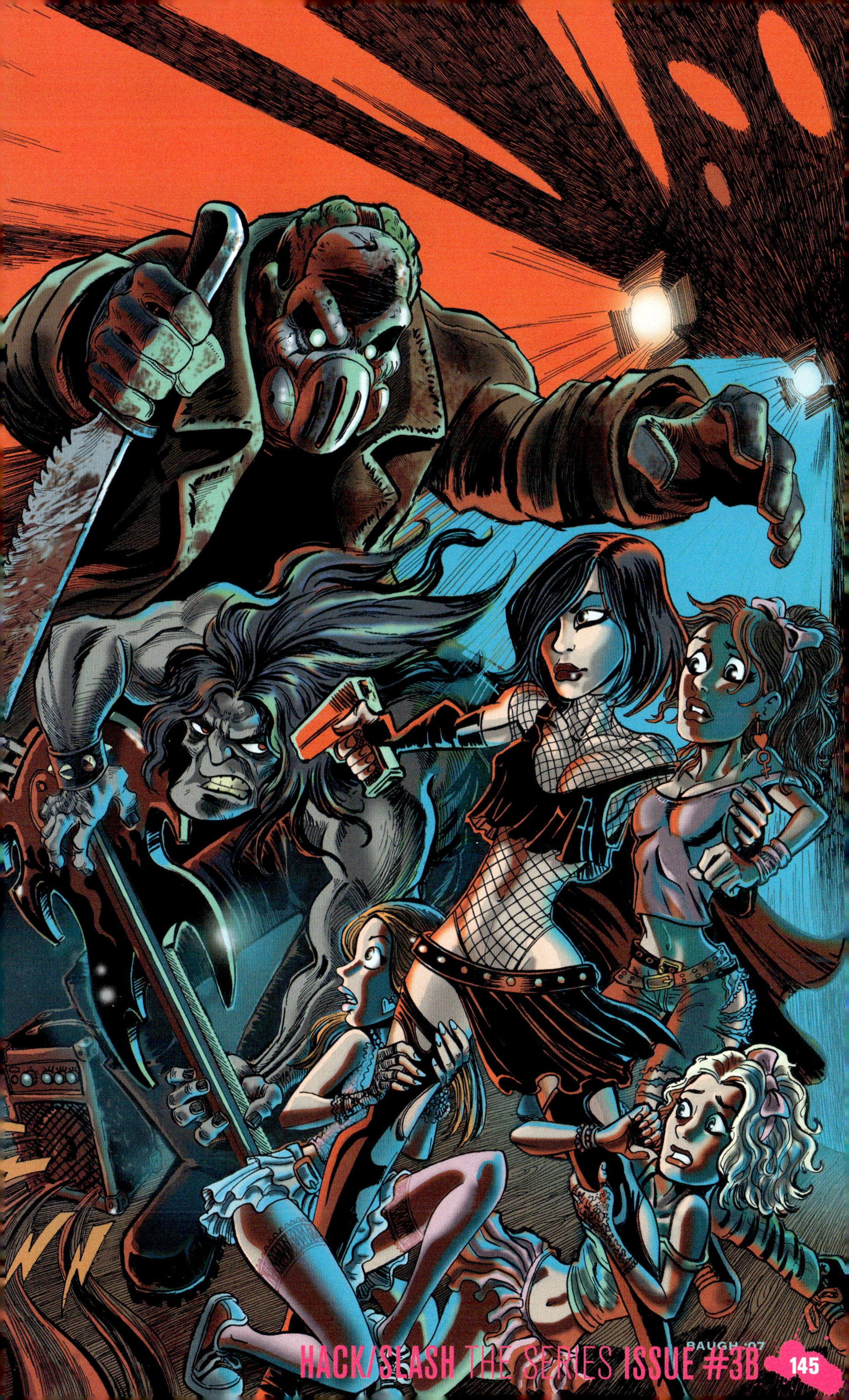
BAUGH '07

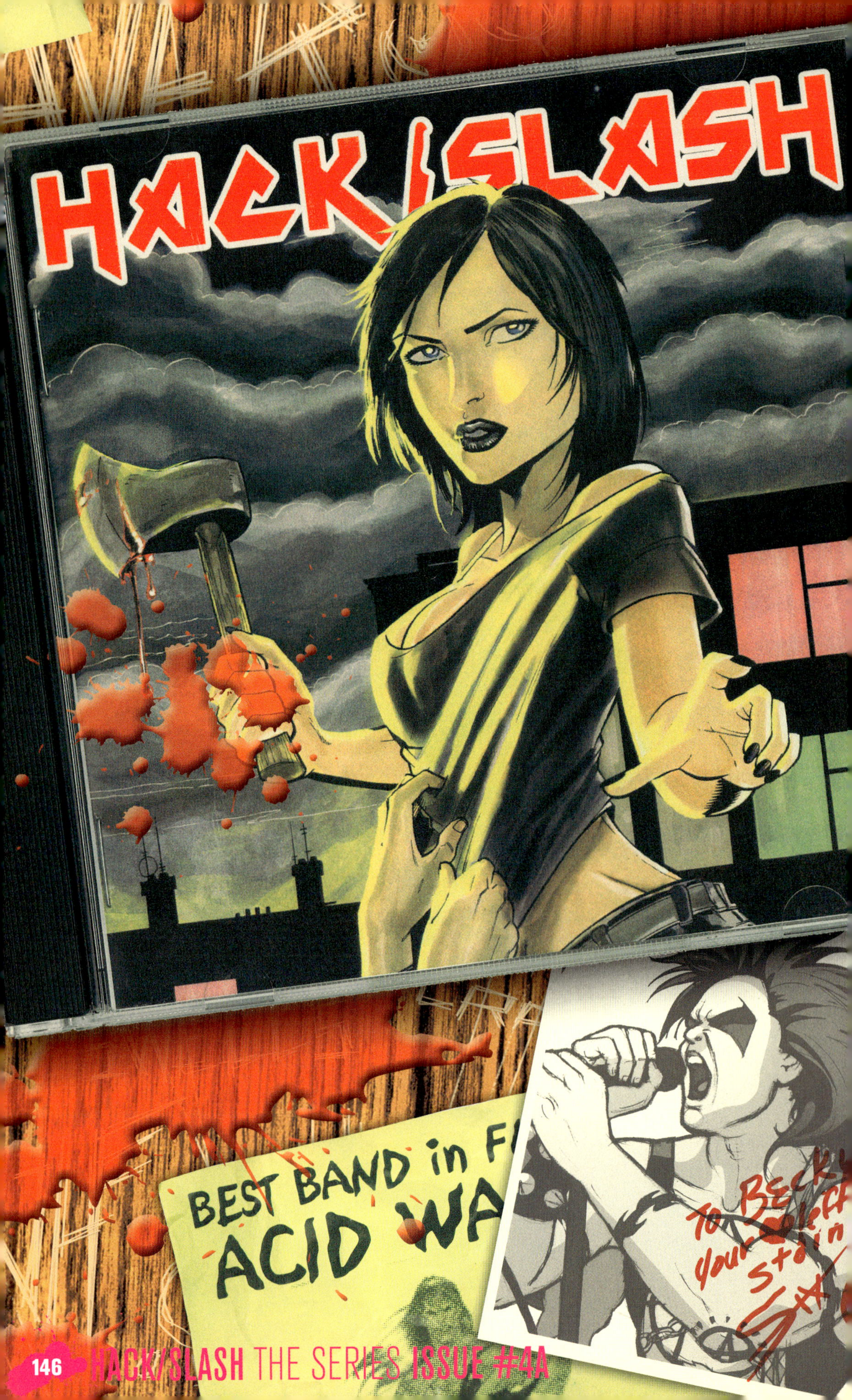
HACK/SLASH
BEST BAND in F
ACID WA

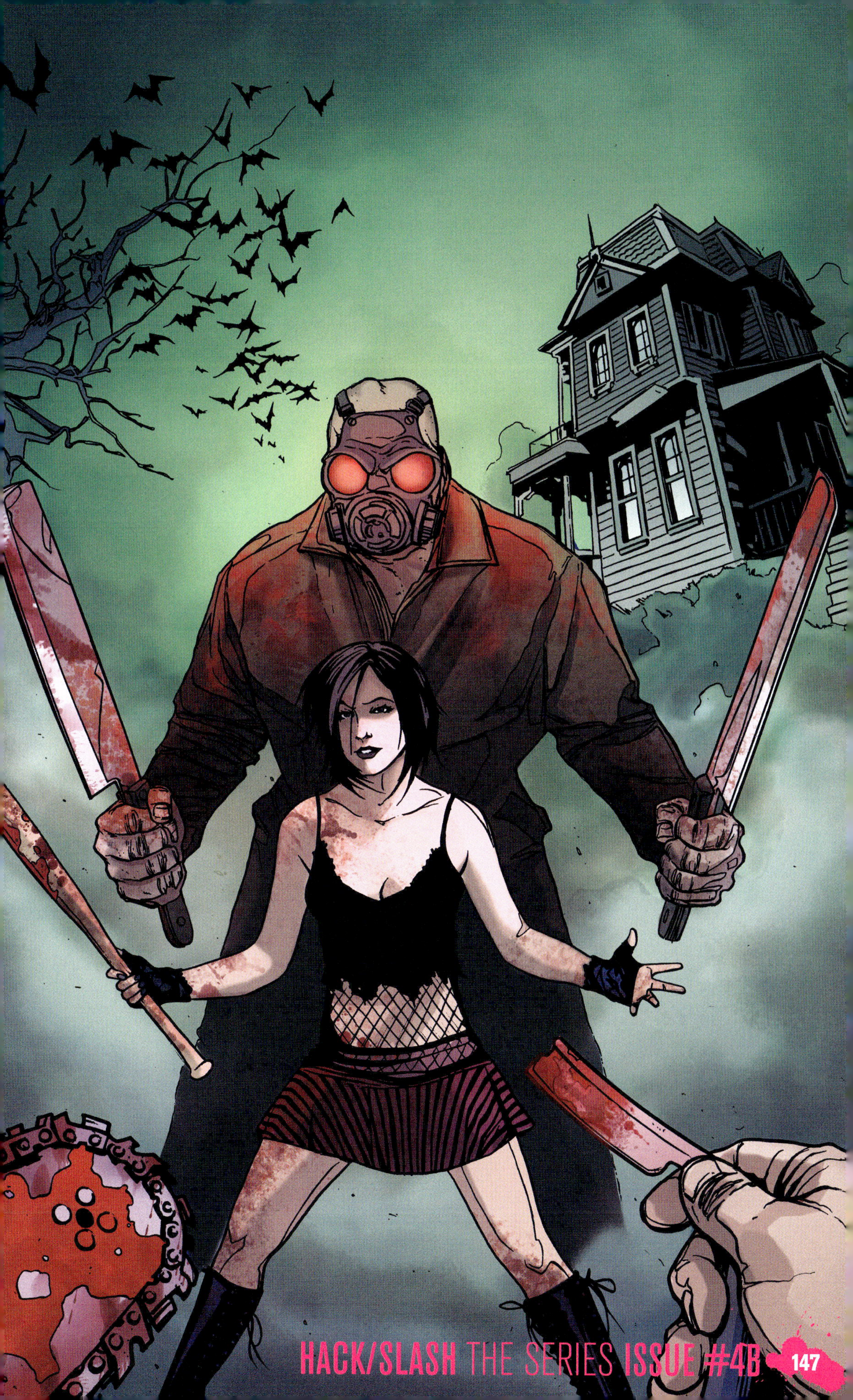

CHUCKY

Real Name: Charles Lee Ray
Death by: Gun Shot
Pre-Slasher Occupation: Criminal, voodoo practicioner
Slasher type: Possessed Object/Vengeful ghoul

Special Abilities: Chucky has a unique phsiology, in that his body is built like that of a doll but contains some organic/human-like organs. He is also adept in the use of Voodoo magic.

Slasher weapon: Anything he can get his hands on, often a knife

Body Count: In the 40s

The Story: On November 9, 1988, while fleeing police, Charles Lee Ray, the notorious "Lakeshore Strangler", was shot and mortally wounded by Federal Detective Mike Norris. Before dying, Charles tooks cover inside a toy store which had a sale on "Good Guy" dolls, and used a voodoo ritual in order to transfer his soul into one of the dolls. The store was then struck by lightning, and it burned to the ground. Before the death of his human body, Ray had randomly murdered several people, many of whom simply got in his way. For ten years he attempted to use six-year-old Andy Barclay's body to harbor his soul because, as required by the magic, Andy was the first person to whom Chucky revealed his identity.
Finding Chucky's broken doll body ten years later, Tiffany, an old girlfriend, reassembled and reanimated him. When Chucky admitted that he never intended to marry her, Tiffany imprisoned him, but Chucky managed to escape. He electrocuted Tiffany, and transfered her soul into a bride doll. After reconciling, the couple embarked on a murder spree, culminating at the cemetery where Chucky's human body was buried, as they needed to get an amulet (called "The Heart of Damballa") in order to transfer their souls into human bodies. But Tiffany had other plans -- she slyly asked Chucky to kiss her before they appropriated human form, but suddenly grabbed his knife and stabbed him. The two dolls fought to the death, after which Tiffany was discovered by a cop. Tiffany managed give birth to a baby doll, dying shortly afterward. Chucky and Tiffany eventually reconciled again to raise their son/daughter, but this also resulted in Chucky being cut into pieces and stored in a police evidence locker. (from WIKIPEDIA.com)

"I searched through a lot of gator shit, and I can't say for sure Chucky is dead.

All I know, is that if he's still alive, I'll spend the rest of my life watching my back... or... well... the back of my calves."

148 HACK/SLASH PSYCHOFILES

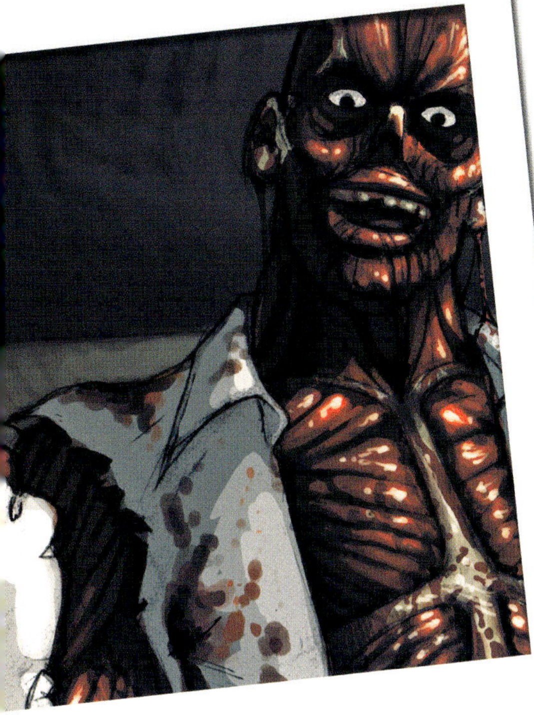

DR. GROSS

Real Name: Dr. Edmund Gross
Death by: N/A
Pre-Slasher Occupation: Psychologist, College Professor.
Slasher type: Obsessive Nutjob

Special Abilities: Dr. Gross possesses a resistance to pain and a keen intellect.

Slasher weapon: Surgical tools

Body Count: 12

The Story: Dr. Gross was a professor at a prestigious Atlanta university, who regularly used hypnosis to sexually assault his students. When several students discovered photos of what he'c done to them, they decided to turn them in. Gross prevented this by killing each of them. Gross was arrested, placed on trial and sent to jail. While imprisoned he began a bizarre self-analyzation which ultimatedly led to him skinning himself in order to be closer to his "true self." Gross was removed from prison, and taken to a psychiatric hospital from which he escaped. He then set about murdering a number of his other students, occasionally convincing them to commit suicide or skin themselves.

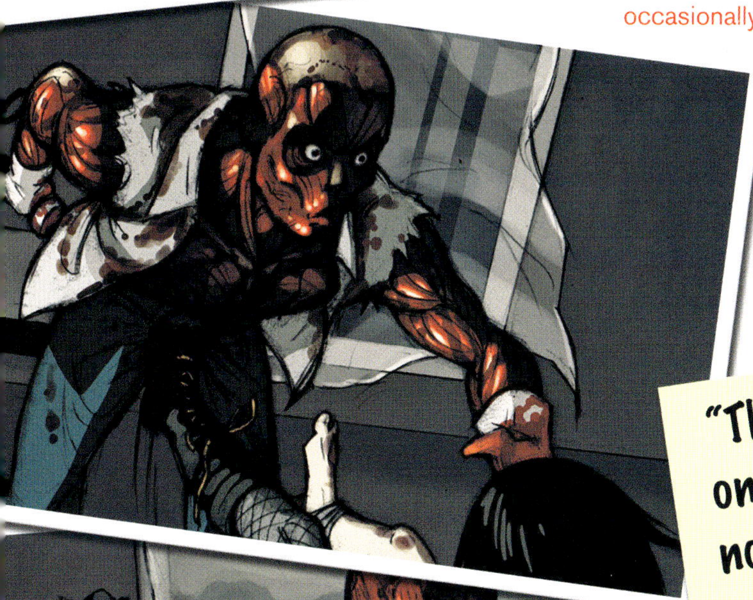

"This asshole was one sick fuck, and now I get to think of him anytime I try to wear sandals."

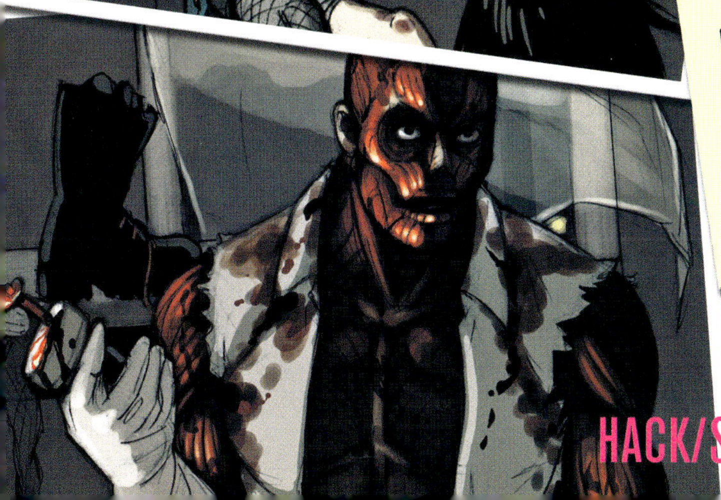

SIX SIXX

Real Name: Jeffrey Brevard
Death by: N/A
Pre-Slasher Occupation: part time musician, part time lawn care specialist
Slasher type: Faust

Special Abilities: Six is able to manipulate a variety of otherworldly magicks which appear to alter probabilities in his favor as well as granting him musical skill. The same magicks allow him to open interdimensional portals, and fire bolts of destructive energy.

Slasher weapon: Black Magick Guitar

Body Count: 14

The Story: Jeffrey Brevard was a small town Floridian with big dreams of taking the musical world by storm. A terrible student, who largely got by on his looks, Brevard formed Acid Washed, a decidedly retro hair metal band, intended to evoke the halcyon days of rock n'roll. The band, largely known for it's unispired musicianship and terrible song lyrics booked only a few shows around Florida in three years until they met the mysterious benefactor who introduced them to a dark power.

"As bad as this guy sucked, I'd still rather hear Acid Washed than anything by Avril Lavigne."

150 HACK/SLASH PSYCHOFILES

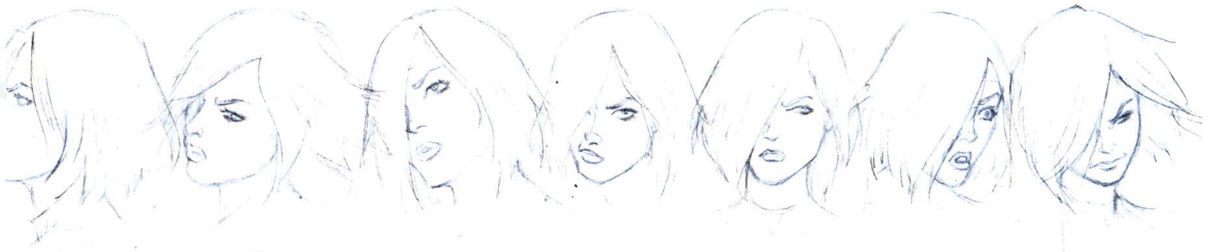

Here you can get a good look at Emily's early sketches for Cassie and Vlad. She nailed Cassie right away, and the "Paper Doll" is one of my favorite drawings she's done. Her early sketches of Vlad show him sort of more "realistically" deformed.

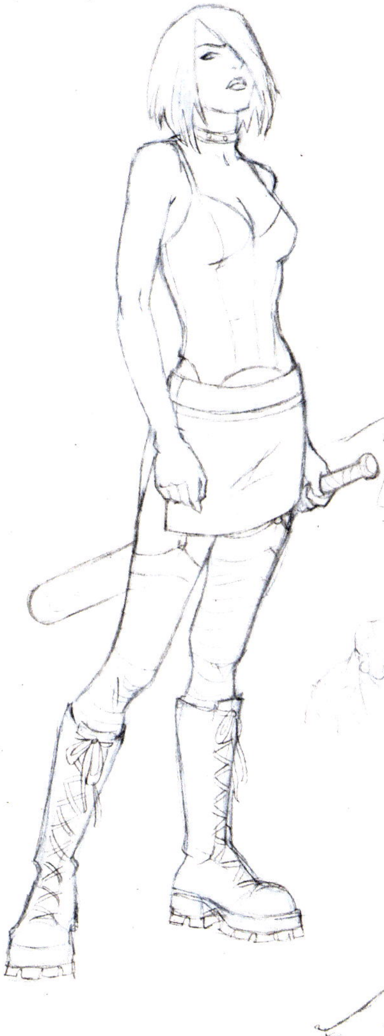

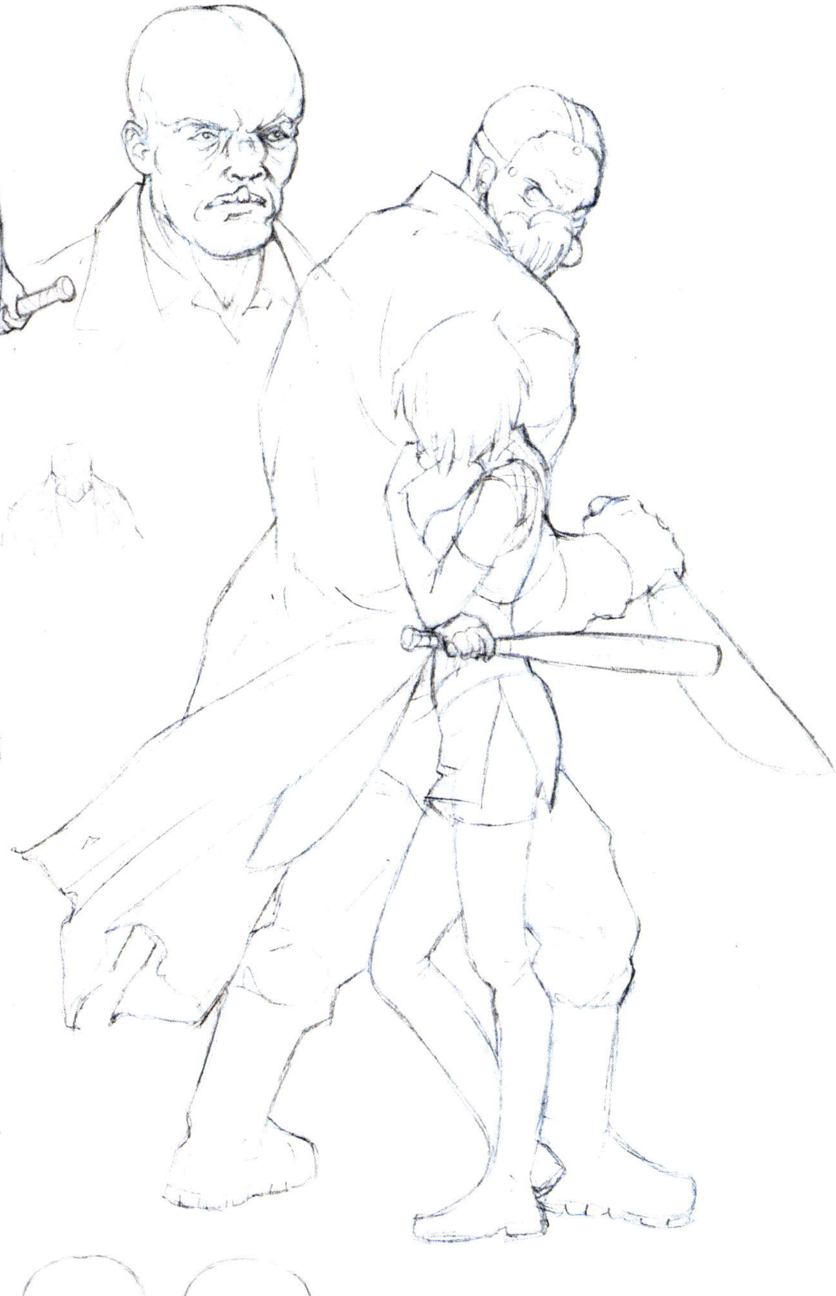

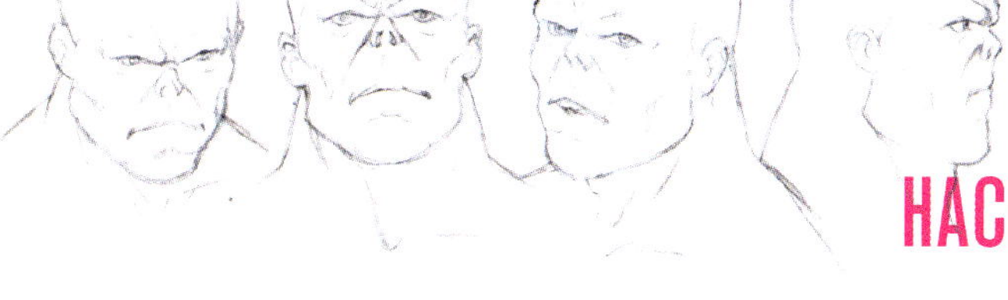

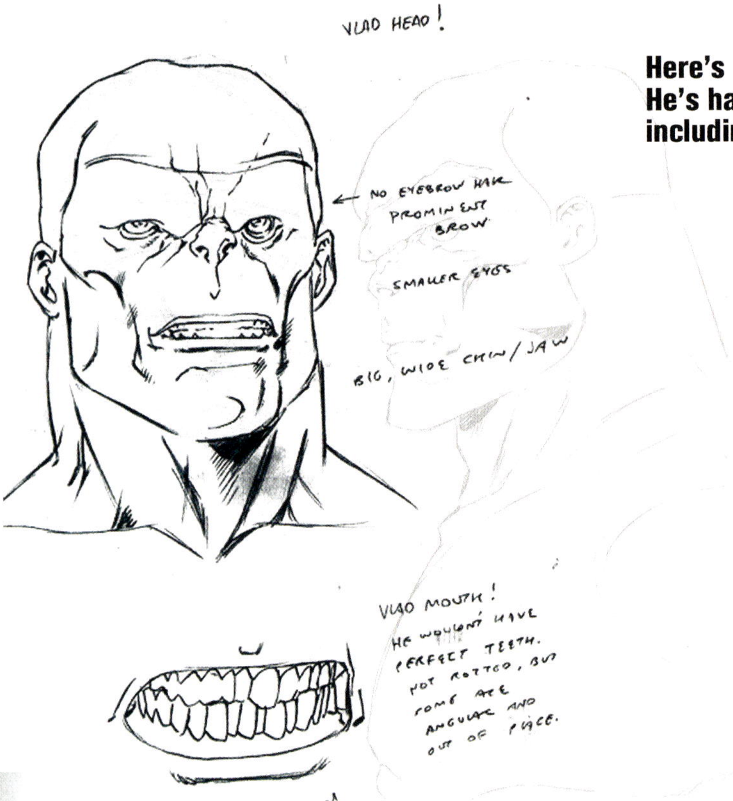
VLAD HEAD!
NO EYEBROW HAIR
PROMINENT BROW
SMALLER EYES
BIG, WIDE CHIN/JAW
VLAD MOUTH!
HE WOULDN'T HAVE PERFECT TEETH. NOT ROTTED, BUT SOME ARE ANGULAR AND OUT OF PLACE.

Here's my "model sheet" for Vlad. He's hard to draw for a lot of people, including me.

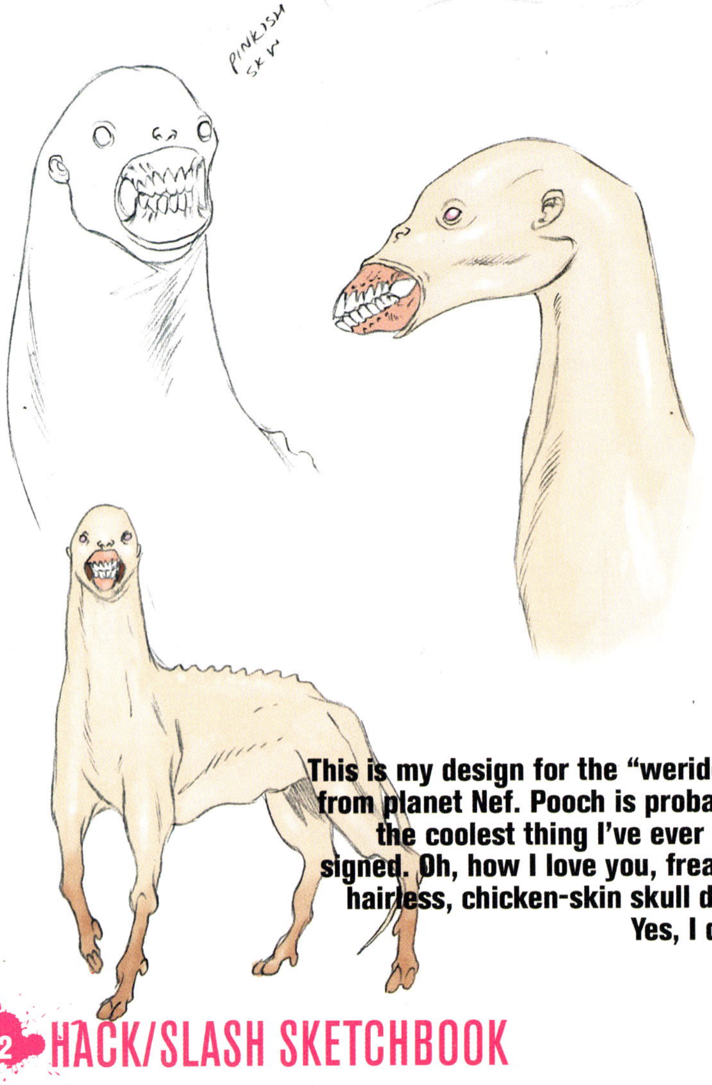
PINKISH SKIN

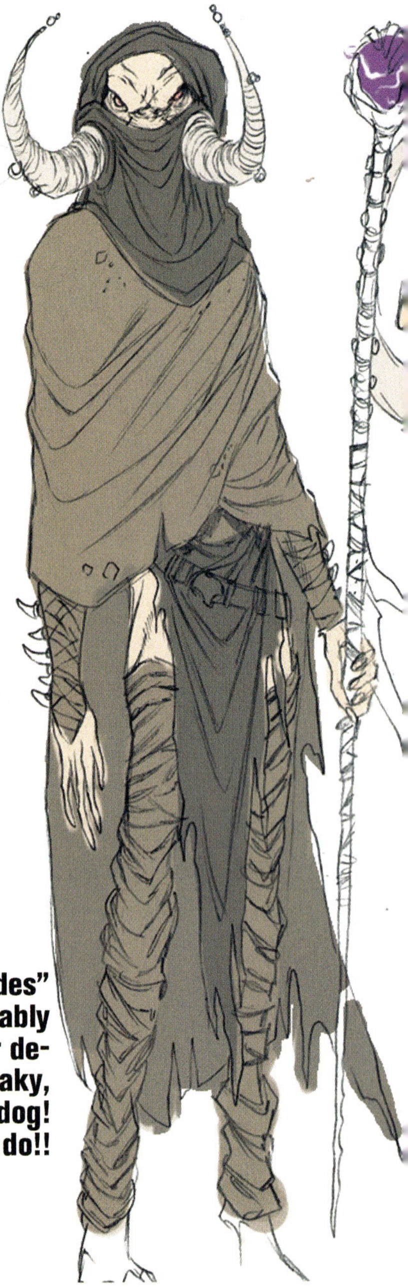

This is my design for the "werides" from planet Nef. Pooch is probably the coolest thing I've ever designed. Oh, how I love you, freaky, hairless, chicken-skin skull dog! Yes, I do!!